"These are the times that try men's souls . . ."

Beautiful *Bonnie Logan*, with her baby daughter, *Dorothy*, is safely ensconced at her sister-in-law *Meg*'s house in New York City, determined to keep the war that rages around her from touching her. But the dramatic events of 1776 threaten to disrupt and change her life forever. Her brothers, *Bayard* and *Thomas*, are fighting with General George Washington in the battles on Long Island, while her third brother, *Josias*, openly sides with the British, winning an appointment to the Royalist government in New York. And the man Bonnie loves—dynamic, enigmatic publisher *William Whitestone*—must deny his true loyalties to protect Bonnie from a fate she has little imagined.

Suddenly Bonnie is faced with choices she never imagined she'd have to make—between her family and her lover, between honor and complacency, between her safety and her duty. And as she faces the greatest test of her loyalty, two nations prepare for a showdown that will decide the fate of . . .

THESE UNITED COLONIES

Also by Cynthia Van Hazinga:

Our Sacred Honor

THESE UNITED COLONIES

Cynthia Van Hazinga

IVY BOOKS • NEW YORK

Ivy Books
Published by Ballantine Books

Produced by Butterfield Press, Inc.
133 Fifth Avenue
New York, New York 10003

Library of Congress Catalog Card Number: 88-91130

ISBN 0-8041-0195-7

Manufactured in the United States of America

First Edition: December 1988

To Renee Feinberg, Marcia Leizure,
and Patty Withington for help and support.

These
United Colonies

Prologue

Charleston, South Carolina
June 28, 1776

CHARLESTON, THE METROPOLIS of the South. She was a world apart from puritanical New England, commercial New York, or the undeveloped frontiers of the Middle Colonies. Charleston was a jewel in the crown of the British Empire, a proud city set on a lush peninsula where the Ashley and Cooper rivers joined to become the Atlantic Ocean. Visitors found her beautiful, though hot in summer. Her citizens were a sporting, social people who moved between plantation and townhouse, ballroom and racetrack, social club and slave market (for half of her citizens were Africans), well content with their lives, with the beauty of the coastline, and with the city itself.

But now the city was in crisis. She was braced for trouble, braced for attack. British General Henry Clinton had recently been dispatched to Charleston to secure it as Loyalist headquarters in the South, and a British naval squadron under the command of Admiral Peter Parker had taken an offensive position in the bay.

The entrance to the city's harbor ran past Sullivan's Island to the north and James Island to the south—both covered with sandbars and swamps, laced with clear creeks, dense with live oaks, palmettos, and myrtle, buzzing with insects. As the British forces prepared for attack, South Carolina's rebels were bolstering their defenses. Their chief hope was a fort still under construction on Sullivan's Island; their commander was that outrageous eccentric, General Charles Lee, and the attack was expected in a few days.

Irascible, wretchedly profane, and unbelievably ugly, Lee got on with the Carolinians about as well as could be expected. In his upper-class British accent, he called Fort Sullivan a "slaughter pen" and ordered buildings along the waterfront razed and batteries erected in town. His commands were issued rapidly and peremptorily; some South Carolina officers absolutely refused to obey him, but John Rutledge, head of Carolina's revolutionary government, and William Moultrie, a seasoned Indian fighter in charge of the local troops, reinforced Lee's authority while throwing all they had into the soft-sided fort, which was built of sand and palmetto logs, for there was no stone available.

"Preposterous!" fumed General Lee. "Moultrie, do you think you can stand up to bombardment in that bug-infested trap?"

Moultrie gritted his teeth. "Yes, sir. I think I can."

"There are fifty British sail out there! When those ships come alongside your fort they'll knock it down in half an hour."

"Then we shall lay behind the ruins and prevent their men from landing."

"Pfaagh!" Lee scoffed. "Are ye mad? And there's no way to retreat! I confess I don't know why you first began with that island and that fort, but I urge you to give it up."

But Moultrie stood fast.

"We will never give it up!"

Lee made a vulgar noise that fell somewhere between a snarl and a snort. "Then 'tis absolutely necessary to build a bridge of boats for a retreat!"

By this time the British commanders had begun to send troops in small boats across to Long Island, northeast of Sullivan's. Their intent was to wade across to the mainland and take the fort from behind, but they had been misinformed; the breach was too shallow for boats, but too deep in spots for wading, and when the first heavily laden soldiers stepped into the straits, they disappeared in a froth of splashes and bubbles. Behind them, 2,500 men were stranded on Long Island.

There was a favorable breeze from the south, and the British squadron moved up the channel smartly and launched a furious cannonade at the fort at about eleven in the morning. The bombardment was terrific; no one there had ever heard anything like it. There was absolutely no way anything or anyone could stand up to such a shower of metal for more than an hour or two—any naval expert would have told you that. The range was about 400 yards, which for guns of that size was virtually point-blank.

But Moultrie and the men of Charleston fought back coolly and fiercely—perhaps too fiercely, for their supply of gunpowder soon ran low. "Every shot must count!" Moultrie warned. There were only twenty-eight rounds of ammunition for each of the twenty-six guns at the fort. The men fell into a rhythm and kept it up all afternoon, fighting steadily amidst the continual blaze and roar.

The rebels displayed marvelous courage. When a cannonball took off his shoulder and scooped out his stomach, Sergeant McDaniel cried out, "Fight on, my brave boys! Don't let liberty expire with me today!" Never did men fight more bravely; never were

3

men more cool. Their accuracy—and the poor, soft sand walls of the fort, which swallowed the shot without splintering as wood would have done—was their salvation.

It was a blistering hot day and young boys passed grog in firebuckets among the thirsty soldiers. "I never had a more agreeable draught, Davie!" Moultrie called to the youngest of the Montgomery brothers. The eldest, Webb, stood at Moultrie's side, clouds of smoke curling over his head, concentrating his fire on the two nearest and biggest of the battleships, the *Bristol* and the *Experiment*, especially the *Bristol*, Parker's flagship.

The rebels' cannon had inflicted terrible damage on the *Bristol*. Early in the action her cable was shot away, and the tide swung her end on to the fort, which raked her from stern to bow again and again. Seventy balls hulled her; one ball getting so close to Sir Peter that it tore off his coattail, together with his trousers. The top of the *Bristol*'s mainmast was shot clean off, and her mizzen was splintered. Twice, all the men on the quarter-deck were killed or wounded. The firing was so devastating it was nearly unbelievable, and it did not stop until nine-thirty at night. At eleven, Parker at last gave the signal for retreat, and the British warships, shocked and beaten, slipped their cables to drift out with the tide. Risking snarls and recriminations from London, they would sail north to join General Howe in New York.

It was over, and the British were stunned at their losses. On the *Bristol*, upward of a hundred men had been killed, and twice as many wounded. The captain of the *Experiment* had lost his right arm. All the ships had been damaged; one was so far gone it had to be blown up by its own crew. But far worse was the jolt to British pride, the shock that the rebels had done it. They had vanquished the mighty British fleet in a direct battle, defended a ramshackle fort, won "eternal credit," as Lee conceded to Moultrie at the end, generously enough. Only twelve Americans had been killed and twenty-four wounded. The victory was as important as it was spectacular: the notion of a quick conquest of the South had been quashed.

Charleston was "damned rebellious country," and all the world knew it. And the flag waved free over the fort on Sullivan's Island.

Chapter One

NEWS OF THE victory at Charleston soon reached a New York bursting at the seams with soldiers of Washington's Continental Army and daily expecting attack from the British warships and transports swarming into her harbors "like locusts escaped from the bottomless pit," as an observer remarked. The British armada, under the joint command of the brothers William and Richard Howe, was the largest ever employed by a European power outside the Continent. Some thirty thousand strong, the approaching armada included nine thousand veterans from the abandoned occupation of Boston, come by way of a stay in Halifax; along with fresh soldiers from the British Isles and Royal garrisons in the West Indies and Gibraltar, and several thousand husky German mercenaries.

To the American Patriots, the odds were discouraging. In New York City, General George Washington had a mere eight thousand men fit for duty; he had just survived a widespread scheme for mutiny among his own guard and a plot to end his life by poisoning. Many had deemed Manhattan Island physically indefensible. "Burn it to the ground,"

General Charles Lee had advised, "or simply abandon it." At any rate, it was risky territory. An estimated two-thirds of the small city was Tory owned; there were many taverns in town where the King's health was drunk openly, and spies were everywhere.

Yet inside this important, vulnerable city were many Patriots determined to fight heart and soul to save her. Some of these were her natives, men and women born New Yorkers, who felt the city was their own. Others were pledged to her for different reasons. Congress had ordered General Washington to make an attempt to defend New York, and he was determined to make the British fight for every inch.

Victory was foremost in the minds of the New England soldiers who had marched south that spring to aid in the defense of New York. Among them were the Logan brothers: Bayard, a veteran of the battles at Lexington and Bunker Hill, who had already seen much fighting and dying; and Thomas, just sixteen, to whom war was still the best adventure of a lifetime. On the eve of July eleventh, the brothers met at Sam Fraunces's Tavern, The Queen's Head.

Black Sam Fraunces was a jovial, popular host who kept a good table, and tonight his tavern was as crowded as ever. At the tavern rail patriotic toasts were being offered and drunk to, and a new song called "Sir Peter Parker" was being sung by a red-bearded man who always had the latest.

"Listen there," Tom said, and he and Bayard both laughed to hear: "Now, bold as a Turk,/I proceed to New York,/Where Clinton and Howe you may find me./I've the wind in my tail, and am hoisting sail,/ To leave Sullivan's Island behind me."

Both of them knew the tune, as did nearly everyone in the tavern. As a broadside, the ballad had been in all the papers. "Timialderry O, Timialderry Aye, Faith, almost too much for Sir Peter!" went the chorus.

"Listen!" Tom insisted, slapping his knee in amusement as the red-haired man began the second verse. "But, my lords, do not fear,/For before the next year,/Although a small island could fret us,/The continent whole,/We shall take, by my soul,/If the cowardly Yankees will let us!"

At length, Bayard and Tom found seats in a corner where they could talk privately. They were close despite their difference in age—Bayard was twenty-four—and shared a strong family resemblance. Both were handsome, well proportioned and muscular, sandy haired and blue eyed, but Bayard was unusually tall, as befit a member of General Washington's honor guard. He was neatly turned out in a blue and buff coat, a bright waistcoat, and buckskin breeches. Tom, still growing to his full height, wore the homespun brown linsey of the Massachusetts militia; he followed General Henry Knox.

Since they had last met, about a week ago, much had happened in the city, and much more had been rumored to happen. The long-awaited, much-discussed Declaration of Independence had come from Philadelphia and been read to the troops. The massive gilded statue of King George III as a Roman emperor had been pulled from its pedestal in Bowling Green and smashed to bits. The American troops had continued to strengthen their fortifications, all the while waiting suspensefully for what might happen next, nervously looking out over the bay at one of the most formidable fleets ever gathered in one place.

"I heard a report that France has declared war on

England!'' Tom told his brother with a voice full of import and excitement.

"That is what we hope for," Bayard said, "but I fear it is not true—not yet. The town is buzzing with rumors. The air is thick with them. General Washington has issued an order rebuking gossipmongers."

Tom leaned back in his chair and sipped from his tankard of ale. He hated criticism from his brother, but nothing could suppress his eagerness and excitement about the current state of affairs. "They say Admiral Howe will arrive to join his brother any day now. They say General Howe wants no more of war and will agree readily to withdraw the fleet as soon as Washington sets the terms."

"There was a rumor to that effect brought by postrider from Pennsylvania," Bayard said. His eyes drifted around the smoky, dimly lit taproom, which was crowded with soldiers in uniform, a contingent of bewigged older gentlemen smoking pipes, and a few silent Indians. A plump barmaid passed their table with a tray of bottles and glasses and gave Bayard a provocative stare. It startled him; it had been a long time since he had desired a woman, and the barmaid's interest took him by surprise. Laughter rose in the tavern and many of its patrons were evidently in the most riotous of spirits, but Bayard could not escape the feeling that it was only a moment of calm before a great storm must break out.

"How many ships have gathered out there? How many?" his younger brother asked eagerly.

"Too many." Bayard rose abruptly. "Let's get out of here, Tom. The air is close." Without waiting for an answer, he pushed past the table and strode through the crowded tavern. The night air was sultry. Bayard waited in the shadows for a moment as

9

Tom hurried to catch up with him. Crowded Queen Street contained all the bustle and variety of New York life—soldiers passed in every sort of regimental garb, men of every race and color hurried by, talking rapidly and at great volume. Most of them were strangers to Bayard, but then his eyes caught sight of a couple—to all appearances a courting couple—among them who were not.

It was his sister Bonnie, newly widowed and the mother of a baby girl, walking in close step with the illustrious newspaper publisher William Whitestone. There was no mistaking Bonnie; with her gleaming red-gold hair and her angelic profile, her slim graceful figure and erect carriage she would always be the prettiest in a crowd of beauties. She was chattering animatedly with Whitestone—himself an imposing-looking man, well built and broad, handsome in a rough sort of way, but exceedingly civilized in his dress—and though the two of them passed within ten feet of where Bayard stood in the shadows, they had eyes only for each other, and he did not call out to them. He had his own reasons for failing to acknowledge acquaintance with William Whitestone, and as for his sister, it was interesting to observe her as a stranger might.

For a woman of her tender years—she was scarcely eighteen, after all—Bonnie Logan had experienced much, and not all of it easy, but the trials and tribulations of her life had not marked her at all. During the British occupation of Boston, Bonnie had lost her heart to a British soldier, Cormick Walker, a man—in her brother's view—not worthy of her at all. But she had loved him, married him, and borne him a child. All that was past; the man was dead, and Bayard saw no mark of it on his sister. Bayard watched Bonnie's gold-lit green eyes open confidingly to Whitestone, saw a smile play about her sweet rosebud mouth, and marveled at her beauty as if he had not known her as a child and knew nothing of her characteristic determination and willfulness, traits just as strong and well established as her good looks.

Perhaps I should warn Whitestone, Bayard thought fleetingly and then smiled at his own joke. No man in New York was more confident or better established than William Whitestone, a descendant of fine families from both the Dutch and English settlements. No man was better connected, no man more ironic or brilliant, more imposing or independent. As well warn the eagle, as well caution King George! Whatever might happen between his lovely, passionate sister and the young publisher would happen. Perhaps the fire of their evident attraction to each other would burn steadily and long, perhaps not. It was not within Bayard's control.

"Why are you looking so distracted?" Tom asked when at last he rattled down the tavern steps to join his brother.

"How else should a man contemplate New York?" Bayard said evasively. Tom was as clumsy and energetic as a young puppy, and sometimes Bayard tired of explaining life to him; but Tom was nowhere as tiresome as Josias, their middle brother, now a married and settled New Yorker whose way of life and political beliefs were totally at odds with theirs. In fact, Josias was married to William Whitestone's sister, Meg, linking the two families—the Boston Patriotic Logans and the Loyalist Whitestones of New York.

With effort, Bayard put the matter of Josias and the question of family harmony out of his mind. After all, he was a soldier during wartime, on the brink of what might well be a major military engagement. He had enlisted for three years, pledged to follow

11

General Washington, and he believed wholly in the cause of American liberty. It was his duty to keep himself fit and ready, not to indulge in idle speculation or family quarrels.

Furthermore, it was Bayard's belief that the times they lived in were far more significant than any family differences. They were being swept along by the times—to wit—their entire Boston family transplanted, for this season at least, to New York. . . .

"The night air makes me restless," Tom said, stretching his arms above his head.

"I believe I'll get back to headquarters," Bayard said. "Mind you take care, Tom."

"Great care," Tom promised. He had in mind to visit a certain tavern on Water Street, where a certain light-haired serving maid, intriguingly called Isannah, had caught his eye.

The brothers parted with a firm handshake on the corner of Wall and Broad streets.

If General Washington enjoyed moments of respite or distraction that night, they were few. Washington was in a torment of apprehension. The masts of the British fleet filled the harbor like trees in a virgin forest, the red-coated soldiers stationed at their rails like an infestation of red ants. Washington's telescope was never out of his hand and seldom far from his eye. The sudden dawn streaked the eastern sky with pink and orange. By the time the sun was halfway up the ladder of the sky and he had breakfasted on his customary firecake, the sound of cannon rolled down the bay from the British anchorage.

"What word from the lookouts?" Washington demanded.

Bayard Logan, his young captain of the guard,

12

was serving as an envoy between the rooms Washington and his generals occupied at the beautiful mansion of Abraham Mortier, on the crest of Richmond Hill, and the lookouts stationed on the waterfront at Fort George.

"They are firing salutes for the arrival of Admiral Howe, at the sight of his flag, sir."

"Now it will start in earnest," Washington predicted. Admiral Howe had not only been expected, but long awaited. The waiting game Washington had been forced to play with the British—their damned inexplicable reluctance to move—was enough to drive a man out of his head. From his headquarters he had a splendid view of the Hudson River. All precautions had been taken to prevent the British ships from sailing up that river: cannon had been placed on the shores, weighted hulks of wrecked ships sunk into the murky depths, and atop these sunken obstacles, long, sharpened timbers had been mounted just below the water's surface, so that their nasty points would rake the bottom of any vessel passing over them.

All this river work had been the accomplishment of General Israel Putnam and his men. It was a desperate effort, but Putnam assured Washington that it would seal off the Hudson, save for a secret passageway left open for American ships to slip through unharmed. The *cheveau de frise*, as the sharpened spikes were called, would be as effective as a shark's teeth, Putnam claimed.

But now, incredibly, Washington watched as five British vessels—the frigate *Phoenix* with forty-eight guns, the *Rose* with twenty-eight guns, and three tenders—shook out their snow-white sails and aimed right for the city and the mouth of the river.

"Open fire!" Washington ordered. "To arms!" Drums beat to summon the artillerymen, but many failed to respond. Instead they ran to the riverbank and stood there gaping. Washington was both appalled and furious. "They are gazing at the ships," he complained, "like so many lovestruck fools!"

It was as if after so much delay, the American soldiers could not credit their eyes. The British were actually attacking! The civilian population panicked; women's screams filled the air. Finally the batteries on Paulus Hook and Governor's Island and the tip of Manhattan opened fire. But the decks of the *Phoenix* and the *Rose* were protected with sandbags, and the British bombardment was overwhelming. Cannonballs bounced down the narrow streets of lower Manhattan among the people— many of them poor housewives and their children—who had run out of their houses to ogle the ships. The Bowery, the air thick with the acrid smell of powder and black with smoke, was lined with people, and women with children in their arms fled sobbing in fear as solid shot screamed across the river into their homes.

Washington was enraged at the response of the untried troops.

"Curiosity at such a time a makes a man look weak and contemptible," he told Bayard. To all appearances, the patriot guns, when they were finally manned and fired, had no effect on the British ships. As Washington and his headquarters staff watched with open mouths, the ships glided past Manhattan unscathed and moved rapidly up the river before a brisk breeze on a rising tide. They moved past the last shore batteries and approached the sunken obstacles in the river. Then, to General Putnam's chagrin—among others—they threaded their way through the secret passage as neatly as if they had a chart, and proceeded triumphantly thirty miles up the Hudson to the Tappan Zee.

"We've been betrayed," Washington declared, watching the topgallant yard of the *Phoenix* disappear from sight. Adding insult to injury, a sailor perched there nonchalantly, waving as the *Phoenix* accurately ran the gauntlet.

The British had encircled New York. Their troops on Staten Island grew in number, and ships continued to anchor in the crowded harbor. Sir Peter Parker's fleet, with 2,500 men, arrived after their defeat in Charleston. July melted into August, and the Patriots were trapped.

Meg Logan was pregnant, and much as she wanted this baby, she was not sure she would last through this entirely dreadful summer. Although she had been robust and healthy as a child and a young woman, she did not seem constitutionally suited to this, the foremost female role. Sadly, she had already failed at it, for during her first pregnancy she had lost the child. Now, her breath was short, she had little appetite, her hands and feet were bloated and swollen, and she could scarcely sleep for worry and the heat. The city was like an oven—day followed day of oppressive, sweltering heat relieved only by darkness and the faintest of sea breezes—and sickness was rampant all over town. Malaria had broken out among the occupying troops, and camp fever and the bloody flux spread from the soldier's camps and tents to the tenements of the poor and the homes of the rich alike.

Meg's chief consolation was the presence of her sister-in-law, Bonnie, who had come from Boston early in the year and been safely delivered of her own darling child, the delightful baby Dorothy. Indeed, Bonnie's easy delivery and prompt recovery from childbed had provided Meg with an example

15

she was hard-pressed to follow, although Bonnie's cheerful company was much a force to the good.

"You must not let your spirits get too depressed, for your health greatly depends on that," Bonnie cautioned Meg. The two women were sitting together in Meg's second-floor sewing room, for the prospect of a new Logan on earth necessitated an enormous amount of sewing, knitting, and piecing. Meg had hired two young Dutch girls to work on the baby's wardrobe, but she had every intention of directing the embroidery and choosing the laces herself. Despite her disinclination for and lack of talent at needlework, Bonnie had been enjoined to help, and the two sisters-in-law and in-heart had already passed many a muggy afternoon in the airless sewing room.

"I confess I am greatly afraid," Meg said, "of the lying-in."

"Darling Meg, don't be. Your condition is entirely natural and anyway inevitable. I will help you, I promise, as you helped me. It wasn't so bad. You will feel better as soon as the weather improves. And Josias will be home soon to give us the news of the day."

But Meg, who recalled Bonnie's confinement much more clearly than Bonnie did, was scarcely comforted. "It's so dreadfully hot," she complained. "I can hardly breathe. I don't believe I slept a wink last night."

"Poor darling. Let me get you a ginger beer. William has sent us a fresh jug."

"And what news?" Meg asked eagerly. "What news has brother William?"

"There is no news, as ever. Weeks pass and General Howe sleeps on. . . . Since the *Phoenix* and the *Rose* showed their strength, everyone has expected attack every day. I wonder . . ." Bonnie, who had known General William Howe in Boston, could guess better than most what he might be up to; she knew his pretty mistress Betsy Loring, lately of Roxbury, and her hold on fun-loving Howe. Bonnie had learned a lot during the British occupation of Boston that she would have preferred to forget. Sometimes she felt a great deal older and wiser than her brother Josias's wife, even though sweet Meg was her senior by a few years and possessed all the worldly sophistication of a born New Yorker. Meg had taken her in when she had arrived in New York penniless and freezing; Meg had welcomed her and given her a comfortable home, both for herself and her baby. Had it been left to her brother Josias, Bonnie might still be wandering the Atlantic coast in search of her husband. Bonnie shuddered, thinking of it.

How different things were now than they had been just a year ago. Then Bonnie had been in her native Boston, in love for the first time. She had turned her back on her staunchly Patriot family to marry Cormick Walker, a British officer. Too late, she had learned that Cormick was a scoundrel and that their marriage had been a false one. By then she was living in New York—Bonnie had left Boston in search of her husband, whose regiment had traveled south. Once Bonnie learned of Cormick's treachery, she had become more determined than ever to find him, and at last she had, in a tavern on Staten Island. Filled with rage and unhappiness, she had shot him with his own gun. Now he was surely dead.

"Josias is late tonight," Meg commented mildly, bringing Bonnie back to the present.

"He seems to be very busy," Bonnie said, although she could not think what Josias found to be

17

so busy about, what with the port effectively barricaded and business come to a virtual standstill. Her brother Josias had always been close-mouthed about his business, always serious and intense, always white-hot in rivalry with Bayard, and the war had brought all these characteristics into stronger focus. Bonnie marveled at his luck in finding lovely, docile Meg and at the harmony of their marriage; she prayed it would last, even while she was presently quite diverted by the attentions of Meg's brother William, and like all girls in love, full of hope for the future.

"Very busy," Meg agreed. She was entirely delighted with Bonnie as a sister—and as a replacement for her own blood sister, Audrey, who had fled to the country house with their parents. She and Audrey had never gotten on, anyway. To put it squarely, they had been at odds since they peeked out of their cradles at each other. Now, Bonnie was a love—if only she were sure William would treat her well—he was so unsteady with women. "You know, dear Bonnie, I do feel a bit better now."

"I am glad," Bonnie said.

"Yes, much better," Meg promised. "Look at this hood! And it shall be trimmed with pale pink ribbon. Isn't it terribly, terribly sweet?"

"Yes, it is," Bonnie agreed, and just then baby Dorothy woke from her afternoon nap, stirring in the low cherrywood cradle that stood under the window and beginning to make her little calls for sustenance.

"Look! She's awake! Look how she smiles at me! Oh, the precious one," Meg cooed, for she was quite swallowed up with maternal feelings, as was Bonnie, too. For despite the war, the rampant sickness in town, and the imminent threat of attack, in many ways the life of women had changed very little, especially for these two women, at least for the present.

Chapter Two

NEWS OF THE Declaration of Independence had reached Charleston on the fifth of August. At the dinner and dance that night to celebrate the sixteenth birthday of Miss Kathryn Montgomery, the youngest daughter of Dennison and Caroline Montgomery, the talk was of little else.

Among the gentlemen, at least. To Kathryn, known as Katy, the doings at Philadelphia—and the war itself—might have been staged simply to deflect attention from one of the most important nights of her life. Katy was one of those creatures who maintained into young womanhood the childish illusion that the sun was her candle, the world her toy. She was her father's pet, and he delighted in her unblemished self-confidence. Regarding her as an exponent, or at least an extension of himself, Dennison Montgomery took immense pleasure in indulging his youngest daughter to the limit of his considerable means. Katy had always been a willful child, yet a charming one, happy and easygoing. It was only in her young womanhood that she had changed somewhat. Already she had been called wild, an unusual description for a young lady of good birth. And there had been that incident in England, when she and her mother and sister had visited there last year . . .

Katy's birthday party, on this occasion, was held at the Montgomerys' splendid new townhouse in the White Point section of Charleston. The house, designed by the London architect Ezra Waite, was one of the prides of the city's new development. Built of brick, it was surrounded by neat, well-organized gardens bursting with bloom. It was a sweltering evening in that season which called in from their upriver plantations all the cream of Carolina society in search of sea breezes and each other's company.

How much they did enjoy each other's company! And how well they knew each other! It was a small society, the Carolina elite, "full of money," and to call it exclusive was not to say that they did not welcome foreigners—for their diversion—and newcomers—provided they were properly connected and financially secure, of course. Carolina society was one that had enjoyed wealth, luxury, prestige, and political power for decades, and all of these were commodities that, once possessed, led quickly to self-satisfaction, and were not easily relinquished. Although *rebellion* and even *independence* were words on everyone's tongue here tonight, there was little thought of sacrifice.

Through the years, this midsummer birthday celebration had become a regular event, one looked forward to by the family's many friends. Everyone knew that the Montgomerys knew how to stage a party, and tonight the house was looking very splendid. Every room shone with candlelight and glittered with silver. Freshly starched curtains trembled at the open windows. A buffet table was loaded

21

with sweets and treats; a formal supper would be served at midnight.

In the second-floor drawing room, garlands of ivy and bouquets of roses, white lilies and fragrant peonies had been arranged painstakingly and added a spicy-sweet perfume to the air that was almost entirely overwhelmed by the scent of the tobacco smoked by nearly every gentleman in the crowd. Liquor—rum, Madeira, Bordeaux, cordials, and several potent fruit punches—was flowing and had been flowing for several hours.

"Goodness, it's hot!" Katy Montgomery exclaimed, although she was as lightly clad as fashion permitted, in yards and yards of sheer, pink-flowered dimity, styled off the shoulders and cut very low over her small, round breasts.

"Not at all, dear," protested her mother, who thought any complaint in company unmannerly. "Pray, don't mention it! There's a lovely sea breeze tonight."

"Papa and his friends are blocking the windows," Katy said in a sulky tone, and it was actually true: the men had formed a tight conversational huddle between the ladies and the east-facing windows. "I think I'll try to distract them!"

"Really, Katy! Please remember your manners!" Caroline protested, but her willful daughter had spotted a friend arriving through the big, arched front door, and had run off to meet her, herself distracted, complaints and the temperature forgotten.

"Good evening, Mama!" It was Webb, Caroline's oldest son, a calm and distinguished man, already married and living in his own house a short distance away.

"Oh, Webb dear! And darling Susannah!" Caroline offered her cheek to be kissed. "How wonderful you look, Webb!"

Tall and handsome, Webb had always been his mother's favorite, and had not disappointed her by choosing the wealthy Miss Susannah Gridley to be his bride. Webb had the characteristic Montgomery looks: a high brow over deep-set dark blue eyes, strong features, and straight white teeth. His blue-black hair was smooth and glossy, his smile sincere, and he had all the appearance of a happy man. Webb was an ardent Patriot and, like his brother Davie, a veteran of the desperate fighting at Sullivan's Island last June. Tonight he was triumphant over the news from Philadelphia and had obtained a copy of the revolutionary document, which he was eager to show to his father and the other men.

Webb kissed his mother gracefully, bowed, and joined the cluster of men, leaving fair, slender Susannah at his mother's side.

Caroline sighed. It was obvious that the men would just have to indulge themselves in a thorough discussion and analysis of the political news before any of them could turn to socializing. Politics was the only thing that had proved to be anywhere near as interesting to her husband as the price of rice. There were some things a woman just had to bear. She shook out her fan and inclined her head toward her daughter-in-law. "And how is the dear baby, Susannah?" she asked.

"Very well, thank you. He has his first tooth."

But Caroline, upon whom grandmotherly responsibilities sat prematurely, had turned to greet the next guests, the distinguished Dr. Alexander Garden and the colossally wealthy Madame Gabrielle Manigault, who went everywhere and knew everyone. Dr. Garden was not only a prominent physician, but an energetic botanist and a special favorite of Caroline's. Calling his attention to the splendid

23

bouquet of lavender lilies, she led him to the punch bowl.

Susannah turned to greet Liza, Webb's other sister. The two embraced. Being of like and even temperament, they were close friends and shared the role of peacekeeper in the fractious, hot-tempered Montgomery family. Liza was less than two years older than Katy, but possessed a serenity the younger girl was unlikely to attain with the passage of two times twenty years.

"You look lovely," Susannah complimented Liza, who was a very comely young woman with curly dark hair, a sweet, heart-shaped face, and the deep-set blue eyes typical of the family. She wore a dress of green-striped silk and a lace over-bodice.

"It's a wonder I'm presentable," Liza admitted with a laugh. "At the last minute, Katy stepped on her hem and tore out a yard of lace! Her maid couldn't find the sewing basket with the pink thread. It finally turned up in the summer kitchen. Then Davie discovered the cat had just had kittens on his black trousers. I ran so fast I was dizzy! I can't remember if I put my hair up or not."

"Did you mention my name?" Davie, the baby of the Montgomery family, tall and handsome at fifteen, appeared at Liza's side. Susannah stole a covert glance at his trousers, which looked well brushed but damp, and then smiled in greeting.

"Now we are all here," Liza said with an excited and satisfied sigh. "Oh! Except Taylor!"

"Taylor is not happy with the news from the north," Davie said gravely.

"But he wouldn't not come?" Susannah asked.

"Spoil Katy's birthday party?" Liza gasped.

"Oh, Katy would hardly notice," Davie said accurately, "but Papa would. I believe Taylor will come tonight."

"Family! Friends!" bellowed Dennison Montgomery, his blue eyes blazing. He was every inch the patriarch, and each of his children resembled him physically and respected him extravagantly. Carolina-born Dennison had met his English wife on a trip to London; he was fond of both traveling and business, and so successful a planter of rice and indigo that he filled his own ships with his merchandise and had swelled his plantation's labor force to one hundred slaves.

"I give you a toast, dear guests!" he went on. "Firstly, to dear Katy's birthday. A sweeter girl never drew breath!"

Davie winked at Liza so drolly that she could barely contain her giggle.

"And to our nation's natal day, as well! Dear friends, dear children, we have received today the important and long-awaited news of that Declaration composed and ratified by representatives of every single colony. I shall read every word of it to you in a bit. But first I give you the toast! Are you all supplied with a glass and a bit of cheer? Here, then: To the prosperity and perpetuity of the united, free, and independent states of America! God bless us! Hurrah!"

"Hurrah!" Davie led the cheers, as always ebullient and irrepressible. "Hurrah! Hurrah! Hurrah!"

Caroline Montgomery frowned, hoping this would not entirely spoil the party. Katy hardly heard; she had drifted out to the balcony and was leaning over, her curls falling down entrancingly, her half-exposed breasts aching, calling down to Will Streeter, who had just arrived on a high-stepping black stallion. The handsome, devil-may-care son of the Streeters of Tranquility Plantation, Will was Katy's current favorite. She ran down to him now and kissed him boldly, and through luck, no one from her family saw. Katy had that sort of luck, and none of them knew how bold she was.

"Do you still love me, Will? After last night?" Katy demanded teasingly, knowing in her way that he loved her more than ever, was drunk with wanting her, and would find a way to be with her alone again after the party.

"Oh, Katy!" he said.

Dr. Garden thought of war—awful wounds and hasty surgery, gangrene and camp fever, suffering and death. He hoped that it might be a short war, that there would be no fighting in South Carolina, that it would be over by winter.

Liza felt her heart pulled so that it ached; oh, what would happen to them all? She thought of Webb's baby, of keeping him safe at the plantation. How she longed to be there, at Ashley Hall—everything would be better there.

Webb thought of his brother Taylor. No one on earth was more compassionate or just; no one was more moral or courageous. Yet Taylor was opposed to rebellion, opposed to any decaration of independence; Taylor believed it was their duty to work for reconciliation with England at any price. All his life Webb had loved and admired his brilliant younger brother and followed his lead in matters of taste and judgment. Now, for the first time, they were heartbreakingly at odds.

Where was Taylor? Webb had been vaguely aware that he had not yet bumped elbows with his brother at the punch bowl, but Lucinda Carroll, Taylor's redheaded sweetheart, had arrived, and was standing with Liza and Susannah near the musicians' stand. He looked quickly around the room. Taylor was absent.

With no diminuition of volume or enthusiasm, Dennison Montgomery began to read the text of the

26

Declaration aloud to the assembled party. " 'We hold these truths to be self-evident,' " he read, " 'that all men are created equal, that they are endowed by their Creator with certain unalienable rights, that among these are Life, Liberty, and the pursuit of Happiness. . . .' "

Webb's pulse raced as he heard the stirring words. By God! This was it! This was—finally—the setting in motion of the course of events that would shape his life. Suddenly all else seemed to have been in preparation for this moment, this challenge. He strode across the room to Susannah, not noticing that her eyes were filled with tears. Clasping his wife's hand, he faced the open door and was thus in a good position to see Taylor enter.

Tall, handsome, twenty-one-year-old Taylor Montgomery paused on the threshold of the drawing room and took the measure of the crowd with one sweep of his deep-set, dark blue eyes. He had heard his father's voice as he climbed the stairs, heard the provocative declaration. To him, it seemed madness, the madness of mob rule. The excitement and fervor of his friends and family chilled him to the bone, and he saw them all in sudden deep shadow as he felt them surge toward him, calling out his name.

God guide us and save us, he thought. With great effort he dispelled his vision of the cloud over the party and took his sister Liza's outstretched hand.

"Good evening, Lizzy! What a lovely gown. I see you are all in the best of spirits tonight. All signs point to a momentous occasion, do they not?"

Not without forbodings, Washington had entrusted the high command of his troops on Long Island to his second choice, the feisty Irishman from New

Hampshire, General John Sullivan. Ruddy, rebellious General Nathanael Greene, Quaker turned soldier, who was Washington's clear first choice, had fallen ill with a fever. Bayard Logan, who had known Sullivan for many years, spoke up for him to his commander-in-chief.

"Sullivan is absolutely passionate for the cause," Bayard said.

"That is well," Washington said, "and he does not lack abilities, but I fear he lacks the knowledge of men and operations that would compensate for his want of experience to move on a large scale . . . which we all lack. I speak to you in complete confidence, Logan."

"As always, sir. I do not doubt but you are right, General Washington, but I know Sullivan to be brave and spirited and possessed of sound beliefs."

Bayard thought of his own father, who had been Sullivan's friend and was now dead. He remembered Sullivan's fine farm in Durham on the Piscataqua River and a visit he had made there as a boy during maple-sugaring season. He dreaded overstepping his position, but he longed to see Sullivan's strengths recognized. Behind his cool facade, Bayard was a passionate man, and passionate for principles as well as people.

"No doubt," Washington said dryly, thinking how these Yankees did stick together. "But will his politics help him find his way around Long Island?"

In truth, John Sullivan was totally unacquainted with the geography of Long Island, and it was Washington's constant fear that the British would do the logical thing and take a solid position there.

Indeed, on the twenty-first of August the British troops began to move, loading troops onto the ships at Staten Island and swinging east to Gravesend Bay where they were well out of reach of Washington's cannon. Despite a great thunderstorm—which was generally interpreted as the voice of God—the complicated maneuver went smoothly. The soldiers were carried ashore in seventy-five flatboats, eleven bateaux, and two galleys, all built specifically for this operation.

The morning landing at Gravesend Bay made a splendid sight, impressive if alarming. The vessles of the fleet spread acres of white sails to dry in the bright sunshine that followed the storm. The hills and fields of Long Island glittered a bright green. Fifteen thousand men, with all their arms and supplies, were landed by noon, and the crack of American warning guns was heard from Red Hook to Cobble Hill. A few patriot skirmishers set wheatfields on fire, but as the wind cleared the smoke, they could see rank after rank of brightly arrayed British regiments advancing smartly in time with the music.

Troops at the American outposts on Long Island retreated slowly, driving off cattle to keep them from the enemy, burning hayfields to deprive them of fodder, even burning some houses and killing some livestock. They showed no signs of panic, but neither did they hurry to report to General Washington what soon became clear—the thrust of British movement was to the east, indicating that they planned to surround the American fortifications by marching around the American left.

The British objective was the American position on Brooklyn Heights. There, Brooklyn's defenders, less than eight thousand in all, occupied a series of posts on a broken ridge nearly two miles in front of the main fortifications in the village. Despite being outnumbered, the American troops had a tactical advantage in being higher than the British on the plains below. Washington dispatched reinforcements to

Brooklyn, but—personally obsessed with the strategy of striking simultaneously at several fronts—he kept the bulk of his force on Manhattan, fearing a trick.

"I do not understand Howe!" Washington complained to Bayard Logan. "Why does he not attack?"

"He continues to move troops to Long Island," Bayard commented dispassionately, although as his brother was among those joining the defense, he was not feeling dispassionate. He feared for Tom, and he also worried for General Sullivan, who had already irritated Washington with his attitude of vapid self-confidence and his intermittent reports that showed little grasp of the situation. Sullivan had been subsequently relieved of command and was now serving under General Israel Putnam.

"I see that he does," Washington continued, "but I cannot believe that he will not feint and come across to attack Manhattan as well." Having replaced Sullivan, Washington was already almost as dissatisfied with Putnam, particularly for allowing the troops to scatter fire, obscuring the distinction between real and false alarms. Washington was in a dither over Howe's intentions and desperately needed the support of an intelligence network as extensive as the one he had had in Boston.

Howe did have a surprise in mind for the Americans, but it was not the one Washington had prepared to meet. Under cover of darkness, he left half his force in front of the American lines, firing at them sporadically, and with the rest of his troops, he began to march around in a great loop to the right, aiming to cut off the American troops from behind.

* * *

In Manhattan, Thomas Logan had packed up his clothes in readiness for an expedition to the front. He had been engaged in a work detail near Broadway when a sergeant major had arrived, breathless with the news that the enemy had landed a large force on Long Island and that they were ordered to move that night to support the position around Brooklyn Heights.

"Now we shall snuff a little gunpowder!" Tom told his chum, William Knox, who had come with him from Boston and was still his best friend. Knox frowned. The thought gave him quite a disagreeable feeling, although he agreed with Logan that this was what they had come to do.

"But, Tom," William suggested, and from his lewd smile it was easy to see what was coming next, "before we go . . ."

"Have we time?" Tom asked. He was stalling, but already the thought of it had hardened his loins.

"There's always time," William said reasonably. "How much time does it take? Besides, we might never come back. We might never have another chance in all our lives."

That dire thought was enough to send both young men scurrying to the house of Fancy Nan. Fancy Nan was not awfully young, but she was exceedingly buxom, and from the minute Tom laid a hand on one of her warm, soft breasts, he was glad that he had come. After all, a soldier's life was a risky one—to think of going to the grave without a bit of fun.

"Aren't you a sweet boy?" Nan whispered, opening herself to him, her long auburn hair spread out on her blanket like a russet shawl. Nan shared her house with a dozen other jills in the district behind Trinity Church, which everyone called the Holy

31

Ground. Tom had made her acquaintance almost as soon as arriving in the city, and having once made it, had made it a habit.

At this time of his life, young Tom's sexual appetite was huge, nearly insatiable, and his frequent draughts of satisfaction had kept him quite content with army life. But today, he had to tell Nan he was leaving town.

"You'll be back," she predicted. "Nancy knows."

"How do you know, how?" Tom demanded, grabbing her around her slender, supple waist and pulling her to him for one last thrust—so wonderful he gave a real shout of joy, hardly heard in the clatter and clamor of the house where anything might happen, and nightly brawls were the rule.

"You've got too much juice to die so soon," Nan said, and smiled broadly, revealing her prize possession, a prominent gold tooth.

From the roof of Nan's house it was possible to see a good distance, and so Tom ran up to take a look across the East River as soon as he was able. Brooklyn Heights was clearly visible, and over it hung the smoke of field artillery, distant puffs that floated neutrally, robbed by distance and the course of the wind from any sense of the horrors of battle or any sounds of explosion. It was an odd sight, and Tom vowed right there and then to do his duty as well as he was able and leave the rest to Providence.

The Long Island ferry left at the foot of Maiden Lane. At the lower end of the street, Tom and William Knox spotted some casks of sea bread, formed of canel and peas-meal into biscuits as hard as musket flints.

"Take some!" William urged. "Take as many as you can carry."

"Well, I guess I will!" Tom said. "I seem to be a bit hungry!" And they both laughed as he stuffed his shirt with the biscuits and clutched an extra handful to his buttons, stowing them in his knapsack as soon as they reached the ferry stairs. A crowd had gathered, as crowds did at almost any excuse in Manhattan, and as the young soldiers piled into their boats, they gave three cheers, which were echoed by the spectators along the wharves.

"Good luck to ye, ye bonnie lads!" called out one white-headed woman in a pink cap. For a fleeting moment she reminded Tom of his own good mother at home, but the feelings of homesickness that thought aroused threatened to become powerful ones, and he swallowed them as fast as he could.

Their crossing was swift, and they soon landed at Brooklyn and marched eagerly up the ascent from the ferry to the plain. Tom was following close behind his friend William and then nearly collided with him. William had stopped short at the sight of what was ahead—it was a sight to stop anyone cold. Coming down the slope were the wounded soldiers being evacuated, some white and silent on stretchers, some moaning awfully, some with broken legs, and some with bloody head wounds.

"Oh, no!" William gasped, and Tom was daunted, too.

" 'Tis a sight to make me think of home," William began, but Tom hushed him.

"Poor fellows will soon have doctoring," he said optimistically. "It's only that we are not used to the sight."

"Pray God we don't become accustomed to it."

A short distance along the plain, a halt was called for the soldiers to rest and refresh themselves. "Let's give those biscuits a try," Tom suggested, digging one out. Within sight of skirmishing between British and American soldiers below, now easily heard as well as seen, he tried to bite one of the biscuits, but gave up, laughing.

"Hard enough to break the teeth of a rat!" William declared. "Don't I wish we had some water."

"It will rain soon enough," Tom told him. The sky was pewter gray.

"By God, they are close by!" remarked their lieutenant colonel at one particularly loud report. Officers of the new levies wore cockades of different colors to distinguish them from the standing forces. He now ripped off his red cockade, saying, "I'm willing to risk my life in the cause of my country, but I'll be damned if I'll provide a brilliant target for their sharpshooters!"

"Colonel Arnold makes good sense," Tom said to William. Another young officer, unsettled by the firing so nearby, had lost his nerve, running among the resting troops sniveling and blubbering, praying for forgiveness if he had injured anyone. Pray that I do not so lose my courage, Tom thought, not blaming the man so much as feeling glad that it was not himself.

"He's a fool," William said in a low voice.

"As the poet says, 'Fear does things so like a witch—'tis hard to distinguish which is which,' " Tom said, quoting his father and feeling rather clever for having recalled the whole couplet.

"Your father was a clever chap," William acknowledged. "Pity you don't take after him!"

"Nor you, yours!" Tom joked, and the two young men had enough spare energy to rough and tumble.

The gray skies soon opened up, and the Massachusetts regiment marched on in the driving rain.

The fighting below them intensified without seeming to be in focus. To a man in the middle of it there was no apparent plan or purpose. Tom's regiment arrived at a mill pond where a regiment of Maryland volunteers was in desperate straits. They had been cornered by a British regiment and driven into the millpond at high tide. Those few who could swim had gotten across the pond; those who could not swim had sunk or made easy targets as they floundered in the weeds and mud.

"They look like water rats," William said, seeing the remnant of the regiment of southern gentlemen shivering on the banks. As the tide fell, Tom went into the water and helped remove a number of waterlogged corpses and a great many arms. One man had gone mad and was sobbing insanely.

"The grapeshot fell upon us like hail," reported one of the Marylanders who had survived. "Jesus, it was dreadful. The enemy had set up field pieces by that brick house there, and they poured it on us. 'Twould have been worse but for the twelve-pounder we got set up! Aye, it 'twould have been worse!"

Tom could not imagine worse, but he shared what was left of his biscuits, softened now from marching in the rain, with the dripping soldier. They spent the night on the ground near the millpond, without tents or anything to eat or drink but what they had carried with them or could pick up.

All night the scattered firing continued. Tom slept at last, but all his dreams were of sudden ambush. He woke hungrier than he had ever been in his life.

Inevitably, the first business of the next day was to find something to eat. Remembering a field of Indian corn a short distance from the creekbank where they had spent the night, Tom crossed the creek with a few of the others and headed for it. But near it, just abreast of a neat row of haystacks, they walked into a shower of British shot.

"Get behind the haystack!" the lieutenant with them called out, and Tom dove into the soft, sodden rack of hay as grapeshot whistled over his head.

For a few moments there was a brisk exchange of fire between the few Americans and an equal number of British, then some forty or fifty Americans came rushing across the creek in reinforcement, only to be followed by some forty or fifty Redcoats. The sound of firing alerted the rest of Tom's regiment, which came along in good time to meet a British force of equal size. By the time Tom's entire regiment was engaged they were in good shape to drive the British out of the field and across a split-rail fence.

"Now they are routed!" Tom exulted, but he was chagrined to see that several of his fellows had sustained severe wounds. One was a plump farmer from Brighton, another a redheaded man from Lincoln who could not have been more than sixteen. Their cries were piteous to hear as darkness fell. The entire regiment lay upon a rise covered with young trees, and all that could be done for the wounded men was to build a fence of saplings to prevent the approach of the enemy's horses. There were no other regiments in sight and no doctors, and as they lay there a day longer, three of the wounded men died. In the late afternoon of the second day, heavy rain began to fall. Soaked to the skin, still hungry, and unable to protect his ammunition, Tom was very discouraged.

"I wish I knew what the devil has in store next," Tom muttered to his friend William.

"Even Satan has abandoned us," William replied, for there was a strange suspension of all activity that made all of them feel cut off from the main thrust of the engagement. But at about sunset, when the storm had passed over, the colonel in charge rallied them, ordering them to parade and discharge their pieces, which they did awkwardly. The sound of gunfire brought General Putnam on horseback, dashing along at top speed wearing only a soiled shirt and a sleeveless waistcoat.

"Good work, lads! Onward!" Putnam shouted, and then, after conferring with the officers, was off at top speed, leaving the regiment as much in the dark as to the general plan as before.

"Now our muskets are as empty as our stomachs," Tom commented bitterly.

"And with half the trouble," William said.

"And not half the trouble to reload them."

"Unlike our stomachs."

So hungry was he that at dusk, Tom set off with William and a few others to find food at some nearby farm. Near a stand of fine, straight red oaks he saw a snug Dutch barn and a matching stone farmhouse. The property seemed deserted, and so it proved to be, but Tom found a one-horned milk cow which had been driven off but found her way back home and was sorely in need of a man's hand. Milking her into a pail, he drank gratefully, and then milked her again. With the contents of the pail and a few raw pumpkins they found in a neatly walled kitchen garden, he and the others filled their stomachs and made it back safely to the place where the rest of the regiment was sleeping on the ground, hard earth and wet leaves serving as their beds.

* * *

Meanwhile, the surprise General Howe had engineered was on. At nine o'clock that night, Howe dispatched a column of ten thousand men under General Henry Clinton and Lord Cornwallis from Flatlands with orders to surprise the undefended Jamaica Pass and then swing west to get at the Americans from the rear. Guided by three Tory farmers who had been born and raised nearby, the light dragoons, regiment after regiment of red-coated infantry, four battalions of grenadiers, a regiment of Highlanders in kilts, and fourteen pieces of artillery moved carefully in the dark, passing solid Dutch farms and neat cornfields ready for harvest. They moved stealthily, in complete silence, in some places reduced to single file across a narrow bridge or causeway. Even the most rudimentary American defense would have thrown them off course, but there were no roadblocks, no opposition, and they encountered no colonials except a small patrol that surrendered without a fight.

While the main guard advanced, Howe was launching a diversionary feint on the right of the American position, threatening the Flatbush and Bedford Passes with Hessians. The effect would be to corner both Sullivan's and Stirling's men, who were now spread out on the hills, facing the harbor, expecting attack, but ill-prepared to face the main body of the British army.

The sun rose on a long column of British, spread like a red ribbon on the horizon. They had occupied all the high ground along the ridgeline and astride the Jamaica Road, which ran along the top of the ridge. They were advancing steadily down the Bedford Road.

To one American scout, the sunrise was "red and angry." The rest of the day that followed was equally so. The news spread like wildfire along the heights from one post to the next, and the American line began to fold back to avoid capture. Soon a full two thousand men were scrambling down the slopes, racing through the woods and across tilled fields, some holding their formations in companies and batallions, some fleeing singly, shrieking "Every man for himself!"

Chapter Three

WASHINGTON HAD BEEN asleep in his Manhattan headquarters when he was awakened by the sound of firing from Brooklyn. He was informed that an action had started along the shore on the opposite side of the American position from Jamaica Road. Exactly what he expected! His conviction that this was the major battle was strengthened when dawn showed him British warships in full sail hurrying to the battery on Brooklyn Heights.

Gripped by a sense of the moment, Washington ordered more regiments to Long Island and jumped into a small boat with a few members of his headquarters guard, including Bayard Logan. It was a cool, clear day, and when they first arrived in Brooklyn, all seemed to be in order. Washington was told that the American left was undisturbed. In the center, Sullivan had advanced across the continuation of Jamaica Road to the edge of the hilly spine and was looking down at the Hessian regiments. To all appearances, the main action was still on the right, beside the harbor.

Mounted on a splendid gray stallion, Washington rode to the right to encourage the troops, many of whom he knew to be rookies. As ever, he gave the impression of great physical power, and was tremendously graceful on horseback. Cheered by the sight of him, many of the soldiers waved and smiled. "Quit yourselves like men, like soldiers, for all that is worth living for is at stake!" Washington called out.

Then, all of a sudden, a cannon boomed to the left, deep in the American position where no cannon ought to be. Washington's hands jerked on the reins. His horse responded by rearing and wheeling. A second shot came from the same direction, followed by a burst of marching music, and then, at the signal, the dreaded Hessians suddenly began charging up the slope toward Sullivan's center.

Bayard rode desperately to Washington's side, thinking only of protecting the commander in chief from gunfire. "Sir," he said urgently, "your place is inside the fortifications!"

Despite his dismay, Washington did not despair, nor did he panic. "Let them approach within twenty yards before you fire," he ordered a colonel.

"Sir, a messenger!" Bayard said.

The frightened messenger could hardly speak for the horror of his information. "Sir! The main British command has mysteriously appeared on the Jamaica Road, sir! They are at Sullivan's rear!"

"Steadfastness will save the day," Washington declared. After all, he believed, an enemy soldier was no more than an enemy soldier whether he was on your front or your rear.

This attitude did not seem to be widespread. The back road to Brooklyn Heights was soon filled edge to edge with running men. The sound of firing on the hills sank to a whisper and then died away. Almost surrounded and badly outnumbered, the Americans fled, hid when they could find a place to hide, or surrendered when they were cornered. There were many instances of bravery: Colonel Smallwood's Maryland regiment, tiny and determined, clung to a hillside buying time with blood. Washington looked out over the walls of the fortifications at Brooklyn Heights and watched them with his emotion clearly visible on his sunburned face. "Good God," he exclaimed, "what must my brave boys suffer today!"

General Stirling and his brigade were totally exposed, pinned between attack from the south and the British general Cornwallis at the rear. They stood firm for four hours. Between them and camp were Gowanus Creek, two large millponds, and a vast expanse of marsh. Although they could be seen by the rest of the American army, there was no way to get aid to them. Heroically, Stirling advanced to attack Cornwallis, and kept up a stubborn fight for about half an hour while the bulk of his men plunged into the swamps under desperate fire. The officers swam their horses over; some of the men swam and some of them floated, clinging to logs; but many drowned as they floundered, and many others, including Stirling, were left behind to the enemy.

Horror-struck, wounded, filthy, exhausted fugitive soldiers straggled into the fortification. Washington had his hands full keeping the ramparts manned and the spirit of resistance high. But the fort was held by four thousand of the greenest soldiers in the entire army of amateurs, and they were terrified both by the sounds and sights of the battle outside and the influx of battle-weary soldiers. Many bore gruesome wounds, many were twitching with pain, gushing blood, falling down dead. All was building to a last, totally devastating assault.

And as Washington looked over the ghastly scene, the British converged on the open space just beyond the ramparts. They halted—British in red, Hessian regulars in blue, and Yagers in green—fanning out like the spokes of a multicolored wheel. Their firing slackened and they ignored Washington's cannonfire. It was the largest assembled army Washington had ever seen together in one place. Through his spyglass he watched officers on horseback move among the troops, saw preparations for movement. In the fearful silence he heard orders called out.

"By God, now they will attack," Washington said grimly. His army was in complete confusion, scattered, frightened, and tired. From Howe's point of view, it was a tremendously favorable moment. Washington braced himself.

And then, incredibly, the thousands of red- and blue- and green-coated soldiers shouldered arms, lifted their knees in perfect unison, wheeled, and withdrew. In a few minutes they were out of cannon range. An expression of confusion crossed Washington's broad, handsome face and clouded his gray-blue eyes.

"What is happening, sir?" Bayard could not resist asking.

"General Howe has decided not to attack. Today. Unless . . ." Washington was wracked with suspicion, still wary of a trick. What might it be? A sneak attack tonight, under cover of darkness? A naval attack as soon as the wind and the tides were right? Dear God, the more one knew of military science, the more confusing it became. At any rate, there appeared to be a respite, however temporary, and the present need was to establish order.

"Double the sentries!" he ordered. "Rum and water for all. The men must be returned to their formations, and they must all be fed." All the afternoon, all the evening, Washington moved through the encampment, laboring to pull the army of wounded and terrified men together again.

"Where is General Sullivan?" Bayard asked of some Massachusetts soldiers he knew. The reply came that he had been captured. "Have you seen my brother Tom?" Bayard inquired of the same men.

The colonel seemed shocked to realize that Tom Logan was missing. He had led his men through a thicket of blueberries, across a sandy brook, and through a wheatfield. All of them were soaked with mud and exhausted; most of them were almost broken down. "He was right with us when we hightailed it into the woods. Knox was with him. Where's Knox?"

"Knox just came in, sir."

Men were still straggling into the fort, and Bayard kept an eye on the gate for the rest of the night, but there was no sign of Tom.

As the battle raged on Long Island, spies and counterspies in Manhattan turned their attention to the eastern skyline, watching the smoke and the movement of ships, making notes, and listening to rumors and reports with avid attention. Nearly all the spies among the Patriots, and their counterparts among the Tories, took scrupulous care not to attract attention to their lives in any way. Certainly each of them possessed great strength of character. It is an undeniable fact that the man or woman who enters upon the career of a spy must have all the qualifications of a good soldier and a commanding officer besides. A spy must not only be courageous, he must also have poise, self-possession, absolute self-control of his expression, tact, and discretion.

For a spy, discovery means death. His is the most dangerous of wartime undertakings.

44

* * *

At a coffeehouse called The Lark's Song, near Wall Street in lower Manhattan, it was the busiest hour of the day. As The Lark's owner and proprietor, William Whitestone was both well known and popular. His clientele included both Tories and those known to be sympathizers with the Patriot cause, as well as a good many soldiers in uniform. His own politics seemed clear to everyone—surely his newspaper had an obvious Royalist point of view—and yet a few who endorsed the rebellion trusted him with their lives. All in all, William Whitestone was one of that breed of men who attracts attention and admiration by his energy and originality without truly entering into the hearts of his fellows. Many men knew and liked Whitestone without really knowing him.

William Whitestone was a man ruled by many passions. Foremost among these was his desire to be entirely independent of restraints and good examples. His first rebellion had been against his extremely fashionable, extremely wealthy and domineering father. As a very young man, William had struck out on his own, emphatically separating himself from his father's realm and setting out to guarantee his own support.

Some years ago William had opened a bookstore in Manhattan, having visited London as a young man and taken the example of booksellers there, as well as the advice of the famous Dr. Johnson, who assured him that there were none of this trade worthy of note in all of the backward colonies. But from the start, William had diversified in his merchandising efforts, offering fiddles and fiddle strings, sheet music, writing paper and sealing wax, slates and chalk, as well as books. He sold jars of pickled sturgeon and patent medicines, both imported and home brewed. Indulging his own passion for gambling, he raised gamecocks in his back garden and offered them for sale. Indulging his love of cards and drink and for conversation and recreation of every variety, he had opened a coffeehouse adjacent to his bookstore and print shop, and from the start The Lark's Song had done very well.

Doubtless, there were spies among the men clustered at sturdy oaken tables and belly up to The Lark's long, curved walnut bar. Doubtless, because there were secrets to be discovered in the gossip of the tavern's diverse clientele, and where there are secrets, there are spies.

Josias Logan, successful merchant and father-to-be, was among the civilian New Yorkers who had come to The Lark's Song looking for news. With a slight wave to William, his brother-in-law, Josias took a seat at a round table of men he knew from commerce and from society.

The men looked grim.

"Harrumph! Good evening, Logan," said Richard Harrison, a sallow, powdered man of considerable wealth. He sat with Doctor Bard and John Moore, all of them cronies from the Moot, the Debating Society, and other elite hangouts.

"Good, you say?" Josias quipped.

"Disastrous," hissed Doctor Bard. "Dreadful!"

Josias ordered a rum, his usual drink. His voice was low. "I seek advice. Has the hour come, do you think, to evacuate the ladies?"

"That hour is either past, or not yet here. Besides, the Virginian has seized small craft on both the Jersey and Long Island shores."

"A more impudent, false, and atrocious commander never lived," Moore said.

Josias looked over his shoulder nervously. Moore's

46

statement was too bald for a public place. Neutrality was the pose of the wise, certainly in this place, where Continental soldiers were as likely as not to be sitting at one's elbow. And a more vulgar, violent lot had never drawn breath. A drunken soldier would draw a knife in a split second. Josias had seen it.

"Watch your tongue, Moore. And you, Logan, must take into account that your wife is delicate," Doctor Bard said.

"You all assume Howe will turn his guns onto Manhattan," Harrison said. "He may never need to."

"What have you heard?" Josias asked. Harrison's opinion interested him more than Moore's.

"Heard? I heard the cannonfire. I saw the smoke." Harrison lowered his voice, and Josias leaned forward. "That battle's over. Sullivan and Stirling have been taken prisoner. The Yankees are scrambling through the marshes like muskrats, and Howe has the ridge surrounded. It's my opinion the war is over, if you must call it a war."

Josias felt his heart pounding. More than anything, he wanted an end to this conflict. He longed to know for sure that there would be no more war, that ordinary life and ordinary commerce would begin again.

The heat had driven Bonnie and Meg from their house. Taking a little carriage and baby Dorothy in a basket, they drove north toward Turtle Bay, past the freshwater Collect Pond—so named by the Dutch and rumored to be not only bottomless but home to a sea monster. To the west rose the commanding Bayard's Mount, a sugarloaf hill crested with cedars that stood a hundred feet high. Past Delancey's

47

Square the city proper ended, and old Dutch farmsteads and orchards stretched calm and green in all directions. Here, they left behind the crooked, cobbled streets, the spicy aroma of the waterfront, the fly-covered sewage in the gutters, the shouts of peddlers, and the rumble of iron wheels.

"I do enjoy going out to the country," said Meg, a city girl through and through.

" 'Tis a lovely day," Bonnie said. She felt dreamy; the night before she had walked out with William Whitestone on the Mall and the grassy slope behind Trinity Church. They had sipped sweet wine and watched shooting stars, and she thought she was quite in love. Sometimes it seemed so symmetrical she could not believe it true; her sweet friend Meg married to her brother Josias and Meg's own brother William . . .

But William was different—a different sort of man from her own brothers and the rest of the men she knew socially. There was something so imposing about him that Bonnie was a little frightened of him, even though she could tell that he admired her. He knew so much, so many facts and so many people, so much about life that he made her feel lucky to be at his side. She was convinced William was the most brilliant, handsome, and marvelous man alive. She was sure she loved him. But she was not sure he loved her. He seemed always to be holding back, always seeing past the moments they shared, and he left her yearning, always yearning, for more of him.

"Meg, let's stop here and walk in the orchard," she proposed as a particularly handsome orchard of red apples and golden pears came into view. The trees were set in neat lines, and soft yellow light fell through the leaves in a lacy pattern on the grass below.

The sights and sounds of war, the battle being fought across the wide East River was far from their minds at this moment. Leaving Dorothy sleeping in her basket in the care of their driver, they walked together down the alley of red-laden apple trees.

"Whatever should happen, let's always be friends," Meg said sentimentally.

"Whatever could happen?" Bonnie wondered.

"Promise," Meg insisted.

"I do promise," Bonnie agreed readily enough.

"We must pick apples enough for sauce and pies," Meg said, beginning to gather fallen apples and those which hung low enough for her to reach. Although she was already grown large with her baby, she moved slowly and gracefully, almost like a ship in full sail. "Help me, Bonnie."

Bonnie began to fill a basket. "Someday," she said dreamily, "I should like to have an apple orchard of my own."

"And would you live in a tree?" Meg teased.

"No! In a house in the midst of the trees. With a pond, perhaps, and a snug walled garden. With roses."

Meg cut right to the point. "I don't know, Bonnie, if William will ever marry."

Bonnie was startled. It was as if Meg could read her mind and see that in her dream house, William must be the master and her husband. "What do you mean? Why do you say so?"

"I say so only because I know my brother. A bit. I wonder if anyone really knows him."

Bonnie was relieved, for though she felt that she knew him as no one else did, and that he admired her greatly, she agreed that William could be a mystery. Still, she was insecure, and Meg's mild advice troubled her a bit. "He has been most kind to me," she remarked, suffering a little at the suggestion that her suitor's attentions might not be trained toward the sacrament of marriage.

"He is kind," Meg said stoutly, "and I've never seen him care for any woman more than he seems to care for you. It's just that he's so independent. I don't know if he'll ever marry, that's all."

Bonnie relaxed. William was independent, that was surely true; anyone could see that. And he was stubborn and complicated. He had never promised her a thing, but she felt surely that he liked her, and she knew that he could never bore her. But for now, she reasoned, perhaps it was best not to build such hopes for the future. These were uncertain times for all of them. The thought of seeing him again was enough, for now.

"Don't be silly," she told Meg, shivering a little for no reason at all. "Do we have enough apples? Shouldn't we go back? Oh, see those rosy pears. Let's gather some, and I will try to make pear preserves as my mother always did!"

In the blackness of night Bayard Logan accompanied General Washington as he rode the ramparts, looking out to the edges of the woods where the British had raised their city of white tents, listening for a sneak attack. Dawn arrived, robed in a foggy drizzle, but it was just possible to see that something new had been added to the picture: the British had dug a trench, sixty rods long, parallel to the American works, so angled that it could not be fired into.

"A foreseeable scientific approach," Washington said to Bayard. "Soon they will set cannon in that trench, then dig another, even closer to our redoubt."

Bayard agreed that it seemed likely, but he could hardly listen for worry. He was consumed with anxiety about Thomas. Bayard had been waiting for two days for his brother's return, or any word of what had happened to him. None came. His duty as a soldier was to guard the commander in chief and to follow orders, but how could a man not take personal responsibility for his own younger brother? He was surrounded by drenched, starving, sick, and frightened men, but at least these men were safely inside the fortifications. Tom was out there somewhere. Was he still hiding out, trying to make his way into the lines? He could not bear to think of the other possibilities—that his brother had been taken prisoner, had possibly been tortured, or was already dead or lying moribund, but these ghastly possibilities were alive on the fringes of his imagination and would not dispel themselves. He tried to keep his mind on his duties, but it was hard.

Following Washington as he inspected ammunition boxes, Bayard heard a chorus of bitter complaints from the exhausted soldiers. Much of the gunpowder had been spoiled by the driving rains. Rations were scarce and what there was, was moldy. In every corner of the fortifications, wounded men moaned and died. The men were dreadfully dispirited, although the imposing sight of General Washington on a tall, gray horse encouraged them for a time.

"I am determined that it is time to retreat," Washington told Bayard. "Damn it, I'd say it's unavoidable. How can we ask more of men who have already given so much? Call a council of general officers so that we may resolve this and make an immediate plan."

"Yes, sir," Bayard said. "But, sir?"

"What is it, Logan?" Washington's face was lined, his voice tired and sad. Bayard felt the chill he always felt in the presence of the commander in chief, one to which he would never become accustomed. He felt, unmistakably, that he was in the presence of greatness. Although he, as captain of Washington's honor guard, had more opportunity than most to see the general engaged in ordinary human activities—eating, weary, discouraged, bored, homesick, even angry—this had done nothing to dispel the mystique that surrounded the tall Virginian.

Never had Bayard known a man so thoroughly a gentleman, so thoroughly kind, yet completely courageous. Bayard had come to feel for his commander the love and respect he had used to feel for his own father, so recently dead of heart failure, and still there was more—a more mature respect grown of witnessing Washington on duty, seeing his dedication, idealism, and efficiency in matters of life and death to thousands of men. Bayard had no doubt but that he was loved in return, and yet, on this occasion, he hated to add one more concern to the great burdens of the day.

"Sir, my brother Thomas is missing."

A frown passed over Washington's broad face. "I am sorry, Logan."

"I don't believe he is dead, sir. I don't believe it!"

Washington listened calmly. During the six months or so that Bayard had served him, he had become very fond of the handsome young Yankee and trusted him completely. He valued him for his tact, modesty, and good sense. Although he was not a Virginian, he was well bred and educated. Whatever Logan wanted, Washington was inclined to go along with him; Logan was not the sort to cry wolf.

"It may sound a long shot, sir, but I want to go look for him."

Washington considered it. No one could doubt

young Logan's intelligence, yet how could he think that one brother could find another in an occupied war zone? And then he saw that Bayard's face was set with misery and longing. It was in his power to release him on this heart's errand, and he would do so. "I cannot do without you, Logan," he said at length. "Do not risk your life. You may go, but return by nightfall."

"Thank you, sir. I will return directly; you may count on that."

"Take a good horse."

"Thank you, sir."

But in the end, Bayard slipped out of the fortifications on foot, carrying a pack of damp biscuits, a flask of brandy, a knife, and a standard Brown Bess. He knew that the Massachusetts regiment had straggled into the fort after crossing a millpond past a stand of alder; he headed that way, making every effort to be both swift and silent. The ground he crossed was slick with blood-soaked mud trampled into a mire by the retreating soldiers.

Chapter Four

THANKING GOD FOR the cover of a dense ground fog, Bayard headed into the grove of young alders and passed within thirty feet of a manned British cannon. He slipped across a trench, smelling a cooking fire and the odor of grilling meat that wrenched his empty stomach like a vise. In the stillness of the forest, the sound of dinnertime conversation was loud; he heard one young voice complain that the bit of meat he was allotted was all gristle, then heard a chorus of "God Save the King," as the soldiers passed round their ration of rum.

Proceeding stealthily, Bayard moved through the trees toward the gleam of a body of water. He did not doubt that it was the millpond the Massachusetts men had described. He must be moving closer to Tom. Dear God, don't let him perish, his heart asked. He let his instincts guide him, let his bones and blood decide to turn left rather than right along the mucky, reed-choked shoreline.

The near-full moon rose, resembling a chagrined face looking down upon the battlefield. Bayard stopped when he saw strange pale blue shapes ahead. Standing absolutely still, he thought he heard someone moving nearby. At length he realized the noise was the beating of his own heart and advanced deliberately. The pale shapes resolved themselves as the bodies of two Americans, half-submerged in the mud, their swollen faces looking like scarecrows. He forced himself to look until he was satisfied that neither was his brother, and kept on.

Here the mud was knee deep and the going was slow. The surface of the pond was still. He paused, listening. Bullfrogs croaked and he saw the curved silhouette of a pair of nesting loons amid the rushes. Mosquitoes whined at his ears. And then he heard the tramp of a party of soldiers coming toward him from the alder grove. He dared not splash into the pond to hide. Spying a massive fallen pine, he carefully lay down behind it, hidden in a thicket of raspberry brambles and ferns.

And there, stilling his breath, he lay and waited.

Two, then two more red-coated soldiers splashed along the edge of the marshy pond, smelling of gunpowder and meat. Bayard had never felt more foolish, more helpless, in his life. He willed his breath to still itself, and prayed to God to save him now. He had been reckless, coming out alone. He was shirking his duty as an officer on this brotherly crusade.

Two of the soldiers sat on the log, their coattails hanging back, nearly brushing Bayard's face. They were sharing a flask of grog.

"Give it here!" one of them demanded nastily.

"Wait yer turn."

"Hurry up."

"Ah . . ."

"Hurry up."

"Here's to King George and victory!"

The flask, emptied, sailed over Bayard's head and

landed with a splash in the pond. The soldier who had thrown it belched and exclaimed, ''Damn me if I don't like this fighting! I'd like to be forever tanning the Yankees. Their dead officers shall make our fortune.''

''Aye, Alister, we've epaulets and gold braid, purses and watches. So why did you kick out that poor sod's false teeth?''

''Why? Because they're ivory and worth plenty, you damned fool, and the taking of them's a soldier's right, same as the lockets and charms.''

''I'd not want to answer to God for it.''

''Fine talking of God with a soldier, whose trade and occupation is cutting throats! Our King is answerable to God for us! I fight for him. My religion consists in a Brown Bess, good flint, well-rammed charge, and seventy rounds of powder and shell, and my prayers are for fresh dead to loot tomorrow.''

''Then pray the Yankees don't ferry across the river.''

''The only river they'll ferry over is the river Styx.''

Bayard lay without moving, without breathing, listening to the British soldiers bray and squabble like children, his mind lurching between fear of death and appreciation of the absurd. He felt the minutes pass, each as long as an hour, until one of the soldiers exclaimed, ''Hark! Hear you that?''

Bayard felt the earth under him shake as they stood up, the backs of their legs pushing against the fallen log.

''They'll not have our pickings, by God!'' one muttered. They feared their own, other looters who might take their treasure from them.

''It came from over there,'' a soldier hissed, ''in the ferns.'' And with those words he stepped over

56

the log, his heel missing Bayard's sleeve by a fraction of an inch. He had but to turn his head to see Bayard, but he looked forward. Stealthily, Bayard gripped his musket and tensed.

"Hello," the soldier called back to his comrades, "here's one we nearly missed, not quite gone under, I daresay. He'll not have much, by the look of him, but . . ."

One of his companions stepped over the log to follow, and saw Bayard in the first instant. As he opened his mouth to shout Bayard jumped quickly to his feet and struck him in the chest with the butt of his musket, and he collapsed like a wet sack.

The soldier who had noticed the body in the ferns turned and discharged his musket, but missed. Bayard then immediately struck him and touched him with the muzzle before he discharged his Brown Bess. He staggered backward, mortally wounded. "Jesus, my God," he exclaimed, "I am a dead man." He fell back into the mud, clutching Bayard's musket in a death grip.

A musket ball tore through Bayard's coat as he turned. Cursing, the soldier fixed his bayonet and stepped over the log. Bayard drew his knife and ran at him.

They met; as the soldier gave Bayard a slash across the face, Bayard ran his knife into his throat. His blood spurted over him, and he fell to the ground.

The remaining Redcoat was now too close to raise his Brown Bess. Bayard raised his knife but the soldier clubbed his right side with his musket. Bayard fell, the wind knocked out of him, and the soldier pointed his weapon at his face.

Bayard thought himself dead, but the blast did not come. The dead soldier in the ferns had come to life, jumped up, and seized the Redcoat; together they fell struggling to the ground. The Redcoat tried to use his musket, but Bayard pounced and used his remaining strength to pin his arm to the ground. In desperation he bit Bayard's finger to the bone before his other opponent struck him senseless with his fist.

The sudden silence seemed unreal. The all-too-familiar, commingled smell of gunpowder and blood pervaded the little clearing as the two men, both on their hands and knees, fought to catch their breath, their heads nearly touching.

And Bayard gasped, "Thomas!"

"My God, Bayard!"

With a twisted grin, Bayard said, "Fancy meeting you here!" as the brothers fell into an embrace.

Sheets of rain continued to fall, and it was dark long before night.

General Washington was sustained only by his nervous energy. He had not slept for days, and was in that condition in which a man could drink gin and know no effect other than that of water. Exhausted, he had at times caught himself dreaming on horseback, and once he had almost issued an order for Bayard Logan to convey before remembering that Logan had not returned. The longer Bayard was gone, the more likely it was that he would not return. Washington regretted letting Logan go. Logan was worth a dozen other men to him. It had been an error, and he blamed his own judgment. Waging war was naught but a progression of mortal errors, it seemed; the greater general was merely he who made fewer mistakes.

Washington was deeply involved in the problem of how to move his entire army across the East River to safety without attracting the attention of the British. On the surface, it seemed to be impossible. Spies abounded and the British army was within earshot and eyeshot of both the ramparts and the river. A mile of water to be crossed, ten thousand men to be moved . . . and what if the British army caught them in mid-stream?

Any error would lead to disaster. Washington's plan was to tell a series of brilliant lies. Not even high officers were told the truth. Fresh troops were needed, he said, to relieve the tired men trapped in the Brooklyn Heights fortifications. He summoned John Glover's Massachusetts fishermen, the most rugged of sailors from Salem and Gloucester and Marblehead, to man all the small boats on the rivers. He ordered the troops in Brooklyn to prepare to be relieved at midnight by troops from New Jersey. Everyone was warned that safety in so complicated a shift of forces required complete silence.

Silent in the drenching rain, the troops waited on the Brooklyn shores. As regiments were withdrawn from the lines, the men still in position were ordered to spread out and fill in until the fresh troops should arrive to take over.

In Manhattan, the Yankee fishermen gathered by the East River in all manners of small craft—every sloop, yacht, fishing smack, yawl, scow, and rowboat that could be found in any water from the Battery to King's Bridge or Hell Gate. Every one of these men, expert at oar and sail, stood looking out for the mythical troops from New Jersey, and then were amazed by their orders—to take the boats across the river empty.

"And keep yer oars quiet!" Glover commanded.

"Blimey, is the man mad? Sending us out without the Jersey troops?" muttered a wizened little fellow from the Massachusetts north shore, nicknamed "Cod."

"The captain's more than right, as usual," another, a free black man, said. "He's for pulling our men out of a place where they're dead as decoy ducks."

Favoring the crossing, the harvest moon found a path through the clouds and shone brightly on the flotilla of tiny boats scurrying across the mile-wide river. Nothing could entirely still the splash of so many oars or the low voices of ten thousand men embarking with their heavy guns and stores, but somehow, the British slept, not even sentries wakening, either on shore or on the fleet.

All through the night the troops were ferried across the water, loads of men and cannon, small arms, ammunition, tools, horses, and all the larder besides. General Washington seemed to be everywhere at once, appearing suddenly through the darkness and silence, a tall, glimmering figure on a tall gray horse.

Inevitably, there were moments of panic. Men who could not see the trail ahead of them and marched to the whispered instructions of invisible guides stumbled and fell; some of them tried to climb onto the backs of men ahead of them. Cows, used to being driven with cries, refused to be driven in silence, and had to be left behind. The rain beat down unceasingly. Some of the guns were so heavy they sank in the mud, and even teams of oxen could not extract them. In the wee hours, the winds turned fickle and some small crafts collided mid-river. The strong current spun the tiny craft in its whirlpools. But the men were valiant.

"Don't leave 'em as much as a biscuit," Glover advised and looked the other way as seaman Cod tipped up a cask of Medford rum to lighten it.

As the final regiments slipped out of the Brooklyn ramparts, a skeleton force slipped in to keep the campfires burning and give the cries of sentries.

Dawn was near and men were still crowding toward the shore. Washington rode to the shore, hurrying the last of the troops, fearing that dawn's light would expose them to the eyes of the British, but like a miracle, a heavy fog came over the water, swallowing the little boats before they had gone six feet.

Washington rode back to the ramparts to alert the last of the rear guard. In all the struggle and confusion, his young captain of the guard had never been far from his mind. Sad to say, Bayard had not yet come in. It was unlikely now that ever he would. Damn the fellow! He should not have taken the chance!

As Bayard and his brother struggled back toward the ridge-top fortifications, Tom told his story in the lowest of tones: "All was confusion when they turned our flank. I tried to stay close to William, but we ran through a cornfield, and when I came out the other side, I was alone, but for a few British. I'd wrenched my knee, you see. I ducked back into the corn until dusk. I've been crawling and playing possum. . . . Sweet Jesus, I lost track of the time!"

"All these days look like nights," Bayard growled. "But I reckon two have passed, at least."

"I thought I was dead. I thought I was dead," Tom said over and again, marveling in his existence, shaking with the glory of being cold and wet, hungry and tired, and yet still alive. "I thought of Mother. I thought of you, too."

Seeing the grove of alders ahead, Bayard knew that safety was not far. The wound on his face was bleeding freely, and he had wrapped his bloody, throbbing finger in a piece of his coat lining. His ribs ached from the blow he had taken from the musket butt. Still, he was triumphant that he had found Tom; finding Tom made anything worthwhile.

As soon as he approached the fortifications, Bayard sensed that something had changed. A dense fog hung over the encampment, and it seemed strangely silent. He gave the password—"starlight"—to the sentry and slipped inside. The fortifications were nearly empty.

"What? What?" Bayard asked, almost frightened. Staggering, he struggled to make sense of it.

"All the troops is goin' down to the ferry," muttered the sentry. "Best you two git there quick!"

"General Washington?" Bayard asked. "Where is the general?"

And out of the fog loomed a massive gray stallion, and Washington leaned down. "Thank God you are returned to us!" he said, and Bayard felt his commander's familiar voice like a benediction. "Good heavens, your face is a mask of blood!"

"I'm fine, sir!" And he really was.

"Make haste, Logan! Make all haste to the ferry slip. The sun is an hour high already, and the last of the army has been moved."

Calling on the last of his strength, Bayard obeyed, carried along the muddy path to the ferry steps by the eager rush of the last regiment to leave the trenches. At the ferry, the boats had not yet returned from their last crossing, but they came in good order, and with the commander in chief, the Logan brothers stepped into one of the last boats to leave Long Island, and were swallowed by the fog.

In the week following Katy Montgomery's birthday party, the city of Charleston suffered a heat wave of proportions unusual even in that semitropical town. Day after blistering day, night after airless night passed without relief, and the tempers of her citizens flared even hotter than the rays of the summer sun.

Although Taylor Montgomery was not immune to the discomfort of the weather, he was far more disturbed by the clouds of war that he glimpsed on the not-so-distant horizon than by the ferocity of the late-afternoon thunderstorms that blew across the Carolina coast. By nature a peace-loving man who loved and was loved by a wide circle of friends and family, Taylor found himself increasingly and uncomfortably at odds with nearly everyone he knew.

It was a situation that suited him not at all, for Taylor despised dissent. Above all, he was accustomed to approval and easy conviviality, used to courtesy and easy conversational exchange.

Not that Taylor—beloved second son, fearless horseman, natural gentleman and scholar, most graceful of dancers and wittiest of raconteurs—could have been said to lack character. It was blue-eyed Taylor whom his Princeton classmates had dubbed "Squire Worthy, Lord of the Ladies," well-appointed Taylor who had been elected to lead the opening march at the St. Cecelia Christmas cotillion, reckless Taylor who, at the age of sixteen, lost one hundred pounds at the track in one day, and won it back on the next.

Taylor and Webb. Webb and Taylor. Since boyhood, they had been a charming, invincible team, their allegiance hardly strained by Taylor's traveling north to the College of New Jersey at Princeton, or Webb's marriage, two years ago, to the amiable Miss Susannah Gridley. Webb and Susannah had settled chiefly in town, having had designed and built for them a splendid broad town house with a wide sea view. The plan was that Taylor, when he had chosen a suitable bride, would undertake the construction of a matching house, adjoined to Webb and Susannah's and sharing a spacious backyard with tropical garden.

The matter of the suitable bride seemed an easy one to resolve, for among all the comely and charming girls of Charleston, Taylor had ever preferred red-haired Lucinda Carroll, and it was evident to everyone that Lucinda loved him.

But Taylor had come south this summer with a mind and heart full of beliefs and opinions that set him in direct opposition to his brother Webb, and for the first time in their lives there was a coolness between them that threatened to affect all their well-laid plans.

One hot and humid afternoon, during that hot and humid week, Taylor left the house to meet Webb at the waterfront Merchants' Exchange. Although there were two carriages and a sulky available, he set out on foot, waving farewell to his sister Liza, who was engaged in some needlework on the shaded side gallery. All the rest of the family had retired to dim, cool bedrooms to rest.

For the time being, he was resident at his parents' summer house in Charleston, a house bursting to the seams with projects and parties, women and their conversations. The life of the house, like the life of the city, was underlaid by a small army of black slaves who spent their days carrying and fetching, dusting and polishing, washing clothes and concocting dishes for an endless procession of bountiful meals. There was scarcely a quiet corner in the entire three stories, and Taylor missed his privacy, privacy he had enjoyed in his quarters at college and had come to relish. But, until he decided what course his life must now take, he would remain at home, where his mother and sisters were delighted to have him, delighted to see him and spoil him with attention and all his favorite dishes.

The city Taylor strolled through was sultry and subdued. Nearly everyone who was not obliged to perform physical work had retreated to some shady corner to escape the sun and heat. Most shops were closed on summer afternoons; the fish and produce stands were draped in lengths of cotton cloth, and a yellow dog slept in the slave market where a prime shipment of healthy Africans had paraded past the auctioneer only that morning.

Even after the sophisticating experience of travel, after seeing Philadelphia and Baltimore, Taylor greatly admired his hometown. Some said that it had a foreign flavor unlike any other American city, with its broad streets and lawns laid out in a gridiron design and set neatly along them the great number of genteel homes of wood and brick, most of them festooned with balconies or piazzas. Nearly all the fine houses were quite new; a building boom had taken place during Taylor's lifetime, following the devastating hurricane of 1752.

The Merchants' Exchange, one of the most famous buildings in America, was only five years old. It stood near the waterfront, across Meeting Street from St. Michael's Church, and, with its pilasters of imported Portland stone and a roof of Welsh Carnavon slate, was extremely grand. Dennison Montgomery had been one of the planters involved in its commissioning, and the whole family had witnessed every stage of its construction and was as proud of the Exchange as if it had been their own house.

Webb had business there, and had sent word to Taylor to meet him. During the years Taylor had been up north at school, Webb had taken over more and more of the family's business concerns, dealing with shipping and factoring while the affairs of the plantation itself, the planting and harvesting of rice and indigo, had been left to their father. The understanding in the family was that Taylor would eventually take over his father's duties at Ashley Hall.

As he approached the Exchange and the meeting with his brother, Taylor's steps slowed. He was apprehensive. The last thing he wanted to undertake was a political discussion with Webb; he sensed how far apart their loyalties had spread, and suspected Webb had not yet realized the true extent of the division. He had missed his brother, his comrade, during the school year, and longed for a restoration of their easy, amusing partnership. But over the course of the summer, such a reconciliation had become increasingly unlikely.

Gulls wheeled overhead in the bright blue sky, and the scent of low tide greeted him as he crossed a floating wooden bridge that stretched out to some of the docks. Scores of children—black and white—could be seen scurrying through the reeds and splashing through the mud flats, gathering oysters and clams in the ebony sands. He turned back inland a way and saw his brother through the huge, many-paned glass windows of the Merchants' Exchange.

Webb saw him, too, slammed down his brandy glass, rose, and came outside.

"Hello, Taylor! Glad to see you come along! Let's take a walk, I've had enough of ciphers and cylinders for any one day! On my word, it's hot!"

The brothers clasped hands in a salute, then swung into a stroll, their gaits matching easily. Webb was an inch or two taller; Taylor a shade more elegantly dressed, but the family resemblance was strong. No one seeing them could fail to conclude that they were brothers; the high brow, the deep-set dark blue eyes, the aristocratic bone structure marked them as members of the Montgomery family.

Across the water the low islands in the harbor shimmered and trembled in the hazy light, and Taylor allowed his eyes to rest on them for a moment. Webb broke the companionable silence as they turned into a narrow, curving street lined with sailmakers' shops. To make the most of the sea breeze, the craftsmen and their apprentices had pulled their sails and bolts of cloth out into the street, covering it with yards of white like drifts of snow.

"Let's go to Taggart's for a cool drink," Webb suggested.

"That old pirate's still alive?"

"More or less."

Eli Taggart, who was or was not a retired pirate but who, with his peg leg and golden earring, certainly looked the part, ran a garden cafe near the Exchange that was known for strong drinks and an exotic atmosphere. At this hour, the cafe was nearly empty, and it was as cool as a jungle hut, built as it was in a ring around a massive poinciana tree, whose spreading branches formed a green roof. Taggart kept parrots; green, yellow, and red, that chattered and complained on low hedges around the tree, and grew his own fruits, which he mixed with dark rum for his famous drinks.

"Taylor, there's something I've been meaning to say to you," Webb began, when they were seated and had sweet-smelling potions on their table.

"Say it," Taylor urged. Sitting in Taggart's backyard, he felt as if he were sixteen again. Nothing here had changed in five years.

"I think you ought to join our militia," Webb said. "You know I've started up my own guard unit—jolly fellows, you know most all of them, and

67

what's happened recently makes me think there really is going to be a bit of a fight."

"We must do everything in our power to prevent it," Taylor said quickly. "War would be a catastrophe."

Webb scowled. "What do you mean? You know what happened on Sullivan's Island in June? The war's already on. We were attacked. Against great odds, we sent them packing! It was an awful fight; Davie and I were there. We saw it, saw men killed."

Taylor snorted. "Webb, you sound happy about it."

"Well, I'm not sad. It had to be. The situation's intolerable!"

"So say some. But the situation is, Webb, and pray do not let your temper guide your tongue, that we exist in a compact with the King, that compact is our agreed foundation of government, and that compact has not been broken. These are very serious matters, precisely, as you say, because they involve men's lives."

"Taylor, you sound like a periwigged judge!"

Taylor laughed, but he continued seriously. "Whatever or whoever I sound like, my point is that I consider it a matter of individual conscience. Every man must exercise his own reason these days, and decide for himself what to do. At this point, I am far from inclined to join the jolly fellows. You make it sound like the Monday Night Club—cards, feasting, and plenty to drink!"

"It is pretty much the same membership," Webb admitted. "But it's no joke, Taylor. I hope you don't misunderstand. People in town are taking heed of who's loyal and who's not . . ."

"By loyal I assume you mean disloyal," Taylor said stiffly. The rum was making his blood race; he felt the heat uncomfortably for the first time that day.

The suggestion that he was already the subject of gossip annoyed him.

"I mean loyal to Charleston, to Carolina, to ourselves. What the rebels, what the convention in Philadelphia is saying, is that we ought to be independent and that we can fight for ourselves."

"That's just what I mean to do—stand up for myself. I consider myself a British citizen and I am pleased and proud to be one. I don't fancy being coerced into any positions, any declarations, least of all war, which would bring down madness and mob rule."

"Mob? Don't you see, Taylor, the mob you fear is us!"

"Maybe. Maybe you think it is."

"This is rebel territory, Taylor. If you refuse to join the militia, you'll be asked to sign a loyalty oath."

Taylor lost his temper. "You mean a disloyalty oath? Good Christ, Webb! How can you be so sure you are right? How dare you have the presumption to lead fathers and sons off to their deaths for some idea you have of liberty?"

"We have to defend ourselves!"

"Not if you don't start trouble."

"So you think we're all wrong? Me and father and all our closest friends?"

"Men of principle and integrity may think differently from other men of equal good intent. I can consult only my own conscience."

Webb rose slowly to his feet and swayed there. "I am sick to hear you talking so, Taylor. Damned if you don't sound like a coward!"

"Shall I draw a sword to prove I am not?" Taylor demanded, jumping up. His face was white and his eyes blazed. "What will you do to prove you are not a fool?"

"Enough," Webb said with obvious effort. "Brother, let us cease right here. Neither of us is about to change the other's mind. Let us part at once, for now. But I warn you—sign the loyalty oath."

"I cannot and I will not," Taylor said in an awful voice, but Webb had already stridden out of the cafe, setting off a chorus of parrot talk as he rushed through the shady courtyard.

Chapter Five

BAYARD AND THOMAS Logan were among the very last of the wet, weary, and bedraggled troops to arrive on the East River shores and straggle through the narrow streets of Manhattan in the chill of that foggy morning. It was wretchedly, unseasonably cool as it so often is at August's end.

Surgeons moved among the scores of wounded who had been transported across the river on litters and now lay in rows, their bloody heads bandaged, the stumps of their severed arms and legs being quickly stuffed into canvas sacks. It was a gruesome sight, and the moans of the sick and dying made a low accompaniment to the clash of guns being moved and the rattle of iron wheels on the cobblestones. Drums and fifes had met the vanguard of the retreat, but now a general dampness—of spirits as well as skies—prevailed, and only a few citizens lined the streets to see the fighting heroes home.

Among them, to be sure, were Bonnie and Meg, Meg great with child, swollen and proud as any *grande dame*, and seated regally in a smart black carriage with Bonnie and a careful driver. Bonnie called

71

out delightedly when she finally spotted her brothers.

"Bayard! Tom! Over here! Oh, how glad I am to see you!"

Without thinking, Tom cut out of ranks and headed for Bonnie's voice. Bayard only saluted at first.

Bonnie chattered away, the sound of her voice a wonderfully optimistic sound in the general gloom. "Why were you so late? Goodness, we had nearly given up on you two. We reckoned you had come and gone already. Good heavens! What happened to Bayard's face? He looks dreadful! Oh, my word!"

Meg began to cry at the sight of them both so wet and filthy, so exhausted and cast down. Then she saw the bloody scar crossing Bayard's face, from nose to chin, and let out a shriek.

"Oh, hush, Meg, oh, please don't take on so," Bonnie chattered. "Josias will have my hide for letting you come out with me! Oh, do stop! Bayard! Please come and show you're all right."

Bayard worked his way through the crowd of soldiers and spectators toward the women's carriage. Out of the corner of his eye he thought he saw William Whitestone watching the disembarkment from a vantage point. Bayard bowed when he reached the black carriage. "Good morning, ladies. I'll live, Miss Meg, sister. But you two would do well to get home and stay out of harm's way."

"We only came out of concern for you," Bonnie informed him. "Praise God you are safe and alive. We have heard the most dreadful rumors about the fighting in Brooklyn. Promise me you will come to us as soon as you can and tell us the truth. You, too, Tom!"

A lone fifer struck up a tune and the two Logan brothers remembered they were soldiers. All around them, men fell in automatically to make their way to dry quarters and a long-delayed hot breakfast. All the soldiers were hungry, with the sort of hunger that drives out any other questions until it is satisfied. As they crossed the island the sun broke through the clouds, and the wind shifted to the south. It would be a beautiful, clear day, the sort of day when the British fleet would be able to move swiftly into position to stop their retreat. They had been lucky, although most of them were too tired and hungry to consider their good fortune. Some of them just lay on the cobblestone streets in the sunshine, drying out and catching their wind. Soggy clothing and blankets were draped over fences to dry in the sun.

The men were disheartened, despairing, downcast. Many of them decided then and there to leave the army and go home. As regiments gathered, they sadly counted their numbers and reappropriated beds and blankets. The troops were back in Manhattan, but for how long?

Surely, this was the question uppermost in the mind of the army's commander in chief. When ten days had passed since the retreat from Brooklyn—an orderly retreat, one that had established without a doubt the efficacy of a soldiery able to think for itself, to survive swirling currents and dense fog in brave silence, one that would long seem miraculous to trained military minds, but after all, a retreat—Washington was no closer than before to knowing what on earth General Howe's plans might be. There had been no indication whatsoever of an impending British assault; there had been no clue as to what was happening behind their breastworks.

Washington was torn and confused. He saw

clearly that remaining on Manhattan was courting total disaster, what with the British throwing up entrenchments from Brooklyn to Newtown Creek, all the way north to Hell Gate and Flushing. He had seen the frigate *Rose* sail up the East River and enter Turtle Bay, absolutely oblivious to the bombardment of the American guns on shore. More and more warships circled Long Island, came down the Sound, and settled in the East River. The enemy on Montresor's Island was so close that American scouting parties could insult them without raising their voices. The noose was tightening.

On the other hand, Washington feared that his diminished, discouraged army could not survive another humiliating defeat.

Bayard, who had himself heard outrageous, near-mutinous grumbling in the ranks, sat in on a council meeting of the general officers. Washington's headquarters were in Richmond Hill, celebrated as the most delightful country seat on Manhattan Island. Its builder, Abraham Mortier, was now paymaster for the British army. Richmond Hill was lovely in summer, its gardens brilliant with roses, its circular lily pond fragrant with teacup-sized lilies and shaded by ancient oaks.

The house itself was splendid: a massive frame building with a portico supported by two Ionic columns and decorated with carved pilasters. Bayard enjoyed extremely comfortable quarters in a little room off Washington's second-floor bedroom, which had a railed balcony looking west across checkerboard grounds planted with grass and grain, and south to the city a mile and a half away.

"An immediate evacuation is in order," argued Israel Putnam. The veteran general was not tall, but was very stout and strongly built and had a remarkable head of bushy white hair. Bayard had heard

Washington refer to Putnam as "the old gentleman." No one could argue with Putnam's logic when he said, " 'Tis manifestly impossible for our depleted forces to defend sixteen miles of coastline!"

But Heath, Spencer, and Clinton were loath to abandon the city they had fortified at such cost and effort. " 'Twould dispirit the men," they asserted. General Greene, recovering from his fever, advised Washington to abandon the city. Washington had gone so far as to ask Congress for permission to burn it down—there was increasing precedent for this, as the Virginians had torched Norfolk a few weeks earlier to prevent Lord Dunmore from using it as his base of operations—but Congress had refused.

"Congress has made a capital error this time," Washington had confided to Bayard. Bayard kept his own counsel, as was completely appropriate, but he was relieved. He had only to think of his sister-in-law's condition, or the fine houses along the Mall which he had visited, to envision the terrible turmoil a fire in the city would cause.

"Congress wants New York held at any price, at all hazards," General Washington continued. "I believe the British want it served up to them whole. They can settle in beautifully and supply themselves with every luxury from the many wharves and docks."

The generals all agreed that the obvious military move was north, thus they discussed the defensibility of Harlem Heights, the rough, hilly, northern end of Manhattan Island. They would pursue a compromise course: nine thousand troops would withdraw to Harlem Heights, five thousand would remain in the city proper. Work would be speeded up at the three forts under construction: Fort Independence at Kingsbridge and the two forts on the

Hudson, Fort Washington and Fort Lee. Lookouts would be stationed on all high places, and every effort would be made to penetrate the British lines and obtain information about their plans.

"I regret my network of intelligence is not as efficient as in Boston," Washington complained. "Leave no stone unturned, and do not stick at expense, to improve this situation." Heeding this plea, Bayard now proposed a young soldier who might make a useful agent; a former Connecticut schoolteacher whom he had met at William Whitestone's bookstore, a man named Nathan Hale. Washington agreed to interview Hale in the hexagonal room at Richmond Hill.

Meanwhile, General John Sullivan, who had been taken prisoner on Long Island, had been released by the British, exchanged for a prominent Tory, Benjamin Franklin's son William, who had been Royal governor of New Jersey before the Patriots had overthrown the Tory government in that state. Sullivan had been held aboard Lord Richard Howe's ship and had there received the most courteous of treatment, the finest of wines and meals, and constant assurance that the Howes wanted nothing more than an honest chance to work out a peaceful settlement with the rebels.

Washington could not swallow the news. "Preposterous!" he swore to Bayard.

Still, Bayard's allegiance to Sullivan was deep. How could he forget the days when his father and Sullivan—and Bayard's Uncle Dugald, too—had shared a bottle, laughing and telling stories at his family's table long after the boy Bayard had fallen asleep? How could he forget Sullivan's hospitality at the farm on the Piscataqua River in Durham? "Sir, none is more anxious to whip the British than John Sullivan!" Bayard insisted. "I know it!"

"Then he is naive, and they have hoodwinked him!" Seeing the stricken look on Bayard's handsome face, crossed now and forever with a scar from a British sword, Washington was sorry he had spoken so roughly. He decided to spare Logan the report that John Adams had said he regretted that "the first ball fired on the day of our defeat had not gone through Sullivan's head." Adams, too, was not impressed in the least by the stories of British change of heart.

Washington tried to soothe his aide. How touchy all these Yankees had turned out to be! "At any rate, the decision is not mine. The matter is being debated in Congress whether or not to meet the Howes and discuss peace."

"It is certainly worth a try," Bayard said stiffly, and was pleased to find out, in due time, that Congress thought so, too, for they sent John Adams and Ben Franklin to meet with the Howes on Staten Island in a confrontation that accomplished naught but the consumption of some excellent clarets.

When the reports of the meeting reached him, Washington dismissed it as "a meeting of the powerless and the misguided." The congressional committee was not authorized to make any promises, nor were the Howes empowered to treat the colonies as an independent state. The last attempt to make a peaceful settlement had ended. The last stall was over.

"Now is the hour upon us," Washington predicted. He called another council of his generals, and they voted ten to three to evacuate New York as quickly as possible. It was the twelfth of September. Bayard went that night to the house on Broadway where his brother Josias lived with his wife Meg and their sister, Bonnie, and Bonnie's baby daughter, Dorothy. All of them would be in danger if the enemy moved in; it was up to him to caution them.

The house Josias Logan and his wife Meg occupied had been built for Meg's parents, Albert and Patricia Whitestone, old New Yorkers and staunch Tories, who had retreated for comfort and safety to their country estate in the Hudson Valley. Albert Whitestone, a wealthy merchant, had been a member of the Royal Governor's Council for the Colony of New York; his wife, who was of Dutch background, had brought to the marriage extensive land holdings in the Hudson Valley as well as a great fortune based on sugar and ale. Their youngest child, Audrey, had gone with them to the country.

The house was handsome and solid, built of brick with huge Palladian windows, ornate cornices, and a carved front doorway. When Josias had first seen it, coming to New York in search of his fortune some years ago and befriended by Albert Whitestone at once, he had loved it at first sight and determined to live, if not there, in just such a house. When it had come to pass that he became accepted, first as a friend of the Whitestone family, then as a son-in-law, he had been delighted with his luck.

When Bonnie Logan first saw the big house on Broadway, coming alone on a frosty January day, pregnant and abandoned, she thought it astonishingly grand. Now, safely delivered of her baby, satisfied that her husband was dead and would trouble her no more, she knew herself to be an essential member of the household—dearest friend and companion to her brother's wife Meg. (And special friend, as well, of Meg's brother William.) She was very comfortable and felt entirely welcome here.

78

Bayard was no stranger to the house, either. He had first come here, invited by his sister, to admire his niece Dorothy, to smooth over strained family ties, to attempt a reconciliation with his brother Josias that had not been successful, but had, at least, been honestly faced. He had come here mostly to see Bonnie, and had tried to reconcile with Josias for their mother's sake, although he differed politically—and in nearly every other possible way—with Josias. And to please Josias's wife, kindly Meg, who so earnestly desired peace in the family, Bayard had attended dinners here.

But now Bayard had come to warn all the residents of this house to abandon it, to pack up and leave. He looked up at the lighted windows as he approached, strode quickly up the graceful front walk lined with a hedge of roses, and knocked on the massive door.

For a long time there was no response, although Bayard could hear music from the second story, where there was a parlor frequented by the family on intimate occasions, and a porch large enough for a cotillion party. The maid who finally answered the door was a rosy-skinned Negro with a frilly white cap.

"Oh, Mister Bayard! You're late! They're all upstairs!"

Only as he climbed the stairs did Bayard recall that it was, being September twelve, his brother Josias's birthday. The recollection saved him from complete surprise when he walked into a festive gathering in the upstairs parlor. The candlelit room smelled of spices and rum. A sumptuous buffet was laid out on a long mahogany sidetable, and its array of meats and breads, fruits and sweets reminded Bayard that he had not dined.

He looked quickly around the room. Meg, the

source of the music he had heard from outside, was seated at the cherrywood spinet. She looked, Bayard noticed, extremely round, and as pale as she was plump. Bonnie and Dorothy were chatting with friends on a low sofa upholstered in yellow silk. As ever, pretty Bonnie had attracted a flock of male admirers who entirely surrounded her couch like the bright petals of a flower.

Across the room, a group of well-dressed men, his brother Josias among them, stood around a huge silver punch bowl. Other guests had gone out onto the porch to admire the stars and enjoy the fragrant night air. Bayard noticed that their brother Tom did not appear to be present. He took the pulse of the crowd, felt himself quite out of tune with it, made an effort to swallow his irritation, and was relieved to see that, at least, William Whitestone was present, a great giant of a man among these foppishly dressed civilians. Ever since his arrival in New York several months before, Bayard had been amused by the extravagant tastes of New Yorkers. As ever, William looked handsome in a rough sort of a way, imposing, but slightly untidy, despite the best efforts of his tailor. Their eyes met, and both men nodded.

Bayard was not alone in his admiration of William Whitestone. Loyalists and patriots alike could not help but respect William's calm manner, his great intelligence, and his sound reasoning, whether or not they agreed with his politics. But of the assembled company, Bayard alone knew where William's true sympathies lay. In fact, it had been Bayard who had approached William last spring, soon after meeting him at his sister's home, about using his knowledge and influence to aid the rebel cause. William's information had more than once proved invaluable. But William's effectivess—and safety—depended on secrecy; thus Bayard could not acknowledge more than a passing acquaintance with the publisher.

"Bayard! How lovely!" Meg called out, turning from her music.

"So you have come," Josias said, coming across the room on unsteady feet, looking as if he had already drunk a good deal.

"Birthday congratulations," said Bayard quickly.

"I am so glad you could come," Bonnie said, handing Dorothy to a surprised young man and floating over to greet him. She was slim, graceful, and confident. Her blue eyes shone, and her remarkable red-gold hair was arranged in a tower of curls and black ribbon bows. She kissed him lightly. "Dear Bayard!" Her fingers traced his scar delicately. "You look handsomer than ever, I swear!"

Josias had not seen his brother since before the battle on Long Island, had not seen the long scar that marked his face from nose to chin, and in his surprise, he stared frankly. Bayard took advantage of the slightly unbalanced moment to address him in a low voice.

"Might we speak privately, brother?"

"Of course. My study."

"Excuse us, ladies," Bayard said, noticing Bonnie's disappointment as he turned away.

Josias strode, listing just a bit to one side, to the book-lined room at the head of the stairs, and Bayard followed. Bayard and Josias, whose boyhood rivalry had not been assuaged, but rather aggravated by the differences of politics they had developed in adulthood, rarely indulged in discussions *tête à tête*. In fact, the last they had attempted had been months ago. Now, Josias wrongly suspected Bayard had come to ask for money; Bayard correctly feared that his brother was too far gone in the consumption of birthday toasts to restrain his temper, no matter how polite he might try to be.

"I'll be blunt," Bayard began.

"You always are."

"I have come to offer you some advice."

"Thank you; I need none."

"A warning . . ."

"Get on with it!" Josias snapped.

"I think the time has come for you to leave Manhattan, Josias. Please hear me out. There will be fighting here very soon, perhaps burning and looting. I am worried about the ladies and Dorothy."

"Your concern is touching, if belated. Creditable, if inappropriate. I have considered the situation, I assure you. Despite any fighting, I have decided that we shall stay here."

"I think that would be most unwise. You could go to Mother's house in Boston. Or to Meg's parents. Perhaps that would be best; Meg looks unwell, Josias, and that would be an easier journey."

"I am perfectly aware of how delicate my wife is—far too delicate to be moved at this point. I have consulted her doctor. He says she must remain close to him and to home. Bonnie, who is an adult woman in possession of a majority of her faculties, has elected to stay with Meg. We're all staying."

"I fear I will not be able to offer you my . . . protection much longer," Bayard said in a distressed voice. This interview was going less well than he had expected, far less well than he had hoped. While there might be some sense to Meg's not being moved, it was obvious that Josias's resentment of him, his dislike of him, far outweighed both his reason and his willingness to consider the matter.

"Oh, spare us your damn protection!" Josias said in a furious tone. "I am relieved to be rid of it!"

"Restrain yourself," Bayard pleaded. "In the

name of all that is honorable, for the sake of the family, of the ladies!"

"Let me tell you this," Josias said, gripping the back of a solid Sheraton armchair for support. "I have restrained myself. I resent your coming here, uninvited, to spoil a social occasion. I resent your presumption in offering me unwanted advice. I resent your assumption that you know what is best for me better than I. It's an attitude you have always had toward me, Bayard, and I will stand for it no longer. This is my house. Now get out!"

"I will most certainly and most promptly," Bayard said, "but I refuse to say I will not return. I commend my sister and my niece to your care. Use your best judgment, Josias. Perhaps your information is better than mine, and they will be in no danger here. At any rate, I wish you all well. Please give my farewells and my respects to all."

And before Josias could add a word, Bayard turned on his heel and descended the stairs to the first floor. He crossed the rich red carpet and opened the front door for himself. He was angry, but even as his blood hummed with injury and resentment, his perspective was reinforced on this family quarrel by the enormity of the experiences he had so recently endured on Long Island—and the thought of what still lay ahead. He pitied Josias more than he disliked him. Compared to the raw reality of war, compared to the knife edge between death and life that had cut every hour, every minute of those days into a series of priceless last chances, all this seemed almost comic.

He took a deep breath as he headed down Broadway. The air was sweet and kissed by the salt spray of the harbor. Crickets sang; voices rang out. He decided he would relish an ale. As he disappeared into the nearest tavern, he wondered again, Where was Tom this night?

Tom was with Isannah.

Tom had a new lady love.

For Tom, as for his brother Bayard, the recent proximity of death had added a clarity to life. As he had lain in the mud in Brooklyn Heights, he had promised himself that at the very next opportunity—should God grant him another lease on life—he would lie instead, in comfort and probably rapture, in the arms of a warm, clean woman. Not in the mud.

Preferably a decent woman, he had thought. Oh, Fancy Nan was kind, and she had been a sort of mother to him, but now that he had come so close to dying, he was a different man, with a new appetite. New aspirations, manly ones. He admitted to himself that there was a one he fancied. She was a very young indentured girl; he had often seen her at Drake's Tavern, and admired her slim, almost childish form and her shiny white-gold hair, straight as straw, always escaping any tie or cap. He had never spoken a word to her. But as he had crossed the East River in the bottom of a leaky dory, shivering with cold and frightened for his life, things had become increasingly clear and simple, ambiguities had evaporated, and he had decided that he loved her, the wench Isannah.

Ashore, he had pursued his goal, his vision. Like so many of the best visions, it was a simple one, and as Tom was a young man who rarely stopped to consider his actions, he set about attaining it directly. As soon as he had rested and bathed in the river, he pulled together the best of his clothes and set off for Drake's Tavern. It was a tavern where a man in a Continental uniform was welcome and in good company, thank God for that.

And Isannah was there. She was there! Untouched by war or suffering, her sweet round face as dear as he remembered it, her violet eyes even more like the twilight, her cornsilk hair in two long braids that made her look even younger. She wore a dress of blue and a white apron. An apron! It was charming in its simplicity, a reminder of the normalcy of women everywhere, even in wartime.

Inclined to be tongue-tied in the face of immediate possibility, Tom had reminded himself that he was Tom Logan of the Boston Logans, an honest soldier in the Continental Army. He had a bit of money saved from home, and he ordered supper: oysters, then salt pork with beets and potatoes and cabbage. Isannah brought it to him and watched him as he ate it with wonderful enjoyment.

When he had finished, he ordered an ale. When she brought it to him, he addressed her directly. "Miss Isannah? That is your name?"

She smiled shyly at him. "Yes, that is my name."

"Have you a sweetheart, Miss Isannah?"

At that she frowned. "No, I am not old enough yet!"

"Things are different in wartime."

And, to his surprise, she sat down next to him. "What is your name? No, don't tell me. I shall guess."

Tom flushed red and gulped his ale.

"Not Benedict. No, not Hiram. Not Eleazer. Not Enos, either. Not Elswyth, nor Emery, not Theodorick! Not Gottfried!"

"There's no one named Gottfried!"

"Oh, yes, there is! The man who delivers Red Hook ale! He's a German man!"

Tom's heart was full to bursting. Things were going well. "Oh," he said. "Things are different in New York."

"Aren't you from New York? Of course you're not! I thought not. Where is your home, Tom?"

"How did you know my name is Tom?" he demanded.

"Why, I just divined it, I guess!" She giggled. Her master, the tavernkeep, a massive curly-headed man, called out for her.

Tom reached out and held her arm. "When you are old enough to have a sweetheart, do you divine that he might be me?"

"I'll tell you later," she promised.

That had been two weeks ago, and since that night, Tom had spent every night with Isannah, first in the tavern and later, under the stars.

And he had learned that she was not shy, but saucy, and not yet fourteen. She had left her little village at the age of twelve, and was bound for two more years, a total of four, to Jasper Drake.

"I'll wait for you, Isannah, I promise," Tom had vowed.

And every night they played, like a pair of puppies.

Chapter Six

B Y THE NEXT morning, Friday the thirteenth, the evacuation began and the city was in a state of turbulence. General Washington's orders were to shift military supplies and equipment north to Kingsbridge. At dawn, soldiers began to move them in horse-drawn carts and by water. The quartermaster was not equal to the demands of this desperate situation. Wagons were needed and wagons were in terrible shortage. First priority was given to the evacuation of sick and wounded soldiers. As quickly as possible, they were emptied out of the hospitals and piled into wagons that jolted and jostled as far north as Dobb's Ferry. Forts were quickly dismantled and defenses torn down.

And in a new policy decision, Washington caved in to the demands of the women. Wives of soldiers, some with squads of children, would be allowed to accompany the army. If the men ever received their pay, Washington figured, they could pay the women for doing their laundry. Until then, he put them on rations and accepted responsibility for them. Their number increased until there were a full two hundred.

The civilian population responded quickly to the mood of the day. Shops and offices opened and closed within an hour. Men and women hurriedly packed their household goods and treasures, tossing featherbeds from the windows, stripping mirrors and family portraits from the walls, removing even the lead window weights and brass knockers on their front doors to be weighed and valued and deposited for safekeeping. Many bade tearful farewell to their homes, sure they would never see them again. Livestock were led to the rivers' edges to wait for ferries. Bells were removed from the city's churches and public buildings and taken to Newark for safekeeping, and through it all the steady cannonading by four British warships enforced haste as they moved slowly up the East River, impervious to fire from the American batteries.

Regretfully abandoning Richmond Hill, Washington and his staff packed and moved north to set up headquarters on Harlem Heights in the extensive, well-placed estate of a loyalist, Colonel Roger Morris, who had left suddenly for England the year before. The house had been built as a summer villa ten years earlier, and was one of the most remarkable and architecturally curious buildings in America, with its double-storied portico, gigantic columns, and triangular pediment, and a large octagonal room at the back.

For Washington's purposes, the house was ideal. From his office, he could see the Harlem, Hudson, and East rivers. From the front balcony, he could see twelve miles south to the tip of Manhattan, see all of New York's harbor and Staten Island.

From across the East River, the British watched the flurry of activity. Josias Logan watched everything from the second-floor corner windows of his offices on Queen Street. William Whitestone had a busy day, getting together the news for the next edition of *Whitestone's New York Messenger*, constantly interrupted by friends with news or gossip and invitations to drink a farewell cup. Through it all he was as cheerful and calm as ever. Meg and Bonnie, with all their servants, remained strictly cloistered in their fine house, waiting for the furor to pass. They would go nowhere, Josias had said, and both women were relieved that he had made the decision for them.

All day the streets were clogged with carts and horses and people on foot. The air ran with cries of complaint and farewell. By dark, nineteen-twentieths of the population had fled. The once-busy, cosmopolitan city was a ghost town.

When he looked back on the army's evacuation of the city, Washington could not help but feel discouraged. There was a pattern of retreat and loss, retreat and confusion, cowardice and lack of discipline that did not bear constant reexamination. It had not ended so badly, after all—they had been saved on some scores—but the price in pride and confidence had been dearly paid.

The British offensive had started on the bright, sunny morning of September fifteenth. Although the massing of warships in the Kip's Bay had been visible since dawn, no one had notified the commander in chief. He had been out early, occupied with the withdrawal of the last of the troops, when he heard the cannonade, saw the black smoke rising, and determined that it was coming from a point on the shoreline defended by extremely inexperienced troops—some had served only a week. He had set off at a gallop.

At Kip's Bay, four hundred and fifty raw farmboys in shallow trenches watched in trepidation as eighty-four barges full of Redcoats and Hessians swarmed across the river. They looked, to one boy, "like a clover field in full bloom."

The clover blossoms landed in a blast of fire and marched through the shallows with their shining steel bayonets extended. Some of the militiamen were armed only with scythes tied to poles. The gunfire was deafening, terrifying, blazing from the riggings as grapeshot and cannonballs roared over their heads. Most of the farmboys took to their heels.

And Washington had come upon them in full flight. He had confronted them running as if pursued by the Devil on horseback, the dust from their feet throwing up a choking cloud in the hot, windless air. Abandoning all formation, fleeing in the greatest confusion, throwing down their guns, muskets, powderhorns, coats, and knapsacks, they had run pell mell through the fields and into the woods.

"Take the fields, take the cornfields!" Washington had shouted, urging his horse into the midst of the milling men, but his words were unheeded.

Then the commander in chief had lost control of his temper. Galloping after some of the men, he had struck at them with his riding whip, shouting at them to turn and stand fast. When they ducked and continued to run, he had thrown his hat into the dust and cried out, "Are these the men with which I am to defend America?"

Bayard had come up then, had seen enough of it to know what was happening. He saw Washington alone at a crossroads, heard him call out, "Good God! Have I got such troops as these? Good God, what am I to do?"

Bayard saw a party of enemy troops, about fifty of them, coming from the east and advancing at a run. Washington stared at them without seeming to see them; he did not move. Instead he sat motionless in the saddle, his head bowed in defeat. Bayard galloped up, grabbed the bridle of the commander's horse, and turned him around, forced him to withdraw to safety.

"Sir, you forget yourself," Bayard said mildly, and the crucial moment when Washington had sought death in his despair had passed.

"Good Christ, what a bungle!" Washington swore, regaining his composure almost at once. "What is now to prevent Howe from cutting the island in two?"

But perhaps bungle had attracted like, for while Washington struggled to make the retreat as orderly as possible, Howe's high command had paused, watching as the next wave of troops was securing a beachhead on the East River, while General Putnam managed to round up about three thousand of the scattered troops and set them on a twelve-mile forced march up the Greenwich Road on the west side of the island.

Bonnie Logan would ever remember that day as the time she spilled tea on General Howe. It had been an unusual day, from the beginning. Early that morning she had been awakened by the maid Katie, saying, "Miss Bonnie! It's dreadfully early but your brother is in the kitchen, and he says he needs to see you."

Rising carefully so as not to wake Dorothy, who was sleeping like an angel with one curled fist outside her coverlet, Bonnie had slipped down the back stairs. What could Josias want?

But when she reached the warm kitchen, fragrant with the smell of baking bread and the deliciously provoking smell of coffee, it was not Josias, nor Bayard, but Tom who sat at the well-scrubbed wooden worktable. And he was not alone. He had brought a young girl.

Bonnie was delighted to see Tom, who had been her favorite playmate as a child in Boston. He looked young in his uniform and felt thin as she hugged him. "Dear brother," she said.

"Bonnie, this is Isannah," Tom said, pulling the slim young woman to her feet. "Isannah, I told you—this is my sister, Bonnie. Bonnie, I'll be leavin' town and I want you to know Isannah."

To Bonnie, not much past eighteen herself, Tom's young sweetheart seemed no more than a child. Seeing her, seeing clearly how exhausted both of them looked, how madly in love, how frightened of what lay ahead, the excitement and sadness of her own forbidden love affair with dark-haired Lieutenant Cormick Walker came rushing back into her mind. In a second she felt the pangs of first love and love ended.

"Hello, Isannah," she said softly and smiled.

"I can't leave her and I can't take her with me," Tom said miserably. "She's bound to Jasper Drake. We have orders to be ready to march at a moment's notice, Bonnie, but . . ."

"Katie, give these two something to eat," Bonnie said. "Is the coffee ready?"

"Yes, ma'am, it is. And there's biscuits aplenty," Katie said, all eyes and ears for this latest development.

"Well, take a minute, Tom, and sit down," Bonnie said. "Isannah, you are most welcome and welcome to come again."

Tom beamed. "I knew you'd understand," he said. "Me and Isannah are pledged. We intend to be married as soon as she's free, and her family was all Congregationalists, too. Isannah's indentured to

Drake, as I said, and she was brought to the city two years past. They say you can't take a woman with you on march unless you're wed.''

Bonnie nodded, sipping the strong coffee. She had been sixteen herself, the age Tom was now, when she had fallen in love with Lieutenant Walker, so foolishly in love that she had ignored the wishes of her family and betrayed their convictions to follow her heart. There was no undoing any of it, now; now she had darling Dorothy, and Walker was dead. She had pledged herself to him in good faith and yet did not mourn him—after all that had happened she could not—nor did her heart hold any grieving or guilt for a marriage (albeit a false marriage) which had given her a daughter and a good deal of wisdom, to boot.

''When did you say Isannah's indenture will be expired?'' she asked kindly.

''In two years' time,'' Isannah whispered. She was a pretty thing, Bonnie mused, so pale and petite, with lovely violet eyes.

Two years at their age is forever, Bonnie thought, but she did not say so. ''Well, then, she should stay with her master till then,'' she said. ''That is my opinion. But she should visit me often and play with Dorothy while I stitch a dress for her wedding day! A fine wedding is a fine start for a happy marriage. I will visit her master very soon and tell him how pleased I am at your intentions. Perhaps our mother would come to New York to see you wed, Tom. When the time comes.''

''But what may happen by then! I may be kilt!'' he wailed.

''Don't even think so,'' Bonnie scolded. ''Isannah, do you agree to wait?''

Shyly, her hand still in Tom's, Isannah nodded, and Bonnie leaned over to give her a hug. It was just then, when it already seemed certain that more would happen on this day before rising time than on most days from start to finish, that William Whitestone came in the door from the kitchen garden, and smiled to see the happy domestic scene.

"I thought not to find you stirring at this hour," he said to Bonnie when she had offered him breakfast and Katie had hurried to find him a mug.

"Come to the garden to say farewell," Tom whispered to Isannah, and they slipped out, leaving Bonnie alone with William.

"Who did you expect to find at this hour?" Bonnie asked frankly. She found powerful William quite the most interesting man she had ever known, and felt that she was still learning more about him. In a way, she loved him dearly, but she could not tell him so—and he, although he was the most worldly and sophisticated of men, seemed to be equally shy with her. Each time they met, it was wonderfully stimulating, if inconclusive, that much was sure; never had he left her less than eager to see him again. And the last time they had walked along the Battery in the evening, he had kissed her so sweetly. . . . No one would ever know to look at him how tender he could be. With effort, she put the thought out of her mind; it seemed too early in the day to have entertained it, but she could not stop the blush that crept up her neck and across her cheeks.

"You are the only woman I know who looks lovelier in the morning than in the evening," William said coolly. "But . . ."

"But you did not come here to flatter me," Bonnie said. They both laughed.

"In fact, I did not," he said. "I came to ask you to visit a friend of mine and take her a note."

"I will do it," Bonnie said readily, "only kindly

allow me to dress first and to brush the tangles out of my hair.''

"I will allow you that," William said. "And take the carriage. Mrs. Murray lives on Incklenberg Hill.''

Bonnie had taken not only the carriage, but Dorothy, and Isannah to hold Dorothy. As they rode through the quiet streets, the city woke to life all around them. It was astonishingly changed since the departure of most of the troops and nearly all of the population. Bonnie had an odd, unpleasant feeling that she was a guest who had overstayed, but she told herself that she had stayed to help Meg, and had already been able to help William as well.

Mrs. Murray, who turned out to be an old friend of Meg's, as well as William's, and to whom Meg sent her regards and regrets that she was too unwell to visit, was a charming Quaker woman who received her visitors, and William's note, with smiles and repeated requests that they stay. Nearly as soon as they arrived, the sound of gunfire on the shore began; it was near, but not dangerously near.

"The British are attacking from the river," Bonnie said in a scared, hollow voice. Everyone had expected this for weeks, but that did not make it less frightening.

"God help our boys," said Mrs. Murray, and closed her eyes in a moment of prayer. "It will be safer for you to stay here than to go home at this point," she said, and in spite of her concern for poor Meg, Bonnie agreed.

Mrs. Murray was the most gracious of hostesses, and the women did their best to keep busy. Mrs. Murray played her violin for the guests. Isannah, who had made a pet of baby Dorothy, took her to see the ducks and lambs in the barnyard. After a tour of the grounds and the gardens, Bonnie and Mrs. Murray sat in the downstairs parlor and occupied themselves with needlework, at which Bonnie had never been proficient and seemed increasingly unlikely to be so. There was only distant gunfire to be heard, but the big grandfather clock seemed to halt, and time passed slowly.

"I am so glad you are here with me," Mrs. Murray said.

"I am pleased to be able to keep you company," Bonnie said.

There was an undercurrent of tension in the afternoon, although Mrs. Murray was as calm as only a Quaker dame can be.

It was nearly tea time when Sir William Howe, General Henry Clinton, and Governor Tryon arrived at the Murray mansion, all of them magnificent in brilliant uniforms. If Mrs. Murray was surprised, she did not reveal it. Bonnie was very surprised. She had never met Clinton nor Tryon, but General Howe recognized her at once.

"What an astonishing surprise!" he said, bowing low.

"Quite," Bonnie agreed.

"We have not met since Boston," General Howe said simply.

"It seems long," Bonnie admitted, lowering her eyes.

Both of them remembered the last time they had met. Bonnie had gone to Howe at Province House, British headquarters, and asked a great favor—that she might go by sea to Halifax to join her husband Cormick Walker. Of course Howe could not know that the ship he had put her on would be stopped by a privateer, that after a dreadful voyage she would eventually land in New York.

"And how is Captain Walker?" Howe asked,

compelled by courtesy to inquire of her husband. His large, dark, fun-loving eyes were truly curious. As usual, Howe looked to be in the pink of health; evidently warfare agreed with him. Tall and slim, he was always slightly rumpled in his dress. His dark hair curled in unruly knots and escaped from the ribbon which fastened it behind his neck.

"I believe him to be dead," Bonnie replied, lowering her eyes even more resolutely. She had told no one and would never reveal that he had not been dead long. In fact, she had seen him alive only last month in the British camp on Staten Island. She had told no one and could not what had transpired between them at Rowe's Inn after their meeting. And evidently the whereabouts and welfare of a certain single officer had not come to the attention of the supreme commander, for Howe appeared to be surprised at the news.

"My dear, I am sorry," he said, although in truth he had not liked Walker when he had known him socially in Boston. He had considered the captain a surprising rascal to have enthralled the lovely Miss Logan. Howe had seen a good deal of crudeness in Captain Walker. Perhaps she was better off so, he thought briefly. It was a small matter, compared to those at hand, but Howe was ever tuned to the finer details of life and the mysteries of love.

As Bonnie well knew. Seeing him, she was curious about her acquaintance, Betsy Loring, who had been such a constant companion of Howe's in Boston that ballads had been written about them. Was she still staying with Howe? Was she here in New York? She dared not ask, nor did she ask what the British commander was doing here. In fact, it was obvious. The invasion of Manhattan had begun, and the officers had come to warn Mrs. Murray, in deference to her wealth and position.

"How lovely that old friends should meet here at my home," Mrs. Murray said, smiling. Circe-like, she held open the door to her elegant downstairs parlor. "I insist that you gentlemen stop for tea. Such a hot day! Do come into the parlor. Or would you prefer the porch? Tell those soldiers out there to sit down and rest! Do you like tea, or something stronger?"

"Have we time to stop?" Governor Tryon asked anxiously. He was a fine, bluff soldierly fellow who, after enduring month after month of delay, wanted to get on with it. His old friend, General Henry Clinton, stood apart from the others, somewhat aloof, as was his way. Bonnie observed that Clinton was a good-looking man in his late thirties with a full, round face and large eyes set unusually far apart beneath black eyebrows.

Clinton was a man who took himself very seriously, and he was an ardent violinist. When he saw Mrs. Murray's old violin at the music stand, he smiled and wandered into the parlor ahead of the others.

"Of course we must stop for tea," Howe said enthusiastically. "Or whatever. For myself, I will take Madeira, if you have it, good lady."

Smiling ceaselessly, Mrs. Murray sent for wine and cakes, and the British high command ate and drank as the women chatted and poured. Clinton was persuaded to give them a little music; all the officers looked cool and gay, and Bonnie made every effort to keep up with Mrs. Murray—a woman of supreme composure and charm. The hot afternoon passed as pleasantly as any late-summer afternoon may pass.

Finally, the clock struck five. It was at just this hour that Bonnie had spilled tea, quite by accident, on General Howe's snow-white trousers. Howe had stretched his long arms above his head and yawned, and Bonnie, whose attention had wandered, had started abruptly and upset a tiny pie-crust table.

"Oh, my goodness, I am so sorry!" she exclaimed, brushing at the stain with her handkerchief.

Howe laughed. "No matter, no matter. Dear me, I have nearly lost track of the time. We must be on our way, dear Mrs. Murray, with all thanks for your gracious hospitality."

When they had ridden away, Mrs. Murray sank into a chair and sighed. "What a trying, exhausting afternoon," she sighed. "Thank goodness you reminded that man he was supposed to be fighting a war!"

"I did?" Bonnie laughed. "Is this to be known as the battle of the teacups?"

But Bonnie couldn't help wondering about the odd events of the day. What had William's note said, and did it have anything to do with General Howe and the others? And what was Mrs. Murray's place in it all? Out of politeness, Bonnie refrained from questioning her hostess. But it was all quite puzzling indeed.

By the time Bonnie, Isannah, and Dorothy drove south again, the garrison of rebel soldiers had passed to the north. Howe had secured his beachhead on the East River, as he had fully intended to do, and the nine thousand men of his second division had been ferried across the river and had arrived in Manhattan. Now Howe would proceed on the next phase of his carefully worked-out plan—he would send a brigade of Hessians south to raise the Union Jack over the abandoned city as he belatedly dispatched the main body of his troops up the Post Road toward Harlem.

It had been a sultry day but it ended with a cold

shower at dusk. For the rebel soldiers, who had just marched twelve miles, fearing attack at every step, who had tossed away their tents and blankets and overcoats in their haste to retreat, it was a miserable night. They were cold and tired and hungry and, above all, ashamed. Whole regiments had stampeded without firing a single shot; their commander in chief had called them a disgrace. And they had lost New York.

All that night, Washington and his staff worked and planned in the small, elegant dining room of the Morris mansion. A chilly wind rattled the windows in their frames; candles burned out and were replaced; the general's cook came up the stairs from the downstairs kitchen with trays of bread and meat and bottles of cider and ale to refresh them. Bayard knew that his commander in chief was greatly discouraged by the disastrous events of the day, but he spoke only of the future. Consulting General Greene, whom he regarded highly as a strategist, and General Putnam, who had just led the disorganized, desperate retreat, he prepared orders for the troops to be placed in a strong defensive posture and to dig fortifications along the bluffs above the Hudson as soon as the sun rose.

"Should they attack, which I would suppose they will," Washington guessed, "we might thus score a small victory. Even a small victory would be vastly encouraging."

"The advantage of higher ground can't be overestimated," General Putnam agreed, "but will the men now stand and fight?"

Bayard longed to speak out, to urge the generals to trust the men, but it was not his duty. Instead, he made careful notes of all that Washington wanted to include in the orders of the day. He took comfort from the presence of General Henry Knox, a friend of his and his family from Boston.

"Where is General Lee?" asked Greene, who had been confined to his bed throughout the Battle of Long Island. Greene was recovered but still pale. His blue-gray eyes sparkled; he was delighted to be back on duty.

"Had Lee been on Long Island, matters would have worn a very different appearance," Knox muttered. Harry Knox, enormously bright, was also enormously fat, and had eaten the lion's share of the sandwiches. This dreadful day past was one he would never forget: amidst the confusion, no one had given Knox the order to retreat, and his brigade had been cut off. Retreat had then seemed impossible; they had taken desperate refuge in the earth redoubt near Bayard's Mount, had been led out of sure death only by an upstart of twenty, the arrogant young Aaron Burr, one of Putnam's aides. Knox had been furious and embarrassed; he was determined to put the whole experience behind him.

"Lee is still in Savannah, I believe," Washington said, "but I have sent word to him through Congress to come north as quickly as he can!"

"Lee's talent for fortification is sorely needed now," Greene said.

"No doubt," Washington agreed. "As soon as possible we must send out the volunteer rangers to scout on Bloomingdale Heights. I fear a major British advance on that high ground."

"Before light?" Bayard asked. His brother Tom had volunteered for ranger duty with Knowlton. It was a vital reconnaissance detachment, assigned also to "secret duties, either by water or land, by day or night." Tom was proud to be a ranger, and Bayard was proud of him.

101

"Before it is completely light," Washington ordered.

"You will send Colonel Knowlton and the New Englanders?" asked General Greene.

"That is correct," Washington said.

"Better soldiers never drew breath," Greene promised.

Well before dawn that next day, Colonel Knowlton and his rangers—about one hundred and twenty brave men—crept across the Hollow Way, a flat break in the cliffs above the Hudson, and climbed the heights to see what was hidden under the thick foliage on Bloomingdale Heights. Knowlton, a favorite of his superiors and an idol of his men, including Thomas Logan, was extremely competent. A farmer from Ashford, Connecticut, he had been a ranger in the French wars, had taken part in the capture of Ticonderoga, fought in Cuba against Spain, and had served with valor at Bunker Hill. Erect and elegant, he was a tall, handsome man in his late thirties.

British pickets guarding the Bloomingdale Road set off an alarm when they detected Knowlton's rangers, and the rangers took cover behind a stone wall, where they stood off nearly four hundred light infantrymen for half an hour. It was scarcely eight in the morning when the squeal of bagpipes sounded, warning them that heavy reinforcements, the famous Black Watch regiment, were hard on the way.

Tom, hearing the unearthly keening of the pipes, felt an inner chill and looked anxiously to his more experienced mates. Hard-shelled Yankees, one and all, the rangers were short-spoken and blunt, and their courage sparked his like a flint to tinder.

102

Knowlton ordered a careful retreat, sending his rangers back up the bluff, keeping the British at a distance with well-placed shots from their long rifles. Washington had heard the gunfire and arrived on horseback to witness the skirmish. Jeering scarlet lines poured into the Hollow Way. The rangers' fire was steady, the withdrawal deliberate, but when the Americans had reached one edge of the Hollow Way and looked over at the other, a red-coated bugler stood up on the heights in full view and blew the fox hunter's call that announced the end of the chase: "the fox has skulked into his den."

Washington's face went scarlet. The insult was plain, even more to the Virginia aristocrat than to the plain Yankee farmers. Tom had never ridden a hunt in his life, but he recognized the call. Implicit in it was all the scorn the British regulars had for the mismatched, shabbily dressed rebel volunteers, and the insult was aggravated by the feelings of crushed pride the Americans had suffered during the rout the day before.

"Damn them," Washington swore. He had slept scarcely an hour; he was exhausted and nervy, and now he felt keenly disgraced.

Bayard, who had ridden up to guard the general, saw this. "How many are they?" he asked in a hoarse voice.

"Find out," Washington said grimly.

Knowlton informed Bayard that he thought the infantry was three or four hundred strong and far in advance of substantial reinforcements. Washington decided on a strategic counterattack. He sent one of Greene's brigades to feint at the British front, hoping to draw them into the Hollow Way, then sent Knowlton and three Virginia companies—showing his habitual prejudice toward Virginians—on a cir-

103

cuitous march to attack their rear on the opposite cliff.

It began well, but one of the Virginia companies opened fire too soon, exposing Knowlton and the rangers before they had gained cover. Grapeshot scattered among the rangers as the British turned to protect their flank. Tom felt a musketball graze his shoulder and heard it snap off a tree branch inches behind him. He saw Major Leitch, who was commanding the Virginians, fall mortally wounded, saw Colonel Knowlton leap up to the granite ledge where Leitch had been standing.

"Forward!" Knowlton called, his blue eyes blazing.

Tom rushed forward with the others. The British were scrambling up the cliff. Washington had ordered reinforcements; now they were fanning out through the woods.

Then a musket ball caught Knowlton, snapping his backbone. Tom jumped to his side and caught him as he fell. "I do not value my life," he heard Knowlton whisper, "if we do but get the day."

"Please God, we will," Tom promised him. Eyes smarting, he laid Knowlton under a tree and took his place with the other rangers, pressing the attack.

The fighting went on for four hours, but the sun was still high when Tom saw the British retreating across a green field of buckwheat, and the Black Watch scurrying through an orchard. He screamed with joy to see their backs. They had forced the enemy as far south as Stryker's Bay, inflicting heavy losses, and the way was lined with collapsed Redcoats. "Huzzah!" the rangers cheered, and the cry was taken up throughout the rebel lines, "Huzzah! Huzzah!"

Hearing the guns on the frigates anchored in the Hudson, Washington had sent an order to break off the attack, and the men returned to Harlem Heights in orderly ranks.

"By God, we did it!" Tom exulted. He had never been so tired or hot in his life, nor as cheerful. A double ration of rum did nothing to spoil his good mood, although the news of Colonel Knowlton's death affected him strongly.

"He'd have been proud," one ranger said.

"He is proud," another insisted.

The rangers clicked their tin cups together in a defiant toast: "Rather death and jack boots than dishonor and wooden shoes!" Tom slid back, fast asleep, and dreamed of Isannah.

Josias Logan was by nature, persuasion, and lifelong experience, a secretive man. Even those who knew him best knew him only partially, and he had endeavored so far to keep his political opinions a matter of personal counsel. True, his friends and family knew him to be a Tory sympathizer, but he had assiduously masked his allegiance to the King in avowals of non-involvement, insisting that his concern was for business only, that he had no desire to become involved in the fighting on either side. And in fact, that was the truth.

But as the months had passed this fence-sitting position had become increasingly difficult to maintain, and now, in the last hours of the revolutionary regime in New York, in the first hours of the British possession, he abandoned it. When Bonnie and Dorothy returned from their afternoon with Mrs. Murray and the generals, they found Josias at home, celebrating.

"It's the hour of deliverance!" he announced to his sister when she had put the baby to bed and joined the others in the downstairs parlor. "Howe has come into the city! We are saved!"

Bonnie's day had begun early and been filled with surprises already. She honestly did not know how to respond. Her family was sharply divided: two brothers in the Continental Army and the third a Tory. In her heart she felt sure that America was strong enough and ought to be independent of far-off Britain; it was a position to which she felt heart pledged. But she was pledged, as well, to living out the war peaceably in Josias's house and to caring for his wife, her dear friend Meg, who had taken her in and was now so much in need of her support. And then there was the question of William! She was almost sure she loved William, but she was not at all sure where his loyalties lay. Personally, she trusted him completely. How could her instincts be wrong?

Oh, how she wished to be left out of the arguing! To have the fighting itself ended at once! She crossed the room to the mahogany sideboard and poured herself a glass of Madeira with a hand that trembled more than slightly. Like others before her and since, Bonnie was determined to try to banish political strife from her personal life.

"Yes, General Howe has come at last," she said mildly, her back still turned to Josias and Meg.

"Listen to the people! They are wild with delight!" Josias said. He strode to the front window and opened it onto the street, which was thronged with citizens. When a group of British officers from the fleet had rowed ashore, women as well as men had taken them onto their shoulders and were parading them through the streets.

"I do hope there won't be violence," Meg said quietly.

"Dear Meg," Bonnie said, "how are you feeling tonight?"

106

"Well," Meg promised.

"They have raised the King's colors again in Fort George," Josias reported, leaning out the window to wave at a friend passing by. "I was told that a woman pulled down the stars and stripes and danced a jig on those poor threads!"

"A new order entirely," Meg said. She drank her wine quickly and felt better. The war, she thought, was like a theatrical performance: one set of actors would leave the stage, although the scenery would remain in place; another set of actors would begin to perform a different play. Many who had been waiting in the wings would come out tonight.

"You'll see a lot of changes in the near future," Josias predicted. "I daresay trade will pick up at once. There is always money to be made at a time like this. Supplies must be obtained and dispersed. Quarters must be found for thousands of men." Josias seated himself next to Meg, who was embroidering a baby's robe, on the low yellow couch. "General Howe must have a fine house."

"And one for Mrs. Loring, I suppose," Bonnie commented.

"Certainly General Howe is entitled to have a mistress," Josias said.

"Josias!" protested Meg.

"Everyone knows about it, Meg," Bonnie teased.

"I wonder who will be named commandant," Josias said.

"Major General Robertson, I have heard," Bonnie said carelessly, for it was one of the items of conversation that had been aired at Mrs. Murray's that afternoon.

"Impossible!" Josias sneered. "Why, the man is nearly eighty, sickly, infirm, and paralytic! Besides, he has no important friends. Friends are very important at a time like this."

"How true," agreed Meg. Whenever Josias said "at a time like this," she assumed he was referring to her pregnancy, which was the period of time of supreme concern to her. Josias, too, was pleased about their expectations. He was one of those men who strives to look and seem older than his years, who seems suited at a tender age for fatherhood. But he was quite distracted tonight, and had not once cautioned her not to drink too much, not to sit too close to the fire.

"Kingsmen will be streaming into the city from all directions," Josias suggested. "They will flock home."

Meg found herself wondering if her family might return from the family estate in Westchester. The thought gave her an odd twinge. Of course she was devoted to her parents, but she had not missed her sharp-tongued younger sister Audrey for a minute. Their relationship, never an easy one, had worsened when Josias Logan appeared. Meg could hardly bear to think of it, but before their marriage Audrey had been dreadfully flirtatious with Josias, and he had seemed to enjoy her company. It was a painful recollection, one she had no need of at a time like this.

"What's wrong, dear?" Bonnie asked Meg, whose anxiety had registered on her usually placid face.

"Oh, nothing! I was just wondering when Reverend Inglis would come back!" Meg lied, referring to the pastor of Trinity Church.

"We shall be needing him before too long, eh?" Josias said, thinking of the christening that must take place sometime in the next month. God willing, the child would be a boy. He had in mind to name him George William, after the King, of course, and General Howe.

"You are right, husband," Meg said happily, and

108

before too long, Katie had come to tell them that dinner was ready. As she left the room, Bonnie took care to close the front window, and looking out, she saw that the house across the street, which was the property of Henry Rutgers, had been marked with a huge G.R. as a sign that it had been confiscated and dedicated to the King's service. Howe had mentioned, she clearly recalled, that he intended to appraise and possess all rebel property in Manhattan, then sell or grant it to Loyalists, so long intimidated in this city, who were now to enjoy the spoils of war.

Chapter Seven

EVEN MORE THAN the rest of the Charleston Montgomerys, young Davie was distressed by the
quarrel that had taken place between his two idol-
ized older brothers. At fifteen, Davie was already
pledged heart and soul to revolution, but he was
angry, confused, and heartsick that his brothers had
taken positions so far apart. Davie was torn. When
he heard Taylor talk, he thought Taylor was right.
When he heard Webb talk, he knew Taylor was
wrong. He was in the habit of going from one
brother to the next for information and approval;
now he felt both of them diminished by their quarrel
and their strongly opposing views. Both of them
could not be right. Did that mean both might be
wrong?

It had never before occurred to Davie that there
could be any lasting quarrels in the family. The family had seemed to him to be an invincible unit, one
no family member could escape—or would ever want
to. Now all he could think of was leaving the family
and their quarrels behind.

Webb and Taylor had not made up their differences since that day when they had met in Taggart's

back garden; they had taken care not to come together again, either in business or in society. No one knew whether it would continue or how it would end. It had set the family on edge; everyone wanted it over.

"Speak to them, Dennison," their mother pleaded. She had received a brief account of the quarrel from Liza who had wheedled it out of Susannah, who had heard from Webb that his brother was a "damn fool Tory and the stubbornest in a stubborn family."

"Do speak to them," she begged her husband. "Tell them they must behave."

"They are too old to be scolded like puppies," Dennison said, "and this is a serious matter. I respect Taylor's thinking, I honestly do, but I think he is inclined to put too scrupulous a point on the matter. I can't think why he believes the British will stand up to their word. Taylor has gotten too fine minded for Charleston. He is too idealistic."

"Perhaps he should go into the church," Caroline suggested desperately. "Then we could ask him to forgive his trespasses and those who trespass against him."

"Taylor is far too worldly for the church, even the English church," Dennison said flatly. "Think of how much he relishes cockfights. How he appreciates horseflesh. And woman flesh."

"He does?" Caroline gasped.

"Oh, good heavens, he is a healthy young man," Dennison said impatiently.

"Where did he get his notions? I am afraid it was up north." Although born and raised in England, Caroline was not a Loyalist.

"His opinions are held by other Charlestonians," Dennison explained. "His friend Rutledge, for instance, is just as hesitant to join the war. I admit;

there is a case to be made for our resolving the problems of our own province before taking on the British empire.''

"I really don't care for politics, not a whit," Caroline stated emphatically, "but I won't have the family fighting like Sicilians. I can't bear it. Promise me that you'll try to talk to Taylor."

And Dennison did try, inviting Taylor to meet him for dinner at the Smoking Club, one of the all-male societies so popular in town. But he found Taylor dealing with the sad prospect of bidding farewell to Lucinda Carroll, his long-time sweetheart, whose father, a prominent clergyman and British sympathizer, had decided to move the entire family back to England.

"Perhaps it is time . . . ," Dennison suggested to his handsome son. "The Carrolls are a fine family."

Taylor had drunk more than was his habit and he laughed bitterly at his father's suggestion. "I quite agree, Papa. The Carrolls are among the finest of Carolina families, but we do not satisfy them!"

"We what? What do you mean?"

"How could I not prevail most earnestly upon Lucinda to make me a happy man?" Taylor asked. "Lucinda is a lovely woman; she has been my special friend since she was ten. She is admirable in every way. In short, I do love her."

"So what is the matter?"

"Lucinda has been forbidden to accept my suit. Her father now thinks our family too rebellious," Taylor explained tightly.

"What nonsense! How irrational these churchmen are!"

"I think you will have to agree that these are not rational times, nor rational issues."

"I am sorry, Taylor," Dennison said honestly. "I suppose Canon Carroll is determined?"

112

"He is. Lucinda has said that she will wait until the war is over. I have urged her not to feel committed to me. They sail this weekend for Portsmouth."

Dennison regarded his son with sympathy. It was apparent that Taylor was deeply unhappy, but Dennison knew that there was nothing he could do to help in this situation. But perhaps mending the rift with Webb would take some of the weight of these last unhappy weeks off Taylor's shoulders. Caroline was right. It was Dennison's duty as a father to help his sons.

"Taylor, why not make it up with your brother?" Dennison pressed. "Put an end to it right now."

"All I have left are my convictions, Papa. I respect Webb's point of view; it is he who does not respect mine."

"Nonsense! Nonsense!" Dennison sputtered.

"Nevertheless, that is how I see it, Papa." The subject was closed.

The day after Dennison and Taylor had dined at the Smoking Club, Davie saw a way out and he took it.

Responding to Congress's summons, General Charles Lee had left Savannah and was heading north. Congress not only needed his expertise at a disappointing time of defeat and discouragement, but also wanted to have a competent commander available in case anything happened to Washington. Lee's stop in Charleston was brief but pleasant; he was a hero in that town, having led the Charlestonians in their glorious victory over General Henry Clinton and Sir Peter Parker in late June. Since then, he had taken a regiment of Carolinians to Savannah.

In Georgia, Charleston's near southern neighbors were in double danger, for not only were the Cher-

113

okee Indians on the warpath, but the British still held St. Augustine and Pensacola in Florida. Georgia was sparsely settled and weak. The British sent out parties of regulars, Tories, and Indians to carry off cattle, seize Negroes, and kill the frontier people. Lee had done what he could to organize resistance, both in Congress and on the local level.

On this stop in Charleston, Lee appealed for help for the Georgians. Lee was, more than ever, a curious figure—thin as a stick, "impossibly ugly," utterly impassioned. Davie Montgomery heard him speak to the city's fathers at an open meeting of the council, heard him call America "liberty's last and only asylum" in his curious upper-class British accent, and recognized a man of action. He was determined to join up with this man if it was the last thing he did.

"Sir, I would go north with you, right away," Davie said, accosting General Lee outside the council chambers. Lee was accompanied by his favorite dog, Spada, one of a pack of twelve that kept him constant company.

Flattered by the obvious admiration of such a handsome young man, Lee admitted, "I could use a quick, strong, young aide-de-camp. Do you ride?" Lee's last aide had succumbed to malaria in Georgia.

"All my life, sir."

"Can you shoot?"

"I was in the front line at Fort Moultrie, sir."

"Good for you. Fond of dogs?"

"Yes, sir!"

"Good. I prefer them to most men I know. We'll ride at dawn tomorrow."

Davie gave the news to his father as a thing already settled. "I can't stomach the opinions and arguments the others like to chew on till they're all

114

pulp. Only thing for me is to go! Don't tell Mother till I've gone."

Dennison knew he couldn't stop his exuberant youngest son, short of locking him up. Davie had always been independent. In some ways he was the steadiest of the boys; he did not chatter like Webb or run as deep as Taylor. His mother would be sad at this news, but she would get over it. Dennison remembered being fifteen—he, too, had been ready for action.

"For Christ's sake, be careful!" he told him. "Here's my pistol. Keep it in your belt and make sure you stay alive, no matter who the other fellow is. Lee's a great general, I suppose. You know we have kin up there in New York."

"I'll be careful, Papa," Davie assured him.

"Come home for Christmas, you hear?"

"I'll be here," Davie promised.

As the American troops on Harlem Heights held firm, vastly encouraged by their victory, one who would have been of their number, a former compatriot of poor Knowlton in the rangers, in fact, named Nathan Hale, made his way secretly across Long Island Sound in a little sloop. The night was dark; no moon shone on the ghostlike craft; no lights beckoned on the eastern shore.

Hale had met with Washington and had agreed to undertake an intelligence-gathering mission, posing as a Tory schoolmaster who had fled Connecticut to seek employment on Long Island. He had stripped off his ranger uniform, even to the silver shoe buckles. As evidence of his profession he carried his diploma from Yale.

No man had ever been more alone than was Hale on his mission. He waded ashore to Huntington in the pitch blackness and slept in a hollow log. From Huntington he hitched a ride to Oyster Bay, adding a Loyalist's red ribbon to his costume.

From the potato farmer who gave him a seat in his wagon, Hale learned that the rebels had deserted Manhattan and retreated north. He was very surprised, but did his best to appear nonchalant.

"Did the rascals set fire to the city, then?" he asked.

"Bless me, no! They run so fast they didn't take the time, I guess."

Hale had a sense of missing out on all the action. Here he was, marooned on Long Island; he had arrived too late. Now the information that would be most valuable to Washington would be in the city. Ought he proceed across the East River and try to glean information about the current strength and position of the King's forces in lower Manhattan? It was dangerous; he might be recognized there, but he guessed he ought to go. From Oyster Bay a market boat crossed to Manhattan every morning.

Hale met dragoons at every crossing, gave his identity again and again in a voice gaining confidence. To get on the market boat he had to be hired as a crew member; to be hired on he had to contact a vital member of the conspiracy, a man who himself had just been arrested, and forced to swear a loyalty oath, but who had perhaps one last favor to collect from the Dutchman who sailed the market boat.

As the market boat made its deliveries, Hale began to hear interesting details. More food was needed for the two artillery companies due for the march through Throg's Neck. A thousand Hessians would eat all the cabbage the Dutchman could bring. The East River bristled with British craft; Hale made mental notes of their names and strength. He saw the headquarters flag flying over the Beekman mansion. So that was where General Howe had taken shelter! It was dark when the market boat, after two more stops, landed at Whitehall Slip, and Hale slipped off into the streets, an invisible man—or so he hoped.

He skulked through the familiar streets with his schoolmaster's hat pulled low to hide his face. There were many here who would recognize him if he showed full face. He saw the changes that had taken place in the city already: Some stores were closed; others had been looted. He saw that doors on patriot residences had been marked G.R., that bright British uniforms hung over windowsills to air, fine black boots stood on some of the stoops. The whores at the Holy Ground had a new clientele; the taverns were busier than ever.

He turned up Queen Street, avoided the public entrance at The Lark's Song, and stopped at a dark doorway that led to William Whitestone's private rooms. He took a deep breath and looked carefully right and left. Then he seized the moment and ducked inside.

Chapter Eight

IT HAD BEEN a hot, dry summer in New York.

Not a drop of rain had fallen in the city since the stormy night the American army had retreated to Harlem Heights, the night of the British occupation, and it was now very dry, indeed. The best—in fact, the only pure—drinking water to be found in New York was in the Collect Pond, north of the Commons, and rich families like the Logans purchased that pure spring water from peddlers who hauled it in carts and stopped at their back doors. The poor, of course, could not afford such a luxury. They dipped their leather buckets among the bullfrogs in the reedy coves of the East River or drew water from the public wells. Now that the drought had begun to lower the level in those oft-contaminated wells, the water began to taste brackish and to smell like soup.

Most houses in Manhattan were wooden, and most roofs were shingled with cedar; baked by the summer sun, they were now bone dry. Many of the trees which had long shaded the city's streets had been cut down by the occupying Americans, and the barricades they had erected still spanned some of the streets between the Mall and the East River, which were poor streets, anyway—there were many wretched dwellings on this side of town. Here, in narrow lanes and filthy crooked alleyways, were the homes of the poor—log huts with dirty floors and rickety wooden tenements of three or four rooms.

Manhattan had long been a village, but its village days were doomed. On Friday afternoon, September twentieth, a hot wind blew from the southwest and increased until it was of gale force. As darkness fell, the wind warningly whipped branches against windows, tossed dry leaves, and stirred up the dusty streets.

Somehow, in the secret hours of that tense, dark night, a fire started. There were many who wished to see the city afire. Nathan Hale was one, although he was not the only American soldier skulking around in town that night. The majority of the New England soldiers were eager for the city's destruction, and they had made that sentiment perfectly public, although the New York and New Jersey troops thought it would be too drastic a move. General Greene had urged it, reminding everyone that two-thirds of the property in the city was Tory-owned. Militarily, it made a certain sense: Why willingly hand over comfortable quarters to the enemy while you were confined to leaky tents on Harlem Heights? The British had expected it earlier, searching for flames from Long Island while they prepared to invade.

At any rate, on this night fires started simultaneously in about five places in the crowded downtown streets. One began in a popular whorehouse on the wharf near Whitehall Slip. It spread immediately to an adjacent tavern, racing through the flimsy wooden structures, feeding on kegs of hard cider and sawdust and rickety furniture and sending up both buildings like exploding bombs which scattered sparks onto the dry cedar roofs next door. Another fire broke out in the old Fighting Cocks Tavern on the Battery; a crowded inn on Broadway called The White Hall burst into flames as its patrons ran screaming; and two or three other fires were reported in other parts of the town.

Had not all the church bells in town been carried away by the retreating population, every bell would have carried the alarm within minutes; as it was, the alarm was effectively spread by women's screams. There were fire companies—all volunteer—but they were disorganized and undermanned; the engines and pumps were out of order, and water itself was in short supply. Pumped up by the south wind, the fire spread as fast as the panic among the populace.

Women and children were wakened from sleep and rushed out of burning houses, some of them half-naked, to watch helplessly as the flames leapt from roof to roof and combined in a wall of fire that moved hungrily up the island. From Dock Street the fire crossed to Bridge Street and Stone and Field Market. Flames sucked the air from narrow streets and alleyways; rickety tenements went up like kindling, and showers of sparks fell everywhere. The heat was intense. Men and women formed bucket brigades, but they were belittled by the size of the fire.

The fear and suffering was terrible. No one knew which way the fire would go next, which way to run, how much time they might have left to save themselves or some of their property. Horses trapped in their stables rolled their eyes and shrieked in fright, kicking at their stalls; some of them broke free and stampeded through the streets. Some people ran barefoot from the fire, beating at the sparks that fell from the sky, igniting their hair and night-dresses, and took refuge in buildings that seemed out of the fire's path, only to have those shelters burst into flames as they huddled there trying to catch their breath.

A warehouse full of guns and gunpowder on Stone Street blew up, turning the immediate neighborhood into an inferno. In the midst of the dark, windy night, the sky was red, and people scurrying through the streets in the red light looked like figures in hell.

Suddenly the path of the conflagration forked. One branch roared up Broad Street, consuming the prim old Dutch houses, some of which dated back to Peter Stuyvesant's day. The other swept north along Broadway, setting off the dry leaves of the famous lime trees along the Mall and jumping from house to house along the city's main thoroughfare before shooting west down the side streets to the Hudson. At this point, one of the houses that caught afire was the splendid Georgian residence of Josias Logan and his family.

William Whitestone had been presiding at the punch bowl at The Lark's Song when the fire broke out. It was a busy night, busier than usual.

The cry, ''Fire! Fire! Fire!'' changed everything. The crowd in the coffeehouse fell silent for the space of a few heartbeats, and then everyone rushed for the door. From the street outside, smoke and flames could be seen to the south and southwest, but at some remove; it seemed that through some chance

121

or miracle, this particular street might be spared, unless the wind changed.

The air was acrid and thick with smoke. Coughing, William filled his pockets with the night's profits, seized his pistol, and ran out into the city.

Above, the southern sky was a hideous red-orange. Black smoke rose in great swirls and hung in dense clouds. The streets were jammed with people running back and forth, some trying to carry off their possessions with handcarts and horses. Everywhere was confusion and panic.

A market woman William knew stopped him and threw herself into his arms, shrieking, "Help me! Help me!"

"Quiet yourself, Abby," he told her brusquely. "Take yourself to the commons."

If there be a Hell, this must be it, William thought. There was an acrid smell of human panic and death amidst the smoke and brimstone smell of the fires. The terror of people running for their lives, the din of roaring fires and collapsing buildings, was dreadful. It seemed the end of everything. What would be spared? Where best to run?

Slowly, William moved through the streets like a man in a trance, affecting a calm and authority he did not really feel, urging people to go to the commons, where at least they would be near a source of water.

William steeled himself to be calm and purposeful, to direct people out of the worst streets and head them north. Many people had lost their heads entirely—a man tried to run with a grandfather clock, another staggered under the weight of a hindquarter of beef. There were packs of children running wild; dogs ran barking, and the hogs that always rooted in the sewers had joined the melee, tripping people and squealing in fright as they charged through the streets.

All the houses on the east side of Whitehall Slip were gone; all the west side of Broad Street as far as Beaver. William came upon a bucket brigade on Beaver Lane and joined it, passing leather buckets up to a soldier on a ladder until suddenly the building collapsed, tipping the ladder backward into the crowd.

William was near the ammunition depot on White Street when it exploded. The deafening sound—louder than cannon—accompanied showers of sparks that flew into the sky and onto surrounding rooftops. The sound of fires igniting dry timber was like the roaring of waterfalls; it seemed as if the very earth trembled in response, and then the windowpanes from the burning buildings began to burst like scattered shots, sending off a shower of deadly, needle-sharp shards.

Above the roaring and snapping of the fire, the high screams of women and children cut like vinegar through oil. One explosion followed another in horrible succession. The city was an inferno. William moved on. He saw a shed burst into flames, exploding with chickens. He saw a dog completely wreathed in flames running toward the river.

As quickly as he could he was making his way toward lower Broadway, toward the family house where Meg lived with Josias and Bonnie. Until the wind changed, at about midnight, it seemed unlikely that the fire would reach lower Broadway, but then the wind suddenly veered to the southeast and changed the fire's course to the west. William saw it, understood what it meant, and began to run, cutting through an alleyway off New Street.

* * *

When Bonnie Logan woke, the midnight sky was blood red, and the air felt as hot as noon. She had gone to bed early with a slight indisposition and slept more soundly than usual; when she woke to the smell of smoke and the sound of screaming, she was frightened at once.

Looking down from her windows she saw a vision of the end of the world. The sky to the east was red; the air was thick with smoke. She saw a flock of gamebirds on the wing, their feathers cruelly ablaze, and when they settled on the roof of the Abernethys' carriage shed, it began to smolder at once. She was too frightened to run; her mind had stopped in shock. She stood rooted there at the window, not even thinking of trying to escape.

"Miss Bonnie!" the servant woman Katie screamed, beating on Bonnie's door before she burst in. "Get dressed, miss, at once, and come!"

"Where's Dorothy?" Bonnie gasped, coming into her senses at last.

"I took her down already," Katie promised. "Hurry yourself, Miss Bonnie!"

Bonnie obeyed, her fingers stiff with fear. She ran first to Dorothy's room, then found the baby safe in the arms of Peggy, a slight mulatto woman, and although her eyes were round with wonder, she did not cry out. She ran through the house, to Meg and Josias's room. Meg was dreadfully pale and bathed in sweat. Josias, for once, looked confused and helpless.

"We are lost!" he moaned, his eyes rolling.

"We must get out," Bonnie said decisively. Meg, still in bed, was clutching her stomach and lay as if incapable of moving. Tears coursed down her face. Josias, with one last look at his wife, moved decisively toward the door.

"Stay with Meg!" Josias ordered Bonnie. "We must get a cart to carry her."

Josias and a few of the men servants ran out to the side of the house, and Bonnie took Meg's arm to help her out of the bed.

"The city is on fire," said Meg in a strange voice. "Oh, Bonnie, I think my time is upon me. The pains have come! I think I'm breaking into pieces! Oh, dear Lord!"

"Darling, you will be all right," Bonnie assured her. "You will be all right. I will take care of you." Good heavens, she thought, what a night to have a baby! She stifled a sob as she reached out for her own, taking Dorothy from Peggy just as the child began to howl.

The little alley William cut through was narrow and dark with smoke. Putting his sleeve over his mouth, he pressed on, but before he reached Broadway, he heard a feeble cry for help from the top story of an old Dutch windmill which had been shorn of its blades and used for storing hay.

"Where are you?" he screamed, looking wildly at the open loft windows. It was completely dark except for the glare of light cast by the burning buildings on Broadway, and that was a flickering light that cast dreadful shadows.

"Help! Help!" came the cry from the top of the old windmill.

"Where are you?" William cried again, and then he saw her—a wraith of a child-woman, her thin arms outstretched, her white-blond hair standing out like a halo. The entire first floor of the windmill was on fire.

"Jump!" William shouted, opening his arms and standing as close to the flames as he could, and jump she did, soaring through the smoke like an angel, and landed safely in his arms, as he staggered backward.

To his surprise, he recognized Isannah, the indentured girl at Jasper Drake's tavern.

Sobbing hysterically, Isannah clung to William as he carried her out of the alleyway. "Where is it safe?" she gasped in her lilting Scottish accent. "I went to hide in the loft, I thought to be safe, but the fires came after me! Oh, dear Lord, am I dead?"

"You will live many more years," William told her and set her into the back of a wagon moving up Broadway full of women and their children. "Go with the others to the Commons," he told her hurriedly, rushing on to his family's house.

But when he got there, it was gone—entirely consumed in flames.

The city was full of incendiarists and vigilantes. There had been so many and such detailed reports of the rebels wanting to fire the town that everyone was suspicious. Everyone was looking for persons setting fires. Suspicious figures were seen scrambling across rooftops; men were caught with bundles of faggots dipped in melted resin and brimstone; smoldering rags were found in empty houses and shoved beneath staircases in tenements. People dealt with these arsonists swiftly and directly; a spirit of vengeance possessed the fire fighters and those who had seen their homes and all that they owned go up in flames.

A carpenter named White was accused of cutting the handles of fire buckets. Apparently quite drunk, he had slashed at a woman fighting the fire; a mob slit his throat before hanging him upside down from a tavern signpost on Cherry Street. A man seen setting fire to his own home was locked inside, where he perished. A woman seized with matches and combustibles was tossed alive onto a bank of flames. A man caught with an armful of smoldering straw was bayoneted and hung by his feet.

The British military command did all that they could to stop the fires and to catch the incendiaries— mostly in their usual cautious fashion. General Howe had been roused to watch the gruesome scene from his veranda at the Beekman mansion, a disheveled Betsy Loring at his side.

Howe was sleepy and annoyed; he was certain the fire had been willfully set, and by some Yankee villains, of course. He had behaved as a gentleman, but naturally the wretched rebels could not—they must ruin his army's winter quarters. Howe ordered General Robertson to put two regiments to work fighting the fire and evacuating prisoners and the sick. That would be all, he decided; he could not spare more men until after daylight, lest the rebels on Harlem Heights use the fire as a cover to launch a full-scale attack on the city.

General Robertson hurried to move patients out of burning hospitals and prisoners out of the jails. He set guards in the streets, wherever he could, stationed patrol boats in the rivers, and sent search parties racing all over town to round up suspects. Robertson personally caught a few arsonists just as the mob was about to throw them into the flames and saved them for ''the Deliberate Hand of Justice.'' He spread a dragnet over the edges of the city and on the major roads to halt fleeing civilians. Any one of them might be an incendiary or a spy.

* * *

Before the flames reached their house, the Logans and their servants had piled into an iron-wheeled hay wagon and were headed up Broadway. The heat was searing, and all of them were streaming with sweat. Bonnie was very frightened for Meg, whose labor was progressing quickly, too quickly, or so it seemed, for it was hard to judge time. Time seemed to be passing slowly, so that each minute was a small eternity, but also too quickly—there was not enough of it.

"I think the wind is changing!" Bonnie shouted to Josias above the din. From the movement of the smoke, it appeared to be so. The wind shift turned the path of the fire away from the main part of the city. It was now confined to those neighborhoods between Broadway and the river where nearly every structure was ablaze.

"Make haste! We must make haste!" Josias shouted at Peter, who was driving the wagon. Meg lay collapsed, drifting in and out of consciousness.

Peter had done all he could to control the horse. "Whoa, Lady, pretty Lady, good girl," he crooned, bending over her neck. He had fitted out the creature with blinders, but it was spooked and danced nervously, threatening to break the traces and upset the wagon. Their progress was very slow. Every block seemed unending.

Trinity Church was afire. As the wagon drew abreast, the ancient structure was in its death throes. Bonnie saw the skeleton of its tall spire appear transcendent in the moment before it crumbled into its foundations. Only a few blocks to the north, the congregation of St. Paul's was standing on that church's roof with buckets, struggling to douse flying sparks and save their house of worship.

"God damn the devils who have done this!" Josias shouted.

"Josias, we must find shelter for Meg. She cannot bear this much longer," Bonnie said, suddenly calm. Ever since she had absorbed the enormity of the disaster, she had been praying for the strength to take care of Meg, and now it had come to her.

"Shelter?" Josias shrieked, his voice high with fear. All the world seemed to be falling down around them. Smoke was rolling down the streets in every direction.

Oh, who can guide us? Bonnie thought desperately. Where is William? She could see that Josias had no more idea than she where to go.

"Drive to Delancey Square," she directed Peter impulsively. He obeyed at once, and the frightened eyes of her brother and the servants held relief that a plan had been made.

Now they made slow but steady progress up Broadway and across the southern edge of the Commons to Division Street. The sky was livid, and every side street was filled with real and unnameable terrors. Bonnie held Dorothy clasped to her breast and cradled Meg's head in her lap. Meg was conscious now, and writhing in pain.

"I shall die," Meg whispered.

"Not at all. You will live," Bonnie promised her.

A line of fire fighters with buckets stretched from the Collect though the tanyards to the Commons. Here the air was clearer, and Bonnie began to hope she had made a good decision. They passed an orchard; the smell of ripe apples was sweet. They turned into Elizabeth Street. Like the rest of the city, it was full of frightened people and abandoned houses.

Anywhere, anywhere will do, Bonnie thought, and then, in a cobbled courtyard off Elizabeth Street, she caught sight of an old windmill with a well and saw that its front door stood open.

"There, Peter, take us in there," she ordered. Peter turned the wagon into the courtyard and stopped it.

The interior of the mill was cool and quiet. Bonnie instructed Peter and Josias to carry Meg to a low bed covered with rough blankets.

"Go for a midwife! Go!" she ordered Josias, and he ran off.

Meg moaned. "Oh, has the world come to an end?"

"Not yet," Bonnie promised. "We'll be safe, dear. The fire is across the island now. You are safe here, safe to give birth to your baby."

Meg was never able to entirely recall the hours of that long, hot night. She remembered the pain, though, waves of it, curling her up tightly and then letting her go. The pain went on and on. The fierceness of her own screams frightened her. It was dark, and she was frightened of the shadows.

"The dark! The dark!" she whispered. Bonnie found a candle.

"There is nothing to fear in the dark," Bonnie promised.

Meg remembered that Bonnie stayed with her through all of it, holding her hand, wiping her face, and murmuring prayers. Bonnie set the servants to drawing water. Josias had gone to look for help. Just after he left, the pains got much worse, so that Meg felt sure she wanted to die.

"You won't die," Bonnie assured her. "This night will end, I promise. Already the fire is burning out, and the sky is light with dawn. Please, Meg. Please try to hang on."

"I am trying," Meg promised, but she had used-up her strength, and felt coldness and numbness in all her bones.

130

Josias returned on the run. He was alone. "There is no one!" he cried in a frightened voice. "No one!"

"We will do the best we can," Bonnie said and she and an ashen Josias tried to hold Meg and help her. After another hour or so, the little boy's head emerged into the world, but he did not draw breath.

"Why has God done this?" Josias moaned.

"God has not set the city afire," Bonnie said positively, but the same bleak sadness and confusion filled her heart. Meg's screams ceased, but she began to sob, a sound that echoed in the dark hollow of the mill, gasping and keening her sorrow with all the last of her strength.

And finally, what seemed like eons later, she drifted off into a deep, merciful sleep.

"It's all over," Bonnie whispered. "My poor Meg. Poor child."

Josias went out again, leaving Meg in Bonnie's arms, and when he returned at sunrise, he had found Doctor Bard.

"The child died of shock," Bard said, and told them that it was God's will, and that they should put all their hopes into strengthening the mother so that she might do better next time she was brought to bed. Bard left at once; there were so very many in need of his help as a result of the disastrous fire.

"It is so terribly sad, so sad," Bonnie wept. "She has been living only for the day she should be a mother."

"God's will be done," Josias said tersely.

Very early that morning, General Howe was awakened from the soundest of slumbers in his bedroom at Beekman Mansion. He was annoyed to be disturbed, and when he was annoyed his full-lipped mouth collapsed into a childish pout. (In fact, General Howe's features were remarkably like those of his King, a fact that had been often observed and was held by London gossips to be more than coincidental.)

"What is it? What is it?" he snapped. He was already furious that the city was burned, and as usual, he and Betsy Loring had indulged themselves royally in liquors and wine with their rich dinner. He had hardly slept. For hours, he had paced the terrace of his headquarters, scowling at the reddened sky and the dense pall of black smoke that hung over the lower third of the island.

"A spy has been caught, sir!" an aide called out. "Major Loring has caught a spy!"

"Joshua is here?" Mrs. Loring asked in confusion. Was she having a bad dream? She groaned and hid her pretty head under the feather pillows. There was supposed to be an agreement that this would not happen.

"It's nothing, dear. I will take care of it," Howe assured her. He sounded murderously annoyed. Head throbbing, he pulled on a wig and a dressing gown and went to deal with the interruption.

The man apprehended was Nathan Hale of Connecticut, cousin of Samuel Hale, who was deputy commissar of prisoners under Major Loring. One of the patrol parties had caught the man attempting to escape through the lines to Harlem, had found drawings of the British fortifications hidden in his shoes. Hale had been brought before General Robertson and had insisted that he was only a Yankee schoolteacher trying to get home, but Robertson had recognized the name. Ever eager to show his acuity, Robertson had summoned Loring's assistant, Samuel Hale, who had identified his cousin by the birthmark on his neck and the powder burns on his face.

"They say he's the one who set the city afire!" the aide informed Howe.

"Where is he?" Howe asked, at last.

"Downstairs, sir."

Howe trudged downstairs in his dressing gown. As he passed the door of his chamber, Betsy Loring poked her head out. "Is Joshua here?" she asked again, referring to her husband.

"Of course not!" Howe snapped. "Pray go to sleep."

Nathan Hale was bound and guarded by four stout Welsh guards. He was a well-built man, Howe noted, dressed like a schoolmaster, but with a soldier's bearing and patriotic fervor. Hale looked intelligent; his eyes were bright with passion and determination.

"Did Washington command you to burn New York?" Howe demanded.

"I cannot disclose the orders of my superior officers," Hale replied firmly.

Howe shrugged. Unfortunate, but there you were. "Lock him in the greenhouse for the night," he ordered. "Hang him in the morning. And for Christ's sake, do not disturb me again tonight."

Nathan Hale was hung the next morning in front of the British Artillery Park. He went to his death with great composure and resolution, yet looking around in vain for a single expression of respect or compassion among the crowd of onlookers, who included Josias Logan, not the only outraged property holder who was convinced that the major incendiary was about to be snuffed. The executioner was Richmond, the teenage mulatto who did this job for the British army.

Hale had gone to war quoting Horace: *"Dulce et decorum est pro patria mori."* Never was a young man more thoroughly idealistic or better grounded in the classics. As he was about to be hanged, he made a little speech upholding the sacredness of duty and the rightness of the American cause. In conclusion he summoned a quote from Cato. None who heard it ever forgot him say, "What a pity is it—that we can die but once to serve our country!"

As a lesson to others, Hale's body was left hanging for three days. Some soldiers, with grisly humor, found a wooden garden sign, a sort of scarecrow, in the shape of a painted soldier and hung it next to him, inscribed "George Washington."

General Washington himself, as he had watched the fire from the balconies of the Morris mansion on Harlem Heights, had not been entirely displeased, nor did the New England troops in their tents below attempt to hide their joy at the sight of the destruction of Tory headquarters.

He had not ordered it, Congress had advised against it, but somehow, it had happened anyway. Washington stood calmly on the upper balcony for hours that night, watching the red glow spread and new fires break out like searchfires on the southern tip of the island. Bayard watched with him, obsessed with thoughts of the safety of his family in the city.

"How sad," Washington said, at last. "But at

least it is settled. Providence, or some good honest fellow, has done more for us than we were disposed to do for ourselves."

"Many will be homeless," Bayard felt compelled to say.

"Aye, no doubt," the general agreed, at this late hour inclined to think of himself as in that condition. He dreamed, night and day, of resigning his post and returning to his beloved Mount Vernon. He often begged his aides to tell him that things would go better without him, but to a man they assured him that if he were to resign all would be entirely lost. He was in a constant state of division, unable to quit this command, and unable to act effectively in it. He was enormously discouraged by the state of affairs and alarmed that the latest committee sent by Congress refused to be alarmed.

"At least, the city's destruction will result in confusion and delay their attack," said Washington, who expected a major British affront at any moment. "If I am given time to consolidate and train the men, I may be able to stand ground."

And then he added in a voice of profound gloom, not having nearly recovered from the humiliation of the retreat from Kip's Bay, "Stand ground, that is, if the men will stand by me, which, bye and bye, I despair of."

Never had Bayard suspected that wars were fought so, in such helter-skelter uncertainty, or that great men had such grave doubts. But apparently such was the case.

Bayard's youthful instincts—for attack, for the offense in which courage, spirit, and honor all counted, which paid off in fame and glory—were being tempered by harsh experience. The most important thing, it turned out, was to stay alive.

Washington was fighting a defensive war, trying to hold the army together and avoid a general action which might well result in massive defeat. Sometimes he called it "my war of posts." His overall object was to concentrate his strength, to hold to his posts, to persuade the young American soldiers to do their duty, and to stay alive to go home to Mount Vernon.

Chapter Nine

OVER A QUARTER of New York City was in ruins; eleven hundred shops and homes were destroyed, their occupants homeless and in most cases reduced to beggary.

Not so for the Logans. Meg's family, the Whitestones, had owned not one or two, but twenty good houses of various design and antiquity, and although the one on Broadway which they had so comfortably occupied had indeed been totally destroyed by the fire, it remained only to look over the rest of the family's real estate, make a choice, and evict the current tenants. Which Josias, entirely comfortable in his position as acting head of the family, did in good order in the days following the fire.

Josias was relieved to find his offices in good order and that most of the family's warehouses and wharfs had been spared. True, Trinity Church was gone, but Fraunces Tavern had escaped the blaze. The heart of the commercial district lay in ashes and the so-called holy ground, the sinful quarter behind Trinity which had housed most of the city's prostitutes, had gotten its punishment. All the towering old elms were burned, but many of the fine mansions of the rich stood intact.

In fact, the most inconvenient loss to Josias's comfort and peace of mind was that of his tailor, for Hercules Mulligan, well known as one of the original Sons of Liberty, had been detained by General Robertson while driving north along the Greenwich Road, and Mulligan was now residing in Bridewell Prison, awaiting trial. Josias, who had lost all his clothes in the fire, determined to press Robertson for the tailor's immediate release. Damn the man's foolish politics, Mulligan was the finest tailor in town! He was everyone's tailor; even General Washington had commissioned a suit while in town, and Josias had been referred to Mulligan by his father-in-law, than whom there was no one more fashionable.

Josias had never liked fussy, peculiar old General Robertson—he had been indeed distressed to find out that Bonnie was right about his appointment as commandant of New York—and he took the matter of Mulligan as a cloak for his resentments. Robertson's many problems included controlling the widespread looting by British soldiers that had begun as soon as they entered the smoldering city, and the more complicated one of finding housing for the soldiers, their wives and children, the sick and wounded, and the growing number of American prisoners.

When Josias approached doddering old Robertson to argue for the release of his tailor, Robertson agreed at once. Strange, he thought, that the spry little tailor had such powerful friends, but so it seemed he did—that clever publisher, Whitestone, had also put in a good word for him. Robertson took the opportunity of a favor granted to ask Josias Logan for a favor: Could Josias supervise the appropriation of the warehouses on the East River to store the goods that would be needed for the army and navy? It would be a great deal of work, but Robertson felt sure he could offer compensation. It demanded a man with great energy and organizational skills. Could Josias find it in his heart to consider the position?

Josias could, and gladly. Nothing pleased him more than to requisition his competitors' warehouses for Royal use. Proudly, he drew up a map of the wharfs and warehouses, and soon workers began unloading ammunition, clothing, food, wines, and crates of good West Indian rum into the Kip, Wright, De Peyster, and Giles warehouses on Water Street and the Byvanck and Pearson warehouses on Dock Street. And always, it was clear, a sampling of the best would find its way into the Whitestone-Logan buildings on Murray's Wharf. Josias's family would lack for naught throughout the course of the occupation, that was now sure.

Returning home on a cool, windy afternoon, followed by a servant carrying a sack of oranges and tea and some choice bottles of old Bordeaux, Josias saw an unfamiliar but handsome carriage at the front gate—a remarkable, cream-colored carriage affixed with flowerpots on each side and in the back. Inside, he found his wife Meg—who had been unalterably dispirited since her loss—seated in the downstairs parlor in conversation with a most fashionably dressed young woman.

"Good evening, dear wife," Josias said, standing hesitantly at the door. He could not see the visitor's face, but he saw Meg's, and Meg's was strained and unenthusiastic.

"Hello! Darling Josias!" exclaimed the visiting lady, rushing to greet him.

"Audrey! Good heavens, my dear. What a surprise!"

"Indeed," said Meg, and from her tone it was amply clear that she was far from delighted to receive her sister.

Josias ignored Meg's inhospitable attitude and did his best to make Audrey Whitestone feel at home at once. "At first I did not even recognize you," he said admiringly. "You are prettier than ever . . . I mean, more grown up."

"Do you think so, dear Josias?" Audrey asked, pulling herself to her full height, which was not a remarkable one despite pink satin shoes that tied at the ankles and were perched on three-inch heels. "I am so pleased, so delighted to be back in the city! I thought I should wither, I mean positively wither up and die, so bored was I in the country with Papa and Mama."

"At least you were quite safe there," Meg said flatly.

"Oh, safe! I suppose so. But all the excitement has been here. I am quite satisfied to be back home."

"And your parents? How is their health?" Josias inquired eagerly. His feelings and motives on this score were quite mixed; on the one hand, he admired his rich and powerful father-in-law Albert Whitestone and thrived on his approval and attention, but on the other, he had become accustomed to full control of the family business concerns during the months that the elder Whitestones had been in residence at their country estate in the Hudson River valley. It was splendid to be in charge; he relished it absolutely. He hoped that Audrey's sudden return did not mean that her parents would soon follow.

Albert Whitestone's son William took no interest in family business matters; he had his own concerns: his print shop, his newspaper, his coffeehouse. William had early made clear his intention to be independent of his father's advice and protection and had done so consistently.

There was something extremely odd—even baffling—about William, to Josias's mind. Although he had been kind to Josias when he was new in town, Josias was always uncomfortable in William's presence. There was something superior and intense about the publisher's attitude. One never really knew what he was thinking or where he stood, but at least—and from Josias's point of view this was crucial—he stood clear of the family businesses.

"Oh, they are well," Audrey assured him, having taken a seat on the blue brocade settee, arranged her skirts around her, and accepted the glass of Madeira Josias had poured for her—Audrey had ever liked her drop. "Although Mama and Papa are thoroughly disinclined to leave the country at this point. They have barricaded themselves into that isolated farm and hardly dare to poke their heads out of the doors. For fear of the Skinners, you know. It took me nearly a week to persuade Papa to let me come to the city, and I should never have succeeded, had I not assured him, Josias, that I would be entirely safe in your protection."

Audrey looked beseechingly at her brother-in-law as she spoke and lowered her voice confidingly. To Meg's ears, she sounded entirely false, but Josias was flattered and highly relieved to hear that Albert Whitestone had no plans to return to the city.

"How long will you stay?" Meg asked.

"How long?" Audrey smiled. "Oh, I am here to stay, dear sister! Here to stay."

"Splendid!" said Josias.

Before joining up with General Lee, Davie Montgomery had never traveled more than thirty miles from home. Now he would see all the Middle Atlantic Coast. Lee took the coastal road north, passing through low country, a region of sandy soil, and low, scrubby pines. To the northeast, the low hills began, and further north, were great enough to be called mountains. This was the "Up Country." Here the trees were tall hardwoods, and the forests teemed with deer in incredible number.

General Lee traveled in a solid black coach, drawn by four powerful horses. On fine days he rode alongside the coach, leaving the windows open so that he could call to his dogs, all twelve of which rode inside the coach, leaping and yelping, their tongues hanging out as the countryside slipped past. The road was narrow and deeply rutted; when it crossed a swollen stream, the carriage had to be floated across, and all the dogs swam behind General Lee.

Most of the days were mild and sunny. For miles and miles they passed among hardwoods bright with fall-colored leaves: the clear yellow of hickory and chestnut, beech and poplar, the red-and-gold of maples and sweet gum, the blood red of black gum and dogwood, and behind them all the oaks—massive, towering oaks fading from red to bronze to brown. Davie was surprised by the lack of pines and the infrequent meadows in North Carolina and Virginia. He delighted to see flocks of green parakeets and small alligators in the marshes.

Birds called as the coach rattled over the rough spots—it was a well-worn, well-traveled road, consistently pitted with chuckholes and treacherous stumps, which by law had to be less than eight inches high. Lee's driver was a burly Georgian named Jake Mashall. "Bear left!" Mashall would shout when he was forced to take the coach up onto its two right wheels to miss some huge ditch or stone, and then "Bear to th' right!" he would bellow a minute later.

Davie was thrilled to be seeing the country, but he was homesick from the start. An eccentric Englishman, General Lee was quite unlike the casual, courteous aristocrats of Charleston who had peopled Davie's life up to now. With his sharp eye and an even sharper tongue, Lee set out to instruct his young recruit in the ways of the world and some of the strategies of soldiering. Ridicule was one of his chief weapons. There was much of the poseur in Lee, a man so physically odd, so skinny and chinless, that he had early learned to deal with involuntary withdrawal from those who did not suffer him long enough to form a mitigating impression of his intelligence and personality. He was fond of overindulgence in drink—a characteristic common in all localities and walks of life, of course, but carried to hearty excess with Lee—and without a doubt he was slovenly. His personal habits had deteriorated as quickly as his manners during his life in the New World.

Lee was well read; Shakespeare was his favorite, and he liked to tell stories. Many of them were about himself. To Davie, they were as fabulous as the tales of Sheherezade. Was it possible that Lee had married a Seneca woman? "Oh, she was a chief's daughter, a very great beauty," Lee told a wide-eyed Davie. Was it really true that Lee had been taken into the tribe of the Bear, given the name Ounewaterika, meaning "boiling water," or "one whose spirits are never asleep?" Lee claimed that he had twin children as a result of this, his only marriage, a copper-skinned pair, a boy and girl who lived in Quebec.

Lee told tales of his adventures in the Ticonderoga campaign, nearly twenty years earlier. He had been badly wounded by a musket shot which shattered two of his ribs as it passed through his body. Although thought to be mortally wounded, Lee had recovered under the care of Madam Schuyler, whom he recalled thankfully, though he condemned Abercromby, his commander, as "our booby in chief" and a "damn'd beastly poltroon." Lee's language was the most colorful Davie had ever heard.

Nightly, the coach and Lee's entourage stopped at small wayside inns of the sort known as ordinaries, usually run by a man and his wife who offered bed and board to both men and animals. Lee insisted that his dogs be given seats at table, served cooked meals of the same quantity and caliber offered himself and his staff, and then shared his bed with the pack of them. One of his favorites was a Pomeranian, as big and furry as a brown bear, which Lee took great amusement in presenting to ladies for a handshake. "Had I seen it in the woods I should have fired without hesitating," the driver Mashall confided to Davie, and Davie had to agree. Small wonder the great general emerged for breakfast covered with matted hairs and smelling strongly doggish.

Day by day they rode north, and by the first of October arrived at New Castle, Delaware. Davie marveled at the flourishing plantations of the German and Quaker farmers, at their surprising architecture, and huge barns. He noticed great gray owls and flocks of bright red birds. By night there were sweet-singing frogs. It was a fair land, and such a big one! Philadelphia, the greatest American city, lay just ahead.

A few days after Audrey's arrival and installation in the east bedroom on the second floor, Bonnie left

Dorothy with Meg and set out to visit William in his print shop.

She had seen him only very briefly since the great fire; Josias had sent him word that they were all safe as soon as he had been able, and he had come to them late the next night, filthy and tired from fighting the fire, his cheeks and hands blackened. He had spoken a few words of consolation to his sister Meg that seemed to help her, although Bonnie knew not what they were. Bonnie herself had scarcely had a private word with him, and she missed him. Only later had she learned of his courage on the night of the fire, how he had rescued young Isannah, how he had found a new home for the Newton family.

William had come once to visit his sister Audrey, but Bonnie had not been at home. Bonnie was surprised by the introduction of Audrey Whitestone into the family circle. Audrey was seemingly so unlike Meg and also very unlike William; so unrestrained, so flamboyant, so artful. It was hard to believe three so different people made up a single family, and yet, perhaps families were often so, Bonnie thought, remembering how different Bayard and Josias had turned out to be, although when Bonnie recalled them as boys, they had been as like as two coins.

She could clearly see, too, that Meg was not fond of her younger sister, or was at least wary of her, and in a way that seemed to go far beyond sisterly rivalry. Meg had not confided in her about it, but perhaps she would in time—Meg was not yet feeling herself either physically or spiritually. Bonnie had only to consider how she herself felt about baby Dorothy to understand Meg's depression, and preserved toward Meg's grief an attitude of respect and sympathy.

Still, it was a beautiful fall day, and Bonnie's spirits soared as she left the big house on Fair Street in which they had all been living since the fire, and walked across the North Ward toward the East Ward. This was a neighborhood of unpretentious houses and businesses which had been spared by the fire. Now, like the rest of the city, it was a garrison, and the streets and houses here were crowded with British soldiers and their families. More soldiers were arriving every day—more than fifteen thousand had marched into town already.

Bonnie well remembered Boston when it had been occupied and knew that some of these troops were, in fact, the same ones who had sailed from her hometown last March. She recalled some of their faces, some of their names, but she had put all that behind her. For Bonnie had taken it upon herself to end her marriage (which had never been a legal marriage), and to her it was almost as if it had never taken place. It was her secret, and hers alone, what she had found when she traveled boldly to the British camp on Staten Island in July to seek out Lieutenant Cormick Walker, the man she had loved and married in good faith.

No one knew that she had found him. Not even Meg knew—although Meg knew that the marriage had been a deception. Meg had been with her when she had encountered Cormick's friend Bridge Thompson and recognized him as the man who had posed as the preacher that dark night in Boston which she had thought to be her wedding night. Bridge Thompson had told Bonnie where to find Lieutenant Walker, and Meg and William both knew that Bonnie had set out to find him.

But it was Bonnie's own secret that she had found him, and found him unchanged in character—still false, lecherous, and unscrupulous. No one else knew that she had found him through an unfortunate woman great with his child, another deceived woman. Oh, the poor, toothless young woman, sick and far from home! Meeting her, seeing evidence of Cormick's true nature, had convinced Bonnie that Cormick must never know of the existence of dear Dorothy, that he did not deserve to know! Meeting her had set Bonnie firmly on the course she had followed through to its end.

No one who thought they knew pretty, light-hearted Bonnie even suspected what she had done. Not even her sister-of-choice, her bosom friend, Meg, knew. But when Bonnie had found Walker, she had gone with him to Rowe's Inn, had risked her honor. And then she had acted boldly, and had shot him with his own gun.

She had done it, and did not regret it, nor did it trouble her conscience, for she was convinced that he deserved no less. But free of guilt, she still could not be free of memory, and the sight of the regiments of red-coated soldiers in the streets of New York triggered all these haunting memories.

By the time she reached William's printing shop on the corner of Wall and Queen streets, Bonnie's good spirits were somewhat strained. She paused at the corner. William's printing offices were marked with a hanging sign of wrought iron in the shape of a printing press. The office door stood open, and the shop gave off a sour, tart smell, the odor of printer's ink. The smell reminded Bonnie of her Uncle Dugald's shop in Boston, reminded her of times long ago and gone forever, for her Uncle Dugald was dead, caught and hung by the British.

William caught sight of her from within and came to the door. ''Good day, Miss Bonnie! Why on earth do you look so stricken? Pray do forgive me, whatever I have done to make you look so!''

Bonnie dimpled. Seeing him, she was instantly

cured of the malaise of memory and felt instead all the opportunity of the moment and the promise of the future. She did not bid it; it happened quite naturally and mysteriously, causing her eyes to sparkle and a shy smile to cross her face. "Good day, William. I assure you, you are guiltless—so far. I was reminded of someone I used to know."

"Well, the fellow had better look out, if I ever meet him," William joked, having little idea of the real complexities of Bonnie's past. "Come in, come in. We are just putting a lively edition to bed, relating all the details of the calamitous fire and naming the wretched incendiarists who caused it."

William's newspaper, which he ambitiously called *Whitestone's New York Messenger; or the Connecticut, New Jersey, and Hudson's River Weekly Journal*, was a four-page folder, seven by nine inches. Just now the upcoming edition was locked into wooden frames on a marble-topped press bed. Proofs of advertisements and broadsides and charts of type sizes hung on the walls. The entire operation was William's pride and joy, for he was a man who delighted in forming opinions and proclaiming them; he enjoyed having power, he relished taking an editorial stance, never minded a few enemies, and he made money on it besides.

In all his endeavors, William loathed advice and doted on independence, and in the first days of its existence, the *Messenger* had maintained a stance of political impartiality. But the events of the past summer, including the violent attack on the print shop, and on his own person, led by the rabid rebel and famous Son of Liberty, Isaac Sears, had turned William openly toward the Tory cause. He no longer spared his readers any detail of the disorganization of the rebel army, of the disgrace of their retreat from Manhattan. He solicited satiric poems ridiculing the

148

rebels, gave an ecstatic account of the invasion at Kip's Bay, and devoted considerable space to bits and squibs of Tory society news. Never losing sight of the fact that the first goal of a journalist is to sell papers, he took care to make his news exciting first, and much later paid his respects to the truth.

As well as current events, William frequently indulged himself in commentary and news of his friends. In this vein, he had some weeks ago published a charming account of Bonnie and her baby daughter entertaining friends for tea in their garden. Bonnie had been delighted; she was typically delighted with everything William did. She did not yet know him well enough to find him less than surprising, and his enigmatic mien fascinated her.

Just then a man came into the shop to speak to William, and Bonnie spent a contented half hour or so wandering around the print shop, snooping at the social columns yet to come, examining the advertisements, and in general feeling satisfied that she had an advance on the news.

In that time, William had finished with his visitor, added a few lines to his editorial, was satisfied with the lockup, and turned again to Bonnie. "His hold on Manhattan is not a firm one, and Howe does his best to shake his hand," he said gleefully.

"Whose?" Bonnie asked.

"Why, Jolly General George!" William joked. "That man has brought word that two warships, the *Phoenix* and *Roebuck,* have just forced passage up the river, with the rebel batteries playing their loudest tune, to no avail."

"I do hope no one was hurt!" said Bonnie, who must always think of her two soldier brothers.

William was touched by her womanly reaction. Her tender heart was so loyal; a man could not fault her for that. "Someone will always be hurt, my dear," he said sadly, "but we must take great care that it is not us."

Bonnie studied his face. His intelligence shone out of his large, bright eyes. Never had she known a man like him. He smiled at her and reached out for her hand.

"Don't look so worried," he said. "For the time being, we are all of us safe, and the future is in God's hands. Isn't there enough talk of war and politics so that we two need not carry on such a gloomy debate? I will spare you my opinions this day, if you will spare me yours!"

Bonnie was glad enough for the suggestion. She had worries enough today.

"Let's go now to tea, dear pretty lady," William proposed. "Have you been to Madam Cummings' Florida Tea Gardens? You have not? Well then, come along at once! Madam's peach tarts are close to heavenly."

And riding to the tea garden in William's shiny black phaeton, Bonnie determined to forget the war and the presence of British soldiers and to enjoy herself.

William adored Bonnie's bright company, and he enjoyed his outing with her tremendously, as he did all the times they were together. But when they parted again, when he had halted the black phaeton in front of the house on Fair Street and kissed her cheek in farewell, he was left with an uncomfortable feeling of helplessness.

Damn it all! William thought as he watched her run swiftly and gracefully up the brick steps. She was so lovely. He longed to call out to her, to stop her, but knew he must not. Shaking his head in frustration, he snapped the reins and jerked sharply at the bit.

How pretty she is and how sweetly patriotic, he thought. Although Bonnie rarely discussed politics, it was obvious where her feelings lay. And her devotion to her soldier brothers was extremely touching. I do hate to see her go, he admitted to himself. My God, I do love her!

William drove off in a gloomy frame of mind, an unusual one for him. He knew well enough that it was because of Bonnie, who had touched his heart as no other woman ever had. He loved her, but he must not reveal it. He admired her sincere patriotism, but must poke fun at it and pretend to despair of her politics.

For William was caught in a lie, a deliberate lie he had chosen to live, and he could not be truthful with Bonnie for her own well-being. She thought him a fervent Tory, and so she must think him—she and everyone else, for his usefulness to Washington and the army depended on it. For Bonnie to know the truth would surely endanger her life. And so far, she did not. No one in his family did. So far, his very public pro-British position had brilliantly hidden his private convictions, and he must see that it continued to do so. He reminded himself that a report on another glorious British victory would be timely. It would set off the story he had just set into type—that Ethan Allen had deserted the rebels and claimed all Vermont for the King. Of course that was a total lie, but it was amazing what men would believe, seeing it in print. Even William, a man with no illusions left, or so he hoped, was amazed at that.

Washington's office at the Morris mansion was a small room at the end of a short second-floor corri-

151

dor above the famous octagonal drawing room. From its smallish windows he had clear views of all approaches to the house and both rivers. It was furnished with a blockfront desk, several chairs, one Windsor chair facing a small fireplace set with shining brass andirons, and a surveyor's table holding maps.

Late one foggy night Bayard knocked on the general's door. When bade enter, he found Washington studying his maps. "I wish to God I were more familiar with the land around here," he said to his aide. He was extremely fond of Logan, a young man but steady, a man who would hold when told to hold, and move when told to move. He preferred his company to that of most of the generals.

"You are more familiar than the enemy," Bayard said truthfully. "Sir, it is very late."

"So it is. I left the dinner table brimming with energy."

"General Lee stimulates you."

"As does news of Virginia. Logan, when this war is over, you must visit us at Mount Vernon."

"I would like that, sir."

General Lee had come riding up that very day, accompanied as always by his dogs. Everyone was so glad to see him that it was easy, for a time at least, to overlook his tempers and eccentricities. True to form, Lee had collected thirty thousand dollars from Congress to guarantee he would not lose by his service in the Continental Army, ever mindful that he had relinquished his pension as well as his command in the British army.

Together, the two generals had seemed more like two southern planters than two soldiers in the midst of war. Washington was greedy for news from home, and Lee had stopped at Mount Vernon. While the others ate and drank, Washington had pressed

Lee for news of the tobacco harvest, the neighborhood, the horses and dogs, and, of course, of his wife and family. Lee had an eye for details and an ear for gossip; his sharp-tongued reports had Washington laughing like a man free of cares.

Bayard had watched and listened, realizing how rare such an occasion was for the general, how often he sat alone with a heavy heart, his mind "on the stretch," his feelings wounded "by a thousand things," as he admitted to Bayard. Lee's arrival seemed the occasion for a gala dinner, and Washington's cook had risen to the occasion, sending up a meal of pigeon soup followed by boiled beef with mushrooms, well-seasoned chicken custard, wilted greens and peas, and cream biscuits with wildflower honey. Several bottles of fine old wine from Roger Morris's excellent cellar had come up the stairs and gone down the throats of the assembled generals and their aides.

And although Lee professed weariness, Washington had cornered him in his office after dinner for more conversation. Washington knew that Lee was widely regarded as his next-in-command, and thus tried to acquaint Lee with the gravity of the hour: the shortage of men and materials, the horrible sick count, the desertion rate keeping pace with enlistments, the prospect of a cold winter. When Lee retired to his bed, Washington had the sense that he had not quite succeeded, that Lee did not yet realize the full danger of the situation.

"Howe will not attack," he had assured Washington, and if Washington were not thus convinced and reassured, Lee predicted also: "They will throw all their strength into the fortification of New York City. Then they will advance toward Philadelphia."

"We must confer again tomorrow," Washington said now to Bayard. "I am not sure Lee realizes that we have only one possible exit from this island, should an exit be necessary."

"Knightsbridge," Bayard said. "A bottleneck."

"And Congress harps on the necessity of preventing the fleet from sailing up the Hudson. So far we have thrice proved ourselves helpless before the fleet. Congress . . ."

"General Lee will make a good advocate at Congress," Bayard reminded him.

"Already he is frustrated with them. Already he understands how slowly they move, how hard it is to rouse them, how they may declare and proclaim from dawn to dusk, but it is for us to do the fighting!"

"No one could handle them—and the soldiers, too—as you do," Bayard insisted.

"I am blessed in my staff," Washington said graciously, and he did not protest as Bayard banked the fire for the night.

Chapter Ten

IF WASHINGTON FINALLY slept that night, Howe did not. After a month of baffling hesitation, Howe had chosen this night to move north, and move he did, sailing stealthily under the cover of darkness and fog, landing unopposed—but as Bayard had guessed, guided by maps which were crucially inaccurate.

Leaving Percy in charge on the west side of Harlem Heights, Howe had sent the British fleet up the East River, through the treacherous rapids at Hell Gate and landed them on Throg's Neck, which was also called Frog's Neck by the men who farmed nearby. Howe's maps showed that the Throg's Neck peninsula was firm and solid; in fact, it was a soggy bit of marshland which became an island at high tide, and American detachments guarded its exits—several fords and a causeway over a freshwater creek. Howe's men, who had come to set a trap, found themselves in one, at least for the time being.

When Washington got the news, he was up and out immediately. Tall and erect on horseback, ever unmistakably the commander, he galloped through the dawn with his aides racing behind him. He was happy to discover that the territory between Throg's Neck and Kingsbridge was strong and defensible, that is, cultivated farmland crisscrossed with stonewalls. Hastily, he called a council of war.

Lee and Putnam, Knox and Stirling, McDougall, Clinton—all were there. Never could so many military geniuses gather together without a great deal of debate. Bayard hovered in the background, making notes when asked to, supplying information that he had, calling for spirits as needed.

"Howe has landed four thousand men!" Henry Knox reported. "And they're only a few miles from here. I assume it's the origination of a pincer movement." Knox, the former Boston bookseller, had read all the books about modern warfare and studied closely the campaigns of Frederick the Great. Significantly, so had all the British generals. Bayard was comforted to see Henry Knox, whom he had known most of his life; he was robust, and fatter than ever. Bayard realized that every time he saw Knox, he had gained weight, no small feat in these times.

"Landed them in a stinking swamp," said Alexander McDougall, his heavy, stuttering brogue clearly identifying his Scottish ancestry. One of the original New York Sons of Liberty, he was a self-made man who had made a fortune delivering milk, and now commanded a brigade of about eleven hundred men. McDougall was feeling particularly lucky—he had received word that the devastating fire in the city had stopped two doors short of his home.

"Don't you see we must get to higher ground?" General Lee sneered. Lee was one who would never overlook the humble accents and humble origins of men like McDougall.

"What sort of fool d'you take me for?" McDougall roared. Two-thirds of his men were sick; those who weren't diseased would soon be, from sleeping in the mud. From the soldier's point of view, since the retreat from Long Island, things had gone downhill fast, and McDougall wasn't far from sharing that sentiment.

"The entire army is in grave danger," Lee insisted. "Unless he is a fool, Howe will move to surround us. Retreat is vital."

Everyone but George Clinton was in agreement: There was no holding Throg's Neck or Harlem Heights, either, against many thousand healthy, well-equipped men. The only sensible action was to retreat in good order. But Congress had ordered them to obstruct the navigation of the Hudson "at whatever expense," so a force must be left to hold Fort Washington.

Lee fumed. "Don't you see that Fort Washington will then be isolated and vulnerable?" he demanded.

White Plains, an interior town in a hilly area, consisted of little more than a courthouse and a scattering of homes. Nonetheless, it seemed to Washington the first "and most convenient" stage of his retreat. It was agreed; the army would withdraw to White Plains.

This decision set off a furor of preparation on Harlem Heights. The orders had come down in each mess for the butchers to keep killing, and the cooks to keep cooking until enough provisions had been prepared and packed up to feed every man for four days. A long line of wagons, men, firearms, and supplies began to move north across the Harlem River and up the right shore of the flood-swollen Bronx River in the direction of White Plains. Because there was a severe shortage of horses, the men themselves had to pull the artillery. Although it was only a day-long march, the removal took four days.

Howe was a soldier who made a plan and then followed through—in his own good time. Steadily, he landed more men and shifted others off Throg's Neck in flatboats; his strength was now estimated at eleven thousand. As fast as he could, he set the troops marching north on a road only a few miles to the east of the one Washington was using.

Led by Stirling, leaving parties behind on every advantageous piece of ground, systematically drawing in the detachments as they climbed the plateau, the Americans got there first, if by only one day, and set up camp.

News of military maneuvers on the northern end of the island made its way quickly to the city on the southern tip. Josias Logan, as he left his house to walk to his office in the morning, was greeted by fellow merchants who always knew the latest news.

As ever, real news came interspersed with fabulous and idle reports, which propagated daily and lived about as long. Josias had learned to believe a story only after it had made the rounds and survived. But on this day, his informant was a fellow merchant trader, the well-dressed and reliable Captain Copeland. Copeland greeted him with a broad smile as Josias stopped, en route to the office, to look out across Albany Pier where the Long Island Dutch farmers were unloading their market boats, heaving sacks of corn and potatoes up to the broad wooden wharfs.

"Have you heard? Howe has landed at New Rochelle."

"New Rochelle? So Washington has evacuated Manhattan altogether?"

158

"Altogether!"

Josias was, of course, pleased. It seemed imminent that the Royal army and navy would soon annihilate Washington's feeble forces and restore the authority of George III. He thrust out his chest a bit in anticipation of that victory, a day that should justify all the inconveniences of wartime, a day when men who had been loyal, such as himself, should be praised and rewarded for their faithfulness to the mother country.

It was a beautiful, sunny autumn morning, and the wind was variable, bringing to his nostrils at one moment the smell of the open sea and at the next the dreadful stench of the prisoners crammed like dogs into the stone sugar refineries, now dismal jails for the large and increasing number of Americans taken captive. Josias gasped at the smell and looked up at the sky. A huge bald eagle circled, presenting a tremendous wingspan. He took it as a good omen.

It was only one of many. These were good days for Josias. Rid at last of the uncomfortable proximity of his rebel brothers, politically vindicated by the retreat of the Americans and the triumphant occupation of the British, singled out by Commandant Robertson to manage the military warehouses—all this at a time when his own and the Whitestone family businesses were prospering. Josias was in a good position to take advantage of a curious loophole in the customs law. The Prohibitory Act of December 1775 had suspended the authorities of customs officers to collect duties, a prohibition that was supposed to accompany a general trade ban, but had survived it. Thus, importing was more profitable now than it had ever been.

Josias was a busy man and a stimulated one, the more so for the arrival of his sister-in-law, Audrey Whitestone, whom he found a most enchanting, di-

159

verting addition to his household, especially now that Meg seemed always unhappy and withdrawn.

He found himself whistling as he proceeded to his office on Queen Street and climbed the stairs. His clerks were there ahead of him, and a pile of correspondence waited to be read. He set about it with goodwill. Nothing pleased him more than finding a check or a sum of money inside an envelope, and his rents alone were a considerable source of joy. Since the town had begun to fill up with Loyalist refugees from Dutchess, Bergen, and Westchester counties—and even further, for a group of Loyalists from Virginia had sailed into town with Lord Dunmore—housing was in great demand, and, of course, since the fire, there was less of it. Josias's reaction had been to raise rents, and in a matter of a few weeks had nearly doubled the income from his town properties.

Even, or perhaps especially, in a besieged city, there was quick money to be made. Commerce was lively; many of the refugees were artisans who had carried in with them the tools of their trade, and the tavernkeepers alone were making small fortunes. Josias was well pleased as he looked out of his corner windows at the bustle on Queen Street, seeing that the tin man Thomas Thomas, at Number 30, had signal lanterns hanging out today, as well as his usual stock of stewpans, tureens, plate warmers, and all sorts of tin, copper, and japanned ware.

There was a new man at Number 55, John Barr, a saddler and cap maker who sold saddles and saddle cloths, bridles, trunks, and saddlebags, whips, spurs, and portmanteaux. Up at Number 176, near Peck's Slip, Daniel Hartung, lately of London, had hung up the sign of the Cap and Muff and had in stock muffs and tippets, fur-lined gloves, squirrel linings for cloaks, and handsome gentleman's trav-

160

eling caps. Josias made a mental note to look over his stock; winter was not far off.

From his second-floor windows, Josias had a good view down to the front doors of his brother-in-law's enterprises: the *Messenger* offices and the coffee-house known as The Lark's Song. Even in the late morning, business was brisk at The Lark, which was frequented these days by officers of the Royal force, both British and German. Josias watched with interest for a few minutes, seeing deliverymen and officers go in, soldiers and officers reel out, seeing the usual New York assortment of well-dressed and well-wigged gentlemen and ragged, shabby, unwashed sorts, Negroes and Indians, artisans in leather aprons, barefoot children and, now, even wives of the Hessians in their quaint dark-skirted Bavarian costumes with braids and little white aprons.

"What's that? What's that?" Josias asked suddenly, startled by the approach of one of his clerks.

"I asked, sir, if I should go to the De Kuyper warehouse and begin the count?"

"Yes, of course. Go at once, and mind no loitering, McWilliams."

Josias returned to the large mahogany desk that had been his father-in-law's, and took out a notebook. He had been making notes since the day he arrived in this city, and they made interesting reading, if no eyes but his own ever saw them. Josias took a distinct pleasure in keeping a record of his life and times. Sometimes he compiled some of the information he had acquired and wrote a letter to a friend; sometimes he just closed the notebook and put it safely away.

The streets are full of riffraff today, he wrote. *The town is full to brimming and the markets are beginning to show produce of the season: the vegetables look mostly*

161

good. Reports are that His Majesty's troops landed this morning on the continent from York and Long Islands, about Morrisania in West Chester County, and penetrated into the country a considerable way with little or no opposition.

I shall meet with Commandant Robertson this afternoon upon the matter of the disposition of food to prisoners. The ancient one depends heavily on me for guidance.

Josias's opinion of General Robertson had not improved much although he—and the rest of New York—were forced to accept his authority. Old James Robertson was both dull and persnickety, and though his health in general was feeble, he was an unrestrained lecher and exposed himself to criticism, in some instances ridicule, by his attention to women of any age or condition. Still, like most vain men, Robertson was not immune to flattery, and Josias energetically courted his favor.

It was in this vein that he intended to invite Robertson to dine when he met with him this afternoon. He also intended to ask for a dispensation, an exception from the Prohibitory Act which forbade New York merchants to export goods without General Howe's permission. To Josias, this act was not only completely distasteful, it was unwieldy and unwise.

If the merchants of New York could not continue—and build up—their trade, how would they deal with the necessary stream of imports from the West Indies and Britain?

"Hunger and nakedness will result from this threatened suffocation of trade!" Josias muttered, taking up his pen to record this sentiment in his journal, just so.

"What on earth did you say?" a feminine voice asked. "And whom are you addressing? There is no one here but us!"

Josias jumped and slammed his notebook shut, causing ink to splatter on his starched white shirt-front. There, although he was not expecting her, was his sister-in-law, Audrey.

"Oooh! Dear Josias, I have startled you! I meant no harm!" Audrey cooed, rushing at him with her pocket handkerchief. As annoyed as he was to be interrupted, Josias could not help but notice the sweet fragrance his petite relative gave off, and the confiding softness of her eyes.

"No matter!" Josias mumbled. "The clerks have gone out, I see. You let yourself in?"

"I did. I bade my driver wait and climbed the stairs all alone, dear Josias, and let myself into your offices . . . all to have a word with you."

Josias overlooked the fact that words between them were not a restricted commodity, as they lived under the same roof and met almost nightly at the dinner table.

"A word in private, I meant," Audrey qualified, as if reading his thoughts. As she spoke, she paced the room dramatically, her pink silk skirts swishing, her lovely yellow hair piled nearly a foot high in a turban of powdered curls. Josias admired her as if she were an exotic bird. He was a young man, although he did not consider himself so, and he was not experienced with women; far from it. Audrey had always unsettled him. The younger of the two Whitestone sisters, he had thought at first that he loved her more than Meg, and perhaps he had. Certainly Audrey had seemed more receptive to his attentions than had her quieter sister. But at the critical moment, their father had offered him Meg, claiming that Audrey was engaged to an officer, which perhaps she had been, although if so, nothing had ever come of it.

It was Audrey who had been a belle, and Meg the

163

shy one. Audrey was possessed of definite physical charms, and no man could be insensible to them. Slim, long necked and high bosomed, she had wide blue eyes and a round pink mouth that was nearly always open—in smiles or in ceaseless charming chatter spoken in the softest and sweetest of voices. Her dress and makeup were as fabulous as might be expected of a young lady of her station and means, and quite regularly took her the whole morning to assemble. She was out early today.

"Well, you shall have it. A word, or any number of them, my dear," Josias said graciously. "May I offer you a seat?"

"Oh, no! I should rather stand!" she declared, and continued to pace the room, every so often rushing to the window to peer down into the street. "But perhaps . . . ," she began, and then hesitated.

"What? You have only to ask!"

"I had only wished I had a drop of wine. For courage," she confessed.

"At once," Josias said, pleased, as she had intended him to be, to be able to satisfy the whim of so lovely a lady. He kept wines both at home and at the office for his guests. Nearly all New Yorkers, he had learned, drank a good deal, and he had learned much about wines and liquors since he had come to the city. Indeed, while Josias had been almost puritanically abstemious in his Boston days, in New York he had become a drinking man. Now he poured Audrey a fine sherry, straight from a rival's warehouse, one he was confident she would relish.

"Oh, thank you!" Audrey cooed, sipping at the sweet wine from a handsomely etched wine glass. "I am so thankful to have found you alone. My errand is such a foolish one, I am afraid, and yet . . . it is so much on my mind."

Josias was horrified to see Audrey's pale blue eyes

164

swim with unshed tears. He rushed to her side, inhaling her perfume, and touched her arm kindly. "What is it? Are you ill? Tell me at once!"

Audrey gulped her sherry and set the glass down on the windowsill. "It's your sister . . . and mine!" she admitted. "Josias, please don't think I am foolish, but I feel it most keenly. They don't like me and are united against me. They have formed a cabal!"

Josias was taken aback. He had not noticed it, but was it not possible that Meg, who had not recovered her spirits or her health since losing the baby, should entertain foolish jealousies of her lovely young sister—so delicate, so pretty, so defenseless? And as for Bonnie! Why, she had no right!

"Oh, my dear, I am so sorry you feel this way," he said. "I think perhaps you are too sensitive."

"I have tried to be cheerful about it, Josias," Audrey confessed, batting her eyes in a remarkable way that compelled him to stare into them. She leaned close to him and spoke in a low voice. "But they whisper against me, and they plot. Bonnie is cold to me, terribly cold, and Meg has now told me that I should leave your house and take up residence in another place."

"Nonsense! I should be most unhappy if you ever did! To say nothing of the fact that I have promised your father to be entirely responsible for your safety. Let me hear no more such talk, Audrey!" The sound of her name in his own voice gave him a strange turn, and when she fit herself into his arms and clung there, he felt his heart beat faster than—for a moment—he thought he could bear.

"Oh, thank you, dear Josias! Oh, thank you!"

"I am your protector, Audrey," he said. "And I ever will be, my dear."

* * *

Davie Montgomery had never felt so far from home. After his arrival at Harlem Heights, Davie had been temporarily assigned to a unit of light infantry under Lee's command which comprised the rear guard during the retreat to White Plains. There was a great need for reinforcements in this unit, for its ranks had been greatly depleted during the retreat from Kip's Bay. Many of the men had gone north on the Boston Post Road and not been seen since.

Davie's first march was nerve racking and disorganized. There was an early frost that October, followed by a week of bone-chilling rain. He tried not to recall the soft sweetness of Carolina autumns. Many of the men had abandoned their tents and blankets during their hurried retreat from Manhattan; as day followed rainy day, their thin summer clothing grew soggy and clung to their shivering bodies.

Although he had not yet seen any fighting, Davie had already changed. On the ride north he had grown taller and stronger, hardened from boyhood into something approaching maturity, his body filling out as fast as his mind. Already he had heard stories and seen things he never dreamed existed; on this White Plains campaign he was sure he would see more.

Davie was with McDougall's brigade when the main body of the British army approached White Plains. At their right flank was Chatterton's Hill, rising one hundred and eighty feet above the Bronx River. It had taken Howe's men a week to march thirty miles, and they had done it in good comfort. Everyone heard the British coming. Their drums and fifes played a merry tune. It was like a full-dress parade, and the Hessians in their huge fur hats resembled marching bears. Davie and the other men were spread out in a little wood, taking cover from the oaks and maples just turning red and yellow and still dripping with rain. The ground underfoot was saturated and slimy, where it wasn't trod to mud.

After the week of rain, the sun finally broke through.

"Good day for a fight," commented one of Davie's new pals, a soldier from Connecticut.

Davie laughed, but he felt his heart tighten.

The skirmish began at midmorning. McDougall's brigade was ordered to defend Chatterton's Hill. In the bright sunshine, the men there could clearly see the approach of the enemy—the red and blue uniforms and the groups with horses, artillery which they unlimbered to train their guns upon the hill.

Among the men formed behind a stone wall on Chatterton's Hill, Davie Montgomery suddenly heard a sound that was new to his ears—the sound of something swiftly approaching, whistling overhead. Three more cannonballs followed in an orderly succession and crashed to the rear. It took Davie a moment to realize that the cannonballs had been meant for them. Once the royal artillery had their range, the cannonade began in earnest, and the air was rent with a hellish din.

As the men lay behind the stone wall, a brace of frantic wild turkeys, so paralyzed with fright that they were incapable of flying, ran toward them and tried to hide among the men. As the roar of the bombardment increased, flocks of little birds fluttered and circled above them in a state of utter bewilderment, and scores of rabbits fled for protection to the men lying down in line, nestling under their jackets, and creeping under their legs, as perfectly tamed by fright as household pets.

Davie was soon demoralized by the heavy artillery fire. He had imagined himself exchanging musket fire with the British on a fair field, but here the enemy was remote, safely beyond the range of American musketry, striking at them with impunity, and his only defense was to lie still and pray that a random ball would not destroy him. It was that very random, impersonal quality of the British massed artillery fire that frightened him most; it would have been easier to cope with an enemy that aimed at him specifically. It seemed such an unfair way to die. Amid the smoke, dust, and flying debris that filled the air, Davie felt totally alone, isolated from his companions and abandoned by his officers.

Davie looked up to the beautiful calm sky, at the sun shining as it would upon a scene of peace and happiness. He wanted to be with his mother. He thought he should wish for nothing in the world if he were home, but death was whistling above him. A moment more and he should never see this sun, the apple trees before him, the home where he was loved.

A shell burst deafeningly, and a Connecticut man was hit in the thigh. At the sight of the gaping wound, the spray of blood, at the sound of his groaning, more than one recruit took to his heels and fled. Swallowing his panic, Davie knelt beside the wounded man and tried to hold the leg together. He felt sick, but he also felt lucky that he had been spared. Four feet to the left and it would have been his leg.

"Dear God," he prayed fervently, "spare this man and get me out of here!"

But the man was already dead, grown cold with incredible swiftness.

The urge to flee became a madness in Davie's legs. Other men flew past him, and finally Davie joined them, convinced he had heard an order to retreat. An officer met them. His sword was drawn, but he did not threaten them with it. Instead he addressed some of the men by name, and the men soon rallied and let the officer lead them back to their positions. Davie thought: Now I am a coward.

An age passed before the cannonade finally lifted.

Two British and two Hessian columns moved slowly through the flaming autumn trees and heavy brush, their weapons glittering under the bright sun, looking like lances of light. Then the columns halted, and the soldiers sat down in position to eat.

When the advance resumed, the left column forded the river and moved to the left under the cover of Chatterton's Hill, their column now a line of skirmishers. They then turned and moved up the hill. Davie lost sight of them, but knew when he saw them again they would be much closer.

He could not have said how much time passed before the American artillery went into action. Alexander Hamilton directed the fire of two light artillery pieces with especially good effect. Colonel Smallwood's regiment made forays down the hill that slowed the British attack. Davie moved with the others, rushing down the hill, then rushing back up it. As long as he was with the others, he felt safer.

For a few moments, it appeared as though the British attack had been halted. Inexplicably, the enemy had ceased firing. A hundred yards in front of the stone wall behind which Davie crouched and lower down the hill was an apple orchard. Beyond the orchard, the ground fell off sharply. His mates cheered when Davie demonstrated his recovered nerve by going to pick some apples. He found some big red ones, filled his shirt, and when he returned he tossed them out as if he were throwing feed to a flock of hens. Everyone laughed at him, and he felt warmer than he had in weeks.

Davie looked to the far edge of the orchard. Men he had not seen before were walking there, approaching him. Suddenly a ball thocked into the tree trunk behind him. He felt a jolt of panic. They were trying to kill him. It had started again.

A line of British and Hessian troops would advance until they could see the Americans behind the stone wall, fire, retreat out of sight to load their muskets, then once more move up the hill to fire and fall back. The Americans, in turn, would fire on the British and Hessians as soon as they showed themselves above the level ground or aimed at the flashes of their guns. The fight was carried on in this fashion for what seemed a very long time, and for all the danger, became monotonous, until the moment when everything changed.

"Rall has turned our flank!" someone shouted.

Davie's unit suddenly found itself in danger of being surrounded by Hessians coming up the other side of the hill. They fell back, making stands in detached groups. Seeing themselves heavily outnumbered, they moved down the hill in a body. But Davie had not noticed the retreat, and in a moment he found himself alone before the Hessians, large men wearing high shakos. Some of them had gathered around a group of Americans who were kneeling and begging for mercy, as the Germans began to beat them with their musket butts. Without considering consequences, Davie fired into the knot of them, and it broke apart. He never knew whom he had hit.

At dusk, the British stopped and began to dig entrenchments overlooking the main American positions. They had gained the high ground on the American right, forcing an extensive realignment of the American defensive positions. During the night they brought artillery on Chatterton's Hill.

The Americans hastily dug makeshift entrenchments, but found that water soon seeped into shoe-top level. Davie had perspired heavily, and after his feet were soaked he took a violent cold.

Sent back to the baggage, he found some dry leaves and made a kind of bed to curl up in. Chilled and miserable, without food or water, he alternately burned and shivered.

"You'll be better in the mornin'," his sergeant promised him, and in his fevered dreams, Davie began to recover his spirit. He knew they had done well. Hell, just to be alive was to have done it all, and they were alive. They had fought well against a determined and well-planned British attack, and had survived.

Chapter Eleven

B ONNIE HAD SET herself to doing all that she could to comfort Meg and to help her recover spiritually as well as physically from losing the baby. For months, she knew, Meg had set all her hopes on the baby's birth, living only for that day and the years of motherhood to follow, and with all that swept away from her, she was rudderless, adrift, and nearly inconsolable.

Remembering all that Meg had done for her when she first arrived in New York, Bonnie pampered her, insisting that a fire should burn in her sitting room both day and night, instructing the cook to prepare special puddings and flips to tempt her appetite, and taking her out in a carriage for air and diversion as often as she could persuade Meg to go.

One autumn afternoon which promised to be fair, but carried with it a seasonable warning chill, Bonnie prevailed, and with a reluctant Meg at her side, left the house on an expedition. A brisk wind blew off the harbor, and fleecy white clouds dotted the bright blue sky.

"I really don't care if we go," Meg said weakly

when the two women were seated in the big blue carriage. "I'd just as soon stay home today."

"Nonsense," Bonnie insisted. "The air will do you good."

Afterward, Bonnie was to wonder what evil impulse had persuaded her to go out, why she had overruled Meg, but overrule her she did.

"Where are we going?" Meg asked, settling back with a slight smile.

Bonnie called out to the driver to take them to the wharf at Peck's Slip. "And by way of the Battery, Peter," she ordered, "so that Mistress Meg may see the harbor."

"See the harbor? I have seen it all my life," Meg said fretfully.

"It's changed," Bonnie said simply, and she was right. The stimulus to trade provided by the British occupation was proved by the view across the wide harbor where almost five hundred vessels, including military transports, now lay at anchor. The panorama was stirring, and Bonnie felt her spirits rise at the reminder of how strong were New York's ties to the rest of the civilized world.

"They say this is the largest array of ships ever to be seen in America," Bonnie said.

"I daresay," Meg concurred. "Josias says business is very brisk."

"Josias has ever been a great one for business. Like our father," Bonnie said mildly, thinking back to Boston days, when Josias had worked with their father, James Logan, building a great firm from a small one, overseeing the construction of one of the finest wharfs in Boston. Sometimes it felt very strange to be so far from Boston. Bonnie was quiet for a moment, remembering, but Meg's next words brought her sharply back into the present.

"And now you will show me Peck's Slip?" Meg

inquired. "Good heavens, Bonnie, what business have we there?"

"Most vital business," Bonnie joked. "You will see."

But Meg was troubled, and could not leave her worries behind her. Taking advantage of the privacy the carriage gave them, she began to cry softly and voiced her greatest concern. "I fear I do not please him . . . your brother . . . anymore," she said in a small, sad voice.

"Oh, Meggy, don't say such a thing! It's just that you are not well yet! And he is cross and tired at night after working so long at his offices."

"He is not too tired to laugh and talk with Audrey," Meg said bitterly but accurately.

"Audrey is not sincere," Bonnie said, dismissing her.

"But she is very pretty."

"That is why we are going to Peck's Slip," Bonnie said.

Meg's curiosity grew as their carriage rolled and bumped northward along Water Street. Many of the side streets they passed had been burned in the fire and lay in ashes. On some foundations, tents had been stretched to provide makeshift homes—poor enough shelters now, but destined to be wretched when winter came. And everywhere there were soldiers: soldiers on and off duty, soldiers in bright red coats, Highlanders in kilts, Hessians in high brass shakos and quaint German dress.

Peck's Slip was a scene of confusion and excitement. Horses and wagons, handcarts and porters, merchants and tradesmen all jostled for a place on the narrow pier. At the end of it, a tall-masted cargo vessel was the focus of the activity, her hold being emptied with ropes and gangplanks down which sailors and porters scurried with crates and bales.

174

"It's the ship *Catharine*," Bonnie announced. "She is just in from Glasgow with lots and lots of dry goods and dress goods!"

"So that's the surprise!" Meg said, amused and decidedly cheered. No one liked fashionable clothes more than Meg. Leaving the carriage at the end of the slip, the two women walked to the landing stage and joined a small crowd of ladies who had been similarly alerted to the arrival of this cache of treasures. In an hour's time they had selected and bargained for a full score of dress-lengths in opulent fabrics: silks and satins in shades of pink and apricot, lilacs and aquamarines more fabulous than nature—some of them dyed in the Orient, velvets and tiffanies and Cantons and Florentines, moreens and crepes—and a set of more useful multicolored calicos and cambrics to fashion gowns for daily wear. And then there were lutestrings, buttons, and ribbons, silver lace and gauze, silken and morocco shoes, clocked silk stockings, hats and bonnets and caps and plumes and bows and fichus and bandeaux.

"I am quite fatigued," Meg complained when they were satisfied and had called the driver to load their purchases into the back of their carriage.

"Then we shall go straight home, darling," Bonnie promised. Meg took her arm, and together they walked the length of the pier. When they had nearly reached the end, Bonnie's eyes fell on a unit of red-coated soldiers escorting a high-ranking officer toward the *Catharine*.

What she saw left her cold and took her breath away. At the head of the unit was the very last person on earth she wanted to see, or ever thought she would—a man she had presumed dead. Cormick Walker. She stopped short. In another minute she would be near enough so that he would see her.

"What's wrong, Bonnie?" Meg asked in a voice

175

of sweet concern. "You look pale—all of a sudden, you look quite pale!"

Bonnie froze, unable to move. But it was too late to run, anyway. There was nowhere she could hide; she stood out in the open on the deck. Was it possible she might be mistaken?

Meg shook her arm, her concern mounting. "Speak, dear. What do you see?"

She was not wrong; it was he, unmistakably—broad shouldered, erect, his shining hair dark as a seal. She knew him too well to mistake him. But she had shot at him with his own gun and left him for dead in that inn on Staten Island! She had thought him dead, wished and wanted him dead.

Bonnie swayed, weak kneed, and then he turned and she saw that although she had not killed him, she had hideously wounded him. One side of his face was badly scarred—healed into reddish-brown splotches—and, horribly, one ear had been torn away. He was hideous, now, but out of that poor, ruined face his bright brown eyes looked piercingly, and with all the acuity of an eagle, they fastened on her.

Bonnie gave a low miserable cry, and fainted. When she came to, Peter and Meg had lifted her into the carriage and Meg was holding her hands and begging her to speak. For a minute she kept her eyes closed and considered if she might be better off dead herself. Then she opened them wide in fright.

"You are so cold," Meg said. "Please, Bonnie! What is wrong?"

"It was him!" Bonnie gasped. "Meg, it was him! Dear Lord, it was Cormick Walker!"

"Who was?" Meg asked, bewildered. She had heard much of Walker, who was Dorothy's father, but thought him long dead, thought Bonnie a widow.

176

"That soldier!"

"The one with the scarred face?" Meg asked, for she had noticed Bonnie staring at him just before she had fainted.

"And he saw me!" Bonnie sobbed. "He looked right at me, I know he did! Dear God, he will try to find me now!"

It was all Meg could do, when she and Bonnie were safely back in the house on Fair Street, to comfort Bonnie and to persuade her not to flee.

"I am not safe, I shall never be safe, as long as he lives," Bonnie wept. She was terribly shaken. She had spent the last several months tying to forget her marriage to Cormick Walker, trying to forget his very existence. But now it seemed she would never get the sight of Cormick's terrible face out of her mind, and that she would never have peace again. "And neither is dear Dorothy! Oh, perhaps we should ride out of the city by night!"

"Bonnie, 'twould not be safe to go! No one can pass through the lines. Much better stay here. And, remember, he does not know where to find you," Meg argued.

"I will be in constant danger, as long as I am in this city," Bonnie insisted.

"Perhaps we should ask William for advice," Meg said.

At that suggestion, Bonnie became more upset than ever. "Never! Not a word of this to William! Oh, promise me you will tell no one, Meg, not even Josias. And especially not William!"

Bonnie's feelings for William, though they were very tender, were a bit confused. She could not deny that she was fond of him, but his latest newspaper editorials had upset her—he had described General

177

Washington as a traitor and murderer and demanded a general execution for the rebel soldiers blind enough to follow him. Despite her residence in Josias's house, Bonnie increasingly considered herself a Patriot, and she had no desire to ask William for help.

And even if she chose to ignore William's Tory sentiments—which in truth might not prove so difficult; after all, she had overlooked them many times before—how could she admit to the man she loved so fervently that her husband, whom William believed to be dead, was alive? How would he react when he learned that she had shot her own husband and left him for dead? More distressing still, what if he learned that she had never truly been married to Cormick at all? Bonnie feared that his tender feelings for her would change, that he would turn away from her, shocked and disappointed by her deceit. And that, Bonnie knew, her heart could never bear.

Meg, in the end, had to promise not to tell William or anyone, although she thought it rather a great secret for keeping. But weeks went by and there was no further sign of Cormick Walker in the town, and certainly no word from him. As the time passed, Meg all but forgot about it, for she had many concerns of her own. But Bonnie could not forget.

Josias had known no woman before Meg, and no other since. This condition, coupled with his appetite for flattery, born of insecurity, made him easy prey for his crafty sister-in-law. Audrey had always been flirtatious, and she had ever enjoyed inflicting discomfort upon her older, shyer sister. Perhaps for these reasons alone she had set out to confuse and captivate the affections of her brother-in-law. Perhaps she was jealous of her sister's marriage, or perhaps she acted chiefly from boredom and idleness. Human behavior and motivation are proper studies for the philosopher—to the player at life they are most often obscure.

At any rate, Audrey had devoted herself to the care and capture of Josias's heart, and she had set about it with great energy, trying to convince him that he was quite a splendid and remarkable man, who was bound—worse luck!—to a drab and unworthy woman. It remained to Josias to conclude that she, Audrey, was much more deserving of his attentions.

On a certain November evening, Josias and Audrey were alone together in the front parlor, a handsome room furnished with Chippendale and papered with scenes of Naples and its famous bay which had been painted in France. Josias had returned early from his offices in the hope of seeing Audrey, and had been pleased to find her, elaborately dressed and coiffed, waiting for him with an opened bottle of claret and a tray of cheese biscuits.

"Oh, Josias!" Audrey cooed when he appeared, rushing to him with a flurry of her lavender silk skirts. "Oh! I am so extremely glad to see you! I had just been thinking about you, dear."

Few men can resist the chance to learn more about themselves. Josias was not one of them. "About me?" he asked. "What were you thinking?"

"Oh, just how very hard you work and how grateful I am to you," Audrey said. "Are you weary? Do have a seat by the fire and a glass of wine. After a hard day's work, a man . . . I declare, though, you do not look tired. You look, as ever, quite robust and elegant."

Robust and elegant! Josias sat down gratefully and thrust out his chest. He had been rather tired lately; the knots and tangles of the official import docu-

179

ments, the constant scramble to take a percentage of the imports for himself, the management of his clerks, the obligation to exert his authority over the troops assigned to requisition goods was all more complicated than most people realized, and he often felt unappreciated.

But not by Audrey. "Poor dear," she cooed. "Put it all behind you tonight! Now you must relax and enjoy yourself—a good dinner is on its way. I have seen to it myself."

"Where is Meg?" Josias asked, a trifle nervously.

"Meg is not feeling well. I think perhaps she has the grippe," Audrey said sadly. "And Bonnie has elected to sit with her. So you must try to be satisfied with only me to entertain you, Josias."

"I thought Meg was a bit glum this morning," Josias remarked, wondering if he should go to his wife's bedside.

"I do believe my sister is sometimes quite deliberately glum." Audrey said.

"Poor woman, she has not recovered from . . . from her confinement," he said, and he truly felt some pity for her. Although he had married Meg hardly knowing her, he felt a strong affection for her. At times he had even felt it to be love.

"La! She may never recover!" Audrey said cruelly. "She thrives on sadness. Frankly, my dear brother, a man like yourself deserves better. A man like yourself has certain needs, certain desires. Or so I would imagine."

"You understand me so well," Josias murmured.

"She is not looking her best these days," Audrey continued. "I don't think her appearance does credit to you, Josias. You are a very important man in this town."

"Oh, really! Not really! Oh, my!" protested Josias, but he was very well pleased with Audrey's opinions and attentions, and he soon forgot his impulse to visit Meg and settled down to a jolly evening with her sister, an evening of wine and sympathetic chatter, and after a fine dinner, brandy and draughts and more pleasant conversation. And perhaps, when the hour grew late and the candles burned low, Audrey would allow him to kiss her and hold her in his arms, as she had now once or twice, an experience so stimulating and delightful that it seemed in no way wrong, no way at all.

Since Davie had left to go north with General Lee, the Montgomery family had broken still farther apart. It was the custom for the families of planters to spend the summer months in Charleston and then return to their inland country plantations for the winter, except for the holidays, when society was again apt to gather in town.

Webb Montgomery, occupied as he was with the business of shipping and selling the rice, and involved as he was with the continuing construction of his splendid seaside townhouse, had not wintered at Ashley Hall, the family rice plantation, for a few seasons. His parents followed the usual model and would this year, but partly to escape the tensions that had built up in the family over political questions, it was decided that Taylor and Liza Montgomery should leave town early, that fall, and return to the country.

Ashley Hall was seven miles by land from Charleston, but seventeen by water. Taylor and Liza traveled by water. At its mouth, the Ashley River was too shallow to permit the passage of oceangoing vessels, but for every other sort of watercraft, it was a broad and generous highway. Surrounded by bales, bundles, and boxes, their personal servants, and heaps of provisions, Taylor and Liza left Charleston in a broad, shallow riverboat made by hollowing out a huge cypress tree, sawing it apart down the middle, and fitting a keel and floor between the halves.

Such boats were common on the river because they were essential for the transportation of passengers and cargo, but they were few compared to the number of pirougues, canoes, and small rowboats that crisscrossed and followed the narrowing river up country to the broad, fertile, inland plateau. The first white settlers had learned to make canoes from the Indians by hewing out the trunks of long-leaf pines and the thick cypress trees that dominated the coastal swampland. Now expert African canoemen were the backbone of the transportation system, and boat-building was a thriving local industry. The boat that carried the Montgomerys had been built by the master boat builder at Ashley Hall, and was rowed by a sextet of muscular, broad-backed Angolans and Ibos, clad only in loincloths, who spoke among themselves in Gullah, the Creole language which had emerged as the tongue common to slaves of various African races.

Liza sat quietly in the stern of the twelve-oared boat, entirely swathed in linen shawls and scarves to protect her from both the burning sun and the hordes of mosquitoes, which although at their ebb in autumn, were still of a thickness and ferocity to inspire madness. As a repellant, she had dowsed herself in her mother's favorite imported Cologne water.

Its strong, tart smell made her brother Taylor laugh and wrinkle his nose in distaste. "You do not smell like a lily, Liza," he teased.

"Nonetheless, I do not intend to give all my blood

to the winged creatures of the air," she replied, smiling at him.

Both were happy to be leaving the busy city and returning to the plantation where they had been raised and which they loved. Already the beauty of the river had soothed their nerves and lifted their spirits. It was a dark, peaceful river, its smooth surface belying the strength of the current that ran beneath, and it cut through a land that was a virtual paradise. The shores and bluffs were wild and thickly wooded; game abounded in the forests and on the river's edge; white heron lifted like huge flowers into the blue sky. When their boat neared the banks, Liza could see trailing smilax and bright, trumpet-shaped bignonia, huge crabs scurrying sideways through the shallows, and freshwater oysters clinging to half-submerged rocks.

"It's so beautiful!" Liza called to Taylor, and he nodded happily. Both were glad for the quiet of the journey. And both were glad to escape Charleston.

Their leave-taking had not been without some difficulties. "Go, if you must, Liza," her mother had said to her privately the night before, "and I am glad that you will be there to look after Taylor, but it would be better if you would stay here and set about choosing a man to marry. Your little sister Katy is ahead of you in that regard. That girl is nothing if not practical! And I am sorry that Taylor will not make up his foolish quarrel with Webb before he leaves! Dear Lord, why have you given me such stubborn, willful children?"

Caroline was fond of addressing the deity whenever it was convenient, and of invoking His supreme authority whenever it seemed her own could benefit from His support.

In this vein, she had complained to Liza about

Taylor, although not to Taylor himself, for she realized that her son was now a man and beyond her management. "I am entirely out of patience with him, I swear it. The Lord has told him to forgive his brother and to love him as himself. I don't know how Taylor dares to disobey both his parents and the Dear Lord, too, really I don't!"

"I don't believe he thinks of it that way," Liza had said. It was her hope that her elder brothers would find a way to deal with their differences, in time. For now, it seemed a good solution to go with Taylor to Ashley Hall.

William Whitestone had published the text of Governor Tryon's loyalty oath in *Whitestone's New York Messenger; or the Connecticut, New Jersey, and Hudson's River Weekly Journal*, and by the end of October about one thousand New Yorkers—of the male sex—had affixed their signatures to the so-called loyal address. Josias Logan signed; William himself signed with a great flourish of his pen.

New York was the heart of Tory America. Within its borders, every citizen who wished to escape suspicion of Patriot sympathies had to wear a red ribbon on his hat, the insignia of loyalty to the king. Now those Loyalists who had suffered insults and indignities at the hands of radical patriots had their day, and many abused their power, ransacking the homes of known rebels who had fled the city, and carrying off their household goods and private possessions. At night armed patrols stamped through the dark streets to prevent crime, stopping off whenever possible at a bright tavern to revive their courage with flip, a mixture of rum and beer, or rum-fustian, a mix of gin and beer.

Signs of the great fire were abundant and inescapable. Acres of lonely chimneys and scarred, blackened walls stood among the houses that were still whole and occupied. Some of the ruins attracted homeless families and helpless vagrants to reinforce their rickety foundations with boards and lengths of woven goods, creating hovels resembling mushrooms at the foot of dead trees.

All of the displaced Loyalists were desperate for news: news of home, news of England, news of the war. William sold every paper he could print, and the constant question was "What news? What news?" All the reports of British advances and American retreats were received with great joy in the city, and everyone was certain that the heart of the rebellion had been broken. Everyone was sure that the whole of the country would soon be reduced to subjection, and shortly afterward, to reason.

Long lines of Americans taken prisoner in the battles and skirmishes near Harlem and White Plains were marched through the streets of the city on their way to the prisons in the churches and sugar warehouses. Both soldiers and civilians looked on exultantly and jeered at them, sometimes pelting them with stones or rotten fruit. The city was packed to the rafters with soldiers.

In early November, William published the text of an address to the commissioners to plead for opening the port of New York to free trade. Josias had drafted it, and it was a document from which he stood to gain greatly, but for the time being, it was merely held under consideration.

For there was always the possibility that the fortunes of war would reverse themselves, that by some unforeseen turn of events the rebels would again

185

take control of the port. Josias thought it extremely unlikely, but, as he recorded in his notebook, *Should they again become Masters of New York, the Consequences would be unpleasant indeed.*

Chapter Twelve

ALTHOUGH ONLY ABOUT one hundred and fifty men had been lost—and Washington did not count that few, except for what might have been—the general was very disheartened by the skirmish which came later to be called the Battle of White Plains. He had been greatly puzzled by the British strategy. He had constantly expected them to attack and had instead seen the enemy infantry sitting down beside their muskets, waiting; seen tents rather than cannons emerge from the forests. Anxious minutes turned into hours while nothing at all happened.

In truth, the British were permanently chastised by what had happened to them at Bunker Hill. Howe could never forget those New Hampshire sharpshooters and the way they had taken down his men at astonishing range. He was determined to avoid another such bloodbath and felt that to force the ground where Washington was installed would lead to no gain, for the rebels had higher ground behind them and would only retreat to it. Howe was beginning to believe that to win this war he would have to utterly destroy the American army; territory in a land so vast had less meaning than it did in Europe.

187

At all costs, Howe knew that he had to maintain his army—reinforcements were thousands of miles away. He could not take risks with his men—and least of all, with himself. Instead, he must rely on his professional skill, bide his time, and wait for a suitable opportunity.

So the night after the skirmish at Chatterton's Hill, the British troops slept on their guns while the Americans were kept busy digging entrenchments. When Howe awoke, he looked over the strengthened earthworks through his golden telescope and immediately deferred action upon them. He debated whether he had time to ride back to his headquarters and visit with his mistress, Betsy Loring; in no time he decided that he did. Fun-loving, aristocractic Billy Howe could never—nor did he seek to—repress his *carpe diem* outlook on life. He was now thinking seriously of where best to spend the upcoming winter, and nothing appealed to him near as much as New York, a decent town, all in all, which offered amusing diversions and the excellent possibility of a good time. At the end of a hard ride he found Betsy Loring still in her red satin dressing gown; she was glad to see him and he was glad to see her.

Washington could not believe that the British did not intend to attack. "I want the troops safely installed in the heights of New Castle," he told his generals. "I yearn to see them in that haven." Everyone who could be spared from the lines was set to carrying supplies from White Plains north into the hills.

As before, as ever, wagons were in woefully short supply, and Tom Logan was one of the men assigned to walk along beside an ancient, rickety hay wagon filled and heaped with forage for the officers' horses. A light rain fell, and the landscape was uncommonly gray-brown and gloomy.

When Tom spotted a flash of red in the hedges of a stubbly cornfield, he thought at first it was a bright bird. Then he was sure it was one of the enemy, hiding, or perhaps wounded or dead. He called to his mate John Scott, an Irishman born who still retained the speech of his native island, and together, they crept along behind a stone wall to investigate.

"Easy, lad, easy!" Scott whispered as Tom rushed forward, "Go slow!" But Tom's blind enthusiasm was rewarded, for when they found the Redcoat, his arms were up and he called out, "Don't shoot! Don't shoot me, I'm on the run!"

"A deserter!" Scott called out.

"Aye, that's right! I've had enough!" the British soldier said hoarsely, and when they had a look at him, they saw that he was very young and walked queerly.

"Had a touch of the lash, eh?" Scott asked.

"More than a touch, and I've done no wrong," the man complained. "So take me along with ye, will you, boys?"

"Send ye to gaol, more likely," Scott said, but the deserter turned cunning.

"I've a bit of information, boys, that yer commander might find some interest in."

"What is it?" Scott asked suspiciously.

"Take me along, and I'll tell yer commander, I will."

"Let me take him to my brother," Tom suggested, and after talking to the man, a good-looking young Londoner who claimed he had been abused by a noncommissioned officer for the human and forgivable crime of drunkenness, Bayard sent him on to Washington.

"It sounds to me like the poor fellow's speaking true," Bayard said.

"The last night of the month. I know General

Howe is planning to attack then, because I heard the orders go down," the deserter insisted.

Washington was forced to take him at his word. He considered the attack inevitable. The night of All Hallow's Eve seemed a likely time for it. He sent the deserter on to a town in central Pennsylvania where he was allowed to live freely on condition that he not fight again.

The night of October thirty-first was exceptionally black and stormy. Sheets of rain fell on Washington's army as he marched them from White Plains to New Castle, leaving a strong rear guard hidden in the caves and rocky hillsides along the way. When they were safe on the New Castle heights, he set fire to a few barns to signal their successful retreat.

The weather was far too stormy for Howe. He postponed his planned action until the weather should improve, and went to bed early in a dry tent. In the morning, he made a show of activity, firing a few cannon in the direction the American army had gone, but again, decided it was not worthwhile to pursue them.

From his new position, Washington saw that the British camp was a long way away. That next night, the chilliest one of the year so far, the British lit a ring of bonfires.

"My God, it's a splendid sight," Tom sighed, standing guard. He committed the beautiful, starry night, the magnificent sight of the blazing fires, to memory. The fires seemed to mix with the stars, and he thought it would be hard to say which were the brighter. One day, he hoped, he would describe the scene to entertain Isannah with his thoughts and observations. One day in the distant future, he would tell the story to their children.

The next day, Howe roused his great army to their feet and marched them south, back toward New

York City. Washington, at first greatly alarmed, was more puzzled than ever. What would Howe do now? And what must he do to counterbalance the British commander's unpredictable activities?

The net of silver stars had caught the golden crescent of a moon by the time Taylor and Liza, surrounded by all their baggage, arrived at the private landing dock near Ashley Hall. It was near midnight. Liza had been dozing, half listening to the deep-toned, rhythmic chanting of the slaves rowing the broad riverboat, half dreaming. In her dreams, everything was just as it had been when she was a child, and she was very happy.

Liza had always been happy at Ashley Hall. She far preferred the country to life in town. She had missed the plantation sorely the year before, when she and her mother and her sister Katy had embarked on the long sea voyage to England, where they visited an aunt, returning through the port of New York, to visit Caroline Montgomery's brother Albert Whitestone and his family. They had arrived in New York just in time to attend the wedding of Meg Whitestone to Josias Logan, and to experience some of the dangers of life in that city for a known Loyalist and his family.

It had been a nerve-racking experience for all of them. Patriot mobs had roamed the city after the news of Lexington and Concord, and the Montgomerys, with many of the other wedding guests, had been virtual prisoners in the Whitestones' house for several days. When they had finally dared to leave—Caroline had insisted on their making a break for the first coastal schooner sailing south—they had encountered a mob in the streets and had only been

191

saved through the intervention of their cousin William.

Liza shuddered whenever she thought of it, but then, any city was a trial for her. She loved her large, lively family, but always felt uncomfortable in crowded city streets and a bit ill at ease with fast-talking, pleasure-seeking city people. Her sister Katy had loved London: the plays at Covent Garden, the races, dining out, meeting relatives and friends at various entertainments, but what Liza had liked best about England were English gardens. She had seen many that she would never forget, and she had some ideas for a garden at Ashley Hall that might rival—or exceed—the beauty of the one at Hampton Court, her aunt's estate in England.

It was at Hampton Court that she had met Trevor Greene.

The day of their meeting had been almost too romantic for belief and had only grown more so in Liza's memory. It had been spring, and the long alleys of flowering almonds and lilacs had perfumed the air, made musical with the songs of hundreds of birds. Trevor Greene, a distant cousin by marriage, had come down from Oxford to meet the visiting Americans, and had, surprisingly, immediately, and obviously preferred Liza to her bolder—and many thought prettier—sister. Trevor was a student of botany, and, as the third son in a Warwickshire family, seemed destined to pursue a scholarly career in that field.

Liza had liked him at once. He was the tallest man she had ever met, and so soft-spoken that she had to rise to her tiptoes to hear him, even when he bent engagingly toward her. Sharing an interest in gardens, they had wandered off together to see the Dutch-style knot garden of privet and roses, and alone together, they had very quickly established a real rapport.

When they parted in London, where he had come to see them off, they had kissed for the first time, and Trevor had promised to write her. Liza had told no one how deeply her heart had been touched, but held her secret to herself, as she had hidden his letters, which had arrived regularly, clever and loving, full of botanical observations and questions about South Carolina plants and flowers, until the war had stopped them.

Liza often thought of Trevor Greene, although she did not speak of him, and all the natural world seemed to contrive to keep him in mind. Had the war not come to interrupt and change their lives, she felt sure he would have come to America to study and record some of the strange native plants of the Carolina lowlands, and she might have introduced him to Dr. Alexander Garden, their friend in Charleston who was also a botanist. It was a strong bond between them, for Liza loved natural things, and without ever having looked into a book of botany, knew every wildflower and had an acquaintance with every bird and creature of the forest.

Realistically, Liza supposed she should never see Trevor Greene again, but she knew in her heart that she would never forget him, and that although he had not proposed or promised her anything, he had set a new standard for romance that was quite unmatched by any of the cheerful, exuberant young men she knew either in Charleston or at the surrounding plantations.

A torch burned at the Ashley Hall boat landing, swathed in a cloud of mosquitoes, but the watchman, Cuffee, who had held his position for as long as there had been an Ashley Hall, was asleep in his hammock. Taylor leapt gracefully out of the boat,

193

calling "Cuffee! Cuffeeeee!" and the oarsmen chanted, "Massa home! Massa come home! Oh, rouse up ever'bodies, Massa home!"

Within minutes there was a parade of men, women, and children on the wide path that ran down to the river from the house. Nearly all of them naked or scantily clad in shifts that hung off thin brown bodies, the African population of Ashley Hall rallied with goodwill, or at least curiosity, streaming out of their quarters, rubbing sleep from their eyes, calling out "Welcome! Welcome back home! Oh, Massa Taylor! Look, Missy Liza come, too!"

Later, when she was settled in her bedroom, which opened into a twin chamber used by her sister Katy, Liza felt perfectly content. Nothing had changed; everything at Ashley Hall was just the way it had been when she was growing up there. The room was exactly the same: tall, floor-to-ceiling windows stood open, white lace curtains blew in the night breeze, stirring the mosquito nettings draped securely around her bed. The posts of the mahogany bed were carved with sheafs of rice, the crop which supported all aspects of plantation life. The yellow moonlight made a path across the bare cypress floor, and somewhere on the grounds, a woman laughed; a long, low laugh of late-night contentment.

Dreadfully tired after the day's long journey, Liza fell asleep at once. But Taylor sat up, drinking whiskey in the shadowy little office downstairs, looking over the Farm Book, the record of everything that happened on the plantation, day by day. He was hours from sleep.

It was Taylor, the second son, who had been destined since birth to take over the management of Ashley Hall, when the day should come that his father was able to do it no more. In his years up north,

Taylor had not forgotten his family assignment, and now, political circumstances being what they were, he welcomed the chance to devote himself to the plantation and put town life and other concerns out of his mind for a time.

Life on a Carolina plantation, although it provided a man with an open heart and robust health with many pleasures, was not an easy life. Dennison Montgomery had inherited the life from his father, one of the colony's agricultural pioneers, and he had taught his children—chiefly through example—much of what he knew. But none of them could have met with success but for their slaves.

Nearly one hundred black-skinned slaves lived at Ashley Hall, including women and children, house servants, and the craftsmen and special workers who performed services. Those who worked on the rice-growing numbered about fifty and worked two farms. Rice was an exacting crop, although well suited to the Low Country cypress swamps, and the Montgomerys owed their success at its cultivation—whether they knew it or not—to a key core of slaves who had raised rice in West African swamps for generations.

Thus, when Dennison and his father had first set up Ashley Hall almost fifty years ago, their newly arrived, African-born slaves had been more familiar with the planting, hoeing, processing, and cooking of rice than they were. A few of the old slaves: Big Benny, now Old Benny, and Joseph, now Old Joe, had set up the rice fields, the team yard, and the rice mill just as they remembered them from their childhoods, and the design was good. It held firm today.

In the morning, Taylor would send for Old Joe and Old Benny, and he would talk with them about the coming harvest, the quality of the crop, the men

195

who were the best workers, and the men who were no good. He had been taught respect for these two men by his father and his father's father, and he had presents for both of them, brought from Charleston.

Bonnie Logan was by nature a determined, active woman, but now, for the first time in her life she felt entirely constrained. Since she and Meg had inadvertently encountered Cormick Walker at Peck's Slip, she had been terribly confused and afraid, unsure of where to turn or what course of action she ought to pursue. In fact, the only course of action that presented itself to her was no action at all. All she knew for sure was that she must not risk meeting Cormick.

Day after day, she stayed inside, usually in her sitting room, chatting with Meg and playing with baby Dorothy, trying to maintain a cheerful facade while she felt most unlike herself. Although Meg knew why she would not leave her room and why her eyes were so often swollen red and stained by tears, she discreetly did not mention it.

Bonnie felt like a woman under house arrest. She dared not go out—she was too conspicuous, she knew, with her unusual red-gold hair. She could not leave town, could not flee home to Boston, for New York was entirely closed. Soldiers were everywhere, and among any group of them he—Cormick Walker—might be. The thought made her catch up Dorothy and hug her so tightly that the baby cried.

"Poor child," Bonnie whispered to her. "Don't cry. You are safe with your mama. We are both quite safe here in Meg and Josias's fine house."

But one lovely, twilight evening, as Bonnie, with Dorothy in her arms, stood admiring the western sky from a second-floor window at the front of the house, she realized that they were not safe.

The streets were very quiet, and the whistle very clear. Its three tones stabbed her to her heart; she knew at once that it was he, for, back in Boston, that had been their signal—three rising tones—just so had he whistled at her father's garden gate. In those days, she had rushed out to meet him, her young heart full of love and hope for the future. But now she froze, cold with fear and panic.

"Dear Lord," she whispered, "let it not be."

But the unmistakable whistle came again.

Bonnie ran from the window, fled from the room, and hid in bed. But while dressing the next morning, she heard it again, and the next evening, while she was feeding Dorothy, again. There was no denying it; it was Cormick. He was there, out there, watching her. She had brought it on herself, and there would be no escaping it.

She feared she would go mad.

The Montgomery family's house at Ashley Hall plantation was good sized but not pretentious. It stood about fifty yards from the river's edge, and was approached from the land side through an avenue of cedars. Taking advantage of a slight rise in the terrain, its builder had provided the house with a splendid view of the bend in the river and a vista out over the rice fields and meadows to the surrounding woodlands.

Most planters reserved their architectural flights of fancy for their Charleston residences, and Ashley Hall was already old—the core of the big house had stood for fifty years. It was a double-sectioned, two-story structure, built solidly and affectionately of the strong local cypress, designed to open to the outside for exposure to the air. Porches ran around it—on the south side, they extended from the dining room, the drawing room, and the parlor. The north side was more secluded, and the gallery running between the dining room and the kitchen house, at a remove of some fifty feet, had been newly covered with a wooden roof and paved with bricks made on the plantation.

All of the rooms, including the bedrooms on the second floor, which were quite small, were high ceilinged and airy, with tall windows that admitted light and air in good weather and could be closed by cedar shutters when storms blew. All the floors were of all-heart yellow pine—bare boards worn smooth and pale by the years and the daily scrubbing given them by the house slaves. Caroline Montgomery and her mother-in-law before her had furnished the rooms with solid, comfortable pieces, mostly of well-rubbed mahogany which had arrived in such great quantity from the Indies. The walls were covered with mirrors, family portraits, and some fine engravings, mostly scenes of harbors and famous seaports which had been sent from England.

Coming from England with her English ways, Caroline had added a card room off the downstairs parlor, and a library, which contained books in Latin and French as well as English, although they were mostly unread. It was Caroline, too, who had imported the sets of Canton ware and English china, some of it rimmed with gold, some of it hand-painted with flowers in every shade nature had ever decreed. Caroline had filled the dining room cupboards with crystal and glass, filled the sideboard drawers—always locked—with silver service for all the family and their guests.

Liza felt perfectly at home in the house, and when she had opened every door and every cupboard, every drawer and cubbyhole, and when she was satisfied that the housekeepers Bella and Harriet had maintained everything in perfect order, she settled down to a routine that was both busy and satisfying. Mornings, after seeing that the servants were working at their respective tasks, she walked in the gardens and directed planting and weeding before it got too hot. Her newest project was a stone-walled bed of lilies. She had brought the bulbs back from England, and had the highest hopes for a multicolored display next spring. If the day were cool enough, she often ventured further, exploring the meadows or forests in search of wildflowers.

By late morning, she was usually forced to retreat to shade. Often, she read for a while, and sometimes wrote a few lines in her diary, then she occupied herself with the amusing, if frustrating task of trying to teach two little black girls to read. Afternoons were spent in music and needlework, but above all, in visiting, for Ashley Hall was not remote from its neighboring plantations, and it was the custom for Carolina ladies to travel from here to there, usually bearing baskets of needlework, and to meet each other to gossip, drink tea, and gossip some more.

Except for Thursdays, when she was occupied with plantation business, Liza was obliged to participate in this local custom, and nearly every afternoon found her visiting or receiving visitors at Ashley Hall, often traveling by river. But what had always been a simple friendly custom was now changed, as Liza discovered during the first week at the plantation, for the neighbors were as divided as her own family, and seemingly as outspoken.

"I am so glad to welcome you," Anne Leah Mason had said when Liza came to visit her at her pleasant riverside home.

The Masons and Montgomerys had long been friends, and the men of both families often hunted together.

"Thank you, Anne Leah," Liza said, without understanding the sadness in the woman's voice.

"I have been lonely of late. Many of the neighbors won't receive us," Anne Leah confided. "And I am afraid it may get worse. They are barbarians, some of them! They hate us, who have always lived here among them, because Papa has been outspoken in his defense of the King and his opposition to Mr. Jefferson."

"Surely you are wrong," Liza protested.

"Oh, no. You will see," Anne Leah warned. "Sometimes I think we would do better to flee to England."

"Leave your home?"

"You will see," Anne Leah warned again. "Passions are running high these days."

Liza tried to put the conversation with Anne Leah out of her mind, but when she returned a visit to the Greens of Rice Hall, the plantation which adjoined Ashley Hall, she met with another such upsetting encounter.

"My dear!" said Clementina Green. "Is it true that Taylor has refused to sign the loyalty oath?"

"Taylor's politics are none of my affair," Liza said stiffly. "I'm sorry, but I can't really discuss it."

"My husband says his principles are impractical," Mrs. Green continued, ignoring Liza's obvious discomfort. "The time has come when we must defend ourselves, my dear. Taylor's holding back so is not of service to your family. It may put you at a great risk!"

"Please, Mrs. Green, don't say more," Liza asked.

"But my dear, it is so!" she insisted. "You should

speak to him of what I have said. Perhaps you can influence him.''

Liza had no intention of doing so, but she wondered if Silas Green had asked his wife to speak, if it was indeed a warning meriting Taylor's attention. She returned to Ashley Hall in a very contemplative mood.

Chapter Thirteen

EXTREMELY WEARY IN both body and mind, Washington was for the moment securely ensconced in the highlands beyond White Plains, but he was acutely aware that he had left part of his army—and desperately needed guns and supplies—behind in a vulnerable spot, in the isolated garrison at Fort Washington on the Hudson. To abandon it without a fight would be to give the enemy control of the Hudson. To defend it would be to risk a great many men.

Although it had been hastily constructed and had some serious limitations, Fort Washington was, apart from West Point, the strongest American fortification. It commanded the lower Hudson Valley, but it had no well—water for use inside the fort had to be windlassed up from the Hudson. The garrison there numbered about three thousand men, but the fort had no east-facing exterior defenses; it was completely focused on attack from the river.

Worse, what Washington did not know and would never know, a certain William Demont, a traitor in Magaw's Fifth Pennsylvania, the regiment inside Fort Washington, had already provided the

British with detailed plans of the fort and convinced General Howe that it was absolutely necessary to take it.

How exhausted the commander in chief really was, can hardly be imagined. He had not taken a full day off in a year and a half, since the day when he accepted his command. Puzzled and depressed over the progress of events, he was haunted by the knowledge that the terms of enlistment of most of his army were due to expire. He knew that he must make the crucial decision whether or not to defend Fort Washington.

As usual, he called his aides and generals into council. Washington depended heavily upon his generals. General Nathanael Greene, whose military expertise and opinions Washington respected highly, insisted that Fort Washington could be held indefinitely, but Washington advised Greene to evacuate Fort Washington. Occupied with moving his troops across the river to New Jersey, Washington left the final decision up to Greene.

Once settled in his new headquarters at Hackensack, Washington drafted a report to Congress. *I propose to stay in the neighborhood a few days*, he wrote, *in which time I expect the design of the enemy will be more disclosed. . . .*

Bayard Logan knocked softly on the door and entered with a pitcher of mulled cider and a bottle of rum. "Sir," he said, "I intercepted the maid with these. It is very late."

"So it is," Washington admitted, rubbing his eyes. Bayard stirred up the fire. "I hope you will join me," the general offered. He was able to relax in Logan's company, as much as he ever relaxed. Logan reminded him of himself as a youth, and he was a handsome lad. The scar on his cheek had healed to make him handsomer than ever, and yet the young man looked tired. "Take a seat," he said.

"Yes, sir. 'Tis a peaceful night."

"Thank the Lord. I relish a quiet night." Both men drank the rum-laced cider. "I expect Howe will soon join us in New Jersey."

"And Fort Washington?"

Washington sighed deeply. "We have abandoned enough ground, fled enough fortifications. Somewhere we must stand our ground." He paused, considering the composition of the army: cold, weary, on the verge of discharge. His distrust of the militia was mixed with an essentially unrealistic notion of what soldiers fired with patriotic fervor could do against overwhelming odds.

"Both forts—Washington and Lee—have value to our morale, if you see what I mean," Washington mused.

Bayard nodded. He understood this well; the forts had proved ineffective at controlling river traffic, but stood as symbols of rebel defiance.

"On the other hand, Fort Washington is stocked with men and munitions of extreme value to the army. I have asked General Greene to withdraw all the stores and soldiers not necessary for the fort's defense. . . ."

"Surely he will then do so?"

"He continues to assure me that they can be brought off at any time. He does not believe the garrison to be in danger."

"Reed is strongly in favor of overriding Greene," Bayard observed. In the last council, Adjutant General Reed, an old friend and favorite of Washington's, had exploded with temper, so determined was he that Greene should be commanded to evacuate the fort.

"Greene is closer to the situation than we are,"

Washington said in a drowsy tone. "And I take my orders from Congress, don't forget. You know I am undecided. But for now I must prepare for the attack on Jersey. I will examine Fort Washington when . . . when I have time."

"Good night, sir," Bayard said, slipping out of the room.

By the time Washington was ready to inspect Fort Washington, it was too late. General Howe sent an officer to the fort under a flag of truce to demand that General Magaw surrender or have his men put to the sword. Howe gave him two hours. Magaw notified Howe that he would fight, and sent word to Greene and Putnam. When Washington got the news, he was panic stricken. He mounted at once and rode with Bayard Logan and one or two others to the west bank of the Hudson.

"What do you hear?" he demanded when they reached the river.

"I hear nothing, sir," Bayard said. The sun had set as they rode the nine miles from Hackensack, and it was getting dark.

"Either it has not begun or it's over," Washington said hopefully. "Perhaps the garrison has escaped! Ride on to Fort Lee!"

Dusk had fallen by the time they reached Fort Lee. Junior officers there informed Washington that there had been no serious combat yet. Greene and Putnam had gone to inspect the defenses, taking even more men into the fort.

"Get me a boat!" Washington demanded.

Bayard rowed as the commander in chief peered out into the darkness. The rowboat's oars made ripples on the black surface of the great river, and overhead, a flock of honking geese flew north up the

205

river in a wide V formation. "By God, I fear the worst!" Washington said in a tense voice.

From midriver a dark shape approached.

"Who goes there?" Bayard called out.

To everyone's surprise, it was another rowboat, this one containing Generals Greene and Putnam. Oarsmen from both boats leaned out to hold the two together, gently heaving in the tide, while the commanders had a conference midstream.

"What have you seen?" Washington called out.

"All is well," Nathanael Green assured him. "I have ordered Magaw to stand fast. The men are in high spirits and will make a good defense." His voice was nearly lost in the sounds of wind and water.

"Nothing more can be done tonight!" Israel Putnam shouted.

"Nothing more tonight!" Greene echoed, and the generals were all rowed back to Fort Lee.

When in the early morning, the generals were again launched on the river, the sound of cannon fire greeted them, echoing from the cliff across the river.

"Hurry! God damn it, make haste!" Putnam cursed, and the oarsmen bent frantically to their work, fighting the rising current. On the eastern shore, the boat's keel scraped ashore on a pebbly beach, and all the generals scurried up a steep path that climbed the cliff into the fort. It was a beautiful, crisp morning, and birds twittered in the bushes and trees, oblivious to the approaching danger. The firing was still about two miles to the south when Washington entered the fort.

Almost immediately it was apparent that there was a real battle at hand. Messengers came riding in with frightening news. The British army was approaching from three directions. The assault from the south was only a beginning. Hessians were approaching from the north. On Long Island, a great force was marching for the Harlem River. Washington had been wrong when he assumed that Howe would not pitch his whole army at Fort Washington.

And Greene had been wrong to think the fort defensible. True, there were fresh earthworks, but the fort was too small to contain the numerous troops now spread out in its defense. There were no barracks, no water, no palisades. The cannon were fixed to fire in the one direction from which no enemy seemed to be approaching.

The generals stood about awkwardly. The only plan for evacuating the fort, should that become necessary, had been to move the men down the cliff to the river's bank and across the river. But no arrangements had been made to activate this plan. There were no boats.

News came that the first line of redoubts at the bottom of the American position had been overwhelmed, but that the second line was holding.

"Your Excellency, you must now come off," Greene said to Washington.

Washington was in great agony of spirit. It was too late to get the men out. If only they would resolutely man the lines, the British might weary of attacking. He hesitated, watching the smoke rising from the fighting to the south.

"Sir, you must come," Bayard said.

Greene and Putnam volunteered to remain at the fort, but Washington refused to let them. "Magaw is in command," he said flatly, restraining with difficulty his impulse to take personal command, still hoping that the firing to the north and the south would somehow prevail against a British force three times its size.

Glumly, the generals filed down the cliff face and

were rowed back to Fort Lee. There, they passed an agonizing day, looking over the river from the high western bank, watching the smoke rising from the middle of the cliff that meant that the enemy had now successfully crossed the Harlem River and penetrated the American center. As they watched, the smoke moved closer and closer to the fort and the American troops retreated into the fort, until three thousand of them were huddled where there was room for one-third of that number.

"I cannot bear to imagine what they must be doing inside that fort," General Putnam muttered to Bayard.

Washington paced the floor of his lookout. "This is most unfortunate, most unfortunate. Send a messenger at once. Direct Magaw to hold out."

A messenger ran down to the river and pushed off in a small boat. When he returned he had bad news.

"General Magaw has entered too far into a treaty to withdraw, sir!"

"Send another messenger!" Washington ordered. "Urge Magaw to insist on liberal terms of surrender!"

But when the next messenger returned, he brought the news that Magaw had been able to obtain no other terms than to surrender his men as prisoners of war.

"I would resign," Washington said to Bayard that night. "I am totally mortified and miserable. We have lost almost three thousand good men! I cannot forgive myself."

"Sir, you cannot blame yourself, you cannot!" Bayard insisted. He was as stunned as the rest of them by the catastrophe at Fort Washington. Anger mixed with sorrow, grief with resentment, so that he felt almost sick.

"I know my tendency toward rashness," Washington mourned, "so have endeavored to block it with deliberation. But in this case . . ." His voice catching, he coughed to hide it, and took a sip of Madeira, which he preferred to all other liquors. He had been drinking since dinner, but he was not drunk. Bayard had never seen him drunk.

"It is not the end of anything," Bayard said reasonably. "They are not dead, only prisoners of war. A swallow does not a summer make."

"Congress has ordered me to consult with my officers, and I have endeavored to do so," Washington said. "My estimate was that the fort was indefensible; Greene's was not. Our army is a small democracy. We are all inexperienced . . . save, perhaps, Charles Lee."

"In the face of the situation, there was nothing else to be done," Bayard insisted.

"Yet, we are growing more experienced every day," Washington said after a long silence. "More experienced and more weary. I am wearied almost to death with the retrograde motions of things. Dear Logan, does it now seem long since Cambridge, when we met?"

"Many lifetimes ago," Bayard agreed. Sometimes it was impossible to believe it was a scarce seven months since he and the general had marched into New York City.

"No man, I believe, ever had a greater choice of difficulties and less means to extricate himself from them," Washington said.

He walked to the window and looked out over the wide river. Darkness had fallen on the water; it seemed to him a pall. This, the worst disaster of the war, coming at a time of increasing setbacks, seemed the blackest defeat. True, he had advised Greene to withdraw, but his order had been discretionary, and Greene had not done so. As commander in chief, the ultimate responsibility was his.

And the ultimate mortification. But before Washington had time to dispatch to Congress his report on the debacle at Fort Washington, that unhappy affair had been succeeded by further misfortunes.

Washington was at his headquarters in Hackensack two days later when a breathless rider arrived with terrible news. It was a bright, luminescent morning—a clear coppery day after a night of cold, drenching rain, but the British had taken advantage of the dripping blackness of the night and had stealthily crossed the river. They had landed six miles above Fort Lee and were already marching toward the fort.

"Good God! Already!" Washington burst out. Roused at once from his depression he called for his horse. Galloping at top speed, he covered the six miles to Fort Lee in three-quarters of an hour. Fort Lee had only two to three thousand defenders; news came that Cornwallis was approaching with about eight thousand.

This time Washington did not confer with his generals, and he did not hesitate. "Evacuate at once!" he ordered.

The little fort went into a frenzy. A great number of men had broken into the sutler's stock of rum earlier and were already blind drunk. Washington ordered them to be lined up as much as possible. Some of them muttered that they would not risk their lives by leaving. Cooks were cooking lunch over a dozen campfires; Washington ordered them to march without taking either the meal or the burning-hot cookpots. There was no time to hitch up the cannon, except for two small twelve-pounders. Much had to be abandoned—two or three hundred tents, about a thousand barrels of flour, much baggage—all of it virtually irreplaceable.

"Make haste!" Washington bellowed, and to a quick drumbeat, off they went at double-time, heading for a bridge across the Hackensack River, six miles away, presumably the same bridge the enemy column would cross.

It was one of the most unnerving mornings of Washington's life. He had every expectation that they would encounter the enemy before they reached the bridge. Urging the men on, urging speed, he rode through the brilliant autumn day, scanning the woods and fields, seeing no sign of the enemy. At last he saw the narrow bridge spanning the river, and he forced the Fort Lee garrison—gasping for breath with parched throats—over into temporary safety.

General Charles Lee was now in command of more than five thousand militiamen at North Castle near White Plains. From there he was to stand guard against a possible British thrust up the Hudson or into Connecticut, which Washington still considered highly possible. Warning Lee, he said, "They may still pay the army under your command a visit."

But Washington had also informed Lee that should the British move instead into New Jersey, he would expect him to move the troops there with all possible dispatch. The commander in chief had only about two thousand men with him, and was plagued with worry not only about their widespread illnesses but their expiring contracts. Washington was in awe of Lee's experience and prowess as a military mastermind; Lee, as ever, was in awe of no one.

Lee had urged Washington to withdraw the garrison from Fort Washington, and when he heard the grim news about the fort's surrender he flew into a flaming passion.

"My God, this is a splendid affair for Mr. Howe," he moaned, "who now has his sores licked by us!" Giving vent to his anger and vexation, Lee wept plentifully and, deeply embarrassed, tore at his hair. Davie Montgomery, who had been taken into Lee's closest circles following his baptism by fire at the Battle of White Plains, was an unwilling witness to the scene.

"Cursed affair!" Lee raged. "Oh, why must men of such inferior judgment prevail? Oh, why?"

Davie, who had never met General Washington, felt only an involuntary tremor at Lee's nightreasonous condemnation of all the other American generals. To hear Lee, Putnam, Greene, and Washington were all fools, blackguards, and utter cowards.

"If only some military man were set at the head of the damn army," Lee suggested, "for you soldiers do not want courage, and are still among the living in goodly numbers, then the war could be won! The Congress disgusts me! Who, young man, do you think should be given a good deal more power? Who?"

"Why, you, sir," Davie answered, as expected.

Egging on Lee's drive for power was a letter he received from Joseph Reed, Washington's adjutant and old Virginia friend, a man whom Washington trusted absolutely. Reed was badly alarmed by the debacle at Fort Washington—and then at Fort Lee. He wrote quickly and secretly to Lee, begging him to come at once.

I do not mean to flatter you, nor praise you at the expense of any other, Reed wrote flatteringly, *but I confess that I do think it is entirely owing to you that this army, and the liberties of America so far as they are dependent on it, are not totally cut off. You have decision, a quality often wanting in minds otherwise valuable.*

Lee was entirely delighted with this insubordination on Reed's part. Hee-hawing in his glee, he read the letter aloud again and again.

And then, Lee refused to join Washington. "Let him stew!" he told his aides. "Let him poach himself in his casserole of indecision!"

Lee was brimming with exciting ideas at this point, none of which involved going to help the main command. Officially, Lee wrote to Washington that he had heard that a detachment of Robert Rogers's Loyalists corps was nearby and that he had decided to linger in Westchester to eliminate them. He had in mind to establish once and for all his military superiority to Washington.

Then he wrote Reed at headquarters, thanking him for his kind words and agreeing that it was certainly true that indecision in war was far worse than stupidity or even cowardice. Unfortunately, Washington opened this return letter, thinking it an official communiqué, and was thus both warned of Lee's insubordination and crushed by Reed's obvious erosion of confidence in him.

Rumors that Lee was about to succeed Washington spread through both the American army and Tory circles in New York. Meanwhile, General Greene brought his demoralized troops to join Washington's at Hackensack. Many of them were half-starved, half-clothed, half-armed, and discontented. Discipline was a problem and desertion was a daily affair.

Washington could do little but continue to retreat

213

southward into the New Jersey countryside. He fled toward New Brunswick on the Raritan River, Cornwallis in pursuit. From there he moved south toward the Delaware River and Philadelphia. Washington was not prepared to face the enemy. He was painfully learning the business of warfare, a science that includes not only military strategies, but formidable judgments of character, and a constant wariness of mind. But Washington was determined to be a democratic leader, and until the end he would take military risks to protect what he referred to as "the essential interests of any individual."

Lee was nowhere to be seen; he lingered at his headquarters in Peekskill, waiting for his sun to rise, lavishing attention on his pack of yapping dogs at the expense of his cold and hungry soldiers.

Chapter Fourteen

ALWAYS, DURING THE darkest days of a war, there are those who live out the finest days of their lives. Such a one was young Audrey Whitestone, a pretty, lighthearted, apolitical young woman in a city packed with men. There were all sorts of men: bachelor soldiers and officers and some who had put their faraway wives out of mind, disconsolate Loyalists in exile, desperately seeking comforts, and the New Yorkers she had known all her life. All of them were eager for diversion and distraction, all felt the urgency to enjoy the moment that war instills in soldier and civilian alike.

Audrey did her best to remain cheerful and to help those whom she fancied forget the rigors of wartime and the horrors of the battlefield. She had a new rose-purple silk polonaise gown that had already been celebrated in a popular song, and it crackled and rustled as she hurried around the dining room on a cool early December evening when General Robertson was to be a guest at the Logans' table.

Humming softly, Audrey lit the beeswax candles in the silver candlesticks and wall sconces. She was delighted to see General Robertson come in early; Robertson was the most powerful man in New York, even if he was terribly old, and he made amusing company. As a moth to a flame, so Audrey was drawn to powerful men—and so to trouble.

"Good evening, General," Audrey said in her sweetest tone, offering Robertson a cool cheek. Kissing it wetly, he reached for her waist and gave it a quick pinch. Despite his age, James Robertson had a remarkable and well-deserved reputation as a libertine.

Audrey giggled. "La, sir, you shouldn't!"

"Shouldn't what?" Josias asked, entering and looking annoyed.

"Oh, good evening, Josias," Audrey said, her full skirts rustling as she whirled to face the door. "Dear brother," she cooed, "are you tired? You look just a bit rumpled and mussed." And then, lowering her voice to a whisper, "Are you out of sorts, Josias? When we have a guest?"

"Of course not, my dear. I have worked well today and look forward to this evening. Robertson, won't you sample the punch? Are you admiring the family portraits there? Those are Meg's and Audrey's ancestors, the Van Rensallaers. Spared by the fire, luckily, as I had just sent them out to Malichai Miller's shop to be reframed!"

"Dutch folk?" Robertson asked, peering at the pale, bland faces in their gold-leaf frames. He was nearsighted and had stood so close to the paintings that he had knocked one askew. Audrey ran to straighten it and to look coyly up into the general's eyes.

"Oh, terribly," Audrey said. She was ashamed of her mother's heritage, preferring everything English. Although she had never been to England, she knew she should prefer it to New York, and

216

since the visit, last April, of her Carolina cousins returning from London, she had felt quite deprived that she had not yet made the tour.

"Here, here, a cup of punch," Josias said, handing round the chased silver cups. "Take care, now; it's a bit strong."

"Just the way I like it," Robertson said, taking a seat near the fire. "Delicious! Last night, by the way, I dined with Ambrose Serle. You know, Howe's secretary. A most serious man, of course."

"Of course," Josias agreed. Everyone knew Serle, who processed pardons for Lord Howe and circulated constantly in the city.

"According to Serle, Howe is of the opinion that all the people of parts and spirit are in the rebellion. I cannot believe this to be true. Think how Howe's army scattered them on Long Island. Think of the recent victories. Have you seen the sorry parades of prisoners from Fort Washington?"

"I have," Josias said. "Sorry indeed."

"Most wretched men," Audrey agreed. Everyone had seen the filthy, ragged soldiers march through the streets on their way to confinement in the sugar mills, warehouses, and prison ships. "So many of them!"

"More than three thousand. What they will eat, I don't know," Robertson said. "But at any rate, Serle did tell me a joke: How is New York like Athens?"

"Not for its literature," Josias hazarded.

"Nor for its refinement," General Robertson admitted, "but instead for its insatiable appetite for the new."

"How true," said Josias, smiling mildly.

Audrey frowned. She did not like the joke, nor did she relish it particularly when the gentlemen insisted on talking about politics. For all her affectations, Audrey was a practical woman, and many practical people are bored by any discussion of principles; they hate abstractions. Talk of the war, she acknowledged, was inevitable; she strove only to remember that it was temporary, and that in her scheme of things, it had its uses. "When will the war be over, do you think, dear General?" she asked with a confiding glance and a laying-on of her round blue eyes.

"Shortly, Miss Whitestone. I should imagine, my dear, by Christmastime. We have that fox Washington on the run in Jersey now!"

"Oh, how wonderful!" Audrey sighed, looking at Robertson as if he had done it himself. Josais could not help noticing, as she had expected he would, and he was annoyed. His relationship with his sister-in-law was a sensitive, if peculiar, one. He had moved from being her self-appointed protector to being her secret and most ardent admirer. More than anything in the world, he looked forward to the kisses she occasionally allowed him, tinged as they were with guilt and a sense of danger. Now, he was forced to see his sweet, pretty Audrey admiring another man, and it upset him.

"Cornwallis has halted at Brunswick, as a matter of fact," Josias said in a grumpy tone. "For some reason, Howe neglected to send him onward. Instead, he has sent Clinton with an amphibious force off to Newport, Rhode Island. I can not imagine why, unless it is because the navy so disgraced themselves in Charleston last summer."

"Oh, Henry Clinton?" Audrey asked. Clinton, an aristocrat by birth, was a New Yorker by upbringing, and he was well known to New Yorkers, although he was not a society man. "Henry Clinton is very clever," Audrey said, repeating a theory she had often heard her father voice.

218

Josias looked more annoyed than before, and he barely adopted a teasing tone as he asked, "What do you know of these things, Audrey dear?"

"Very little, of course, as I am a woman," she said, smiling entrancingly. "Good heavens, let us go in to dinner!"

"And your wife? She is better?" General Robertson asked, for form's sake, as the three of them passed into the dining room. He had dined here thrice lately but had never seen Mrs. Logan, who was still recovering from childbed, he had heard.

"Alas, very little recovered," Josias said. Meg was so dispirited and out of sorts that it was depressing to be with her, and increasingly hard to forgive her her frailty. A man needed a robust, supportive woman, and Meg was not forthcoming in this regard, neither was she physically cooperative, and Josias was quite tired of waiting for her to come around. The early harmonious period of their marriage had been a brief one, and Josais sometimes felt that it had never been, so entirely distracted was he by his wife's sister. Indeed, Audrey could not have timed her visit better.

Dinner was served at once, and the collation was one that did justice to Josias's connections and Audrey's direction, for in this as in other matters, she was deliberately taking over her sister's responsibilities in the household. The roast was seasoned with sage and onion, the ham well smoked, and the jellies shone like jewels in cut-glass dishes engraved with Ws entwined with ships in full sail. Audrey was very comfortable using her family's treasures and at ease in her mother's, or sister's, place at the head of the table. In an odd way, she felt toward Josias as if he were her father, except that he was far more susceptible to manipulation.

And manipulate him she did, taking advantage of

General Robertson's attentions to torment Josias. Robertson lost his inhibitions under the influence of the claret Josias poured, and he reached out to fondle Audrey's shoulder and arm with increasing frequency, and even, when Josias had left the room to see about more wine, her breast. Audrey took her cue to shriek and gasp as Josias reentered, and could tell from his redness of face and stiffness of bearing that he had seen and was in quite a temper, although too indebted to General Robertson, who, as commandant of the city, had placed so many golden opportunities in Josias's path already, to take issue.

"Let us return to the fireside to finish this Madeira," Josias suggested. Both Robertson and Audrey were unsteady on their feet as they rose from the table.

"When will the old goat go home?" Josias whispered as Audrey passed him in the doorway.

"I daresay he is getting sleepy," Audrey acknowledged. "I believe I am."

But Robertson settled himself by the fire and began to tell a tale of the last war, in which he had personally witnessed a remarkable instance of the cleverness of the Indian people and the foolishness of the French. Audrey smoothed her rosy-purple skirts and listened with wide eyes while Josias fumed, and not until the mantel clock had sounded midnight did Robertson relinquish his seat and call for his cloak and carriage.

"Many thanks, Logan," Robertson said in parting. "A lovely woman, your sister-in-law. Lovely!" As Josias stood in the doorway to bid Robertson farewell, he saw that the first real snow of the year was falling, swirling in the wind and coating the dark streets and bushes with icy drifts. He shuddered as he hurried back to the fireside.

Audrey sat there, curled coquettishly on a low-backed settee. "Goodness! What long stories dear General Robertson does tell!" she said.

Josias shut the parlor door firmly. "Interminable," he said. "And I could think only of how much I longed to be kissing you."

Audrey gave a small gasp. "Josias! You are becoming so bold!"

"It's your fault. You are too beautiful and too disturbing." He knelt near her and put both hands on her tiny waist. She smelled of lilies and wriggled like a bird in hand.

"Oh, do stop! Josias, you are my brother, you know!"

"In law only. My heart is yours as a lover, Audrey."

And then he pressed himself on her, fired by passion mixed with jealousy and torment, kissing her face until his tongue found hers. She turned her face from side to side and gasped, growing rosy, which excited him further, so that he kissed her bosom, served up prettily in the low silken square of her neckline.

"Oh, my Lord! My dear Lord!" she whispered. "Oh, please!"

Josias knew what to do and did it, removing her bodice with hurried fingers, parting her petticoats until they could be united wetly with his widespread hands on either side of her tiny frame, holding her steady while he entered her and carried her with him until she trembled, pleading for his mercy and ardor, her eyes shut like a cat's.

Both of them ended with delicate quiverings and sighs from the bottom of their happy lungs. "Oh, my dear Josias," she whispered. "What have you done to me now?"

Josias was very pleased with himself and enor-

221

mously relieved that he had at last made his position clear. "Think of me not as your brother, but as your husband, now," he commanded her, kissing her breasts possessively.

"But what of my sister?" Audrey was naughty enough to ask. "What of her? What on earth shall we do about her?"

"Forget her for now," he ordered, but the thought was there between them.

It was mid-December and still General Lee dragged his heels. He had finally crossed the border into northern New Jersey, but avoided joining Washington. He had written Washington that *I am assured that you are very strong*, though nowhere had he in fact gotten this sort of information. It seemed imminent to him that as Washington's situation was nearly hopeless and the man himself incompetent, that he himself might very soon be called into the job of commander in chief.

I should imagine that we can make a better impression by hanging on the enemy's rear, he wrote, *so as to annoy, distract and weaken 'em*.

Washington found this communiqué inches from insubordination, but replied promptly and politely: *Join me with all your whole force with all possible expedition*. There! Could there be any mistake about that?

Lee chose to make one. Instead of heading straight south toward Trenton, he moved from Morristown to Basking Ridge, where, seeking the best possible accommodations, he set himself up in a cozy hostelry known as White's Tavern, four miles from most of his men, who were ordered toward Germantown under General John Sullivan. Accompanied by a guard of fifteen men and his aides, Lee enjoyed a fine supper at the widow White's table and slept soundly with his canine companions.

The next morning he rose early, but spent two hours squabbling with officers of the Connecticut light horse, ridiculing their old-fashioned wigs and speaking contemptuously of their troops. He breakfasted rather late, and sat in dressing gown and slippers, himself still wigless, by a cheerful fire while he wrote a letter to General Gates, as usual complaining of Washington's deficiencies. It was Friday, the thirteenth, and would prove to be an unlucky day, for Lee at least.

For even as Lee wrote, toasting his toes, danger came galloping up to the inn. The British, guided by local Loyalists, had learned that he was at White's Tavern under a light guard. Davie Montgomery, who had come to carry off Lee's letter to Gates, happened to be looking out the west-facing window and saw a party of dragoons turn the corner of the avenue at full charge.

At first Davie thought he was imagining the very worst, but the sight was persuasive. "Here, sir," he exclaimed, "are the British cavalry!"

"Where?" Lee asked, signing the letter with a flourish.

"Around the house," Davie reported, for in a flash, the cavalry had parted ranks and surrounded the tavern.

Lee was either self-possessed or made a fine show of it, for he only remarked, "Well, where is the guard? Damn the guard! Why don't they fire?"

There was a pounding on the door and the widow White, entirely distressed, rushed in with her gray braids hanging to her waist. "Sir! The British!" she gasped.

"For God's sake, what shall I do?" Lee demanded.

223

"Let me hide you, sir," she suggested. "Up here, between the chimney and the breastwork! I shall say you have already gone!"

Lee tried, but skinny as he was and push as he did, he could not insert himself into the tiny cubbyhole. As he tried again and again to make himself smaller, holding his breath in an effort to shrink, a bullet came through the open window and lodged in the mantelpiece.

"It is hopeless," Lee said with obvious disgust. "Montgomery, may I ask you to go see where the guard might be?"

Davie took up two pistols and ran out of the room. From the back hallway he could see that the guard was absent but had left most of their arms lying about. Through the back door he saw dragoons chasing the guard in various directions. There seemed to be a great many of them.

Lee's dogs were yapping furiously, but the General remained absolutely calm. "I believe we can escape by the back, sir!" Davie shouted, but up the front staircase came a tramping of sturdy boots, and bullets began to rain in through the windows.

"My windows!" shrieked Mrs. White, scrambling under the featherbed where Lee and his dogs had lately rested. "Oh, dear Lord, we shall all be kilt!"

The British were under the command of a flamboyant young subaltern who was beginning to make a name for himself, Lieutenant Banastre Tarleton. Davie did not recognize Tarleton, but Lee did, and in the most annoying way, for Tarleton and the cavalrymen with him were part of the Queen's Light Dragoons, soldiers who had been under Lee's own command in Portugal during the late fighting there, when Lee had made his reputation.

"Surrender at once, and you will be safe!" Tarleton called up, "but if you do not comply with my summons in five minutes, the house will burn and everyone in it will be put to the sword!"

"I beg of you, spare my property," widow White begged, peeking out from the feathers, "I am a poor widow and have no other means, sir!"

Lee was not moved to sympathy, but paced the floor in increasing agitation. Someone downstairs had opened the front door to a hail of bullets. Was he obliged to die here at this obscure tavern, after all he had been through, all he aspired to yet do? The notion seemed to him totally loathsome and of no practical benefit to himself, or anyone else. Making one last attempt to escape by the back, Lee's staff officers were scattered or wounded and Lee was seized.

"So it is you," he said to Tarleton, red with fury.

"You are my prisoner, sir!"

Lee could not speak for his annoyance, and all the more so when he was tossed across a waiting horse and carried off in triumph, bareheaded, in his slippers, with his collar open and his shirt frankly soiled. Davie, hands tied, was one of several aides who were taken along; others avoided capture by hiding in a chimney or disguising themselves in servants' clothes.

It was evident that Tarleton and his men considered this capture a personal coup. Their arrival at Brunswick touched off a general celebration. Two bands played all night, and some of the men contrived to get Lee's horse as drunk as they were in toasting the King. It seemed a prelude to British victory, for if Lee were as vital to the American cause as they believed him to be, and many believed him to be entirely responsible for the few successes that the Americans had so far been able to gain, would not the rebels' defenses now crumble?

* * *

When the story of Lee's kidnapping reached England, it was not at first believed, for it seemed too fantastic. When Washington got the sad news, he expressed the utmost regret, writing that *our cause has received a severe blow . . . I feel much for the loss of my country in his captivity*, but at least General Sullivan knew how to obey orders. Washington sent him word to move the rest of the army south to join him as quickly as they could march.

Sullivan's forces numbered two thousand, and Gates commanded another six hundred or so, all that remained out of seven regiments. Washington needed them at once, for he was acutely aware that nearly all their terms of enlistment would soon expire.

"I am exceedingly distressed," he complained to Bayard Logan. "The good Lord knows I cannot run an army without men!"

"Surely they will agree to stay," Bayard said hopefully.

"You may as well attempt to stop the winds from blowing or the sun in its diurnal as the regiments from going when their time expires," Washington mourned. "Not that I blame them, Logan! I long for home myself. I have just written my estate manager . . ." He brightened as he did whenever his mind turned to Mount Vernon. "I have sent him a stallion that I think will do well. And I have instructed him to plant a row of locusts across from the new garden to the spinning house."

As much as he feared the British army, the commander in chief was actually more worried about the "disaffection," of New Jersey, New York, and Pennsylvania. The natives of these three states were extremely divided in their loyalties. "The army depends on the people," he told Bayard, and it was, to his mind, an irrefutable proposition. The people of New Jersey were infamous in the support they gave to the British.

In his most reflective moments, Washington acknowledged that many New Jersey people of all sorts were simply watching to see where the balance of power lay, their sympathies not firmly pledged to either side. He knew that he had to act decisively, and soon—before the bulk of his enlistments expired and he was left with a feeble force of twelve hundred men in the coldest months of the year.

"These are the times that try men's souls," wrote Thomas Paine, who had come to New Jersey to see the army and arrived to see it in full retreat. "The summer soldier and the sunshine patriot will, in this crisis, shrink from the service of his country; but he that stands it *Now*, deserves the thanks of man and woman."

Fiery Paine was full of praise and admiration for Washington in this time of crisis, observing that "There is a natural firmness in some minds which cannot be unlocked by trifles, but which, when unlocked, discovers a cabinet of fortitude. . . . God hath blessed him with uninterrupted health and given him a mind that can even flourish upon care."

In fact, Washington was not in the best of health, and as ever suffered agonies of toothache, but he was holding together, providing a stable center for the army. He was confident of the virtue of his men and the nobility of the cause, and he was optimistic in his own way—with the kind of optimism that inspires the desperate, for he never pretended that circumstances were not grave.

Washington began to plot a bold and daring strike—under the circumstances only the most extreme measures could produce sufficiently radical results. For a time, he drew into himself, gathering his strength and calling on his inner reserves.

"These are the times . . . ," he said to himself, savoring Paine's powerful, poetic words. "Aye, these are the times . . ."

Chapter Fifteen

BONNIE LOGAN'S LIFE, once so independent and carefree, had changed utterly since the day when she realized that Cormick Walker had found her and was hunting her. Using Meg's illness as her excuse, Bonnie rarely left the upper floors of her brother's house, and when it was absolutely necessary to leave the house altogether, she disguised herself in a servant's dark green woolsey cloak, hiding her distinctive red-gold hair inside its hood, and tried to remain unrecognized. She feared for herself, and above all, she feared for her child, Dorothy.

"But he does not know about Dorothy," Meg said. The two women were alone in the upstairs sitting room on a blustery December day when the pearly gray sky outside was spitting snow. They had taken tea and had enjoyed each other's company all afternoon, talking at great length as they could of so many simple things that were of interest to them: how to dry peaches and preserve cherries in rum, how to turn a collar in the prettiest way, and the delightful, cheerful cockiness of baby Dorothy's smile.

Meg was feeling a bit stronger, although she had developed some internal troubles she could not define, nor could Doctor Bard explain, but which forced her to stay abed at least two weeks of the month and to endure great abdominal discomfort.

"Unless he has seen her and guesses that she is his child," Bonnie wondered aloud. "By her age, perhaps. He may have seen the two of us together, Meg." The two friends had been over this ground time and again, but its danger and uncertainty had not dissipated.

"We do not know what he has seen," Meg admitted. "Perhaps he thinks Dorothy is my baby." The idea forced a tear to escape from her eye. How sad it was that she had no baby of her own. She had not given up hope that she could become pregnant again, although Doctor Bard had sighed and shaken his head warningly when she asked him about it. And now, Josias seemed to have lost interest in her.

"He seems to watch all the time," Bonnie said despairingly. It was true: She had heard Cormick's three-noted warning whistle at all hours of the day and night, although none of the servants, sent out to investigate, had been able to catch him loitering in the nearby streets. Often when she looked from a window, she saw his figure standing in a shadow. And once, when Bonnie had gone on foot to the market, she had seen him again, face to face, and she would never forget the look he had given her— a mixture of hatred and anger that had caused her to scream aloud. She had run home, sobbing.

"I still think we should talk to William about this. I still feel sure that if anyone can help you, he can," Meg suggested, but Bonnie, as usual, shook her head vigorously in refusal.

"Not William," she insisted, still unable to relinquish her pride. She had told him that her husband was dead, and their love was built on starting afresh; their love, and his admiration for her, was the finest thing in her life, the only pure, clean, shining thing (except for dear Dorothy) that she had to cling to. She could not bear to tell him the truth. How could he then love her? No, she could not tell William, and as it was, she did not see him often these days, and the last time she had seen him he had seemed hurried, even brusque with her.

"I am afraid that Walker is mad," Meg said, wriggling her toes by the grate in which burned a cheerful fire. "I am sorry to say it, Bonnie, but he looked quite mad."

Bonnie shuddered. "I have never seen a more dreadful face. He is totally changed, I assure you. I cannot even imagine how he can be alive. How can he have survived those powder burns, and what is his recollection of the circumstances of his injury?"

"Darling, I hope you never know," Meg said. "Perhaps he will go away soon. These wartime days cannot last much longer, do you think?"

"General Howe has come into town—for the winter, at least," Bonnie said. "He is quite confident of a peaceful winter, they say. They say he has sent Cornwallis home to visit his wife. From what I know of General Howe, I should think he will be appearing socially with great frequency."

"Perhaps you should go out of town," Meg suggested. "You could go to my parents' house on the Hudson. You would be safe there."

"If it were not for you, dearest Meg, I should consider that plan, but I will not leave you alone here. I do not want to."

"Still, the day may come when you change your mind. You must not make such important decisions on my account," Meg protested.

"No, no, I will not leave you here in this house. With them," Bonnie said darkly, for both of them suspected the worst, which was also the truth, about Josias and Audrey.

"They cannot harm me," Meg said. "And Cormick might harm you. I think you should consider it, Bonnie."

Bonnie shook her head, but soon she had a new consideration. A young lieutenant arrived at the house on Fair Street with an elegant hand-painted invitation. An official celebration was due General Howe, and a ball was to be given to welcome him, the conquering hero, to the city. It would be held at Roubalet's Tavern, and Bonnie's presence was most urgently requested.

"Shall you go?" Meg asked.

"I don't think I can refuse," Bonnie said.

"My goodness! What will you wear?" Meg asked, getting on to the next important question. "Something will have to be made up for you! Something really splendid. From the new shipment! How about that apricot silk? We could have it trimmed with gold lace. And then you must wear golden shoes."

"Stop, you little devil, or I'll take your head off!" had been the last words Davie Montgomery heard as a free man. When he had seen the number of dragoons surrounding White's Tavern and heard General Lee say, "I will surrender," he had made a last attempt to escape, scrambling over a stone wall near an arbor black with hanging grapes. But the wall was slick with morning frost, and his foot slipped.

And then he was taken. A tall, red-faced ensign

with a black moustache had taken him, swiping at his left arm with his cutlass and cutting it to the bone. Howling with pain, Davie had surrendered and climbed, with some others, onto a wagon that followed General Lee tied across his horse, first to an old Dutch farmhouse near the Raritan River, then to the British base at Brunswick. Lee was kept there, but Davie, with the other enlisted men, was sent on to New York, to one of the nefarious sugar-house prisons.

The sugar refinery turned prison was a bleak, five-story stone building in the northwest corner of Trinity churchyard. Like all the prisons in New York, it was full to overflowing, crammed to its barred and paneless windows with soldiers in varying states of health and preservation, all frustrated, filthy, and underfed. Like all New York prisons, it stank horribly and was surrounded by a heavy military guard.

Davie was marched from the ferry to the prison through a gauntlet of gawking New Yorkers, men and women, old and young, all seemingly fascinated by the misfortune of the captured soldiers. Still weak from lack of blood, although his arm was healing up quickly, he staggered through the unfamiliar streets surrounded by his fellows and a cordon of red-coated guards carrying bayonets. So this is New York, he thought. He had always wanted to see New York, although his imagination had not extended to this sort of disgraceful arrival.

The dense crowds of people, many of them odd and foreign-looking, the press of the buildings—so many of them charred and black—impressed him, and as he was directed in through a narrow gate, through an iron door, into a large room already overstocked with unwashed bodies, he remembered his father's parting words: "New York—remember you have family there!"

Much good that will do me now, Davie thought. Unless I can manage to escape. And from the first cold, noisy night, he thought of nothing else.

If Davie's thoughts had turned from memories of his far-off Carolina family and the easy, pleasant life he had left behind, theirs of him had not ceased. His first letters came to his parents' house after a delay of a month or more, and his last, written from Harlem Heights, had not yet arrived in Charleston when he was captured and incarcerated in the New York sugar house.

In fact, in waiting for these letters, Dennison and Caroline Montgomery had postponed their migration from Charleston to Ashley Hall, and though the first frost had touched the gardens, and the hunting season had begun, they still lingered in town. Their daughter Katy was with them; Webb and Susannah had no plans to travel to the plantation until Christmastime, if then. At Ashley Hall, Liza and Taylor continued to enjoy solitude and peace in their ancestral dwelling.

But something very odd and chilling had happened to change their lives there. One afternoon, Liza had gone alone to the wine cellar, thinking that she would surprise Taylor with a special bottle of old claret to drink with their dinner, which promised to be a very delicious dish of woodcock and persimmons. The wine cellar was one of seven brick-arched cellars that spanned the length of the plantation house.

Liza had found a bottle, wiped it free of dust on her apron, and then wandered through the other cellars, all of them dimly lit from shuttered window vents and redolent of the spicy-smelling cedar beams that crisscrossed the foundation of the house. In one corner, she saw an ancient apple press; in another a bale of straw. Then she thought she heard a small, soft weeping sound, like a stray kitten.

Calling "kitty, kitty," she prowled deeper into the dusk, but the sound had ceased. Certain that she had heard something, she called again, and then in a corner, she was sure she smelled another human being. She was curious rather than frightened. "Who is there?" she called softly, expecting a lost child. "Don't be shy. Come out! Where are you?"

There was no answer, but when she held her breath, she was sure she heard the breath of another. She strode to the dark corner, and there, in the dim light, she discovered a slim black girl cowering on a bench in a dreadful condition.

"Good heavens!" she gasped. "Who are you? What happened to you?"

The black girl was young, hardly more than a child, but her body clearly showed that she was entering womanhood. She was naked except for a skimpy shift and a frilled mobcap which failed to cover her glossy black curls. Her skin had the soft pallor of ivory and her eyes were mad with fear. Liza put out her hand and the black girl shuddered and cowered.

"I'm not going to hurt you," Liza promised. "Come out now, come on."

The girl moved stiffly, but fell forward and Liza saw that she had been badly beaten on her back, which was now festered and oozing. Her legs and feet were scarred and bleeding. Liza had never seen such a hideous sight. She was filled with pity and fear. The girl was not from Ashley Hall. She must have run away. What could she have done to incur such brutal punishment? Liza shrank back, confused and upset. Then, to her astonishment, the girl seemed to recognize her.

"Miss Liza? Miss Liza? I'm Sarah. Mr. Hill's Sary."

"Mr. Hill? The dancing master?" Liza still did not recognize one of the Charleston dancing teacher's slaves in this poor wretch, but she felt suspicion and justification in a rush of blood. She had never liked her dancing teacher. She had always thought him hasty and overfussy, bad tempered and perhaps even cruel. Nicholas Hill was a leading Patriot and a popular member of her brothers' crowd. Liza knew that he filled his dancing school with pretty young girls of mixed blood, especially in the classes for young men, but she had never before given it a thought.

"Don't talk anymore," she ordered Sarah. "Just come with me. You can't stay down here."

Sarah was so light that even Liza could carry her up the stairs to the main floor. Something stopped Liza from crying out for help, and instead she took the girl into Taylor's office, where there was a small couch and a basin which he used for washing when he came into the house after working or riding. There, she very tenderly washed Sarah's feet and legs—although she dared not touch her back—and heard her story.

"Did Mr. Hill do this to you?"

"Yes, ma'am."

"But why, Sary? Why?"

Sarah fell silent, and then she said simply, "I didn't please him."

Liza sighed. She was too innocent to know just what that might mean, but too instinctive not to realize that Sarah was telling the truth. "Why did you come here? How did you get here?"

"I have a brother, works for Big Benny. I hide out in a wood boat, and they bring me here. I came last night. Old Lucy . . . she put medicine on my back."

"So everyone knows you're here?"

"No, ma'am, not everyone. Please? Please, don't send me back to Mr. Hill, Miss Liza."

"I am sure we won't do that, for he does not deserve to have you, Sary. But I must tell Taylor. . . ."

Riding a swift and sure-footed marsh pony, Taylor was moving slowly through a thicket of young pines in the midst of a pine forest transformed by autumnal colors and fragrances into a magic land. Taylor had been out all afternoon, enjoying the wind and the weather as much as the hunt.

Great flocks of blackbirds passed high overhead, sailing south toward the delta where they would roost in the marshes. Small flocks of wood ducks winnowed the air, their strange, shrill cries answered by their kind in the lagoons and ponds of the plantation. Taylor had seen a flock of blue herons, grunting as they drifted overhead with heavy grace, and then spotted the woodcock, absurdly roly poly, rising, glimmering, out of the brakes.

He had thinned out the woodcock, aiming carefully at the fattest of them, tucking them neatly into his saddlebags when his lean dog, Blue, had caught them neatly in his mouth. Now he was lost in the sights and smells of the day, thoroughly happy, delighting in being alone in this world that was mixed of air and earth, all underlaid and crisscrossed with water.

The slave patrol—a pack of eight men on horseback—startled him with their sudden approach along the river road.

"Mr. Montgomery!" the leader called out.

"Hello, there, Perkins," Taylor answered, recognizing him. "What's wrong?"

"Nothing's wrong, sir, 'cept a valuable slave gal run off from her master in Charleston, joinin' up with a crowd of 'em heading to the west. Some say she was seen on your land. Some say your slaves know about it."

"I haven't heard a thing about it," Taylor said. "Everything's quiet at Ashley Hall, gentlemen. What's this about one woman? Why doesn't he advertise for her?"

"Gentleman miss this gal in particular, I guess. He put up twenty pounds for her takin', Mr. Montgomery. Young woman, well trained, light skinned, and pretty."

"I haven't seen her!" Taylor insisted, waving good-bye to the slave patrol as his horse pranced in a circle, kicking up a drift of yellow leaves.

"Name of Sarah. Master's Mr. Hill!" Perkins called back.

"The dancing master?" Taylor asked, "Mr. Hill the dancing master?" but he didn't hear Perkins's answer.

As Taylor rode toward home, he thought about slavery. He despised cruelty to slaves, and neither he nor his father had ever practiced or condoned the barbaric punishments that they both knew were commonplace among some of their fellow slave owners. African-born slaves and their descendants were as common as bluebirds in South Carolina, as ever present as the yellow pines. In this part of the colony, they outnumbered whites. To Taylor's thinking, as the whites were in charge, they had a moral debt to principles of justice and humanity.

When he let himself think about it, Taylor could

see that the day might very well come when the Negroes should become, through education, example, and proximity, enough accustomed to the forms and dictates of civilization, so that they should work as free men, accepting a wage instead of subsistence. It was unthinkable that a rice plantation like Ashley Hall could exist without their labor, whether slave or free. The work was prodigious. In season, field hand and foreman, overseer and even children must all work twelve or fourteen hours a day to get the work done.

Why, Taylor thought, it was obvious that the Africans were born for this sort of work! They were of a race that had not yet accepted Christ or mastered self-government. It was obvious that, although honest and noble in the particular, they were, as a people, woefully ignorant and dependent, as the child is dependent upon the parent. They were immune to the diseases and the draining effect of the summer sun that killed white men. They planted rice, built canoes, and fished with nets as their ancestors had always done. In return for the security of a home and food, they gave their labor. That was the system, and in its ideal case, Taylor found no room for profound regrets or guilt of any stripe.

But it was in cases such as the one the slave catchers had gotten involved in, that he felt great distress and apprehension. Out of fear, out of stupidity, or bad character, some men were cruel to their slaves. And this was utterly regrettable; it lowered both master and slave morally; it cast doubts on the whole system. And the system was essential; he came back to that. All Carolina was built on it, supported by it, and could not exist without it. He came back to that.

Taylor rode through the neighborhood of slave dwellings as he approached Ashley Hall in the twilight. They were extensive and built of the yellow-heart pine which defeats the ravages of rot as it frustrates the termite. The houses were of two rooms—a chamber for each family, and before it, a sitting room with a tall chimney. The slaves were permitted to cut all the firewood they needed, and tonight nearly every chimney sent forth smoke into the lavender night. Out the back door of nearly every house was a small garden or orchard which they were free to plant and tend, as soon as their day's work was done, which was far earlier in this season than any other.

Food was given to these slaves, they raised more, and nearly every man had his own dugout canoe from which he could catch fish, shrimp, and oysters. The slaves at Ashley Hall were not cold or hungry, and Taylor wondered if they were content. At that moment, he heard a slave woman call to her child, and heard a man somewhere begin to beat on a deep-toned drum. He told himself that these two, at least, were not unhappy.

Those who had just arrived, on the other hand, he knew often had problems and made trouble. Freshly imported slaves often took some time to settle down and become productive workers. Some suffered from diseases encountered on the long voyage; some suffered suicidal melancholy. But most put their pasts behind them and accepted life as was, glad to be alive, happy to be fed and clothed and to feel the wind and sunshine. Or so he supposed.

Taylor was frowning at the development of his thoughts as he stamped into the front hall of the big house. The hallway was dark, and as was his habit, he crossed first to his little office, where he was accustomed to record, every afternoon, the events of the day in the Farm Book, while drinking a glass of whiskey or rum.

240

But this afternoon, to his surprise, he found Liza sitting there, holding a cloth to the head of a woman stretched across his couch, a very pretty, very young slave woman with a cascade of tousled black curls. The slave girl was wearing one of Liza's nightdresses, open to the back.

"Taylor!" Liza said. "Don't say anything till I explain."

He took it all in at a glance: the dreadful condition of her back, her age and pretty face, Liza's gown. What's more, the girl looked familiar; all the Montgomerys had studied dancing with Mr. Hill during the last few years, and he was sure he remembered the girl from the dancing school. He recalled that she was especially pretty and spirited. Her master was a brute.

The young woman opened her eyes and then shut them helplessly, but in that instant Taylor saw that she remembered him, too.

"We must hide her! She's been most cruelly beaten," Liza explained. "She came upriver from Charleston. Her master . . ."

"I have already met the slave catchers looking for her," Taylor said flatly. He lit a lamp and poured himself a glass of whiskey.

"Oh, no!" Liza gasped. "Oh, dear heavens! We must hide her, Taylor. She can't go back! She needs rest and time to heal, and I think she's taken a fever."

Taylor hesitated. What his sister proposed was extremely dangerous. After all, the slave girl was Mr. Hill's property. But Taylor's sense of humanity, of justice, coupled with his reflections of that afternoon, quickly banished all doubt from his mind. To turn the girl over to Hill would be as good as killing her. The only honorable course was to protect her.

241

"You must be careful, very careful," he warned Liza.

"But you agree that we must hide her?"

"For the time being. When she is better, then we will decide what to do. But she must not stay here."

"No. I thought of taking her to Old Lucy's house."

"But if they come looking again, they will search the quarters," Taylor pointed out.

"Then I shall put her in Katy's room and let Old Lucy come to nurse her."

"Does everyone in the house know about this?" Taylor asked.

Liza smiled oddly. "I think we are the last to find out," she said.

"Good heavens," Taylor said, gulping his whiskey.

Within a few days Sarah's fever was better, thanks to Old Lucy and Liza's careful nursing, but she was no safer. Despite Taylor's efforts to discourage them, the slave catchers had come again and had searched every house in the quarters.

When the slave patrol had gone, at least for a time, Liza knocked on the door of Taylor's office. It was a blustery, rainy day, and he was relaxing with a cup of chocolate, reading a newspaper printed in Philadelphia. According to the reports, the war was just about over. The American army—naked, depleted, almost without provisions—had retreated into the New Jersey hinterlands. A formal surrender would surely come by spring. The whole tragic mistake would soon be ended.

"Taylor, we have to do something!" Liza said in great distress.

242

"About the slave girl?"

"She is not safe here. There is so much gossip; I am sure it will come out that we are hiding her."

"What can be done? Hill should be punished. But that is unlikely to come about." Taylor, a man of his time and his class, could more easily condemn an individual than the system. "Hill should himself be beaten."

"You wouldn't send her back to him?" Liza asked in a horrified voice.

"Of course not. She can never go back." In the last few days Taylor had given this some thought. It was evident to him, as a man of the world, that Hill had an emotional stake in Sarah that went beyond the ordinary master-and-slave relationship; either that or the man was insane. Either way, Sarah would not be safe with him.

"It breaks my heart to see what he did to her. She has told me that her only fault was spilling tea when serving him his breakfast. And after he beat her, he poured melted wax into the wounds."

Taylor winced.

'She is a good girl."

"She is that, and also pretty and clever."

"What can we do? Where can we hide her so that she will not be seen or noticed?"

"Perhaps," Taylor said slowly, for he had a bold idea, one that had come to him from a notice in the newspaper, "perhaps what I should do is take her to the North. She could be free there. The British are granting sanctuary to any Negroes who come to them to aid or join the army. In the North, perhaps in New York, she would be able to begin a new life."

"You? Go to New York?" Liza was astonished.

"Perhaps that is what I should do." In fact, at that moment Taylor decided that it was the only thing he could do. In spite of his love for Ashley Hall, for Charleston and the South, for his family,

Taylor knew that these last several weeks had been but a brief respite from the problems at hand. His disagreement with Webb—and many of his neighbors—would not go away. Taylor realized now that his politics might well cause his family harm. By leaving his beloved home, he could escape the tempest that was brewing around him, and save a helpless girl, who had no other hope but him.

"Taylor! What an idea! I should miss you awfully."

"How soon would she be well enough to travel?"

"She is not really well, but . . ."

In two days' time, they were gone. Traveling as a gentleman and his body slave, they went by carriage to Wilmington, in order to avoid Charleston, and took passage on a coastal schooner to New York. As soon as they left the harbor, a severe storm hit, and they huddled in their cabin for the entire voyage.

Taylor occupied himself with teaching Sarah to read. He found her a willing pupil and a delightful, well-mannered companion.

"In New York," he promised, "I will take you to a dance hall, and you will have a chance to teach me."

Every night Sarah bared her back, and Taylor bathed it gently with an herbal solution which Old Lucy had bottled up for him to take. He had the extraordinary sense that his life had been suddenly lifted off its settled course and dropped precipitously onto another. He also felt that he was doing his duty before God. Taylor believed that his race was famed for its humanity and tenderness. It was his conviction that whatever a man did, he did in the sight of God. At the end, every man would stand alone before God and answer to Him for his actions.

244

He had no idea what they would find in the North or when he would see his home and family again. When he was not tending to the girl, he read the works of Rousseau and wrote an essay on rice planting.

In New York, they were received as just what they were: a southern Loyalist and his servant. The weather in the northern city was abominable.

Chapter Sixteen

NEW JERSEY HAD long been a territory of mixed sympathies. Many of the Quakers of south Jersey, philosophically opposed to war of any sort, were open in their attachment to the British government. The region between the Raritan and Passaic rivers had been settled largely by New Englanders, and these civil libertarians were ardent revolutionists. But the people of Sussex, Middlesex, Monmouth, and Hunterdon were ardent Tories, and in Newark and Elizabeth there were also a majority of Tories, all members of the Anglican Church. The Loyalists were prominent and active citizens, many of them owners of large farms and prosperous businesses.

And now, following the retreating American army, British troops were being stationed in New Jersey in a long chain of posts stretching from Staten Island to Princeton. General Howe ordered them to preserve the "greatest regularity and strictest discipline" and particularly to protect the inhabitants and their property. No one paid the least attention to this directive; instead a program of pillage and destruction was launched that seemed designed to render the King's cause unpopular, to turn every Loyalist into a rebel, and to create a lasting hatred for Great Britain and her armies.

It had been a hard campaign, and the rank and file of the armies were determined to take their fun where they found it. British and Hessian alike set out to harvest the spoils of war. The accounts of their murderous progress through New Jersey spread like wildfire and raised a howl of outrage.

Every incident of British abuse was immediately reported to the Americans, and every scrap of news made the rounds of the taverns and camps. Meeting his brother Bayard at The Lion's Head, a busy riverside tavern near Hillsborough, New Jersey, Tom Logan was full of the latest reports of misdoings.

"I have heard that just yesterday Squire William Smith of Smith's Farm in Woodbridge heard the cries of his daughter coming from her bedchamber," Tom began with the relaxed, satisfied tone of a man who has a good story in mind and a good mug of ale before him.

"She was not alone in there, I'll wot," guessed Tom's friend John Scott, who had come along to meet Tom's famous brother. Scott found Bayard to be a decent fellow, not at all proud, and handsome like Tom, save for the deep scar on his cheek.

"Oh, no, the poor girl was not alone in her bed," Tom continued enthusiastically. "When her daddy rushed into her room, he found a swinish Hessian— an officer, big and shaggy as a wild boar—attempting to ravish her. Smith killed the Hessian with his French pistol, and the girl concealed herself in a cupboard, but the officer's men came running in and killed Smith, after they ruined and plundered his farm."

"Terrible," Scott voted. "Unnatteral villains, those Hessians! Why I have heard that a number of young women of the town of Hopewell, to the amount of sixteen, was flying before the enemy and took refuge from their cruel ravages upon a mountain height. 'Twas near the farm of Ralph Hary, I heard. But poor lassies, information was given to the enemy of their retreat, and they were soon carried down into the British camp . . . where they have been kept ever since!''

''Those troops do more for our side than for theirs,'' Bayard commented. ''What can be said to vindicate conduct so atrocious? I have heard that on Wednesday past,'' he said, and not only Tom and John Scott, but all the rebel soldiers congregated at The Lion's Head leaned forward to hear, ''that three women came down to the Jersey shore in great distress. A part of the American army—the militia, I believe under Alexander MacDougall—went and brought them off, and it appeared that they had all been very much abused. . . .''

''Did you see them?'' Tom demanded.

''Yes, I had the sad duty to take their story,'' Bayard admitted. ''The youngest of them was a girl about fifteen years of age, and she was in a dreadful state, having been ravished that morning by a British officer. She said she was afraid to go home, that her mother would beat her.''

''I saw the Ridge Road in Hopewell was littered with skillets and pots,'' a soldier wearing Connecticut brown reported. ''They had taken them from kitchens for the pleasure of spoil and then thrown them aside an hour later. They say the finest houses of Hopewell and Maidenhead are entirely broken up, stripped of every article of furniture, the cattle and sheep driven off.''

''Some of the plundered houses belong to Tories who are out conducting the army to safety,'' Bayard added. "It seems there is no price for protection; or they are simply wild."

"Aye, they are wild beasts," Tom agreed. "In particular, I would judge, are the Hessians."

"Aye, the Hessians," was the general roar around the tavern. "They are cruel devils!"

"Here's to our side," a soldier called out, loud and clear.

"Here, here, here!"

"Death to the lobsters and Hessians!"

"Here, here!"

"And, soldiers and gentlemen," Tom Logan suggested, "Let us drink to the health and success of the ladies!"

"Aye, to the ladies!" the crowd roared, and the few pink-cheeked ones present grew pinker.

The immediate result of demonstrated and well-reported brutality in New Jersey was a local offensive-defensive. Farmers and artisans, as well as regulars and militiamen, took on the British army with furious determination. Sweeping down from the hills and ridges, often at twilight, they made lightning raids on isolated camps to cut off detached groups of men, intercept postriders, capture baggage trains, and drive off cattle. Whenever the British marched along a quiet road, they had to keep a sharp and constant lookout for sharpshooters concealed behind stone walls, bushes, or thickets. It was guerrilla warfare in the tradition of Concord and Lexington, and, indeed, some of the same men were involved.

Riding back to New York after settling some men in south Jersey, General Howe himself narrowly escaped death at the hands of some farmers. A group of farmers armed with muskets lay in wait for him in a ditch. As Howe rode along, preceded by a guard, one of the guard spied a suspicious glint in a hedge of holly, and the farmers were taken as prisoners of war.

To his mistress, General Howe that night admitted that he had been afraid of the consequences of hanging the farmers. "Damn it, if they won't play by the rules, why should we? My guard, Betsy, wanted to hang the locals on the spot, but damn it, I could only think of the reprisals!"

"They'll perish soon enough in the sugar houses," Betsy Loring said. "Don't think of them, Billy."

Inside New York City, food and fuel were becoming desperate concerns, although there was no shortage of commodities of British manufacture. There were pots and pans and knee buckles, hair powder and rum aplenty, but all food stuffs had to come into the city by market boat from Long Island or New Jersey or by convoy from Ireland or England. The convoys were often delayed; market boats depended on the whims of the tides and weather, and after the hard frosts of November, both local produce and dry firewood were in short supply.

Washington, retreating with the remnant of his army through southern New Jersey, had looked anxiously over his shoulder, fearing that Howe, emboldened by his successes, would attack at any moment, or lead the army in a march against Philadelphia. There was every reason to think he would, assuming that he intended to annihilate his enemies. Instead, Howe, who had just received the gratifying news that His Majesty had conferred a knighthood on him, had decided that it was time to settle into winter quarters in New York. Howe, like all conventional military masterminds of his day, closed his mind to the possibility of winter soldiering. There was a season for warfare, and to the British general that season had ended.

Almost as soon as Sir William and his entourage were settled back in Manhattan, the official celebration of his elevation to the peerage took place. Howe's reputation was at its peak. The King had complimented him lavishly and expressed special concern that he was too fond of exposing himself to fire. "Consider," George III had said royally, "how much the public would suffer by the loss of a general, who had gained the affection of his troops, and the confidence of the country."

The celebration was inaugurated with a noon firing of the guns at Fort George, a tremendous noise that rocked the streets of southern Manhattan. As soon as darkness fell, and that hour, in late December, was not long in coming, fireworks were set off near Whitehall Slip by Colonel Montresor.

"A very splendid exhibition," commented Josias, who watched from his office windows. He opened his notebook to record the same, and added, *The snow, which fell the two preceding nights and day, now melting, has made walking out very disagreeable, yet a vast concourse of people, considering the place and its circumstances, were assembled to see the fire-work. Soon I will go home to dress for the General Lord Howe's Entertainment, when he will be publicly invested by his brother with the Order of the Bath.*

A good variety of success attends all matters of my business and the fine union of my interests with those of the Whitestone family. In fact, from what I have heard, all the colonies, for instance, Pennsylvania, are in such distress without free trade with our mother country, that I have concluded (and told Robertson so) that if the fleet constantly blocks up the rebel ports, during next summer

251

this nasty business might be concluded almost without the intervention of the army.

Here Josias put down his notebook and wiped his pen. He had need to make haste to dress for the evening. His sister Bonnie had also been invited to the dinner and dancing; because of his wife's illness, he would escort his sister-in-law, Audrey. Without a doubt, the event would be remarkable and he would need to make more notes on the morrow.

William Howe liked Americans, and he had invited many of them to share his triumph. With the official personages, the military elite, and a sprinkling of miscellaneous Tory sympathizers such as Josias Logan, to say nothing of the brilliantly attired ladies accompanying these gentlemen, the ballroom at Roubalet's Tavern was full. There was an excellent supper and two orchestras playing, one upstairs, one down.

A poem to Sir Howe was read and applauded: ''He comes, he comes, the hero comes:/Sound, sound your trumpets, beat your drums:/From port to port let cannon roar/Howe's welcome to this western shore!''

Admiral Lord Richard Howe took care of the Royal investiture, proclaiming with fraternal pride that he had ''His Majesty's commands to invest this man therewith in the most honorable way.''

''Never was the ribbon more honorably conferred,'' General Robertson promised Josias.

''Nor more honorably invested,'' Josias replied as politely as he could. He had come to despise Commandant Robertson for his annoying attentions to Audrey. To see the old lecher's fingers on his sister-in-law set off a storm of jealous temper which he was hard put to conceal. "Audrey," he said, "let us descend to the taproom for a bit."

"Oh, Josias," Audrey sighed, "but I have just agreed to dance the very next dance with General Robertson!" Audrey was draped in pale blue sateen, cut very low in front and tied up high behind in an exaggerated style that was said to have come straight from Paris.

"Yes," Robertson giggled. "I shall keep Miss Whitestone in a perfect whirl. Just watch, my good man!"

Josias looked stricken, and turned away to see his sister Bonnie, who had been acting very strangely all evening, head to head in conversation with Mrs. Betsy Loring.

"Billy really is a perfect hero," Mrs. Loring was confiding to Bonnie. She waved a gold filigree fan embossed with her initials. "Bonnie, no one knows him as well as I. I tell you he is delightful company, quite the sweetest man in the world. Our life together is perfect heaven. I know there is talk."

"Many people have nothing else to do but talk," Bonnie said. She was not comfortable, or happy to be there. In fact, she was in a terror that Cormick Walker would appear at this event. Every time a dark-haired man came through the door an unpleasant chill wracked her body.

"Are you cold?" Betsy inquired considerately.

Bonnie shook her head.

"Billy's motto, you know, is taken from the King of Prussia. It's: 'Toujours de la gaieté!' Isn't that a marvelous outlook on life?"

"I expect it is," Bonnie said.

"By the way, darling, whatever happened to that lieutenant of yours—what was his name? Winter? Waters? Or was it Walker?"

"He is dead," said Bonnie in a shaky voice.

"Oh, darling!" Mrs. Loring said sympathetically. "Are you provided for? Is there anything I could do to help? Or perhaps Billy? I know he is very fond of you, and I am, too. Really, you should take supper with us one night. We have some marvelous evenings, you know. I don't know where you have been hiding! We haven't seen you at all."

Bonnie had a sudden impulse to tell Betsy the whole story and to ask for her advice. Surely no affair of the heart would surprise this woman whose liaison with General Howe was so widely known and joked about. But Bonnie hesitated. Further involvement with the British military establishment and their social life was the last thing she needed. Increased visibility, especially in that circle, would mean increased danger of being confronted by Cormick Walker.

On the spot Bonnie made up her mind that she must leave Manhattan. Only thus could she escape from the constant threat of meeting Cormick. If she had any influence at all, any hope of protection from General Howe or Betsy Loring, she must use it to this end. She must ask for permission to leave the city and go at once. Perhaps she could persuade Meg to come along with her—if only for a time, persuade her that they would both be safer in . . . in Boston. That was it! She would go to Boston, to her mother's house. Surely General Howe would give her permission to go through the lines in order to visit her old mother.

"What is wrong?" Betsy asked, seeing the play of emotions on Bonnie's face. "My dear, you look almost stricken."

"I have many worries," Bonnie said in a soft voice that sounded at once sweet and brave and a little pathetic. "That is why you have not seen me lately. I have had a letter that my mother in Boston is ill,

254

and I long to go to her. Do you think General Howe
. . . Sir Howe could help me with that?''

"Your mother, dear?" Betsy tried never to think
of her own mother, or any of the Massachusetts connections she had left far behind, but she could acknowledge that others paid tender respects to family
matters. "Just a pass through the lines? I don't expect Billy would mind. Why should he?''

"Oh, it would be so kind!" Bonnie said fervently,
just as she heard a rustle of skirts and felt a nudge
at her elbow. It was Audrey, swaying slightly on
three-inch high heels, rosy from dancing.

"Hello, Bonnie," Audrey said, looking expectantly at Betsy Loring.

"Mrs. Loring, this is my sister-in-law, Audrey
Whitestone," Bonnie said politely. Audrey bowed
respectfully over Betsy Loring's hand and was rewarded with a smile.

"How d'you do? I have heard General Robertson
speak of you," Betsy said. "Really, he is quite an
admirer of yours!"

"Oh, not really!" Audrey cooed unconvincingly,
and Bonnie slipped away as quickly as she could.
Everywhere she looked there were young British officers in splendid evening uniform, and the sight set
her nerves on edge. Bonnie was by nature impul-
sive, and when she had made up her mind to act
she did not hesitate.

"No, thank you, I am engaged. No, thank you,
sir, I cannot," she murmured to the officers who
beset her, requesting dances, as she tried to cross
the crowded room. Now where was Howe? She
would ask him immediately.

Sir William Howe was engaged in a lively debate
with several British officers upon the subject of the

famous prisoner, the arch-rebel Charles Lee, who was now under heavy guard in Brunswick, New Jersey.

"I believe the man is still an officer in the British army," Howe explained. "He has written me urgently demanding what we will do with him . . ."

"Why, he should be shot, as any deserter!" insisted one officer.

"He expects to be politely exchanged," Howe explained. "He has written me twice, as I started to say, to that effect, but I have returned his letters, addressing him as "Lieutenant Colonel Lee." Howe laughed richly. "I have sent my judge advocate general to Brunswick to prosecute."

"The problem is that he resigned his half-pay commission in the British army," explained one of Howe's legal advisors. "There is no clear precedent for this, nor for a retired officer's liability to the call to arms."

"Oh, stuff and nonsense!" Howe exclaimed. "Lee is a deserter. He has turned his back on his responsibilities. He is a traitor and merits death!"

"Should a court martial acquit him, he would sue you for damages," warned the lawyer. "Should the court find him guilty and sentence him to death, the only conceivable penalty, I do believe, you might be attacked as a murderer. I am sorry to say it, but it is so."

"We are hog tied!" Howe concluded.

"I recommend getting an opinion from a high court in England," the lawyer said smugly. "The British court's opinion will protect you."

"And meanwhile?"

"Meanwhile, I suppose it would be safer to bring the rascal into the city," the lawyer advised, and Howe nodded. Just then he spotted Bonnie hovering on the edge of the conversation. "How foolish we all are," he said smoothly, "to be spending this very special night quibbling over traitors. Miss Logan! I am delighted to see you again. Please honor me with this dance."

"Thank you, Sir Howe," Bonnie said politely, and together they moved into the graceful steps of the dance. "Please accept my congratulations on your elevation."

"Thank you. You look very beautiful tonight, my dear, very beautiful."

"Sir Howe! You are too kind!" Bonnie laughed. "I think you have a special appreciation for Boston girls!"

"Perhaps so. Perhaps I do. You are all so radiant."

Bonnie danced in silence for a measure or two and then, still smiling with her lips, she forced a tear to escape one of her big blue eyes. "Forgive me," she begged, "but the thought of Boston has caused me to feel again the anguish I suffer over . . ."

"Over what, dear girl?" Howe asked, leading Bonnie aside and snapping his fingers at a waiter carrying a tray of punch cups.

"Oh, oh," Bonnie sobbed softly.

"Dear child, take a sip," Howe instructed, handing Bonnie a cup of punch as he reached into his waistcoat pocket for a large linen handkerchief. "You look a tragic angel. Now what is the matter?"

Bonnie explained, very briefly, about her poor sick mother and how she longed to go to her. Peering up at him hopefully through tear-laden eyelashes, she asked directly if General Howe would give her a pass across the lines.

"Anything to be of service, my dear," he promised easily. "Call at my office tomorrow to remind me."

Bonnie's smiles of gratitude were like the sun after a shower, but she was relieved when Howe excused himself and she could slip away. I feel nearly as tired as if my tears were real ones, she thought, and though her anxiety was real enough, she managed to laugh at herself. It was in this mood that she spied William Whitestone standing alone near the door.

Seeing him, her heart rose and then plummeted. She could not help it. The sight of him excited her blood, but the brusque way he had treated her at their last meeting—greeting her stiffly and saying nothing more—the distance he had set up and enforced between them, hurt and confused her. And then there was the extreme Loyalist position he took in his newspaper. She could not help but be upset by it—according to the *Messenger* the rebel soldiers— and this included her brothers—had either deserted or suffered starvation. She stared at him, pretending not to stare. She noticed unhappily that he was looking very well.

Finally he came to her himself.

"Good evening, Miss Logan," he said with perfect courtesy. "You are looking lovelier than ever."

"Then do me the honor of being my partner in the next dance," she suggested, steadying her voice to hide her feelings. It was a reel.

"I am the world's worst dancer," he protested.

"Nonsense, I suspect you simply lack practice. The steps are very simple," Bonnie teased. For her, it was heaven itself to be in his arms. "This is the first time we have ever danced together," she said, thinking aloud as the steps of the reel threw them together and then parted them. As he moved down the hall, she admired him jealously—he was well built, if very big and broad, distinctly handsome in a way that made other men look frail and overcivilized.

"I lack the stamina for this sport!" he protested, although his large brown eyes were shining, and when the dance called for a last promenade, his arm was firm around her shoulders and his grip secure on her waist.

"Thank you, sir! A most pleasant partnering!" Bonnie said, bowing, and then took the opportunity to whisper, "I must speak to you!"

"Of course," he said, smiling, but she thought he had misunderstood, until she found her cloak and had gone alone out the door to find her carriage. He was waiting for her there, his hand out, and helped her into his big black carriage.

"I sent your driver home," he said simply. "I will deliver you myself."

"Oh, William! Thank you!" she said, swept with feeling, for she saw him so seldom and was rarely alone in his company. She sat very near him, so near that their knees touched softly as the carriage rocked along the cobbled streets. "How are you?" she asked. She was shaking.

"I am well enough, dear Bonnie, considering the times we live in. I am very busy."

"Yes. I didn't mean to trouble you, but I wanted to take this chance to tell you that I will be going out of town quite soon and . . ."

"Going? How?" She had never seen him so disconcerted.

"General Howe is an acquaintance of mine. I think you know that? At any rate, I . . . well, I asked him for a pass, and he has promised me one. I am very sorry to leave Meg behind, and I shall try to persuade her to go with me, but . . ."

"I doubt that my sister Meg is well enough," he interrupted, "but, Bonnie?" His voice was low and very serious.

She shivered, and he tenderly folded the carriage

robe around her legs, sheltering her with his arm as he spoke softly. "Bonnie, you know that I am very fond of you. I hope you are able to return my fondness, at least in part. It is because I am so devoted to you that I see you seldom, these days. It is better so, in case any disgrace should fall upon me. I do it to protect you, and it is because I do . . . truly love you that I find it so hard to say what I am about to say."

Bonnie shut her eyes. He did love her! Every word he said had the ring of truth, and she believed him. If it were not for the war . . . It was the war that had separated them, the war which had divided their families and caused such bitter misunderstandings.

"I must ask you to do something that might be dangerous to you, although I hope it will not and I do not think it will prove to be. I must ask you to take something through the lines and deliver it safely to someone you know. It will be only a small packet, like a little tract."

"I will do it," she agreed at once.

"You dear girl," he said, pulling her close at once in a rough, smothering embrace. "Don't ever ask me what it is, so that you need not know."

"But where shall I take it?" she asked.

"Take it to your brother Bayard," he said, most surprisingly, and Bonnie's mouth fell open.

"But," she protested, "how shall I find him?" She did not say, I am going to Boston, and it was only later that she realized that he had not even asked her where she planned to go.

"I will tell you everything you need to know before you go. We will meet one more time. Very soon. But Bonnie, my love, let us waste no more time tonight on this subject." And he began to kiss her.

"Oh, very well," she said, "if you insist!" And she gave in to his kisses happily.

Cormick Walker had arrived at General Howe's investiture celebration just in time to see Bonnie Logan step into a big black carriage and leave the premises. He stood outside Roubalet's Tavern for a moment, watching the carriage move out of sight, snow swirling around him in the wind, the yellow light from a lantern making a little circle in the dark night. He had been close to her, as she stepped up into the carriage—as close as he had been in months, but she was not alone. He had to get to her alone.

The wind was keen, and he shivered, finally, and pulled his greatcoat around him before he slipped back into the darkness and disappeared in the direction of the stables.

Having come so close, his determination to get closer was sharpened. He had to get to her. His madness was two edged; he hated her and he was humiliated. To have been injured and ruined by a woman! The shame of it was enormous, and he was determined not to bring the matter into the public eye. He would punish her, but it had to be in secret, for he had told his commanding officer the story that a unit of rebels had stormed the inn and shot him. He had been rewarded for his courage and compensated for his suffering, and no one on earth knew the truth. When he killed her, no one would know why. He meant to do it soon. Perhaps he could manage to enter her house under some pretext. He would go in, bold as brass, and kill her. Perhaps tomorrow.

A lad in the shadows caught sight of Cormick as he passed to the stables, and did a double take at the sight of his face. From one side, it was perfectly normal and as handsome as you please. From the other side, it was frightening, and Cormick knew this from the way people reacted, again and again, even people who had seen it before. He had gotten used to it, and yet he would never be able to ignore it. Sometimes, people's reactions bothered him deeply, sometimes they glanced off. He had become embittered.

"See a ghost?" he spat at the boy.

"No, sir!" the boy gasped, still open-mouthed in shock.

"Well, mind your stupid face!" Cormick snapped.

"Yes, sir," the boy promised, with fear in his voice. The fear made Cormick so angry that he drew his knife, but the boy had disappeared. Cormick went on to the stables; that was his new charge; he was master of Sir William's stables. Horses never minded an ugly face.

Chapter Seventeen

JOSIAS HAD BEEN thoroughly insulted by Audrey's behavior at Sir William's investiture celebration. Laughing and smiling foolishly, she had danced not only with Commandant Robertson but with a roster of foppish—to his eye—young officers, each handsomer and younger, each more confident and self-satisfied, than the last. Although the sight of it had put Josias in a very bad temper, Audrey had taken no notice of it and appeared to enjoy herself utterly.

Once he had even caught her kissing a young corporal in the corner of the cloakroom. He had gone into the unheated anteroom in search of Audrey, who had disappeared from his sight while he was talking to his crony John Moore. And here he had found her, poked into a corner by the barrel-chested officer, squealing like a barmaid at something he had done or said, and he was almost certain that the damned rascal had had his fingers up her petticoats—at least it was the best sense he could make of the rustling and sighing that was going on when he interrupted them.

"Audrey!" he had gasped in anger and shock.

"Good heavens, man!" the officer had said, obviously disgruntled.

"Unhand her, Corporal!" Josias had ordered. "Leave her alone!" Blue eyes snapping, he had seized the man by his waistcoat and tugged with all the fervor of sexual jealousy.

The officer had fled at once, murmuring apologies. "Zounds, sir, I had no idea!"

"What was he trying to do to you?" Josias had asked, but instead of being thankful for his effort to rescue her, Audrey was annoyed.

"Oh, good heavens, Josias, we were but talking," she protested. "It's a party! Aren't you having a good time?"

"It's late. I think we should go."

"It's not late, it's early," she had protested, and turned, smiling as an aide of General Howe's presented himself for the next dance.

Hours later, long after his sister Bonnie had disappeared from the dance floor, Josias had finally succeeded in getting Audrey into her cloak and packing her into his carriage. Even then, all she could talk of was what fun she had had. The drive back to Fair Street seemed a long one to him, for his pride had been sorely wounded. He wanted pretty Audrey for himself, but he had never thought that he should have to compete for her, and what grounds had he for such an effort?

Silently, white with fury, Josias climbed the stairs and went into his own bedroom.

The room was warm; a low fire still burned in the shallow brick fireplace, glowing with coals and a few sticks of fresh wood that snapped and gave off a good light. There was a sweet smell of roses in the room and he could see the shape of his wife's body in the four-poster bed.

"Meg?" he whispered. They had not lain together of late. Meg had suffered complications after her precipitous delivery; at first she had been extremely standoffish, and then he had been entirely obsessed with Audrey.

"I am here, husband," she murmured in a sleepy drawl.

He hesitated, some of his anger and excitement and agitation remaining.

"Come to bed," Meg whispered. " 'Tis late."

Without another word, he unbuttoned his trousers and loosened his collar, shrugged off his vest and waistcoat. The smell of roses was Meg's own smell, and it took him back to simpler days, when she had been the protected daughter of a rich man, when he had come abegging, a stranger in town.

The sheets were smooth, and the bed was wonderfully warm.

"Your hands are cold," she whispered, shivering slightly at his touch. He held her round, full breasts in his two hands, marveling at their softness. Then he bent to kiss them, and moved over her.

She was much plumper than before, and she had let down her yellow hair which was long and straight and fell over the pillows like a skein. Her eyes were closed, but she did everything in her power to encourage him, and he took his pleasure greedily and with great satisfaction.

She was pleased, too, and spoke his name softly as he held her, intermixing it with "husband," an appelation that was far from unpleasing to him. She was not immodest, did not cry out and toss herself about like her sister, but he was very pleased with her, and he felt entirely calmed and restored when he left her, as he did after a time, for he heard a banging in the lower story.

Meg heard him go out of the chamber and wondered where, but she could not stay awake to ask or even worry. More than anything on earth, she wanted a child, and now she might hope for one again.

Downstairs, Josias found not a loose shutter, as he had expected, but Audrey, alone in the parlor with a good fire and a bottle of claret. She turned on him in a fury.

"Have you been with her? Have you?"

Josias was honestly surprised, but before he could frame an answer, Audrey went on.

"I heard you! I listened at the door!" she raged. "You ugly conniver! What gives you the right to turn from me to Meg? You are a nasty deceiver!"

Josias had long preferred not to consider the moral complications of his relations with the sisters. It was part of the unspoken agreement with Audrey that she would not mention it. Coming as he did from the sweet web of pleasure, he felt unprepared to face Audrey's anger, righteous or otherwise.

"Dear, don't be upset," was all he could manage.

In response she hurled her wineglass at his head. It missed, narrowly, and shattered on the hearth.

"It was nothing," he said in a tone edging toward annoyance. He had been nearly asleep; now he was waking fast, but had no idea how to proceed.

A knock on the door saved him. "Is anyone there?" inquired the voice of the cook, Phoebe.

"Everything's all right," Josias said.

The door opened a crack and he could see that Peter stood behind Phoebe and two more servants stood behind them. "We was wokened, Master, by a crash," Phoebe explained.

"Never mind, all is well," Josias assured her impatiently.

Audrey had collapsed on the settee and was starting to cry. She had drunk a good deal during the long evening and was no more inclined than most to accept any blame for an unpleasant situation. When Josias saw that she was weeping, he took heart.

"Don't mind, dear Audrey," he said blandly, for he felt that he had taken back the power in their relationship. He had punished her good and well for her behavior at the party; she did mind; her tears revealed that she did love him. He felt powerful and pleased with himself. He had not planned it so, but it had worked entirely to his advantage.

Sitting next to Audrey, he began to stroke her heaving shoulders and kiss her neck and soon she was melting into his arms.

Meg slept soundly upstairs.

Many said that it was the coldest December in memory, and for Davie Montgomery, confined in the sugar-house prison, the damp coldness was a mortal enemy, if but one of many.

At first, he had been kept for five days without provision of the slightest amount of food. On the fifth day, two robust, handsome, well-dressed officers had come to him—with the other new prisoners—and offered them a chance to enlist in the British army to avoid starvation.

"Will we be as fat as you, then?" Davie had chirped, for he had been in such good health before his capture that the deprivation had left him more lightheaded than miserable. For the remark, he got a blow to the side of his head that made him dizzy, but he was held as a sort of mascot by the other prisoners after that.

After that, they were given food and water, both

in short supply and poor quality. Much of it was condemned provisions from the men of war that choked the harbor. No one who was not starving would have been able to eat it. The flour was wormy, the water polluted and scummy to the eye.

As he was young and small for his age, Davie was one of those permitted to go out of the prison during the day and—under a guard—carry in water and do other chores about the yard. Several of the guards were Hessians, and one of them, Michael Hildebrand, spoke a little English. To amuse himself, Davie tried to talk to him, trading English words for the German and laughing at them.

The rooms of the prison were very crowded and were never cleaned. The excrement of the sick and a surprising quantity of general refuse built up in them to a depth of more than six inches, and this was all they had to use for bedding. Cooking for the entire prison was done in a single copper vat over a fire of scavenged sticks and twigs, which were in ever-shorter supply. Davie learned to pocket bran from the feed troughs of the officers' pigs when he was out on water detail. Cooked, this made a sort of porridge which was much more nourishing than the common fare.

Sickness spread quickly among the prisoners. Swarms of rats spread the plague and yellow fever, and smallpox raged unchecked. Some of the men Davie knew tried to innoculate themselves against smallpox by scratching the sores of infected fellow prisoners with their fingernails.

Every morning, the first sound from the guards was the cry, "Rebels! Throw out your dead!" Every day there were at least ten men who had not survived the night; often there were more. Davie grew inured to the horror and sadness of waking next to a dead comrade. He adopted a prison personality, a hard outer shell of indifference to the others that served to protect him against the constant grinding fear and sadness and suffering. It saved him.

He survived. Only the men with the strongest bodies survived, and many of them went insane. One night all the prisoners locked in with Davie were awakened by the warning cry: "Madman with a knife!" Davie's eyes snapped open at once. A tattered, disheveled figure, a walking skeleton, was lurching through the room, stepping on and over the prostrate sleepers, lashing out with a knife at anyone who tried to restrain him. To save himself Davie crawled under a fat man, bloated by hunger, and cowered there until daybreak.

But through it all Davie had a fixed idea: escape. He had to escape to save his life. It was cold and grew colder daily. He didn't believe he would survive a winter in prison; there was no heat but the cookfire, and fuel was already in short supply. Slowly he endeavored to gain the confidence and friendship of the Hessian soldier who seemed to like him. Bit by bit, he worked toward the idea of a joint escape attempt, singing the praises of life in South Carolina to the soldier so far from home.

By day, Davie walked with the Hessian on the prison grounds and spoke to him of warm weather and plentiful food, of freedom. At night he was marched back into the prison and answered the roll call taken to be sure that all the prisoners were inside. By night he planned what to say to Hildebrand the next day. Finally, he proposed it, but Hildebrand gasped in fear.

"They will catch us and shoot us!" he said in a low, frightened voice.

"Think it over, think it over," Davie pleaded. He counted it as a real victory that the Hessian had not turned him in on the spot. He took great hope from that.

In great contrast to the quarters provided soldier-prisoners were the large and comfortable lodgings set up for the arch-prisoner, General Charles Lee, who had been moved to Manhattan from New Jersey. Lee was assigned to residence in the council chamber of the city hall where he had a large and cozy living room and two smaller chambers. He was furnished with firewood, candles, and excellent food and wine at British expense.

Lee was confined alone, but he had no opportunity to become lonely. He was guarded by an officer and fifty men, and he was permitted to have up to six friends to share his sumptuous table at dinnertime. When he complained, he was allowed to have one of his pet dogs at his side and also his body-servant, Giuseppe Minghini, whom he had picked up years ago on his European campaigns.

From the start, Lee was swamped with guests, including old friends from the British army and many others who were simply curious to meet this famous prisoner. To army friends, especially after a few glasses of wine, he talked freely of the present war and its military structure. To ladies, he was prone to speak of his exotic travels. Most visitors judged Lee to be cheerful; some assumed it was an expression of his courage.

At the time he was captured, Lee had been wearing his dressing gown, greasy leather breeches, and a filthy shirt; although far from a dandy, he felt underdressed and called for the best tailor in town. When Hercules Mulligan arrived, Lee was hard-pressed to decide what sort of suit best fit his present circumstances, so settled on one of powder blue, which was actually rather like the Virginia uniform Washington himself wore. When it was finished, he was delighted with the cut and fit, and he instructed Mulligan to submit his bill to the British high command.

Lee was hardly settled in his new quarters when he received a visit from General Howe. The two generals were more than acquaintances, but had not seen each other for some years. Although both were British aristocrats, they were utterly unlike, and Howe was loath to abandon his conviction that Lee was no better than a common deserter.

"I am honored, honored by your visit," Lee said in an unctuous tone.

Howe held out his hands to the fire. "I see that you are very comfortable here," he commented, his eye taking in the cushions and candles, the flasks and bowls of fruit left over from a late supper.

"Very kind, very kind," Lee murmured. "Yes, it is well enough, for a prison. I have nothing left to sigh for, except my freedom."

Howe dropped his pretenses. "Yes, for a prisoner. You might have got the gallows."

Lee shuddered, an exaggerated gesture that sent his thin shoulders into a sort of convulsion. "Please, Sir Howe! Please!"

Howe made a successful effort to control himself. He cleared his throat. "With all due respect, sir, all due respect. Hmmm. You will be safe here, and the law will take its course." He did not mention that he had sent to England for permission to court-martial Lee.

"Let me speak frankly," Lee enjoined.

"Please do."

"With all her faults, I love my country still," Lee said.

"Oh, you do? I see. Do you mean to relinquish

your current command?'' Howe was surprised at the man's complete lack of morality. Did he see loyalty as a shifting tide? Which army? Which country? For a traitor, for a deserter, Lee had great nerve.

"An irrelevant detail.'' Lee smiled.

Howe was interested now. He paced the large room, stretching his long legs and whirling smartly at the corners. "It is a feckless war,'' he said with unusual frankness. "The rebels cannot possibly win it. They will never become independent!''

"I agree, of course,'' Lee said simply.

"Well then, what in the devil could get into you to be so crazy as to believe it possible?''

"I never did believe it possible. I never did desire independence—only that the hostilities should cease, leaving America free within the Empire. I am far from being the only one who thinks thus.''

"Oh, the Loyalists,'' Howe sneered. "A feeble faction. For the most part, all the best Americans have gone into the rebellion. Which does not mean they will win, only that the country will suffer when they are eliminated.''

"Not just the Loyalists,'' Lee promised. "The rebel elite seeks only a strong bargaining position. How could this callow, beardless country, this juvenile society, hope to manage without their kind parent? The wiser heads among the Philadelphians—the elite, I remind you if you have forgotten or if you have become exhausted by the money-grubbing New Yorkers—consider their Declaration as an interim statement, not a final statement.''

"As what sort of a statement?''

"A statement of position only.''

"Ah.'' Howe rather liked what Lee had to say, even if as a man he was unsavory and shockingly ugly. But still he did not trust him. "I rather favor giving 'em their heads,'' he said at last. "Giving them as much freedom as possible under the flag. It is a new land, after all. And far away."

"If freed, I should continue to use my influence among the Americans to bring about peace negotiations," Lee said boldly.

"Your release is at this time out of the question. Not a negotiable point," Howe said. Had the wily fox been shifting toward this point all along, or was there truth in everything he had said? He felt suddenly weary and thought with pleasant anticipation of the evening he had before him. Betsy had arranged a small but elegant dinner party. A snug nest was a great comfort to a man during wartime.

He is thinking of his little whore, Lee judged accurately. He scrambled to regain the commander's attention. "I am working on a plan," he said, striding to a side table and pulling open the top drawer to show a thick sheaf of papers. "A plan to end the war."

"Really?" Howe drawled, lifting his heavy-lidded eyes.

"As it must end eventually in British victory, my plan is a humanitarian one to make the best of losses on either side. I think myself not only justified but bound in good conscience to bring the matter to the earliest possible conclusion."

"May I see your plan, then?" Howe asked.

"It is nearly finished. I ask your patience. When I have completed it, as I will very soon, I assure you, I would like to put it directly into your hands."

Howe bowed. "I look forward to that day," he said, leaving the room. "Let it be soon."

"Very soon," Lee promised.

Before Lee had been moved to Manhattan, even before he had been cornered and taken prisoner at the inn in Basking Ridge, Washington had seen the boats on the Delaware River and had begun to consider what use he could make of them.

They were unusual boats, planned and built for a special purpose: hauling iron down from Riegelsville, where it was smelted and cast at the Durham furnace, to Philadelphia. They were huge boats, painted black as ink, great beasts of burden. Some of them were a full sixty feet long, eight feet in the beam and three and a half in the hold, but they drew only thirty inches of water. They were called Durham boats.

Casting about desperately for some way out of his present predicament, Washington tried to estimate how many men, how many horses, how many cannon might fit into a Durham boat, and how long it would take to cross the rain-swollen river. It was cold and raining steadily as he sat under a canvas tent and discussed these questions with Bayard Logan.

"John Glover is our man," Bayard said.

"Glover has saved us before," Washington agreed. He did not like to think how many times: Glover and his Massachusetts fishermen had carried the army across the East River in the retreat from Brooklyn. Glover had opposed Howe's landing at Throg's Neck. Glover had moved them across Tappan Zee to Jersey and then whisked the few survivors of Fort Washington across the Hudson.

"He is a fine man, a valuable man," Bayard said.

"Of course," Washington said, but he hesitated. The fact was that he and Glover did not get along. No two men were more unlike: Glover the consummate tight-lipped, tight-fisted Yankee; Washington the patrician Virginia aristocrat. But Washington was not inclined to let personal differences alter his professional behavior; it was Glover who did so, who let it be known that he despised Washington and despaired of his good sense and efficiency.

"Let us go to Glover together," Bayard suggested.

"At once," Washington agreed.

They met with Glover on the river's muddy banks, in a brief period of sunshine. The cold, oblique sunlight cast the barren landscape into high contrast, revealing stiff dead grass, leafless trees, sodden fields, and a high, muddy river. A stiff north wind blew the waters into whitecaps and persuaded all three men to turn their collars up.

"An early winter, and a hard one," predicted John Glover. He was a handsome man with a high forehead and an outthrust jaw. A Marbleheader, he had been a successful merchant and shipowner before the war and stood to make a fortune in privateering as soon as he left the army. He was a solid man with a fortunate mixture of courage and common sense in his makeup, but he had a redhead's touchy temper. It was not like him to admit he didn't know something, particularly anything that dealt with boats or water.

"Yes, an early winter, plenty of snow," he forecast. "The beaver are fat; the geese are long gone."

"The river is high," commented Washington.

"Course," Glover said. " 'Tis snowin' up north."

"I want to take the army across this river, Colonel Glover," Washington said.

"Men and artillery, of course," Bayard added. "And horses." He was counting on his New England kinship with Glover to help mollify the old fisherman; Glover was like dozens of men he had known on the Boston waterfront; he had the clear, deep-set blue eyes of a man who had spent much time at sea, and even his accent was a reminder of home. But he could see that Glover was on edge with the commander in chief.

"Can't be done," Glover said. "It's too late. The river's high, but it ain't crested, and there's a freeze comin' down. You can see it in the clouds."

"But suppose it had to be done," Washington said.

"In what? You don't ferry an army across a flooded river in a few little rowboats."

"Suppose we found the boats. How long would it take?"

Glover looked fed up. "A week," he said firmly.

"Once the army reaches this bank we would have to cross in a few hours," Washington explained. "The British are ten miles away from here."

"Cross in a few hours? Do I look like Jesus Christ to you?" Glover asked insolently. "Do I look as if I could perform a miracle?"

"It has to be done," Washington said.

"How many guns?"

"About twenty."

"And how many men and horses?"

"Two thousand or so, and one hundred."

John Glover's temper was strained to the breaking point. "Can't be done, can't be done," he muttered.

"Only you could do it," Washington said soothingly. "Come now and have a look at these boats."

Shivering in the wind, the three men walked along the river's edge to a point where they could look down on a fully laden Durham boat. Glover had seen plenty of boats in his lifetime, but he had never seen a Durham boat. His eyes lit up.

"By God! That boat looks like the right boat for this river." He scrambled down the muddy bank, almost forgetting the other two in his curiosity. He sized up the possibilities at once and swallowed his resentments. Bayard jumped down the embankment to stand at his side and watched the old fisherman judging the draw and the keel, the beam and the timbers that formed the hold. Glover was pleased; anyone could see he was pleased.

"This boat is all right," he told Bayard and then he called up to Washington, "If you can get hold of twenty of them, I'll be damned if I can't take your damn army across the damn river in a jig's damn time!"

"Thank goodness," Washington murmured.

Having built a fire under John Glover, Washington then set out to get ahold of at least twenty Durham boats. As ever, he depended heavily on his Virginia countrymen, whom he trusted above all others. He summoned the Virginians Wade Hampton and William Maxwell to his tent.

"Have you seen the Durham boats on the river?" They had.

"I want you to get them for me."

"Do we pay for them?" Maxwell asked, knowing in his heart what the answer would have to be.

"With what?" Washington asked. "Oh, if you must pay, pay. Give them receipts, give them script, give them promissory notes. Whatever it takes. Whatever works." For months, Washington had been paying for things out of his own pocket, out of the pockets of his friends. Congress had no money. Everything, everyone—except spies—was to be paid with promises.

"Yes, sir." Maxwell, the most loyal of "old countrymen," still speaking with the thickest of brogues, was one of Washington's favorites.

"What about the iron works?" Wade Hampton asked.

"I don't give a damn about the iron works," Washington said. "Let them take a holiday. But get a hundred men on horseback to ride with you, and gather the Durham boats. You have three days.''

"A week, sir?'' Hampton ventured, thinking that ten days might be possible.

"Three days at most. And the Durham boats must be the only boats left on the river for, say, thirty miles up and down.''

"Thirty miles?'' Both Virginians, and Bayard as well, were struck by the commander's tense vitality. He had changed in the last weeks. He was more decisive than ever; he was thoroughly in command.

"Burn the rest of the damn tubs and warm your backsides; sink 'em or smash 'em, but get rid of them. When we have the Durham boats, we want to have the river to ourselves.''

"Who else would want it?'' Maxwell asked, and they all had a laugh, but Washington had the last word.

"Get the boats in three days,'' he ordered.

Chapter Eighteen

WITH HER BREAKFAST, Bonnie received a brief note in William Whitestone's bold scrawl. *Will you meet me for tea at Mrs. Shepherd's House at four?* it asked. She sent back word that she would, and spent the day in hurried preparation for her journey, for she had met with General Howe the day before and obtained the promised official pass through the lines.

Everyone in the Logan household was busy assisting with Bonnie's preparations to travel. Bonnie had told Josias that she had received word of sickness in Boston and permission from General Howe to go there. Josias seemed not surprised at all, and although concerned for their mother, rather oddly pleased—perhaps to know that his sister was on such good terms with Howe, or that she would be gone from his house, she was not sure which. He had given her some money. Josias seemed pleased with everything these days, and even Meg was less unhappy, although she had been disappointed that she could not accompany Bonnie or persuade her to leave Dorothy in her care.

Meg had insisted on having the very best horse

and chaise readied for Bonnie, and she packed up a wooden traveling chest with a compendium of practical goods and foodstuffs to last the entire way, in case she found herself outside an inn and in need of comforts. After much debate, it was decided that she would also take along Prudence, the housemaid most used to caring for Dorothy.

"You will come back, won't you?" Meg asked again and again, wiping the tears from her eyes. "I really wish you would not go at all!"

"But you know I must," Bonnie said in a low voice, for Meg knew her decision to flee the city was based on the need to avoid Walker.

"I know that you must," Meg agreed. "But I shall miss you so! Dear Lord, I hope you will be safe! I would do anything to keep you here safely by my side."

"I will be safe," Bonnie promised, feeling even more sure of it since she had agreed to meet William again, and they were connected, at least in the transaction of his business, whatever it might be. It was curious that he should want to send a parcel to Bayard, but there were many things during wartime that defied understanding. The name "spy" never even crossed her mind; it was too dangerous a word, nor did she think of breaking any law to carry a parcel to her brother Bayard. To think of seeing Bayard again! It could not be wrong, for the contemplation of it, of doing whatever William asked, filled her not with fear or doubt, but with happiness, for she would be aiding those most dear to her.

And escaping Cormick Walker as well. Truth to tell, Bonnie's fear of Cormick had swept nearly every other consideration from her mind. She must leave New York, and until she was safe she could not stop to question her decision or William's motives.

But if Bonnie faced her journey without guilt or

fear, William's frame of mind more than made up for it.

It was with the most extreme trepidation that William Whitestone prepared the packet of information which he intended to send to General Washington via Bonnie Logan. It was a departure from his usual routine in every sense—messages to the commander in chief usually traveled a circuitous route from Manhattan to Setauket, Long Island, and from there across the Sound to Connecticut, then down the coastline to the general's headquarters near the border of New Jersey and Pennsylvania. But something was awry with his usual avenues of information-sending—oddly awry, for he had received no messages or messengers from Long Island for more than a week—and he was in possession of some tremendously important, tremendously exciting material that must be sent over the lines to the rebel leader at the first opportunity.

Unwittingly, Bonnie had helped him before—long ago she had concealed a book holding a message in her babe's cradle, and she had visited Mrs. Murray at his bidding on the fateful day the British entered the city, not realizing the import of the message she had carried there. He reminded himself that she was a well-to-do, independent woman, able to take care of herself. Inside the city she was the widow of a British officer and because of her residence with her brother Josias Logan, she was almost above suspicion. Outside the city, she could take on the persona of the sister of two rebel soldiers, one of them close to Washington himself, and wherever she went, her sex and beauty would serve as her protection. Taken impartially, she seemed a good purveyor, but it was impossible for William to take Bonnie impartially, and it had been so from the first day he met her.

Nonetheless, he prepared the document. It had

come into his posession in a singular way, but one that made it impossible to doubt its authenticity. James Andrew Feversham, a gaunt, bearded man who served as scribe and assistant secretary to Lord Howe, had come into the coffeehouse in a great hurry, demanding to buy paper.

Trusting William as he did, Feversham had rambled on about his job and its difficulties. The latest shipment of paper intended for official military use, he complained, had been lost at sea, and there was none at all in Howe's offices. He had an urgent bit of transcription to complete—General Howe wanted it done yesterday, of course—and he hadn't even stopped for a bit of lunch.

William listened sympathetically, sold him the paper, then persuaded Feversham to sample the mutton stew being dished up in the tavern. Feversham followed his nose to the savory stew, leaving his new paper and a bundle of manuscripts in the printshop.

While Feversham ate heartily, William had strolled back into the print shop from the coffeehouse and calmly, as if perusing his own proofsheets, read the papers. The first was astonishingly entitled: *Lt. General Sir William Herbert Howe/His Plan for the American Campaign/For the year A.D. 1777.*

Without a moment's hesitation, William had stood over the document at the open type case and, fingers flying, working faster than he had ever before, set—backward, printer's style—the entire document in type. No man in the colonies set type faster than William; his fingers flew over the open case, selecting letters without looking at them and moving on to the next nearly apace with the eyes on the page. The door to the coffeehouse stood open as William worked and he kept an eye on Feversham, although the sight of a raisin pudding had almost entirely filled the secretary's greedy eyes.

By the time Feversham had lunched, enjoying an extra cup of ale on the house, and enjoyed a smoke, he wandered back into the shop, but the tight columns of standing type meant nothing to him; he didn't even notice them. By the time he returned to his desk, burping happily, William had coolly locked the type into a bed, inked it and proofed it.

It was this he hoped to send to Washington as fast as he could, but he had been at a loss about how to send it until he learned that Bonnie was leaving town. He had printed the document clearly on a sheet of his best paper, then pasted on a false front, a detailed fashion brochure lately received from London showing a splendid *robe à l'anglaise* open over a full petticoat, hand-tinted in apple green and silver. It was the sort of paper a fashionable lady might well single out and save, a keepsake that would not look out of place in Bonnie's trunk of gowns and petticoats.

Entering Mrs. Shepherd's Tea Rooms in late afternoon, William spotted Bonnie in a corner near the fire, completely hidden in a woolsey cloak of most ordinary green stuff with a hood that had been pulled back to reveal her red-gold hair. She looked relieved to see him.

"My dear Bonnie," he said.

"Oh, thank goodness you have come." He assumed she was anxious about her journey, but that was not it; she was never free, these days, of the fear of Walker's getting her. She shrugged off the cloak, revealing a gown of soft gray velvet that set off her blazing hair and angelic features to perfection.

He spoke in a low tone. "I could give you a letter of introduction to use when you get across the British lines, but I have faith that you will do better on your own. Mention my name to no one. Ever. You are what you seem to be: a woman seeking to find and help her soldier-brothers. Just ask for Washington until you find the army, then ask for your brother until you see him. When you find Bayard, give him this paper and he will take care of the rest."

William hesitated. Bonnie's immediate, simple trust had the effect of humbling him. How frail she seemed to be, how small and slim, how excessively pretty, and yet he knew she was remarkably brave and spirited. "I should worry about you," he said teasingly, "did I not recall your passion for precipitous journeys and your cold courage in the face of danger! Will I ever forget the night I found you in the bottom of that fishing boat, having crossed the harbor without permission? You were as wet as a seal and quite drunk, if I remember correctly! A journey with an official pass may seem too tame for your tastes."

Bonnie grimaced at the mention of the fishing boat. It had been that night that she had found Cormick, quartered on Staten Island. Enraged when she had discovered her husband's trickery, she had found the courage to shoot him. But during the miserable ride back across the Hudson; she had been certain she would be caught and imprisoned. But it hadn't happened. Instead, she had been greeted on shore by William. Now, as she was leaving him, she tried to rid herself of worries—and laughed. "I daresay I shall make out all right!"

He turned serious at once. "I shall think of you and miss you every day until we meet again, and wish you Godspeed. Your mission is a very important one. Do not even consider failure, and its specter will elude you."

Bonnie raised her hand to his face and very gently

caressed his cheek. "Until we meet again," she whispered.

He rose to go, pressing a fashion brochure into her hand as he did. "Give this to Bayard; keep it with your nightgowns until then," he suggested.

Bonnie was surprised to see that he had given her a pamphlet about a new *robe á l'anglaise*. It was an awfully pretty one, and she admired it for a moment before she folded it and thrust it into her pocket. But immediately her thoughts turned back to William—now she had to say good-bye.

"I'll leave in the morning," she said, and at that moment he loved her terribly and did not dare even begin to tell her so.

"Farewell," he said simply, and touched his lips to her hand. He left the room at once, his large frame dwarfing the tiny round tables, his greatcoat brushing them as he passed.

Bonnie took a deep breath and decided to have another cup of tea before she left. Her fingers trembled. She scolded herself. Whatever happened, she must remain cool.

Standing in the shadows across the street from Mrs. Shepherd's Tea Rooms, Cormick Walker had seen William Whitestone, the famous Tory publisher, go into the tea room, come out a few minutes later, and walk north. He thought nothing of it. Shifting his weight from side to side, stamping his feet in the cold, he continued to wait for Bonnie Logan.

He knew she was there. He had seen her go in. He had followed her from her house on Fair Street, almost catching up to her before she went into the tea room. It had been a long time since she had come out of her house alone, and he was sure this was his day. He would get her today—as soon as she came out. It was no good going in after her. She would scream when she saw him. He had to surprise her, get her alone. And then he would kill her, and that would silence her forever. Nothing else would satisfy him, after what she had done to him.

But when Bonnie had left the house earlier, Meg had watched idly from the window and had been startled to see a man appear from behind a hedge and follow her. Meg recognized him as the soldier from Peck's Slip—Cormick Walker! Filled with concern for Bonnie, she had followed both him and Bonnie from Fair Street, had waited within twenty feet from Cormick, watched her brother William enter and leave the tea rooms, and now crept closer to Cormick.

Meg was cold with fear and steady with purpose. She carried a small Italian pistol which she had impulsively taken from Josias's desk, and although she had never fired a pistol in her life, she intended to do so now.

"Don't move or I shall shoot you," she said in a low voice.

Cormick Walker was completely surprised. He had not heard her approach. He whirled violently and faced a very small blond woman in a fancy, silver-trimmed velvet cloak who was pointing a pistol at his head. He stared at her without recognition, thoroughly confused: Who was this? Should he know her? Had he somehow wronged this woman?

And then it all flooded his mind: how Bonnie had fooled him, how she had lured him into complacency, used her wiles to put him off guard, how she had fired at him, ruining him, leaving him hideous to face the rest of his life. This was not Bonnie, but it was a woman just like her.

"God damn it, you whore!" he swore blackly, slapping at the pistol as if it were an annoying insect. Meg squeezed the trigger as she lost control of the aim and a bullet grazed his neck.

It completely unhinged his wrath. Twice! To be fired at twice by these damned American women, the most dangerous and treacherous creatures who ever drew breath! Roaring like a wild animal, he seized Meg tightly with both arms and began to shake her like a doll. Meg let loose a scream, loud and fierce.

"Help! Help me! Help!" she shrieked and the dim side streets burst forth with people, ragged tenement folk and all the proper patrons of Mrs. Shepherd's Tea Rooms, save Bonnie, who not knowing it was Meg involved took advantage of the commotion to slip out and away.

"Hey, leave her!"

"Let her be, you brute!"

"Stop at once, I say!" shouted a volunteer street patrolman, oddly official-looking in a banded black hat. The neighborhood had formed up a patrol to protect themselves, and especially their women, from the occupying soldiers and their lusts. There had been incidents aplenty. This was not the first; the damned British, who thought themselves superior, were not much better than wild Indians.

"Stop, soldier! I have the authority, and I shall shoot!"

Cormick fled, dropping Meg on the street, and was pursued up an alley by an army of small boys throwing stones.

"You'll be all right," the patrolman advised Meg, bending over her. "Good heavens, it's a lady!" he exclaimed.

"I am Mrs. Logan. Please take me home to Fair Street," Meg gasped, for she was not really hurt, only shaken.

"That I will, Mrs. Logan," the patrolman said,

recognizing the name and already anticipating a generous reward from this society lady's husband.

"Those officers think they can do whatever they fancy with our young girls," was the comment on the street.

"He was an ugly-lookin' fellow."

"Dreadful ugly."

During the first nights after the army had finally reached the western bank of the Delaware, Thomas Logan still dreamed he was on the march. He was exhausted, filthy, and stunned. For the past weeks his life had been a pattern of retreat and defeat, sleeping, eating, and marching in a state of sustained tension unlike any other. They had marched about two hundred miles, always aware that the enemy was near and that the countryside was full of Tories.

Sometimes he could not remember that there had been a time when he was not in the army, had not slept side by side with these men, huddled for warmth like hogs in the mud, had eaten foul bread and thin meat with them, breathed and cursed and prayed with them and made night fires of nearby fences with the rag-tag brotherhood of soldiers who were his closest friends and dearest family.

There was also his brother, whom he had not seen daily, but saw often enough—when they were in the same camp—to know that they were both pulling the same load. He was proud of Bayard, and he knew that Bayard was proud of him, and both of them loved Washington, would give their lives for him. Washington was almost godlike; he held it all together in their minds, for he was always pleasant to the soldiers, never changing his countenance, but wearing the same in defeat and retreat as in victory.

Tom had come south with General Sullivan after General Lee's capture. Sullivan had marched them south nearly on the double. These troops were unusual in that most of them had shoes, and General Lee had commandeered jackets for them, paying a New Jersey merchant in new-minted Continental specie. Still, they were a ragged, destitute lot, shockingly dirty. Most of them were still in their summer clothes, some nearly naked. Nearly all of them had the rash. Tom's friend William Knox had it so bad that his breeches stuck to his thighs, all the skin being worn off, and at the same time played host to hundreds of vermin. Poor William's feet were so swollen that he had been unshod for weeks; he bound his big feet in strips of raw beef hide, tied on like moccasins with thin strips of gristle. In moist weather, this served, but when it froze the hide rubbed his toes so that they bled freely.

They were not a healthy army. Taken as a whole, six of ten soldiers were sick and three would never recover. Many in Tom's company had influenza or dysentery, or had just gotten over some disease. Bronchitis and pneumonia were common. Jaundice and syphilis and liver ailments were constant. They were tired, very tired. And everyone's enlistment was nearly due to expire; nobody forgot that, not a man of them.

As they approached the rest of the army, Sullivan and his second in command, Alexander Scammel, rode proudly at its head. Both Sullivan and Scammel had dressed up for the occasion—on Washington's command. Both wore clean white shirts, brushed coats, black boots, and cocked hats. Both showed off their bright epaulets and polished swords, and they led their men into camp to the brave sound of fifes and drums. Washington had wanted music—good or bad, tuneful or amateurish, as long as it was loud and clear.

And he got it. In Sullivan's force were four trumpets, seven fifes, and twenty drums and men musical enough to play them. Every one of them played from his heart as Sullivan's two thousand men came stepping smartly along into camp. And seeing them, Washington's own troops broke into cheers, the first cheers in quite a while, yahooing and whistling and yelling "Razza-doodle-doo" at the handsome sight.

Bayard saw his brother at once in the file. Tom's clothes were ragged and as filthy as a beggar's, and his lively brown hair hung almost to his waist. His face was covered with whiskers, but he looked fine, and healthy, and indeed, he had grown even taller. Bayard stared, drinking in the happy sight, letting it fill his eyes and heart. Then, to his amusement, he realized that all the soldiers were covered with hair. In an age where the fashion was long hair tied in a queue at the back of the neck, most men who could not afford a barber and wigmaker kept their own at shoulder length, but these men had gone weeks without washing or shaving, and their hair—red and yellow, brown and black—streamed down their shoulders and backs. Some of them had even twisted it into fat braids to keep it out of the way. Bayard stifled a laugh.

Behind the ragged Massachusetts boys strutted Johnny Stark's contingent from Vermont, conspicuous in fringed shirts and leather leggings and fur caps. When it was their turn to pass Washington they sang: "Oh listen to the singing/Of the trumpet wild and free!/Full soon you'll hear the barking/Of the rifle from the tree!/Oh the rifle! Oh the rifle!/In our hands 'twill prove no trifle!"

Washington watched, tall in the saddle, without moving a muscle, but Bayard knew that he was pleased. He had waited so long for these reinforcements. He looked them over, judging their health, their dress, their spirits.

And then, behind these men were more. It was the army under General Horatio Gates and Colonel Benedict Arnold, eight or nine hundred more troops. They had all come in at once! Washington counted them without moving, his eyes widening, and then he broke into a grin. "Well," he said. "Well done!"

In the next few minutes the armies all came to a halt and broke ranks, shouting for joy to see sons and brothers and relatives and friends again. Tom ran to Bayard and threw himself into his arms. William Knox found his brother Henry, who began to scold him for his lack of shoes. There was weeping and laughing and hugging and wrestling between them, and a raucous rendition of "Yankee doodle, keep it up, Yankee doodle dandy; mind the music and the step, and with the girls be handy!"

"It's been a while since I ate a hasty puddin'" Tom laughed to Bayard. "Can't say I wouldn't fancy one, or a Christmas puddin', black with raisins."

Bayard had good news. "There was a package from Mother," he said, "and she sent you fur gloves."

"Fur gloves! Fur gloves!" Choking on the marvelous idea of them, Tom grunted with excitement as he dug into the rest of his Christmas package from Boston. There they were: gloves of softest fur, plus sweet biscuits, a knife, a little sewing packet, three handkerchiefs and a shirt.

"A shirt!" Tom raved, "a shirt! Look at this shirt!"

While the men were still celebrating, Washington called together his generals for a conference. He met with them at his temporary headquarters, the stone house belonging to William Keith in Makefield, four miles north of Newtown, Pennsylvania. His first shock was the news that the armies which had just been brought to him had only two weeks left to serve. He had assumed that they had already been reenlisted. It was a cruel joke; he had waited so long for them.

The commander in chief turned away from his generals. He stared out over the encampment; men everywhere were building cookfires, carrying equipment, moving horses, erecting huts of pine boughs and mud. The sky was steel gray and threatened snow; it was a sky he had come to know well since leaving Virginia. "This news is both distressing and mortifying," he said in a sad voice.

When Washington requested reinforcements from New England, Benedict Arnold was brusque: to him the situation was next to hopeless.

"New England is begging me for help," Arnold said. "The British have captured Rhode Island and may soon march on the mainland."

"Spencer is gathering men in Providence," Washington agreed. All he could think of was that on January first his force would be reduced to twelve hundred men.

"I request permission to go at once to Boston," Arnold said, and Washington agreed that he should go.

That left Gates. Gates was a man whose reputation far exceeded his usefulness; by this time he had given up all hope of winning this war. Instead, like General Lee, he had turned his mind to calculating how best to bargain with the British. He looked past the war, past the eventual settlement. What would be left for him? Washington would never know, never be able to credit to what extent Gates was his enemy, but he did know that the man was a plotter who considered himself far more fit for the supreme command of the army than Washington. Still, Washington was rigorously polite; he needed help and advice, and he had great respect for Gates's military expertise.

"God forgive me, I am weary," Gates complained.

Kindly, Washington called for a special dinner for two: for his own silver and linen, for some vegetables to vary the diet of salt beef and fire cake prescribed by the army. He sent Bayard to order a decent piece of meat, to find some carrots, some turnip, some parsnips, perhaps, to add character to the stew. He opened a bottle of his best Madeira on the spot and poured Gates a glass.

The Keith house was small and the life of that busy household went on outside the closed door of the room where General Washington dined with General Gates. Gates ate heartily, unbuttoned his waistcoat, wiped his flushed face, and suggested a second bottle of wine. He was a large, heavyset man who looked much older than his fifty years. Soldiers called him "Granny" Gates, for his nagging manner as well as his spectacles, and he heard Washington out with thinly disguised impatience.

Washington now took Gates into his confidence. He had a simple, direct plan. He had done everything to keep the plan a secret up to now. He had made preparations already. They must attack the British, by surprise.

"Attack, my dear Washington? To attack, you will need an army!" Gates blustered, trying to make a joke of it.

Washington was not joking. "We will take every man on the west bank, which I judge to be about six thousand men, and divide the total force into three brigades, cross the river at three separate points, and attack the Hessians at Trenton.''

''My good sir! Your troops always move in one direction! To attack they should have to move in the other direction!'' Gates roared at his own wit.

''We must lead the men to victory,'' Washington said a bit stiffly.

''Everyone is aware that there remain but eleven days until the bulk of the enlistments expire,'' Gates said.

''Certainly I am.''

''Well, then, why should the men involve themselves in a battle at this late date? Why should they? They want only to stay alive until it's time to go home.''

''We must call on them to follow the orders of their officers.''

''They are not real soldiers. They are ragged, filthy volunteers.'' The words caught in Gates's throat; he did not mean all of them; he had a high regard for the New Englanders, a rugged bunch. Nonetheless, Gates did not believe the men out in the Pennsylvania snow and mud were ready to fight. They were exhausted and despairing.

''I think the men will stand very well.''

''Bah! I expect you think that, being in surprise, the attack will succeed. How is it possible to cross the river and keep it secret? Every damn German will see you coming and take good aim.''

''We will cross at night.''

''At night? Impossible! I never heard of such a thing. It would take hours! Long before they all reached shore, the Hessians would be lined up on the bank with all their big guns. Your boats would be shot to bits; men would drown at once in that cold river.''

Washington had the sense that he had tapped the

ravings of a grim prophet. Everything Gates said was true, yet it was absolutely necessary to make an attempt. He believed Gates was wrong when he said the men would not fight. The men who were left were stalwart; they would hold.

Gates went on. "Even if you had enough men to risk it, say fifteen thousand well-equipped soldiers, you could not beat the Hessians. The Hessians are professional soldiers. They are the best. Your ragged schoolmasters and farmhands are no match for them. And guns? How many guns have you? Ten? Twelve? In a proper army there would be a gun for every fifty men. You need one hundred and twenty guns, dear sir!"

The effect of hectoring is to make a stubborn man hold firm. "We must take the chance," Washington insisted. "We have a chance and we must take it."

Gates wondered if he had made a mistake. The New York Committee of Safety had urged him to disobey Washington's summons and take his troops instead to reinforce Lee, create a separate army, independent of Washington's command, to fight in the Hudson Highlands. But he had marched straight south instead, and good luck that he had—Lee had been captured. Or was it good luck? Now he had to deal with Washington, who was about as giving as a stone fence. Washington had begun this conversation by asking advice, but it was obvious that he had already made up his mind what he wanted to do.

"A general must be everything," said Gates, "and that is much to ask of one man." It was his way of acknowledging that Washington was in charge, that it was in the end to be his decision.

"What would you do, under the circumstances?" Washington asked finally.

"Retreat. When you can neither fight nor hold, the duty of the soldier is to retreat."

"We have had a bellyful of retreat," Washington said.

In the morning, Gates and his aides rode off toward Philadelphia, but his brigade of eight hundred men stayed behind.

"General Gates is ill," Washington explained to his officers. "He must go to Philadelphia to comfort himself."

Gates went to look for Congress and found Philadelphia gloomy and silent, the streets clogged with goods and wagons. The city's solid citizens were fleeing the imminent British attack. The mood was one of panic. A rumor circulated constantly that the British would burn the city; merchants would not accept Continental paper money; and a certain element in town was said to "exult" at the approach of the enemy.

Chapter Nineteen

NOTHING COULD STOP Bonnie from leaving New York when she learned what had happened to Meg outside Mrs. Shepherd's Tea Rooms, but she did concede the danger of taking Dorothy with her, especially on a winter journey, and finally agreed to leave the baby in Meg's loving care.

Meg was somewhat bruised from her beating, but bid Bonnie farewell with a calm and serenity based chiefly on courage. "You know that I will care for darling Dorothy, as my own," she promised Bonnie. And then, mixed in with her parting kisses, she confided her news, "and I expect to be a mother myself in summertime."

"Dear Meg!" Bonnie was surprised, although she did not like to show it, for consideration of Meg's feelings. "Oh, my dear. You must take care of yourself."

"I surely will," Meg promised.

"I shall be back long before that," Bonnie said. There was no more time to talk; she was gone, leaving while it was still dark, driving north along the Post Road while the sky lightened and the sun rose and the ground was white with frost.

The chaise was a fine one indeed, and she shared the cozy double seat with the shy young servant girl, Prudence, both of them swathed in warm cloaks. Prudence had not wanted to come, and had shed tears the night before, but this morning she had come willingly enough, although she was silent, wrapped in a bright red cloak with a fur-trimmed hood, and a tippet that she had turned up to hide her face.

"You will be well enough," Bonnie told Prudence. Prudence did not answer but Bonnie believed she was right. She felt nothing but relief until she felt sure that no one was following them, or watching them go, and then she felt sadness and terrible guilt at leaving Dorothy.

"I must go, I must," she whispered to encourage herself.

"What did you say, miss?" Prudence asked in a funny voice.

"Nothing. Fasten that buckle, Prudence, if you please. I think that strap is rattling against the railing."

By noontime, the sun had burned away the morning's fog, and Bonnie's pass from General Howe had produced not only safe passage, but a mounted escort through the lines at Kingsbridge, and their journey had fairly begun.

Audrey had gone to John Ramage's studio on William Street where he had set about painting the portraits of military heroes and other garrison beaux, as well as all the prettiest girls in town. When Audrey had heard that the De Lancey sisters had been painted, nothing would do but that she should go, also, but to her distress, it was a tedious process which consisted of sitting patiently for hours on end

298

while the artist worked silently at the easel. She had endured two sittings already, but always returned in a bad temper.

This time, she came home to the house on Fair Street to find that Bonnie had left and that her sister Meg had settled herself in front of the drawing-room fire, with little Dorothy in a basket at her knee, and was very busily involved in piecing a baby-sized quilt entirely of scraps of blue and pink satin. To Audrey's annoyance, instead of looking wan and sour, instead of hiding in her room, Meg looked not only content and satisfied, but full of glee.

"Whatever is wrong?" Audrey asked aggressively.

"Nothing at all, sister."

"I see you have Bonnie's poor child here."

"Yes, I am delighted to have care of Dorothy."

"I suppose it eases your pain that you will never have a child of your own."

"I shall leave that in God's hands," Meg said serenely.

Audrey could not miss the satisfaction in her voice. She stared at her sister, who looked rosy and, yes, a bit plump. "Do you mean to tell me something?" she asked threateningly.

"Oh, Audrey, I did mean to tell you, but I thought you might guess. It's true. I am expecting a child."

Audrey was far angrier than she wanted to show. "Well, I am sure!" she snapped and left the room.

As soon as Josias came in from his offices, Audrey cornered him. "Do you know that your wife is pregnant?" she asked directly.

"Well. Well, my dear . . . ," he stammered.

"How foolish she is," Audrey said contemptuously. "I doubt if the child will ever be born."

Josias was shocked. "You should not say such a thing!"

"Are you my moral instructor, then, as well as my seducer?" Audrey asked sarcastically, and in that moment, Josias was afraid of her, for she was very angry, and did not seem to feel ordinary things as ordinary people did. He backed away, but her words followed him.

"Mark my word, she will never live to bear a child!"

And after she had decided to kill her sister, Audrey began to think how to do it. Poisoning seemed the simplest and easiest way. From time to time she carried a pot of tea to Meg in the mornings, just so that when the time came, she would be able to do it without arousing anyone's suspicion.

After a few hours of Prudence's silence, Bonnie lost her temper. Whatever Bonnie said, the girl only nodded and ducked further back into her hood, which entirely hid her face. "Why are you such a sulky girl?" Bonnie asked rudely.

Prudence pulled off her hood, and Bonnie gasped in surprise. It was not Prudence at all, but tiny, white-blond Isannah, the indentured serving girl who was Tom's sweetheart.

"I knew you would not take me, so I came anyway," Isannah blurted out. Her voice was saucy and bold, but she was more frightened than she showed.

"You are a naughty girl!" Bonnie exclaimed, but she was not really angry.

"I wanted to come; Prudence did not, so I gave her my best handkerchief and a needle case made of Spanish leather," Isannah explained. "I had to come. Perhaps we will find Tommie."

"But what of your master?" Bonnie asked.

"He will get along without me," Isannah said shortly. She was pleased with herself. During her years in America, she had never left Manhattan, and although she had not the faintest idea of where they were going, or of Bonnie's mission, she was happy to be going somewhere.

Despite everything, Bonnie had to laugh at Isannah's boldness and ingenuity. After all, Prudence was a skilled baby nurse, and she had not wanted to come; perhaps it was just as well that she had stayed with Meg and Dorothy.

"Mind you don't tell anyone you have fled an indenture," she warned Isannah.

"I shall never breathe a word," Isannah promised. And from there on, she was very good company to Bonnie.

Whenever they were alone together, Davie Montgomery spoke to the Hessian, Michael Hildebrand, about escape. Instead of just "no", Hildebrand began to say, "but what if?" and when Hildebrand was unjustly beaten for a gate left open, he began to talk about escaping from the sugar-house prison as if it were a reality.

Davie had a plan that was both bold and simple. Every night at dusk, the roll of prisoners who worked outside on wood and water detail was called as they filed inside the main gate. Hildebrand would hide him during roll call, and then they would go off in the first dark together.

Davie was small, as small as his friend was large, although they were of exactly the same age: sixteen. Davie had no coat at all, but Hildebrand had a thick, rough overcoat the same forest green as his uniform, and it hung nearly to his ankles.

The day came when they could wait no more. The

301

weather was dreary, and everyone was impatient to get to their suppers and fires. It had been drizzling all afternoon and twilight came early. Michael Hildebrand was assigned sentry duty; he stood sentinel near the drawbridge and the big main gate. When the roll was called, and the officer of the day shouted out, "Montgomery!" the Hessian supplied, "He's gone in. That little boy is cold!"

Davie stood right behind the guard, hidden entirely by the warm length of Hildebrand's watch cloak. He stood perfectly still and waited breathlessly. Finally, suspecting nothing, the officer left the prison yard and Davie and his Hessian friend were alone, together, and outside.

"Let's go!" Davie whispered, but before he could move, a captain on horseback rode into the yard.

"What are you doing there?" he demanded.

In German, Hildebrand answered, "Everything in order, sir," and the captain rode away. Davie had climbed Hildebrand's back like a monkey, clinging as flat as he could to the German's broad shoulders and belt, knees tight about his waist.

"We be set to go," Hildebrand said finally, and strode out of the prison yard with Davie still concealed under his cloak.

"Luckily for us it's a rainy night," Davie said in a soft, surprised voice. Fog from the harbor and the two rivers rolled through the streets like thick smoke. He had planned for this moment, staked his life on it, had prayed it would come to pass, but now that he was free in the streets of the city he was unnerved and more than a little frightened.

"We'll run and run," had been the extent of his plan. Now he saw that every minute was filled with an equal measure of hope and fear. Where should he run? To the freezing rivers? To seek passage on a ship? Hildebrand knew the town far better than he did, but Davie was the leader of the two of them; he knew that he had better think fast.

They scurried along a dark alleyway, coming up behind a tavern kitchen. The smell of cooking meat and flowing ale hit Davie like a blow, assaulted his nostrils, his brain, his stomach.

"Oh!" he gasped. Had he ever been hungrier in all his life? He was a bit lightheaded.

"We go first to your family," Hildebrand suggested, and Davie thought it a wonderful idea. In his sudden panic, he had forgotten all about his New York cousins.

"Whitestone," he whispered, for he knew that was his mother's family name.

Hildebrand left him in the alleyway while he went into the tavern to inquire. Davie found a crust of sour rye in the gutter and chewed it with pleasure while he waited, his mood seesawing between joy and terror from moment to moment.

"I know where," Hildebrand said when he returned, and Davie followed his friend through the maze of streets to the kitchen door of the big house on Fair Street.

It was a fortunate moment. Josias had not yet returned from his offices; Audrey was still sitting at the painting studio on William Street; and the servants were in the front of the house, building fires and setting the tables for dinner. Meg, with Dorothy in her arms, was alone in the kitchen.

"Good Lord!" she gasped, frightened at the sight of big Michael Hildebrand looming in the doorway, but satisfied that at least it was not Cormick Walker. She stood her ground, and when he said, "Whitestone?" she nodded bravely, wrapping Dorothy in her shawl, and when skeletal Davie crept around the doorframe, she gave a short sigh of sympathy.

"I am Davis Montgomery, ma'am, your cousin, I believe, from Charleston. May I come in?"

Meg nodded silently. She remembered perfectly well that Katy and Liza, who had visited, had three brothers. This must be one of them. Yes, they were named Webb, Taylor, and Davis. This boy's resemblance to Liza was quite striking.

"But have you come tonight from Carolina?" she asked, still confused.

"No, ma'am. We have come from the sugar-house prison where I would have died. This man is my friend."

Meg felt herself on a point of no return. Oh, if only Bonnie were here! Bonnie would know what to do. She noticed that the Hessian was very wet; steam rose off his cloak as it caught the heat from the big fireplace. Both men looked—and smelled—disgustingly dirty, and yet, could she do less than to take them in?

"Prisoners?" she asked.

"Soldiers first," Davie said. He was terrified that he would have to leave this warm room. He needed the warmth of it to give him strength. He swayed, almost faint.

"Are you hungry?" Meg asked, seeing plainly that her cousin could not keep from looking into the stewpot, where potatoes were boiling with corned beef.

"Oh, no thank you, ma'am," Davie said, with awful restraint. "But Miss Whitestone?"

"Meg," she said firmly. "Mrs. Logan."

"Do you think you could put us up? In secret? For a time?" Davie begged, and in a rush Meg realized what she must do and led the two of them up the back staircase to Bonnie's room. There was a closet there with a false back that opened into a slant-roofed, windowless chimney cupboard that was as dark as it was warm. Her mother had once used it for storing clothes stretchers and curtain rods. She showed both men how to climb inside, wrinkling her nose at the stink of them.

"I will bring you your dinners," she said. "Later, when the others are sleeping, I will call you to the tub," and then with a rare smile, added, "Cleanliness is next to godliness, you know."

"Yes, ma'am," said Davie thankfully, "yes, ma'am."

The next day, in another part of the city, Taylor Montgomery woke late, shivering in the attic room he had found for himself and Sarah in the Bull's Head Tavern, the largest hostel in Bowery Village.

"We will be safe here," Taylor had told Sarah, when they first climbed the four flights of narrow stairs to the cheapest room in the house, but, in fact, the city had so far proved to be less than hospitable to the two Carolinians. Both of them found the cold to be stunning, people's accents to be nearly incomprehensible, and the prices of everything—lodging, goods, and foodstuffs—to be dreadfully high. Food itself was in short supply. At this rate, the small amount of money Taylor had brought with him would soon be gone.

And then what would he do? Taylor frowned. He felt helpless. Was all his education and all his expertise at running a rice plantation of no use at all? He missed his home, his horses, his dog Blue—he missed it all painfully. He did not mention it to Sarah, but he felt very out of place in the city. But New York was the one place in America where Sarah could be safe. For not only must Taylor make his own way in this strange city, but for the first time in his life, he had another human being entirely dependent on him. He felt fatherly toward Sarah, as well as stirred by her. Indeed, they were no longer master and servant—throughout the long voyage north, Taylor had come to look upon Sarah as a friend. Certainly, though she had no education beyond what he himself had given her on board ship, she displayed a sharp mind, a quiet courage, and a sweet disposition. Though he knew she must hate the city, she never complained, nor did she cease to trust him.

Taylor had always considered Sarah a pretty girl, but now he realized that she was a beautiful woman. At last her back had healed and her health had steadily improved, despite the bitter cold. Taylor looked over at her now. She was still asleep, one hand nestled under her pillow, her breathing peaceful. Even asleep, she was the loveliest creature he had ever beheld.

Once they had arrived in New York and secured the lodging at the Bull's Head, Sarah and Taylor had been together constantly as Taylor decided what he must do next. Taylor continued to teach Sarah to read and write, and they quickly settled into a companionable friendship. Cut off from his home and his *raison d'être*—he had been raised to be a rice planter, even if educated as a gentleman—Taylor had succumbed to a melancholy streak in his nature. He had come to depend on Sarah's buoyant spirit to bolster his own. Very quickly it became obvious to him that Sarah meant far more to him than he was willing to admit. He knew he was falling in love with her, and the feeling at once delighted and confused him. Of course, it was not at all uncommon for southern gentlemen to have black mistresses. But Taylor was all too aware that he wanted Sarah to be more than just his lover; he wanted her trusting heart as well, and such a relationship between a black woman—free or not—and a white gentleman like Taylor was just not accepted, was not even considered a possibility in the world he knew. Taylor's emotions made him feel the separation from his family even more keenly; he had turned his back on their politics, he had left home, and now, it seemed, he must reject their traditions and values as well. With every day since he had left Charleston, the division between himself and his family seemed more and more insurmountable.

But for now, he must find a way to take care of Sarah and to keep them both from starving or freezing before this cold winter was over. Taylor thought of his relatives, the Whitestones, who lived somewhere in this cold, brutish city. He would set about looking them up. Perhaps his uncle Whitestone would be able to hire him, or to help him find work of some sort.

"Go back to sleep," he advised Sarah as he noticed her stirring. There was a storm raging outside. He had scraped clear a corner of the window and seen a world covered in frost, and the wind shaking the treetops outside was howling like a wild thing.

"Yes, Taylor," Sarah said, smiling sweetly. She snuggled trustingly down under the heap of thin blankets, and her tangled tresses were like black silk.

New York might be cold and unfriendly, but Sarah had never felt so safe and happy in all her years. For the first time in her life, she was free! The knowledge that she was safe from Mr. Hill, far away from slave catchers and beatings, was enough to give her strength amidst the confusion and uncertainty of their present situation. And she felt sure that Taylor would protect her and help her to build a new life here. It was incredible to her that a man like him could be so tender and caring. And yet he cared for her as no one ever had. She owed him her life; her very existence now depended on his benevolence. It was a debt that Sarah could only repay with her love, and she gave him that willingly.

With Gates gone, Washington continued to make plans and preparations for the crossing and the attack. He would need healthy men and food, but food was heartbreakingly hard to come by, even in this prosperous farmland, even so soon after a bountiful harvest. The problem was money.

New Jersey farmers had wheat for sale, and flour and bran and meat, but they preferred, almost to a man, to trade it for hard currency. A farmer was much more enthusiastic about selling a bushel of oats for three shillings, sterling, than for fifty dollars Continental. It was just plain good sense, and with hard times sure to come, there were many farmers who put their political preferences aside and sold to the quartermaster with the gold.

But Washington sent his men out into the countryside to beg and bargain for food, set the cooks to preparing provisions for three or four days, and began to take a close count of the men left on their feet, of the guns that were in the charge of General Knox, of the ammunition and supplies, and of the boats John Glover had assembled.

Washington worked and planned all day on December twenty-second and twenty-third. He envisioned a three-pronged crossing and then a rather complicated united attack from four directions on both Hessian camps, the one at Trenton under Rall and the one at Bordentown under Colonel von Donop. His generals Cadwalader and Ewing would cross at points a bit south of McKonkey's Ferry and meet him on the other side. He chose as a launching point for his own men a sheltered inlet behind a strip of land called Taylor Island. Here, behind a row of pines, he planned to begin loading the cannon on the day of the attack. He would thus gain five or six hours on the crossing.

As far as was humanly possible, all these plans and preparations were kept secret, for spies were everywhere, and the whole success of the mission depended on the element of surprise. Despite widespread sickness and the grimmest of December weather conditions, men at the camp began to anticipate a move, expect marching orders, although when and to what destination, they could not guess.

It had begun to snow on the evening of Sunday, December twenty-second; it snowed on Monday afternoon, too, and all that night. Under cover of darkness and the storm, boats were brought upriver from Philadelphia that would carry men from the two southerly points of embarkation. Washington dined on Christmas Eve with General Nathanael Greene. After dinner, the commander informed his officers of the plan and its proceedings. Unknown to them, a spy also listened, despite the general's careful efforts, despite his plea for caution and his parting joke, which they all knew, as it was taken from Frederick the Great, who had written the manual of war they all followed. "All precautions, I beg you," he said. "If I thought my coat knew of my plans, I would take it off and burn it!"

The snow and cold weather appalled Washington. For one thing, if the river should freeze over entirely, the Hessians could scamper over the ice, and for another, his intelligence sources had informed him that the enemy was planning to invade Philadelphia "as soon as ice is made." Despite the snow, temperatures dropped, and ice was beginning to form along the shores of the river.

When Bayard went to Washington's room that night to deliver a late shipment of letters from Congress, he found the commander excited and a bit depressed.

"I do most sincerely regret the poor conditions we must offer our brave soldiers," Washington said in a voice full of emotion. "The best of them are ragged. The men under Sullivan are so much out of sorts and in want of everything. Do they understand, Logan, that I would not have it so?"

"I believe the men to be steadfast in their love for you," Bayard said.

Washington looked searchingly at the fire and shivered. The small fire in the shallow brick fireplace did little more than heat the hearth. "As God is my witness," he said, " 'tis unspeakably cold."

"As cold in British tents as in ours," Bayard said.

"True," Washington said, appreciating Bayard's good humor. He rose and strode about the room, rubbing his hands together for warmth. "It is time to tell you about a planned maneuver upon which I have set much hope. We will cross the river on Christmas day in the evening and launch an attack just before day."

"A surprise attack," Bayard said, thinking of all this would mean. Absurdly, he thought of Tom's fur gloves and was glad for them. "The hour, the weather, and the holiday will protect our surprise."

"Also the Hessians' ignorance of English," Washington said hopefully. "But it is hard to believe that they will see or hear nothing at all."

"I have heard that they are great Christmas merry-makers," Bayard said. "No doubt they will have a dance and drink a great deal of beer." Bayard smiled at the curious Hessians. In the Yankee tradition Bayard had grown up with, little secular celebration was made of the great religious holiday; Washington, on the other hand, missed the Yule log and the rich, sweet eggnog that were traditional at Mount Vernon Christmas celebrations.

"Aye, I have heard that, also. The Hessian commander, Rall, is said to be a heavy drinker. And I am glad to face General Grant." The commander of the advance enemy positions was Major General James Grant, a fat man whom Washington remembered with disdain from their time serving together, eighteen years ago, during the French wars. Grant had an oft-expressed low opinion of rebels, and could be counted on to take minimum precautions against attack, especially at Christmas.

"We plan to strike the garrison at Trenton one hour before dawn on the twenty-sixth. God be with us." Sitting down as near the fire as safety permitted, Washington looked preoccupied. He dipped his pen in ink as he spoke, and drew small designs upon small bits of paper.

"If you'll pardon my impertinence, sir, I would say that the plan is so bold and so aggressive that Heaven must grant us success." Charged with sincerity, Bayard stood so straight that the top of his head grazed the room's low ceiling.

Washington looked pleased. "Thank you, Logan. It is bold, and I well know the risks of such a campaign. But God is on our side, and right is on our side. The fate of a nation lies in our hands. We will fight, fight bravely, and we will succeed, because we must. Necessity, dire necessity must justify the attack."

"Yes, sir," Bayard said gruffly. God is on our side, he thought, and every volley of our muskets is an echo of His voice. A piece of the paper Washing-

311

ton had been scribbling on fell to the floor. He bent to retrieve it and saw that the commander in chief had written on it: *Victory or Death*.

Leaving New York, Bonnie did not know where she was going, nor did it concern her, as long as she should escape the city that contained Cormick Walker. She drew a breath of relief when the guardhouse at the Harlem River came into view. From the escort patrol at Kingsbridge, she had heard that Washington and his army were "not far, just in the south counties of New Jersey."

She and Isannah headed south. Tiny Isannah chattered briskly as soon as they had passed the lines, commenting on everything she saw. The size and scope of the countryside amazed her; the fresh white fields amazed her; the pointed spires of village churches reminded her of the town in the western isles of Scotland where she had been born. Cheerful as a bird, she was both dreadfully excited and already homesick for the narrow streets of Manhattan, which she had been so eager to escape.

But during the times they were silent, Bonnie thought of the task before her and the extraordinary events that had precipitated it. In her haste to leave New York, she had scarcely stopped to consider what she was doing. Of course it would be wonderful to see Bayard again. But still the entire situation puzzled her. Why would William be sending something to General Washington? Particularly a fashion brochure! She had hidden the parcel in her trunk without looking at it; now she longed to study it. William must be sending the general information of some kind. But if that were so, what could it possibly be?

As she continued to think along these lines, one

idea became increasingly compelling. Could William be a spy? Bonnie began to remember snatches of conversation, things he had said or done that she had passed over at the time. And that day at Mrs. Murray's . . . his note must have been meant to detain General Howe, not protect him as Bonnie had finally concluded that day. Perhaps his well-publicized Tory sentiments were nothing more than a disguise, a cover for his true loyalties. It was fantastic, but the more Bonnie thought about it, the more likely it seemed. How could she not have seen it before! She blushed as she admitted the reason to herself—she had always tried to separate her life from the war. How foolish that seemed now, how cowardly, when William lay his very life on the line every day to help the army and his country. But despite her shame, Bonnie felt strangely elated. She no longer needed to worry where William's loyalties lay. The last barrier between them was removed, and she loved him more than ever.

She urged the horses on. Where earlier she had thought only about leaving New York and escaping Cormick, now her mind and heart were full of her mission. She was not only helping William, but maybe her brothers as well.

A party of scouts in Continental uniform stopped them in mid-afternoon, and sent them toward Philadelphia. "Washington's near there," the captain said proudly.

"Bayard is with Washington," Bonnie said softly, as much to reassure herself as to explain to Isannah. "And perhaps Tommie is, too."

"Perhaps."

With the much-praised new road, Bonnie had heard that the journey to Philadelphia took only three days. But at the end of the second day, she and Isannah were no farther south than New Brunswick, and although they were prepared, with blankets and cooked provisions, to sleep in the chaise or near it, Bonnie was relieved when a tavern came into view, just before sunset.

"Thank goodness! We shall stop here," she said. The tavern, called The Indian Queen, seemed fit for royalty of any nation with its immense open fireplace and long public table already set with tankards and pewter plates. Bonnie arranged for the last free room and gratefully retired there for a few minutes before supper, and then directly afterward. She was bone tired, and when she repeated her prayers that night, she made a special plea for herself, feeling that her own "errand in the wilderness," though fraught with danger, must succeed.

The morning was clear, but with a ring around the sun that forecast snow before dark. Bonnie and Isannah set out very early, but by noon the snow had begun to fall, and the chaise's wheels cut deeply into the slush and frozen mud.

"Dear Lord, we can't go on! We shall never find the road in this storm," Isannah wailed, but Bonnie set her jaw and struggled to keep the horses moving and the gig on the narrow road. She did not know whether to be glad or not when a unit of cavalry rode up and stopped them. Were they friend or foe? Rebels or Redcoats? Then she saw that the soldiers wore uniforms of blue, and she concluded with relief that they must be Continentals.

"Where might you pretty ladies be going?" asked their lieutenant, wrapped in a thick coat with a collar so high Bonnie could not see his face.

"We are looking for General Washington. Perhaps you can help direct us," Bonnie said, and then saw their uniforms more clearly—these were not rebels, but a unit of Loyalist militia. Her heart fell.

"Washington! The man is a devil!" shouted the

lieutenant, taking a harder look at Bonnie and her companion. "Who are you? Where did you come from? What are you carrying in those trunks?"

Bonnie was badly scared, but tried hard not to show it. As the officer came close to her and grabbed her arm roughly, she burst into tears, which were not really false ones. "Only my clothes and a few coverlets," she said. "We are coming from New York and must go to my mother! Dear sir, I hope you did not believe me—that I am going to the General. Why would a helpless woman such as myself want to do such a thing? I only thought you were his soldiers, and . . ."

"I don't know what to make of you," the officer said slowly, staring hard. He had noticed Bonnie's unusual red-gold hair and the beauty that made her conspicuous wherever she went. "Why should a decent woman drive out on such a day as this?" the blue-coated officer demanded, still holding Bonnie while his men poked through the gig and opened one of her trunks.

"We should never have done it," Bonnie said, and, for the moment, she meant it. "Can you help us? Where shall we go to find shelter, sir?" Bonnie asked.

"Go to the devil, for all I care," the man said. He looked to his sergeant, who was rifling through a small trunk of white underclothes with a smirk on his face. Just then, the sergeant held up a copy of William Whitestone's newspaper, the *Messenger*, which Bonnie had used to line the trunk.

"Oh, I see you are a reader of Whitestone's paper," the officer said.

Bonnie threw all her cards on the table, forgetting that William had instructed her not to mention him. "Of course, sir," she said, "he is my brother-in-law."

"Is he really, miss?"

"Indeed he is," Bonnie said firmly, " and if you should be so kind as to guide us to shelter from this storm, I shall tell him and make sure that he writes a piece on your kindness."

"Nothin' here but women's stuff," declared the sergeant, still holding on to the newspaper.

"Oh, very well," the lieutenant said. "We have business to take care of. There is a farmstead over there, owned by some loyal folk named Gibson. They will take you in, I daresay."

And Bonnie went on, shaking a bit at her error and her close call, and when she found the Gibson farm, she traded the gig for a sturdy covered sleigh, rested the horses, and set out again, anxious to make Pennington by nightfall.

Chapter Twenty

POLISHED BRASS KETTLEDRUMS had sounded deep and loud, and colorful regimental banners had fluttered in the wind when Colonel Rall's German regiments had marched into Trenton to take up quarters there. To many of Trenton's citizens there had been no rejoicing; the steady rhythm of the drums sounded like the knell of doomsday. A prosperous little town fortunately situated at the head of the Delaware River, Trenton was formed of about a hundred houses, many of them of the native stone, and most of those belonging to Patriots had already been deserted by their owners.

The well-known reputation of the Hessian troops preceded them. They were greatly feared for their cruelty and licentiousness. In general, there were three types of stories about their inhuman cruelty: In the first sort, Hessians had stuck a Yankee soldier to a tree with a bayonet and left him there, pinned like a bug, screaming until he died. In the second type of story, Hessians skewered a Yankee soldier through his genitals and drove the bayonet up into his guts; in the third version, Hessians stabbed a fleeing soldier in the back. Everyone had heard that they raped girls and women and plundered indiscriminately; in fact, they had been told before leaving Germany that they were going to a country that was rich in plunder, and they considered all Americans fair game.

It was increasingly a guerrilla war, and the fear and hatred inspired by the sturdy, foreign-speaking soldiers with their bizarre uniforms and bushy mustaches broke out in various ways. The soldiers who came into Trenton expected trouble at any moment and slept with their muskets every night.

Their commander, Rall, was nowhere near so nervous. Rall had his headquarters in a solid house that belonged to Stacy Potts, a wealthy Tory who owned a tannery and iron works. Potts played host at a large white wooden house on King Street, opposite the Anglican church, which his distinguished guest was disinclined to enter. Rall was a fervent carouser; he loved to drink and bought his cards by the case. Nearly every night he stayed up late with whomever would keep him company, then slept till the unmilitary hour of nine or ten so that when the guard arrived on parade they had to wait in the cold for him to get out of his bath.

Rall did love parade, for he was extremely fond of music, and in Trenton he ordered the guard and cannon to be paraded around the fenced-in churchyard every day with all possible pomp as the band played on. One of his junior officers observed that it was "like a Catholic procession, wanting only the cross and banner and chanting choristers." Rall followed the parade every day, just to listen to the band; it was a passion of his, along with drill and inspections.

Fifty-year-old Rall had fought bravely and effectively at White Plains and Fort Washington, but he was no man to put in command of an isolated and strategic point. His nickname, "the Lion," was earned by his aggressiveness and durability in battle, but it might as well have referred to his blustering roar. He spoke almost no English, drank far too much, and was noisy and arrogant, especially with regard to the American army. His contempt for Americans was immense and made no distinction between those in uniform—or what passed for uniforms—and those not. It was this contempt that led to his belief that the Americans were not about to attack, would never attack, and if they did attack—which was not a real possibility—they would turn tail and run at the first firing of Hessian guns. He dismissed the reports of a scout who warned him that the Americans were about to attack as "old women's talk." And it was this belief that caused him to refuse to fortify Trenton in the slightest.

Christmas Eve was extremely cold, and everyone not on guard duty drew nearer to the fire. Sentries outside stamped blood back into their aching feet and wrapped themselves in blankets against the freezing wind. Late that night General Grant, who was still in Brunswick, received a Tory visitor who always had the latest information; the man claimed positively that there had been a war council at rebel headquarters, and plans for a possible attack had been discussed. Grant decided that although the information was most likely true, an aggressive action still seemed unlikely. Nevertheless, he sent a dispatch to Rall.

Rall received the dispatch, but like Grant, could not believe that the rebels would try anything. Not in this sort of weather. Still, he knew his duty; he posted a unit to march up and down the streets in addition to the usual guard detachments.

Snow covered the ground in Trenton on Christmas morning, but the cold sun warmed the air to the freezing point by noon. The swift-moving river was full of ice cakes that had broken off upstream in the recent warmer weather. Rall received a report of some rebels scouting around in the area, but nothing came of it. The weather turned beastly, sleet turning to rain, and by late afternoon Rall returned to Potts's house for a game of checkers and a warming mug of flip. Potts had a pretty daughter who brought them raisin cakes she had baked herself, and Rall rewarded her with a kiss and a promise of another.

Rall and Potts were still playing checkers at seven o'clock when firing was heard. Cursing in German, Rall pulled on his leggings and went out to investigate. Eventually, he found that some two or three score rebel troops had attacked the guards on the Pennington Road and then vanished into the darkness. He sent a patrol after them, but they covered two miles without seeing any of the enemy, so Rall ordered the men back to camp.

"No more than a gang of farmers trying to make trouble," he told his junior officers. "Country clowns, making jokes, no threat, boys, I tell you that."

"Colonel, sir, if the trouble is over for tonight, and as we can barely keep our powder dry in this icy rain, might not we have your permission to take the rest of the night off?" one officer asked, on the general behalf.

"Ja, after all, it's Christmas!" Rall conceded. He knew the men had cut evergreens to remind them of the celebration at home, and he himself had a party to attend.

Rall had been invited to the house of Abraham Hunt, who was said to be the richest man in town. Hunt later held a commission in a local rebel militia, and yet he was presumed by many to be a Tory. At any rate, he was a generous host, and the party was in full swing by the time the German commander arrived. Rall set about making up for lost time. The flip was rich and strong, and the food was delicious. Everything pleased him: the baked pigeon and stuffed goose, the venison stew and the wonderful fruit pies, not to mention the excellent spirits and the friendly, admiring company. How well he remembered the festive, cozy Christmases of his homeland! How he longed to be there tonight! A sentimental tear rolled down his cheek. Happily, he drank himself into the next day.

That same day, Bonnie and Isannah, traveling in an enclosed two-seated sleigh known as a booby-hut, found Trenton. They had been lost, or nearly lost, all day, moving south, providentially protected by the eye of the storm, missing its full fury until late afternoon. After a few frightening hours, they had determined that they were near some settlement. Blindly, they crossed Smith Creek on the ice and entered the little town by the Pennington Road. The roads were entirely snow covered; the streets were empty and hushed. It was clear that this little town had suffered some cataclysmic upset, but not at first evident what it was.

'' 'Tis a strange village,'' said Isannah, whose sophistication had increased by leaps and bounds since leaving New York. ''Where are the people?''

''I suppose they are inside,'' Bonnie guessed. ''I don't know where we are, but I am sure that we had better count ourselves fortunate to be here. Now, if there is an inn . . .''

''It's Christmas day,'' Isannah said, stifling a sob, ''and we don't know where we are or if we shall ever find the army.''

321

"We'll find them," Bonnie said confidently, "but, Isannah, heed my warning: 'tis better not to mention the army until we know for sure the sympathies of whomever we meet here. I shall say we are trying to find our relatives' farm in Princeton."

Within a few minutes, they had glimpsed enough looming Hessian grenadiers in dark blue with great plumed shakos to make Bonnie realize that this must be British territory, and that she would be wise indeed not to ask for General Washington. The Hessians were everywhere and looked as big as giants. When she saw a troop of them, some fifty strong, marching down the street toward her, she turned the horses and sleigh at once into the side yard of a big, white house, just as if she knew where she was.

"Let's try here," she said, appearing as courageous as she could and quite succeeding, although she was frightened nearly to tears.

It was twilight and snowing hard when Bonnie knocked on the side door of the house. Her knuckles were white and her feet so cold that they prickled and stung. I pray we find shelter here, she thought desperately. They could not go much farther. Long minutes passed before the door swung open. A woman, neatly dressed in gray, with a white bonnet and white collar, opened it a crack. She was a young woman, but she looked frightened.

"What do you want?" she asked in a soft voice.

"Ma'am, I beg of you, I wonder if you know where we might spend the night?" Bonnie asked in a quavering voice that gave away her fear and exhaustion.

"Are you out alone on such a day as this?" the woman asked with astonishment.

"Alone but for my serving woman."

"Come in at once."

Inside, Bonnie took the measure of the household she had invaded. She had entered the kitchen, which was low ceilinged and warm. A row of tow-headed children sat at a well-scrubbed table in front of a row of soup bowls, a kettle was boiling at the hearth, and dried herbs hung from all the rafters.

"God bless you, you are a Quaker family," Bonnie said.

"Yes, we are. I am Martha Morris. Do you know that Trenton is the headquarters for the Hessian soldiers? They have taken over my house, but for this one room. We have little to offer you, but you are welcome here, welcome in the name of the Lord."

Eagerly, Bonnie ran to fetch Isannah and her trunk of foodstuffs, from which she extracted dried beans and salt pork. "Please," she begged Mrs. Morris, "add it to the soup. Thank God we found you."

Seated by the hearth, Bonnie and Isannah could very plainly hear the occupying soldiers shouting and singing through the board walls that separated the kitchen from the rest of the house. Every now and then there was a crash that made Martha Morris wince.

"They have been here for two weeks," she explained as she began to boil the beans and crumble dried marjoram into the stewpot. "We are completely at their mercy. They have taken all our food: all our winter stores, all my pickles and preserves. They have built bonfires using our fences, and fed their horses with our stored grain."

"You poor woman, you poor woman," Bonnie murmured, feeling immediately drowsy in the warmth. She had taken the littlest Morris child onto her lap, and the small boy's sweet weight reminded her acutely of how she missed her own Dorothy.

Isannah sat silently among the children, looking like one of them.

"They have quartered twenty dragoons in our meetinghouse," Martha Morris said in a horrified voice. "And allowed their horses to defile it. . . . Dear visitor, they are terrible men. They butchered our hog on the dining-room table! I am thankful that our lives have been spared."

"Where is your husband?" Bonnie asked, aware that she might be asking a dangerous question.

Martha Morris fixed Bonnie with a stare. "He is a good Christian and true to his faith, but he could not stop himself. He will be read out of meeting, but I don't care. He has gone off to join up with the rebels."

"So have my brothers," Bonnie confessed. We shall be safe here tonight, she thought. Her eyelids were so heavy she could not stay awake to eat, but slept on a rug at the side of the hearth with two of the Morris children curled beside her.

Although Bonnie missed her baby Dorothy that night, she had no fears for her safety, nor need she have had. Now that her own pregnancy was established, Meg was entirely happy and determined to bring this child safely to term, and she lavished all possible care on Dorothy in the interim.

"You look as fat as a mother sow already," Audrey had said to her, but Meg only smiled. She knew how furious Audrey was, and did not underestimate the extent of her cruelty. Since childhood, Audrey had been spiteful and jealous, and her temperament seemed to have hardened in womanhood.

Meg watched her very carefully, and when Audrey took to brewing her pots of tea and bringing them to her with a show of solicitousness, Meg was not fooled, but alerted. Nothing would persuade her to taste a drop of anything Audrey had a hand in.

And, with wifely tact, she took care to warn Josias as well.

"Be careful, dear husband, not to drink of any brew or potion my sister might mix for you," she said to him.

"Good heavens! Are you quite serious? Do you mean she might try to poison me?" Since learning of Meg's pregnancy and witnessing Audrey's cruelty, Josias had not taken Audrey into his arms and had once again taken up the mantle of expectant father and respectable family man. Audrey had fumed and pouted and taunted, but Josias had never considered that she might strike back.

"She is angry that I am carrying your heir," Meg said simply, "and when she is thwarted, Audrey becomes a bit mad."

Josias recoiled in horror. "She . . . she must be stopped!" he said.

"Oh, there is no stopping Audrey while she draws breath," Meg said calmly, as one who has had a lifetime to get used to the idea. "Only be warned, darling."

"My goodness!" Josias gasped, feeling much like a fly in a web, caught in a sticky scheme both larger and more dangerous than he had ever suspected. He looked at his sweet wife with new respect. How good she was, so simple and brave, so motherly and tender. How modest and circumspect she was! How lucky he was to have married the good sister, after all.

"Victory or Death" was the password among Washington's soldiers. Early on Christmas morning detailed orders were issued, with three days' cold rations—hard bread and salt beef. This, plus their blankets and muskets, with forty rounds of ammunition was all they were to carry. There was a final word of caution: "A profound silence to be enjoined, and no man to quit his ranks on the pain of death."

The plans Washington had made were careful and comprehensive, but no man could have planned on the weather. They were at the mercy of the worst storm of the winter so far. Heavy snow had fallen continuously for days, piling up on the fields and marshes and flatlands, filling the ravines and gulleys along the river, lying heavily on the branches of trees. After two days of extreme cold, the wind had now shifted and promised another storm from the northeast. The river was full of ice cakes, and it might soon freeze over.

Washington was not in a cheerful frame of mind as he sent several small forces out to create diversions, at the proper moment, up- and downriver, and gathered with the bulk of his troops in a sheltered valley just west of the ferry. At about two o'clock in the afternoon on Christmas day, the first units got underway; an hour later the entire army was marching toward the river.

Watching them pass by, Washington again observed how many were barefoot and dressed in rags; it pained him terribly. Major James Wilkinson, who had been with Lee when he was captured at Basking Ridge, observed that their route to the river through the snow was "tinged here and there with blood from the feet of the men who wore broken shoes."

Washington rode down to the shoreline, to the stone house where William McKonkey ran a tavern for the convenience of those using the ferry. He greeted his men by name. These were his most seasoned, steadfast soldiers. Some of them, like New

Hampshireman Johnny Stark, and of course Knox and Logan, among others, were veterans of Bunker Hill. Washington's own nephew, the cavalryman William Washington, was there. Quiet, eighteen-year-old James Monroe, still a Princeton undergraduate, commanded a rifle company. Also among the tattered, footsore soldiers were Alexander Hamilton, commanding a unit of Henry Knox's artillery; John Marshall, from the Fifteenth Virginia, and Aaron Burr, a veteran of Arnold's march to Quebec. When the chips were down, these men would come through. They were the best he had.

And on hand to ferry them all across the river were John Glover's Marbleheaders. With the Massachusetts fishermen in charge, Washington did not hesitate to load the big, sturdy Durham boats to the very gunwales. The beauty of these boats was their shallow draft; even fully loaded with men and horses and guns, they drew only thirty inches.

Thomas Logan was up to his eyebrows in the effort to cross the river from McKonkey's Ferry. The strong rising wind lashed him with a freezing spray that thickened his hair and eyebrows with a coat of hoarfrost. His boots were wet and white with frost, and his fingers, stiff inside his fine new fur gloves, numbed as they clutched his musket.

Theirs was an ordeal of endurance. First there had been the long wait. Hours had passed while the men in Tom's unit stood on the riverbank waiting for the rest of the army to assemble, stamping their feet on the crusted snow, then crouching, wrapped in their blankets, hour after tedious hour while the storm worsened and the temperature dropped.

It was a black night. The air itself was charged with snow bursts and a wild wind; the moon had risen behind a veil of snow-laden clouds and was soon entirely obscured. No moonlight or starlight would help guide them; in the swirling snow it was all they could do to keep the nearest men in sight.

"If I live through this campaign, I'm goin' home," Tom's friend John Scott muttered.

"You'll never survive, you pigeon," Tom teased him. "This ain't the sort of night you fancy, is it?"

"You bet it ain't!" Scott said. "This the sort of night you was raised on, up in Boston?"

"In Boston this might as well be a summer night," Tom promised him.

"How are we going to find our way across that river?" Scott asked. "It's as dark as the devil's kitchen. I ain't so sure that river's still there."

"It's there," Tom said. "I can hear it." The sound was the grinding and scraping of ice cakes and the eerie whistling of the wind.

"I still can't figure how they'll find the other shore," Scott said.

"Better leave that to finer minds than yours," Tom recommended.

"And than yours, I hope," Scott replied, and in this sort of talk they did their best to pass the waiting hours.

The crossing was the most difficult phase of the attack. The dark, swift river was about three hundred yards wide at this point, creaking and groaning as huge slabs of ice broke off and crashed downstream. When the first of the wide, shallow Durham boats touched the shore, Tom battled the urge to turn and run. How, indeed, would they find the way across the river?

"All aboard," John Scott called cheerfully. Ice cakes bumped and crunched against the boat as the men scrambled to find places inside, and the chilling spray splashed over them, freezing on their faces and fingers. The wind had stiffened, bringing a terrible cold that formed ice on the still water as fast as you could look at it.

Glover's men moved the heavy-laden boats slowly upstream and toward the Jersey shore by means of long wooden poles. The steering sweep, manned by the captain, could be fixed to either end of the boats, and two men with setting poles walked up and down each side, pushing the boat forward its full length from the stern and then going forward to repeat the process. Now, with the wind rising, the sleet-laced wind ripped through tattered uniforms and froze fingers around the poles; Glover's men struggled to balance on the icy narrow decks, all the more so as they had to avoid the sticks with which the other men were poking off the ice cakes.

Henry Knox was known for his powerful, deep bass voice. Now he bellowed out orders, keeping the men moving, keeping the lines of horses and men and cannon together. Perhaps only Knox's voice could have been heard above the crash of the ice, but even he was frustrated, saying that "the floating ice made the labor almost incredible."

The last boat to cross carried two cannon, four horses, and ninety cannonballs; it was so overloaded it nearly went down in midriver, but providentially it did not, and when it reached the shore at last, the men welcomed it with an Indian cheer, taking it as an omen of success.

At about seven o'clock, Washington himself had gone over. On the Trenton side, he got off his horse and was persuaded to sit down on a low wooden box that had once held a beehive. There he sat, wrapped in his cloak, waiting for the rest to come across, silent and patient, even though he was aware that things were badly behind schedule. Instead of midnight, as Washington had projected, it was after three in the morning when the last of the soldiers, shivering in clothes frozen as hard as armor, unloaded the last heavy gun on the icy riverbank north of Trenton. And now the snowstorm struck. It was a wild storm, as severe as any in memory, with rain and snow and hail mixed together.

Despite everything, spirits were high. The waiting men had lit bonfires and tossed on all the fence rails to be found within walking distance; they made a cheerful blaze. "Cozy at last?" Tom asked John Scott, who was taking advantage of the fire to dry his soaked trousers, turning slowly around and around.

"Snug as a hearthbug," Scott assured him.

It was four in the morning before the troops finally formed up for the march. If anything, the weather had worsened; a violent hailstorm struck them just as they rounded Bear Tavern, pelting faces with shards of ice like tiny daggers.

Washington had divided the army into two sections. Sullivan, with Stark and Glover, whose men had taken up their muskets as soon as the last boat was across, would take the River Road. Tom Logan was with them. Washington himself led the men along the Pennington Road, with Greene, Stirling, and Mercer. But they would all go together as far as the village of Birmingham, where the River Road and the Pennington Road split. Birmingham was four and a half miles away, about halfway to Trenton.

It was a ghostly procession. Only a few men carried lanterns, but the artillerymen had fixed torches to their gun carriages, and the faint yellow lights made small circles in the falling snow, or flickered upward to silhouette the bare black branches of the oaks and hickories that lined the narrow road. The men were enjoined to keep silent and to remember the password for the night: "Victory or Death."

Washington, astride a chestnut sorrel horse, rode up and down the columns of men, begging them, "Soldiers, keep by your officers. For God's sake, keep by your officers!"

They had set off at four; at five they stopped to eat a very cold breakfast from their knapsacks. It was still raining, snowing, and sleeting in an icy round, but at least the weather was a cover. It would soon be dawn, but this dawn would be nearly as dark as midnight. When they stopped to eat, several of the men were overcome by weariness and lay down in the snow to sleep.

John Scott was one. Tom was separated from him by a few soldiers, but he saw at once that when the officers came round to get them on their feet again, John did not move.

Tom ran to him at once.

"On your feet, trimmer!" he jibed, and then he saw that Scott did not hear him. "Wake up, you lazy faker!" But still Scott did not move.

"Scott! Scott!" Tom shouted in a horrified voice. He grabbed his shoulder and shook him. "Wake up! Wake up!"

But Scott had frozen to death.

"Keep walkin'!" an officer advised him, coming up next to Tom and laying an arm across his shoulders. "You must keepin walkin'. 'Tis deadly to stand still, boy."

Thomas let out a howl of raw grief.

"I think, after all, we will surprise 'em, sir," Bayard said to General Washington, in another part of the line.

"We must push on in any event," the commander said. On and on the army marched. It was dreadfully difficult to move on the sleet-coated ice, but too cold to stop for even a brief rest. It was still dark. Washington sent out whispered orders to show no light. "On through dark!"

A few steps off the road, Bayard strayed into a barnyard, and realized from the stirring of the cows and the smell of the stored hay that they must be passing any number of little farms and houses. What must they think, he wondered, the good folk of Pennington, if they hear the faint sound of marching feet? How many will look out through their snow-drifted windows? How many will have troubled dreams tonight?

Within a mile of Trenton the sky lightened, and Washington and his men proceeded through an alleyway of leafless trees encased in ice which sparkled like diamonds as daylight broke over the ice-crusted fields. Dawn was a glimmer in the eastern sky.

A rider sent from Sullivan galloped up to Washington with grim news. "Sir, our powder is soaked!" the messenger gasped.

It was true; nearly all the firing pins were drenched, nearly all the muskets were unfit to fire. They had carried their heavy guns and rounds of ammunition for naught.

Washington knew there could be no turning back now. "Tell General Sullivan to use the bayonet!" he ordered. "I am determined to take Trenton!"

Then, as they approached Trenton, a troop of about thirty men came into view, marching in the opposite direction across a hummocky field. After some anxious moments, it was determined that they were Americans, a company of Virginians who had made a premature attack on the guards at the north end of Trenton. They had shot a sentry, wounded six Hessians, and quickly withdrawn.

"Who authorized this?" Washington demanded in a cold rage.

"General Stephen, sir."

Adam Stephen was a junior officer nearly as mercurial and insubordinate as General Lee himself. Washington sent for Stephen and took him to task.

"Damn it!" he shouted. "Damn it, sir!"

Bayard had never seen the commander in chief so angry; he had staked so much on the secrecy of the attack.

"You, sir, may have ruined all my plans by putting them on guard!" Washington told Stephen with both anger and regret, feeling anew the burden of an amateur army. Did everyone feel himself free to act independently? Did everyone think himself in charge? Washington longed to have Stephen fired and sent home, but he needed every man he had. In a controlled voice, he told Stephen and his men to fall in and join the vanguard.

Bayard was riding next to Washington when they saw the first sign of the enemy on the Pennington Road. In the fury of the storm, it was not possible to see far ahead, so they were within fifty yards when they came upon a man chopping wood outside his house. The man dropped his ax and his hat in astonishment at the approaching line of soldiers.

"Can you tell me where the Hessian picket is?" Washington called out, as imposing as ever.

The man hesitated, too unnerved to speak.

"You need not be frightened. It is General Washington who asks."

His face lit up. "Why, so it is," he said, staring as he pointed ahead to a small white house just ahead. When the soldiers looked down the road, they saw a Hessian running out of the house, yelling and waving his arms, followed by four others, who came out firing. Bullets whistled over Bayard's head as the Hessians scattered, some of them yelling to alert the main guardhouse just down the road, some firing, some running into the village.

The weary rebel soldiers felt new heart flow into them, and more so a few minutes later, when they heard a cannon booming to the west.

"Sullivan!" Washington exulted; it was coming together as planned. His enthusiasm and eagerness were contagious. The temper of the army rose to a high pitch; strength flowed into tired legs and arms. Washington's voice was like a trumpet.

"Onward!" he called out, and his voice was answered by a great chorus of cheering. The Americans raced on into the town, as nimble as men who had just rested.

Looking down into the town, Bayard saw great confusion and commotion. Confused men would make easy targets. Surprise was the reward of their stealth and their endurance in the face of the storm. Men were bursting out of the houses and running back and forth, many of them apparently roused from their beds. Officers were bawling out orders, buckling on swords; artillerymen were rushing horses into place, struggling with the depths of crusty snow.

Immediately, the Americans set up their guns and began blasting heavy fire into the center of the town. The big guns had been plugged and kept dry—all of them were in working order. Shells bounced along, hissing, demolishing everything in their path, until they finally burst in an explosion of deadly metal, ripping apart men and horses, crashing through walls.

Bayard had never seen such terror and chaos. Following orders, the Hessians tried to form ranks in the streets, but the streets were full of cannonballs. Many of their weapons, at least as wet as those of the rebels, misfired, and even at point-blank range, they did not hit a man. They tried to find shelter, running like frightened devils, shrieking for help, but their shelters were blown apart as soon as they reached them. When they managed to get two guns set up, a bold rebel charge ordered by Knox and led by Captain William Washington attacked them and took possession of them.

Still, the Hessians fought on.

Chapter Twenty-One

TOM, STILL REELING from the loss of his friend John Scott, had entered the town along the River Road from the west with Stark and the rest of Sullivan's men. Joining up with Washington's troops, they advanced through the streets. Now the storm was at their backs and in the enemy's face. Visibility was terrible, and although repeated shots rang out, none of them seemed to hit any of the Americans.

Hessians were beginning to boil out of the houses along the main north-south road, facing into the wind and straining to see the surprising shapes of the advancing Americans through the blinding, blowing sleet. Accustomed to forming into ranks before fighting, the German soldiers were confounded, not to mention thick headed from their Christmas parties the day before, and many of them ran helter-skelter in every direction, separated from their officers, unable to form into regiments.

Tom saw a pack of them run into a church, saw others dive into cellars. On his way down King Street he passed two great cannon, shining brass six-pounders, lying beside seven dead Hessians and a brass drum. As soon as he stopped to look, a drummer from Boscawen grabbed at the drum, and began to beat at it instead of his own. Tom smiled at the lovely sound of it.

Just ahead was the market, but before he reached it, General Washington caught up with him, on horseback and alone, and cried out, "March on, my brave fellows, after me!" He rode off, and Tom ran to keep up.

Never had the Americans' heavy, unwieldy artillery pieces been more useful. Rising to the occasion, Henry Knox had directed the setting of the cannon, placing them at the head of King and Queen streets to command both thoroughfares.

Though still disorganized, the Hessians were rallying in small groups to the beat of their drums. Those Americans with dry powder and some Patriot residents of Trenton were firing from behind buildings. Smoke, snow, shouts, screams, and explosions all mixed with the wild howling of the wind and the swirling snow.

"Charge! Charge bayonets!" the order rang out. In some places the fighting was hand to hand. Tom's gun was as wet as everyone else's, and he pursued some Knyphausen soldiers in black and silver uniforms down a narrow street with his bayonet outstretched. He was outnumbered, but to his surprise, he kept them on the run.

At the south end of town, part of Sullivan's force blocked the bridge with a cannon and watched the bridge turn red with the blood of the killed and wounded.

Tom had got to within two or three hundred feet of Rall and his men, parading two deep in a straight line. Tom pushed on, passing horrible scenes of wounded Hessians moaning and bleeding in the snow, appalled by the screams of the dying. Then the retreating Hessians turned and charged at the town again, and he grabbed up a sword, taking it from the belt of a dead grenadier. Swinging it wildly, he was shocked when he caught a fierce-looking Hessian on the shoulder and saw the man fall backward, clutching his severed arm.

"Oh, my God!" Tom shouted. "Oh, my God!"

At the sight, some thirty Hessians threw their weapons to the ground. Coming up behind Tom, General Sullivan called out, "Good work, my brave boy! Good work!"

Johann Rall had been fast asleep when the first pickets on the Pennington Road were attacked; he struggled to find his head and his clothes while mass confusion broke out outside his doors and the fighting swirled through Trenton's narrow streets. His greatest hope was that this was not a full-scale attack, merely a skirmish at the pickethouse, like the one the night before. His lieutenant, Jacob Piel, came twice to rouse him, shouting, *"Der Feind! Der Feind! Heraus! Heraus!"*

Rall struggled to the window of his bedroom in a nightshirt calling, *"Was ist das?"* Near midnight, an unidentified man had tried to see Rall, and when the colonel refused, he had scribbled a note to him, to be delivered by a servant. Rall had received the note and stuffed it unread into a pocket. The note had reported that the American army was marching against the town. Rall had forgotten the note, and now, being assured by a subordinate that the Americans could easily be driven out by a determined assault, he went to look for his boots, muttering curses and dire predictions for the day ahead.

The storm raged on. Rall could not see two feet out of his windows; his head ached, but he heard the alarm: "The enemy! The enemy! Turn out! Turn out!"

Rall could not find his boots. His head was splitting, and he felt a bit ill. He opened a window and called out, "What is the matter? What is the matter?"

"Don't you hear the firing?" his lieutenant shrieked, frustration mounting.

"I'll come at once," Rall said.

Two cannon were set up directly in front of Rall's house and got off a shot or two at the rebels on King Street before they were knocked out of action by a contingent of rebels. Rall, undeniably dazed, stumbled out of his house and mounted a horse.

"Forward march!" he ordered. "Advance! Advance!" And to his officers, he asked anxiously, "How many of them are there? How many? How many?"

No one could tell for sure; answers ranged from four to six thousand, but there seemed far too many. Americans were filling the streets in lines of three. It was now about eight o'clock, and all three columns had reached Trenton.

The noise was deafening. Hessian drums beat a call to arms, cannon boomed, and John Stark led his men in blood-curdling Indian-style war calls.

Rall rode furiously up and down, leading a counterattack on the men who had taken his cannon. His soldiers, who had managed to get themselves into a sort of a parade line, were thrown into utter confusion. They faced an army of long-haired, wild-eyed madmen: all soaking wet, muddy, and terribly dressed, some barefoot. Yet they charged, yelling and shrieking, cursing, waving bayonets, seemingly fearless.

The British contingent, the Queen's Own Light Horse, panicked completely and rode out of town, some of them trampling Hessian foot soldiers in their haste.

Rall managed to gather some troops, and led his regiment to the east, stopping under some apple trees; some three or four hundred of his men had rallied around him, including his beloved band, which played desperately as their instruments filled with snow. Rall had been planning to attack the enemy on the Princeton Road, but when he learned that he was cut off and was reminded that his men had left all their baggage behind, he conceived the strange notion to ride back into town, thus trying to attack, with a limited force, the town he had just abandoned and which was now filled with the rebel army.

He drew his sword and gave the order to advance. His horse danced neatly. His men were close around him, ready to fight at last. Their mood had changed; they were wide awake now and tasted blood—their lives were at stake.

At that moment, a Pennsylvania rifleman, one of the very few who had kept his powder dry, drew a bead on Rall and shot him.

He swayed in the saddle. "I am hit!" he cried, and his men formed a tight group around him. Their mood was broken; everyone was shaken again, and the swirling snow made it impossible to see what was going on or even if they were facing friend or foe. Rall's major, Knyphausen, rode out in advance and called for the soldiers to follow him, but they hesitated. Rall was hit! The Hessians broke ranks and ran. Rall clung to his horse's back, shouting orders, but he quickly began to grow weak. He was nearly surrounded, and his guard grew smaller and smaller. Two cannon had been moved into Queen Street at almost point-blank range, and the Americans were closing in from all sides.

"What has happened? What has happened?" Rall asked piteously. He ordered a retreat, but just as he gave the command, he fell from his horse. Two of his soldiers carried him to the Methodist church on Queen Street.

A few hundred of the Hessians had found a bridge across a creek and fled, but most of the Germans surrendered, surrendered in town, on the run, and south of the creek.

Hemmed in from all sides, separated from their officers and divisions, outgunned and outnumbered, the Hessians could do nothing else. Many of them were seriously wounded. It was all over, and surprisingly quickly. The entire battle had taken less than an hour.

Washington saw a group of Hessians gathering in a field just beyond the town and directed that cannon be aimed at them, but Bayard Logan rode up to him. "Sir!" he called out. "Sir, they have struck."

"Struck?"

"Yes! Their colors are down."

Washington found it almost too good to be true. He wiped off his fieldglasses, then raised them again, looking out at the bright figures, bold as cardinals against the snow, some balancing their hats on their swords in a gesture of surrender. The mighty enemy now looked dazed and frightened. He lowered his glasses and smiled broadly. It was one of the broadest smiles that Bayard had ever seen on the commander's face, and it warmed him to the core.

"Why, so they are," Washington said, and then his famous reserve cracked a bit. "This is a glorious day for our country," he said.

When the prisoners were herded together, there

seemed to be too many to count, but finally, Washington's aides came up with a rough count: at least nine hundred and twenty. Astonishingly, the Americans had not lost a single man in the fighting, only the two who had frozen on the march, and had only a few wounded.

"Commander Rall is badly wounded, sir," an aide reported to Washington.

"I must go to him," Washington said.

At the first sounds of the battle, the Hessians occupying the main rooms of the Morris house had hastily slammed out, shouting and cursing. Bonnie and Isannah and the Morris family had cowered in the kitchen, but word soon reached them that the Americans had attacked the town. Pressing their noses to the street-facing windows, they saw soldiers running back and forth but were able to make little sense of the uproar and confusion outside.

"The Lord strikes with a mighty sword," Mrs. Morris said. "Isannah, I want you to take the children to the cellar and hide them there. Do not come out until I call you myself. Bonnie, we must go to help the wounded."

Obeying swiftly, Bonnie pulled on her cloak and followed Martha Morris through the dreadful streets to the Methodist church where several Quaker women were already at work, trying to help and comfort the wounded men lying on the hard pews. Few of them were Americans, but to these women, it did not matter.

Within minutes, the freezing-cold church began to look like an anteroom of hell. The smell of blood was sickening. Moaning, sobbing soldiers were laid out, their garments loosened, and promptly died; others were silent with shock. One man had been

342

shot in the face. A horrified boy came in on foot, but soon died; he had lost his whole hand to a cannonball. Blood covered others so thoroughly it was hard to tell where they had been struck. Frozen, bloodied boots took two women to pull them off. Bonnie had never imagined such ghastly suffering, nor seen so much blood. At first, she thought she might faint, but when Martha Morris called to her to help with a portly major shot through the knee, she marshaled all her strength and courage and did what she was told.

There was a flurry of excitement when Colonel Rall was brought in, pale and bleeding. He had been shot twice through the chest. Rall raised himself on one elbow and tried to talk, asking repeatedly for something.

"What does he want?" Bonnie asked, unable to understand Rall's guttural accents.

"I have no idea," Martha Morris said. "Dear Sir, you will soon face your Maker."

Just then General Washington came into the church to pay his respects to the defeated general. A hush fell over the makeshift hospital as all eyes followed the tall, erect general in his neatly fitting blue-and-buff uniform, stained now with mud and water. Rall roused himself to ask that nothing be taken from his men but their weapons. The two spoke for a few moments, and then Washington turned to go.

Bonnie seized the opportunity and ran after him. "General Washington, sir!" she gasped. "May I have a word with you, sir?"

"What is it, miss?" "Who are you?" demanded two of the officers at Washington's side.

"Let her speak," Washington said kindly.

"I am Bonnie Logan. I have come from New York with a message for you. May I give it to you in private, sir?'' This time Bonnie remembered her promise to William and did not mention his name.

"Logan?" Washington asked. Was there no end to the Logans? He wondered if . . .

But Bonnie burst out with the answer. "Yes, I am Bayard Logan's own sister!" she cried, and at that moment, she saw Bayard at the door of the church, his dear handsome self filling the doorway, and she ran to him with a cry of happiness.

"Logan, bring your sister along," Washington ordered, striding out of the church, for he was to meet with all his generals at once to decide the next course of action.

Exhausted and battle shocked, Bayard could hardly believe that he was seeing his sister, and he was far from making any sense of it. For a moment, he was entirely too surprised to speak. Bonnie made up for it. "William Whitestone sent me," she said in a low voice, clinging to Bayard's arm. "I came with Isannah, Tom's intended. We were looking for the army and were lost in the storm and found Trenton. Oh, Bayard, you look so well! I am so happy to see you!"

"You amaze me," he said at last. "I can hardly believe you are here. Here! My God, here! Do you know that the Hessians surrendered? We have won a glorious victory."

A cloud passed over Bonnie's face. How could it be glorious with so many men in terrible pain? Many more must have died. This was the least glorious mess she had ever seen. How could it be worth it?

But even as Bonnie recoiled from the horrible scene around her, she felt guilty. While she had been in New York, wrapped up in her own life, refusing to take a strong stand, the war had scarcely seemed real. Even the cannonfire and the clouds of smoke during the battles in New York had been nothing

344

compared to this. She looked at her brother, and saw that despite his exhaustion, Bayard was intensely proud of the victory. He believed so steadfastly in the Patriot cause; he—with so many others—had risked his life for it. For the first time, Bonnie understood his feelings. In fact, she suddenly realized, she shared them. Once she had put her own concerns behind her, she had finally understood why people were willing to fight and to die for freedom, why William could take such great risks, how he could live a lie and put his beliefs before their love. The cause was right; it was the only acceptable solution. She could no longer deny that, not when so many had suffered for her.

Then Bonnie thought of her brother Thomas, and a sob caught in her throat. "Is Tom here? Is Tom nearby? Is he all right?" she asked frantically.

Bayard looked serious. "Let us go and look for him and then go to the general. You have done good work here. Come with me, now."

Bonnie followed eagerly, clinging to Bayard's arm. She could hardly believe both her brothers were here, and safe, and that she, too, was safe. "It was a hard journey," she told Bayard, "but I know now it was right. He's wonderful, isn't he? Washington?"

"Yes," Bayard said. "That he is."

Wildly encouraged by the victory at Trenton, Washington called to order a council of war. He was thinking seriously of pushing his advantage, of pursuing the fleeing Hessians and pushing on down the east bank of the Delaware.

As the officers conferred, the men were already celebrating. Some of those who had found warm places were asleep. Others had ferreted out the stores of Hessian brandy and were tasting it. Bayard and Bonnie had found their brother Tom with a unit of ingenious New Englanders who had combined a barrel of whiskey and a barrel of sugar in a feed trough.

"Christmas punch!" Tom shouted, quaffing it greedily.

"Trenton toddy!" his mates exulted, and they stirred it with a fence rail. Those who had shoes, drank it out of their shoes, and some of them drank it out of cupped hands. Tom remembered its taste until his dying day. It was as sweet as the victory at Trenton.

"Drink some," Tom urged Bonnie and Bayard, and they did, just to please him. "I think I need to be a little drunk to believe that you are really here. How did you get here?"

So Bonnie told her story again, and the three of them went back to the Morris house to find Isannah and the trunk that contained the paper Bonnie had to give Washington. Isannah came out of the dusty cellar with the Morris children and leapt into Tom's arms, squealing with happiness.

"Damn it, but I can't stay," Tom said. Drums were beating the call to assemble; all the soldiers and their prisoners were under orders to march back to the ferry, and return to camp.

Bonnie thought quickly. What must they do now? Isannah would not leave, now that she had found Tom. Perhaps if they stayed here, with the army, Bonnie could help in some way. At the very least, she could help her brothers. She couldn't return to New York—not yet, not while Cormick Walker was still there and there was so much important work to do here. She longed to see William, to tell him that she knew his secret and loved him all the more for knowing it. But she need not do that now—she was certain of her love for William, and of his for her; it would keep until more important questions were settled.

Full of her new purpose, Bonnie was smiling to herself when she realized that Tom and Isannah were looking at her expectantly. "We will come along," Bonnie determined. "We will follow the army, for a time at least."

Meanwhile, in New York, where they had no notion of what was happening in Trenton, the members of the Logan household were celebrating Christmas, after the fashion of the day and their particular appetites.

Meg Logan, who had been raised, after all, by a Dutch mother, saw fit to mix and stir, roll and cut out traditional Dutch spice cookies, and to tell Dorothy the story of Sinte Klaas and how he would ride over the roofs of the town with his chariot full of presents for good children and lumps of coal for naughty children. Next year, she thought happily, she would have a baby of her own to tell the story to.

Meg shared the cookies with Davie Montgomery and Michael Hildebrand, who were still hiding in the little secret room. Keeping them hidden had given new meaning to her life; she enjoyed the two young men's company in the hours when she sat in their room, sewing while they chatted. For herself, she wished they would never go, but both were restless.

"I promised my father I'd be home for Christmas," Davie told Michael with a touch of sadness in his voice.

"Next year," Michael suggested. His English was improving daily, as Davie had plenty of time to teach

347

him. In return, Michael was teaching Davie to carve wooden figurines, and together they had made a little wooden creche to give baby Dorothy.

On Christmas Eve, Josias had gone to a party at Hicks's Tavern for General Howe and other high-ranking officers. The collation had been superb: Gloucester cheese, pickled salmon, walnuts, anchovies, and beef; mushroom ketchup on smoked turkey, and mince pies. Josias had drunk a great deal of toddy, far more than was his habit, and the next day he felt distinctly ill. He had put on weight during the last six months and had been forced to order a new set of clothes from Hercules Mulligan; that night he discovered that even his newest yellow brocade waistcoat would not button.

Home abed on Christmas day, Josias heard the constant passage of footsteps up and down the stairways, the frequent opening and closing of doors, the smell of fires and cooking, the murmur of voices, and half-dozing, had the dreamy notion that his house had turned into a wayside inn. When he rang his bedside bell for some tea, Audrey herself carried it to him, but it smelled funny to him, and he remembered Meg's warning. "Bless her," he said, wrinkling his nose. He dumped the tea into the chamber pot as soon as Audrey left the room. Audrey was in a bad mood these days. The fatter and rosier her sister Meg grew, the more pinched and sour she became. She had decided that Josias was dreadfully dull, and too awfully plump besides, and she had inaugurated a love affair with a whippet-lean British corporal. Just last night, she had learned that he, Corporal Greene, already had a wife and children in Yorkshire. She felt miffed, the more so as Greene had forgotten her at the card party they attended, and had left at midnight, boisterously drunk, with some of his fellow officers, leaving Audrey stranded at Fraunces's Tavern and obliged to come home by public conveyance.

Her current distaste for Josias did nothing to mollify her jealousy of Meg, though, and the teapot she carried to Meg's room smelled just as nasty as the one she carried to Josias, but Meg dumped it straight out the window.

"She isn't much of a cook," Meg crooned to baby Dorothy, tossing the little girl in her arms by the fireside. "No, your auntie Audrey isn't much of a cook, is she? No, she isn't. We'll just have to be careful not to gobble up any of her nasty dishes, won't we? Yes, we will, and that means you, too, sweet child."

That night, William Whitestone brought Taylor Montgomery to Meg's for Christmas dinner. The two men had met when Taylor had finally set forth to seek out his New York relatives. Taylor, dreading the moment of casting himself on his unknown Uncle Albert's mercy, had decided instead to approach his cousin William. Remembering that William owned a printing shop and a coffeehouse, Taylor had headed to The Lark's Song and made his cousin's acquaintance.

They had much in common: both were bookish and well educated, both were Loyalists, and they had liked each other at once. After treating Taylor to a good dinner and several bottles of excellent claret, William had offered Taylor a job on his newspaper and had made lodging, a floor of rooms in a decent building on Bridge Street, part of the deal.

William was well pleased with his cousin. He seemed an honest, intelligent man, and though William did not agree with his politics, he realized that

Taylor was acting on strong convictions. Taylor had told William about Sarah, and although Taylor did not say so, William had easily guessed the truth—Taylor and Sarah had become lovers. A sophisticated man, William had not batted an eyelash, but he had sensed Taylor's struggle and unhappiness, and wanted to help him.

As luck had it, he was in a position to do so. He alone knew—for his sister Meg had confided in him—that Davie Montgomery and his Hessian friend, Michael, were still hiding in the house on Fair Street. The more William thought about it, the more he felt he must help Taylor. As for himself, his own family's opinions meant little to him, but it was obvious Taylor was deeply troubled by the division within his family.

So William had invited Taylor to Christmas dinner at Meg's, where he met his plump and motherly cousin Meg, her husband Josias—who was not any too honest, in Taylor's estimation—and flirtatious cousin Audrey, who was full of questions about Taylor's sister Katy, with whom she had corresponded before the war. Taylor began to hope that perhaps he and Sarah would not be so alone in New York after all.

After they had finished an excellent meal, at a nod from William, Meg motioned for Taylor to follow her, telling him she had been keeping a Christmas surprise for him. Confused and curious, he followed Meg as she led him up the stairs and into a room where she proceeded to open a small door.

Taylor was both astonished and overjoyed to behold his brother Davie, and Davie was no less shocked. They fell into each other's arms, and before either could attempt to ask the other how on earth they had come to be there, Taylor cried simply, "It's a very merry Christmas!"

"It is indeed," agreed Davie happily, and all thought of the war, all worry about their conflicting loyalties was forgotten as the two brothers rejoiced to see each other once again, so far from home.

With both Davie and Taylor gone, and no one knew exactly where, Christmas in the Montgomery family that year was destined to be a subdued celebration. As was their custom, the family had gathered in their house in Charleston, and although the holiday season was as brilliant as ever among their circle of friends, marked by hunts and dinners, cotillions and celebrations, none of them, save Katy, had much heart for it.

The day was gloomy and foggy, although of a mildness which would have been envied in either Trenton or New York. Caroline Montgomery had invited the whole family to a roast-goose dinner that night. All assembled, dressed in their best, in the candlelit dining room decked in red-and-white holly and festooned with graceful garlands of pine and white ribbons. The room smelled fresh and piney, and red candles blazed in silver holders on the long, linen-draped sideboard.

Webb, now the only Montgomery son in town, had arrived quite drunk. Teetering on the heels of his shiny boots, he leaned on the mantelpiece and engaged his father in a passionate predinner conversation about the recent battles in the north.

"Howe, they say, has the Yankee rebels on the run," Dennison Montgomery said, draining his glass of sherry. "Good man, I met him in London once. Of course, in this instance, he has taken the wrong side."

"I am beginning to admire any man willing to

take a side," Webb said darkly. "Too many of our neighbors lack any convictions at all."

"They will develop them as the war comes closer," Dennison predicted. "A man must think first of his family."

"I do think of my family," Webb said. He turned as his mother entered the room, rustling with black silk. She had taken to wearing black, as if in mourning for Davie and Taylor, and the sight of it unsettled Webb.

Caroline Montgomery exchanged kisses with Webb's wife Susannah and stared anxiously into the fireplace, where an immense Yule log was ablaze. " 'Tis bad luck, you know, if it should burn out too fast," she said.

"It's burning very slowly, Mother," Liza insisted. She had been summoned from Ashley Hall, and had come regretfully, for she hoped to hear from Taylor that he was safely arrived, and she felt sure that it was there that he would write her, as soon as he could. It had fallen on her to tell the family that Taylor had gone north, although she was pledged to secrecy about why and with whom. Instead she had told them that Taylor feared that his politics might endanger the family's safety, and that he had gone north to stay with a friend from Princeton. Keeping secrets weighed heavily on Liza's conscience, but her loyalty to Taylor was absolute.

"Dear heavens, it makes me sad," Caroline said, "that it's come to Christmastime, and our family so divided. To think that my own sons would be so cruel to their mother."

"Confidence, my dear, cheerfulness and confidence," Dennison said as heartily as he could manage.

"*We* are here, Mama!" said Katy, who was in her

usual high spirits, and had gathered mistletoe and brought it into the house. "And I'll wager both Davie and Taylor are celebrating and cheerful tonight, wherever they are!"

"A foggy Christmas day portends many months of mourning," Caroline insisted, her eyes swimming with tears.

"She blames me completely," muttered Webb, who had stalked across the room to replenish his cup and met Liza near the punch bowl. "I can't stand to see her wearing black! She looks at me as if I had toppled both of them into their graves."

"Of course you did not," Liza said soothingly. "Both of them were following their own consciences, and God asks no more of any of us."

"Mince pies, Papa! We are to have mince pies! Katy told me!" sang out Petie, Webb's young son, adorned for the occasion with a red ribbon bow. Petie was on his toes with excitement, wreathed in smiles, and for a moment his high spirits distracted the rest of them sufficiently for Caroline to say, "I suppose we might as well sit down to dinner. Dennison, will you speak a prayer for a safe reunion of our family."

"Amen, my dear. Indeed I will," her husband said, and took his wife's arm to lead her to her place.

In Trenton, the next day, the storm showed no signs of abating. With regret, Washington had ordered that the hogsheads of rum in the Hessian storehouses be smashed in the gutter, although he knew that some of the men had gotten to them soon enough so that they were quite tipsy when they began their march back to the ferry. All of them were exhausted, but they were in the highest of spirits, many of them wearing new boots, carrying Hessian swords and bayonets, and sporting shining brass shakos.

Recrossing the river was slow—even more floating ice than before had to be fended off the big, black Durham boats—but everyone was in too fine a mood to complain much. After two nights and a day of continuous marching and fighting, they were exhausted beyond sleepiness and were giddy with their victory and the prospect of rest on the other side of the river.

Washington had received the fashion plates that William Whitestone had sent and had taken the papers apart to uncover their message. Whitestone's cleverness in securing Howe's plans was almost too remarkable to credit, but so was the young woman's courage in carrying them straight through enemy country to him. He had already arranged for Bonnie to stay in Pennsylvania for a time, and then, perhaps, take on another mission.

"Our perseverance has accomplished what at first seemed impossible," Henry Knox said to the commander. "And as for the men, they are all liberty mad again!"

"A great victory, a splendid success. I am entirely delighted. Every man pressed forward eagerly," Washington agreed. His mind was already on the future. Howe's plans would give them little time to rest and recover their strength. Perhaps they should push on, attack Princeton at once?

There remained the problem of enlistments. Most of the enlistments would expire in about three days. Now is the time, Washington thought, to press passionately for reenlistment. Now, while the triumph is fresh. I will beg them, he decided. I will beg them regiment by regiment. It is necessary, it is essential.

"This is the crisis which is to decide our destiny," he said in a powerful, persuasive voice. "The cause of liberty and the fate of our nation is at stake."

"The common ties of our kindred . . ."

As the Revolutionary War sweeps through the South, the Montgomery family of Charleston is ripped apart by the chaotic events of the times. At Ashley Hall plantation, *Liza Montgomery* struggles to hold her family together as the British invade her home, but a love from her past tests her loyalties and places her family in danger. In Charleston, *Susannah Montgomery* weathers the siege of the city—but her husband, *Webb*, is taken prisoner by the British. Meanwhile, *Katy Montgomery* risks the wrath of her Patriot family by fraternizing with the occupying Tories, including New Yorker *Josias Logan*, who has come to Charleston as a member of the Royal government. And brothers *Davie* and *Taylor Montgomery* find themselves fighting on opposite sides in the bloody battles for the South that will determine the course of the entire war—and the fate of a nation.

Don't miss the dramatic sequel to
Our Sacred Honor and *These United Colonies*
OUR COMMON TIES
Coming soon from Ivy Books

ABOUT THE AUTHOR

Cynthia Van Hazinga is the author of nine popular novels, including *Farewell, My South* and *The Georgians*. She divides her time between New York City and Hillsboro, New Hampshire.

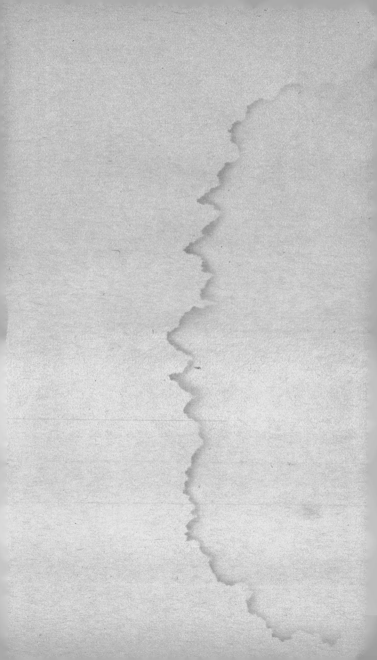